CRITICS RAVE FOR

SEX AND THE SINGLE VAMPIRE

"...an amusing paranormal romance.... Horror romance readers will enjoy this one-bite sitting teeth in cheek (and neck) tale."

—*Midwest Book Review*

"...a truly hilarious and exhilarating read.... Witty and wacky, this is one book you won't want to put down!"

—*RT BOOKclub*

A GIRL'S GUIDE TO VAMPIRES

"...writing that manages to be both sexy and humorous, this contemporary paranormal love story is an absolute delight."

—*Booklist* (Starred review)

"...rich with humor, loaded with sexual tension, and packed with interesting, if sometimes slightly offbeat, characters."

—*Romance Reviews Today*

"Readers who delight in satiric romances will want to learn the rules of *A Girl's Guide to Vampires*."

—*Midwest Book Review*

"Fantastic! It's hilarious, it's sensual, and it's a winner!"

—*Reader to Reader Reviews*

MORE PRAISE FOR KATIE MACALISTER!

THE TROUBLE WITH HARRY

"This is a book you will not put down.... The pages sparkle with comedy, sexy romance, and even a bit of intrigue and excitement."

—*Romance Reviews Today*

NOBLE DESTINY

"Imbued with a delectable sense of wit [this] is an irresistible, laughter-laced treat."

—*Booklist*

"Another wonderful Regency romp. This book is funny and fast-paced...a memorable book. What will Katie MacAlister come up with next?"

—*Romantic Times*

NOBLE INTENTIONS

"This story is a true romp. There is much to laugh at when reading this book and much to miss when it is over."

—*Romantic Times*

"A special one of a kind Regency romp that has simmering seduction, hilarious humor, a mystery, and a divine hero and heroine. A sassy read you don't want to miss!"

—*Reader to Reader Reviews*

IMPROPER ENGLISH

"Two totally opposite people clash with wonderfully amusing and quite sexy results in MacAlister's sparkling contemporary romance."

—*Booklist*

"I'M YOUR BELOVED, DAMMIT!"

I grabbed both edges of the front of his shirt and ripped it open. I think he was as surprised at my action as I was, but I didn't let that stop me from yanking off the rest of the shirt. "Mmmrowr!" I purred, throwing myself on him.

"No! I will not let you do this!" he snarled...in between fevered kisses that came close to melting the fillings in my teeth.

He spun us around so that I was caught between a cold, rough wall, and a hot, hard vampire. I sucked his lip into my mouth and used both hands to clutch his hair. "I'm your Beloved, dammit! You're going to let me save your soul, and like it!"

Other *Leisure* and *Love Spell* books by
Katie MacAlister:

THE TROUBLE WITH HARRY
SEX AND THE SINGLE VAMPIRE
A GIRL'S GUIDE TO VAMPIRES
HEAT WAVE (anthology)
NOBLE DESTINY
IMPROPER ENGLISH
NOBLE INTENTIONS

SEX, LIES, AND VAMPIRES

KATIE MacALISTER

LOVE SPELL NEW YORK CITY

LOVE SPELL®

February 2005

Published by

Dorchester Publishing Co., Inc.
200 Madison Avenue
New York, NY 10016

ISBN 0-505-52555-0

Printed in the United States of America.

Visit us on the web at www.dorchesterpub.com.

It's always a pleasure to share the love of sexy, brooding vampires with a good friend, but when that friend demands that you write a hero just for her (and proceeds to give you a list of the qualities she wants), what's a poor author to do? Diane Hall-Harris is just such a friend, and it's with much gratitude and many, many shared giggles that I dedicate this book to her. I'd also like to thank Lauren Barnholdt for the fabulous title suggestion—good one, Lauren!

Chapter One

"Imps?"

I blinked in surprise at the completely unexpected question. "I beg your pardon?"

"Imps? You are imp removals, *ja?*" The woman who had answered the buzzer connected to an expensive cream-colored stone building didn't *look* insane, but how many people meet you at the door by asking if you were there to remove imps?

Then again, it might have just been jet lag making me think she had asked about imps. What was far more likely was that the jet lag that had hit me in London was still fuzzying my brain. That, or she was speaking in Czech and it just sounded like she was asking about imps.

I shook my head to clear it, held firmly on to my smile despite its lopsided nature, and said slowly, "Good evening. My name is Nell Harris. I have an appointment with Mrs. Banacek."

"Dr. Harris?" another woman sang out as she approached. "How pleased I am to meet you at last. I take it your flight from Amsterdam was an unremarkable one? Please excuse the mess—we've been positively inundated with imps of late, and poor Gertrud is at her wit's end."

The voice—smooth, sophisticated, with just a hint of a Slavic accent—almost perfectly matched its owner. I dragged my attention from the woman manning the door (short, stocky, iron-gray hair, and a no-nonsense attitude that had me pitying the imps—whoever or whatever *they* were) to the graceful creature who floated across the marble-floored foyer. Melissande Banacek was not only the loveliest woman I had ever seen, but her lavish surroundings, expensive address in the heart of Prague, and what I was willing to bet was no off-the-rack pair of crimson and persimmon silk lounging pajamas clearly indicated a woman of no little means. Certainly she was wealthy enough to fly a dirt-poor junior professor of medieval history from Seattle to the Czech Republic on what amounted to little more than a whim.

"Imps," I said, utterly at sea. With my good arm I clutched my bag (beat up with one torn handle) to my chest (stuffed into a bra stretched to its limits to restrain overly abundant occupants), and wished for the tenth time that I had not succumbed to my curiosity (going to get me into trouble one of these days).

"Yes! Do you know how to get rid of them?" Melissande asked, gently pulling her hand from my death grip. "We've tried everything from martins to dragon's bane, but to no good. The infestation seems to be too much for such home remedies, thus we have called the imp-catchers. Come, you must be tired after your long flight. Coffee or tea?"

"Coffee, please," I said, my mind more than a little numb around the edges. Had everyone in Prague gone mad and I didn't know it? Or was I more tired than I thought?

"*Do* you know a good remedy for imps?" Melissande glided over to a cream-colored couch that perfectly matched the cream carpeting and cream satin striped walls. I sat down gingerly on an adjacent love seat, feeling more than a little as if I were cocooned in an eggshell.

"I don't even know what an imp is. You're—you're not joking about them, are you?" The feeling of the love seat, soft and enveloping beneath me, shook off the vague sense of bemusement that had gripped me since walking through the door.

Melissande tipped her head, her silvery blond hair sliding like a curtain of silk as she considered me for a few moments. "How silly of me. I read your file, and I should have remembered that although you are one of us, you have no experience in our world."

The hairs on the back of my neck stood on end. I wasn't jet laggy now, nor was I bemused. The woman in front of me—my employer for the next two weeks—was obviously quite, quite mad. Disappointed though I was at not being able to study a piece of armor from the much-discussed-amongst-medievalists-but-never-discovered Graven Plate of Milan, at least I had my return plane ticket and enough money to buy me a night's accommodation in the hotel at which I'd left my bags.

3

Making no sudden movements, I slowly lifted my battered purse from where I had set it at my feet, and rose from the love seat. "You know, I think I forgot something outside. Something . . . uh . . . important. *Very* important. I wouldn't want the imps to get into it, so I'll just run outside and make sure it's OK."

A smile curved her delicately tinted lips and tilted already exotically tipped gray eyes so the Slavic influence in her heredity was obvious despite her pale coloring. "You think I'm deranged! How refreshing. Everyone here takes me so seriously, it's a wonderful change to be thought mentally deficient."

The warning bells that had been going off in my head went into overtime. "You know, I think we've both made a mistake, Mrs. Banacek. So I'm just going to leave now, and everyone will be happy."

"I'm not, you know," she called after me as I started to back slowly out of the room. "Insane, that is. I've simply introduced the subject to you poorly . . . oh, do mind behind you! Gertrud swore if I squashed another imp into the carpet she'd leave me, and cliché as it is, good help is *so* difficult to find."

I swung around, expecting to see Gertrud with a meat cleaver about to lop off my head, or something equally as gruesome and deranged, but instead found myself staring down at a small creature about three inches tall. It was grayish-green, and was using one set of arms to pull a hairless tail from where it was trapped under my toes, while the other set pounded on my shoe.

"Week, week!" the creature squealed at me, clearly angry.

"Aiiiieeeeeeeee!" I screamed in reply, dropping my bag

as I leaped what seemed to be an inordinate length across the room, landing on the love seat. My weak leg buckled under me, but I caught myself before I could tumble off.

"What the hell is it?" I shrieked, leaping up to do a horrified jig on the love seat just in case the beastly thing followed me and attacked.

"Imp," Melissande said sadly as the tiny green thing shook three of its fists at me before scampering out of the room. "Common Central European Imp, to be exact. There's some sort of Latin name for them, but I never can remember it. Not the brightest beings in the world, but not in the least bit dangerous. Not unless you attack their king, and then they do all sorts of nasty things while you sleep. Or so I've been told."

"I've been drugged, haven't I?" I asked, still standing on the love seat as Melissande closed the door behind the imp. "You were sitting next to me on the flight from London and you put something in my Diet Coke, following which you smuggled me in through customs for some weird purpose, right? Because otherwise—"

"Otherwise you would have just seen an imp and your vision of the world would be radically changed, yes, I know. I'm very sorry I don't have the time to do this properly—indoctrinate you, that is—but my nephew has been held for three weeks, and now my brother has gone missing as well, and there simply is no time to be wasted."

"Indoctrinate?" I asked, stepping down off the love seat and accepting my purse that she had picked up off the floor. I held it at arm's length in case one of those tiny green things had gotten into it. "This is a cult? You're going to brainwash me? I should tell you right now I don't have any money, and—"

"Nell," Melissande said, handing me a cup of coffee.

I took it, trying to covertly sniff it for signs of drugs. "Yes?"

"Sit down. I have a good deal to tell you, much of which you won't accept or believe, but we must be on our way to Blansko in an hour."

"You're not going to let me go, are you?" I asked, ignoring the horribly weak tremor in my voice. I just wanted to put my head down and cry for a long, long time, but suddenly my life had gone so horribly wrong, I was sure I wasn't going to be given that opportunity.

"I will not hold you prisoner, if that's what you are asking, but I am begging for your help." She shoved aside a coffee service and sat on the edge of the glass coffee table, waiting for me to sit down. I did, slowly, not so much because I was wary of her (it was obvious she was the one in power here), but so I wouldn't spill the coffee on the spotless rug.

"Although I imagine an imp stain would be a lot worse to clean than coffee," I muttered to myself.

"A hundred times worse, but common household tips are not why I've brought you here."

I took a tentative sip of the coffee, ready to spit it out if it had the least bit of an odd taste. It didn't. In fact, its smoky flavor was strangely familiar. My eyebrows rose. "Starbucks French Roast?"

"Of course. Is there anything else?"

"I'm a bit partial to their Sumatra blend as well, but you can't go wrong with French Roast."

"Just so. Although don't you find Sumatra a bit spicy?"

"Only after a meal. Alone, or in a latte, it's perfect."

"I've never tried Sumatra in a latte," she mused. "But I will do so at the earliest opportunity."

From imps to Starbucks in ten seconds. I truly was going mad. "Mrs. Banacek—"

"Call me Mel," she interrupted. I looked at her. I couldn't imagine anyone looking less like a "Mel" than the sophisticated, elegant woman before me. She frowned. "No?"

"Um . . . I'm thinking not."

"How about Sandy? Do I look like a Sandy?"

I shook my head. She sighed. "I've always wanted to have a nickname but have never been allowed one. Very well, Melissande it is, although I do think the name Lissa attractive."

"Melissande," I said, setting down my cup and leveling a serious gaze at her. "You hired me to translate the inscription scribed on the inside of an early-fourteenth-century breastplate that has, until this date, remained firmly in the realm of the mythical. You sucked me in with a description and photos of the armor that were so tantalizing, I had no choice but to agree to your offer. I assume you brought me here because you wanted someone who is familiar with obscure European languages, but I'm beginning to feel that you have another purpose in bringing me halfway around the world. I would appreciate it if you would tell me just *what* that purpose is."

She nodded. "A very reasonable request. I applaud both your frankness and your efficiency in going straight to the point. Quite simply, you are a Charmer, and I need your assistance to locate my nephew and brother."

I froze, ice forming in my blood at the word that had so harmlessly tripped off her tongue. *Charmer.* It was a word I hadn't heard in almost ten years. Ten long years. I swallowed back a sudden lump in my throat, my voice suddenly hoarse. "I assume by Charmer you aren't referring to my excellent people skills?"

"No," she said, her eyes serious. "I mean one who has the ability to draw Charms. You are a Charmer. You were born a Charmer, although I understand that you have not used your abilities after an accident during your college years—"

I put a hand out to stop her, blind with sudden grief, a band of pain tight around my chest as I struggled for air.

"I beg your pardon, Nell. That was an unfortunate reference, but it has relevance to the situation."

I shook my head to clear my vision, the memory of the dead, unseeing eyes of my friend slowly dissolving into bright silver-gray eyes subtly highlighted with expensive cosmetics, eyes that were watching me closely. "I am not a Charmer," I said carefully, my voice thick with emotion that I would not acknowledge.

She sighed, her gaze dropping for a moment to her hands as they rested on her legs. "I have a nephew named Damian. He is ten years old, and very dear to me, although I've been accused of spoiling him shamelessly. He was kidnapped three weeks ago. My brother Saer was away at the time, but as soon as he heard of the terrible event, he raced home and began to track Damian. Five nights ago he called me from a small town in the Moravian Highlands to tell me that he had found a clue to

Damian's whereabouts. He believed the boy had been taken to England. Saer left immediately, and I have not heard from him since. I believe he, too, is being held prisoner, quite probably by the same being who is holding Damian. That or . . . another."

The pain in her eyes was not counterfeit, nor did I think she was mad. At least, I believed that *she* believed what she was telling me.

"I'm very sorry," I said sincerely. "Have you contacted the police?"

"Police?" She looked startled for a moment, then shook her head. "No, the police cannot help me. My brother and nephew are beyond their reach."

"I'm sorry," I said again, spreading my hands wide. "I wish I could help you, but I'm no detective, and certainly no expert in tracking people—"

"I do not expect you to find them for me," she interrupted.

"Then what—"

"You are a Charmer. The aid I seek from you—the aid I need—lies in your ability to charm."

"I don't . . . I can't . . ." The pain swamping me was so great I could hardly breathe, let alone speak.

"My brother and nephew are Dark Ones," she said, taking a deep breath. "Moravian Dark Ones. I, too, am Moravian. Do you know what that means?"

I shook my head, too confused and distraught to think.

"Dark Ones have walked the earth all the ages of man, alike, but separate. Vampires some call us, although truly my people are not evil, not the horrible creatures common lore makes us out to be. Dark Ones are created either by a demon lord, or they are born to a father who is unredeemed."

"Unredeemed?" I croaked, wondering if it was too late to change my name to Alice and settle down to a happy life of insanity in Wonderland.

"To each male Dark One there is one woman, his Beloved, who can redeem his soul. Those who remain unredeemed are forever damned."

I opened my mouth to say that sounded like something out of a novel, but stopped. There was no use in agitating her further by pointing out that vampires—damned or not—were fantastical creatures that didn't exist.

Just like imps, a sardonic voice in my head pointed out.

I refused to think about that. "Let me just make sure I have this right—your brother and nephew are vampires, and you're one too; you drink people's blood to survive, but you're not bad or evil or anything out of a John Carpenter movie. Is that right so far?"

She nodded. "There is more to being a Moravian than blood drinking, but since we don't have time to go into the history of my people, we will suffice with the bare minimum."

"Just out of curiosity—how old are you?" I asked. "Since vampires are traditionally held to be immortal and all, I assume you're immortal as well?"

"Only so long as I do not give my heart to a mortal, yes. I was born in 1761."

I did a quick round of mental subtraction. "That would make you two hundred and forty-four."

"Forty-three. My birthday isn't until December."

"Ah," I said, then sat back and waited for the rest of the

fairy tale to unfold. "Go on, please. I'm all ears."

She didn't like the note of subdued sarcasm in my voice, but it didn't stop her from telling me the rest. "My nephew is being held by a demon lord by the name of Asmodeus."

I had a better grip on myself now, so the name didn't freeze me into a block of ice, despite the boundless well of sorrow within me.

"I won't insult you by asking if you are aware of Asmodeus, since I know it was one of Asmodeus's curses you were attempting to charm when you . . ." Her gaze fluttered to the left side of my face where the skin was less taut than the right side. I didn't flinch under her inspection, having learned long ago that if I kept my face immobile, most people didn't notice the slight slackness on the one side. ". . . had your accident."

"What I had was no accident," I said slowly, enunciating carefully.

She offered no reaction to that statement. "My nephew and quite likely my brother are being held by Asmodeus, bound to the demon lord by his curse. I need your help, Nell. I need you to charm the curse."

"I don't know what you're talking about. Even if I did, there's no way I can help you," I said quietly, squelching down the feelings of pain and dread and horror that arose with her words.

She gave me a long look. "I can understand your reluctance to regain a part of your life that I'm sure you thought lost, but you cannot deny the truth of what you are, Nell. You are a Charmer. Most of your kind learn their skills from mages and Guardians, and thus they can only

11

undraw wards and perform simple protective charms, but you were born a Charmer. You are different. You can unmake curses."

"I cannot charm. I never could. I left that all behind me ten years ago." Despite my best intentions to remain calm and collected, my voice rose with each word.

Her eyes glittered brightly at me, so brightly it hurt to look into them. I was vaguely aware that she was weaving a spell of compliance with her words, but I would not fall victim to it. I gritted my teeth as her voice, silken with persuasion, rolled around me. "You are one of the few people who have the power to unmake the most powerful bond known to mankind—a demon lord's curse."

"I will not charm," I ground out through my teeth, anger and fear forcing me to admit something I had worked hard to forget. "Not again!"

"If you do not help me, my nephew will be consumed by the demon lord. Do you know what happens to a Dark One who is thus destroyed?"

I shook my head, sick at heart with the knowledge of what she would tell me. Long-denied memories of a time years in the past tormented me. I wanted to shout to Melissande that it was so long ago, when I was young and innocent, and I believed what I had been told. I was special. I could make a difference. It was all so clear then, so exciting, so easy . . . until Beth died.

"His life force joins with the demon lord. In effect, he becomes him, one of the princes of hell. I would move heaven and earth to save my nephew from that fate, Nell, and all I'm asking of you is your help in bringing Damian home to me."

I shook my head again, blindly reaching for my bag as I stood. "I'm very sorry for you, Melissande. I wish there was something I could do, I truly do wish it, but what you ask is impossible. I can't do it."

"You mean you will not!" The words stung me with the force of a whip. Her eyes were molten silver, glowing hot with fury as she stood facing me. "You have it within your power to help, and you deny me!"

Anger, hot and deep such as I had not known for a very long time, burned in my soul, welling up to overwhelm the guilt that had bound me for so many years. "Do you know what happened the one time I attempted to charm one of Asmodeus's curses? Do you know the exact details of what happened?"

"No, not the details," she answered, her eyes once again moving to the left side of my face, down to my left arm. "It is said the charm backfired, that some trap laid by Asmodeus was triggered when you attempted to unmake it, and both you and a companion were injured."

"You could say that," I said, my breath harsh as I struggled to control it. "If you call death an injury. No, Melissande. I will not help you. You may think I'm your savior, but I assure you I'm not. I bring only destruction, not salvation. I am a murderer, pure and simple."

Chapter Two

You would think that telling someone you'd killed a person (even accidentally) would be enough to put them off, but alas, Melissande was made of much sterner stuff than I had imagined. Which is why forty minutes after I had informed her that ten years ago I had killed my best friend, I was in a car with her, zipping through the night heading north toward the tiny town of Blansko.

I still wasn't quite sure how she had managed to keep me from walking out of her apartment.

"You've cast a spell over me," I accused her. "There's no way I would be here now unless you had cast a spell."

She took her eyes from the road just long enough to toss an amused glance my way. "I wouldn't know how to even begin to cast a spell."

"You've got that vampire thing—what do they call it—a glamour. You've glamoured me into coming with you, but it'll do you no good, Melissande. I never was a Charmer,

14

not then, and I'm certainly not one now. You might have glamoured me, but it won't help. As my very dead friend would be the first to tell you, I can't charm anything."

Melissande sighed, shifting into fourth as her tiny black sports car zoomed around a large truck. "We've argued this all out, Nell. I've accepted that you feel it's impossible to save my nephew, but you did agree to help me locate him."

"That's what I'm saying—you glamoured me or something. There's just no other explanation for the fact that I didn't walk out of your apartment the minute I saw that . . ." I rubbed my forehead, staring blankly into the night, tiny pinpoints of lights blurring into meaningless patterns of light and dark as we raced through the dark. "Oh, Lord, I really did see an imp, didn't I? And you really are a vampire. A female vampire. What does that make you, a vampette?"

She laughed, a pleasant, warm laugh that did much to reduce the panic gripping me. "The term is Moravian Dark One, although in truth only the men are called Dark Ones. I'm just Moravian."

"Yeah, right. Somehow I don't think there's any *just* about you."

Her grin was infectious, even though I hadn't felt the slightest nudge to my funny bone up to that moment. "I didn't use a glamour. It was greed that held you when nothing else would."

"I'd like to dispute that, but unfortunately, the proof is all too evident," I answered, glancing at the back seat where a long, flat wooden case resided. "Brought down by my academic interest. You'll really let me have the breastplate? Free and clear, no strings attached?"

"If you help me locate my nephew, I will gladly give you the piece of armor."

I thought of the object that resided in the heavily padded wooden case. "It's a museum piece, you know. Priceless beyond priceless. No one believes the Graven Plate really exists. What you're offering me is going to rock the world of academic medievalists. I shouldn't be even thinking of accepting such a treasure."

"It comes from Milan," Melissande said, shooting me an occasional glance. "Dating from about 1395, made at the castle of Churburg."

"Italian Tyrol," I said, sighing with pleasure at the thought of it. Every medievalist had cut his or her academic teeth on stories of the Graven Plate. "The armory at Churburg was famous for their exports, mostly to Germany."

"The breastplate consists of nine interlocked plates, each of which is etched with what appears to be the history of the knight who bore the armor."

A little thrill went through me at the thought of those inscriptions. Melissande had assured me, in the calls and e-mails that had resulted in me being in the Czech Republic, that no medievalist had yet laid eyes on the breastplate. I would be the first to see it, study it, translate what I hoped would be a detailed history of a knight-errant who rose to claim the throne of Bohemia.

"It is . . . what is it called—bright armor?"

"White armor," I said absently, my fingers positively itching to touch the breastplate. I'd had nothing more than a glimpse of it before Melissande had bundled it and me into the car. "It was a term used for metal armor that wasn't bound to fabric or leather covering."

Her eyes flicked my way again. "You are very knowledgeable about armor."

I wasn't buying any of her innocent act. I'd already been suckered into doing more than I wanted, all because of that beautiful specimen of armor that sat behind me. "You knew that when you hired me. How did you find out about me, anyway? You didn't do any"—I drew circles around my forehead—"you know, weirdo psychic stuff on me?"

Her lips pursed. "I'm Moravian, Nell, not the Amazing Kreskin."

"Ah. Sorry. I didn't know you couldn't do that sort of thing."

"I can, as a matter of fact, but only under certain circumstances. It's not very easy." She paused for the count of three, then added, "I'm so sorry that I couldn't have done your introduction to our world properly, although really, you were predisposed to believing in Dark Ones and imps. You must have learned something about the dark powers if you were trying to unmake a demon lord's curse." Another of her quick, assessing glances slid my way.

I didn't bite. At least, not the way she anticipated.

"Oh, I don't know. I pretty much had your standard middle-class childhood—divorced parents, school, college, the usual assortment of friends and lovers. There was certainly nothing to warn me about imps and vampires in my future."

"Do you have many friends and lovers?" she asked, her voice polite, but rife with disinterest. I awarded her a few bonus points for not steering the conversation to subjects she really cared about. "A couple of girlfriends, but no boyfriends. Haven't had one of those for a couple of years. All the men I know seem to be so"—I shrugged—"shallow. How about you? Do you have a boy toy stashed away somewhere?"

Her elegantly formed eyebrows rose in astonishment for a few seconds before she gave a little laugh. "I had forgotten how straightforward Americans are. No, I do not currently possess a lover. Like you, I find most men I meet lacking in some way or other."

"Ah." We rode in silence for a few minutes, but it wasn't long before she abandoned the pretense of polite chit-chat and went straight to what she wanted to know.

"Do you mind talking about your past? Not the . . . accident, but how you came to find out you were a Charmer? How you ended up in the position where you were attempting to lift a curse?"

"Yes," I said, rubbing my arms and keeping my eyes fixed out the window. "I do mind."

"I see. Shall I tell you about Damian, then?"

"Knock yourself out."

And she did. The whole of the three-hour drive into the Moravian Highlands, Melissande told me everything there was to know about Damian, from the time he learned to walk, to what he wanted for Christmas.

"That's really fascinating—I don't think anyone has ever shared the potty-training process with me in such vivid detail—but it doesn't really explain much about why a demon lord would want to kidnap a kid, even a junior vampire. I assume it has something to do with his father?"

Melissande shifted gears as the car started climbing

into a mountainous region. "Saer believes that Damian is being held as bait in order to trap him."

"That makes sense. Hold the kid, and make daddy dance to your tune. So why does Asmodeus have it in for Saer?"

"Saer believes that it's not actually Asmodeus who wants him destroyed. That honor, he believes, belongs to Adrian."

"Who's Adrian when he's at home?"

She glanced at me.

"Sorry, it's an Americanism. You haven't hung out around the States much, have you?"

"I like Los Angeles," she said. "Such interesting people. And excellent shops. Adrian is . . ."

I raised my eyebrows as a number of interesting expressions flitted over her face.

"He is the Betrayer," she said finally, not looking at me. "He is a Dark One who has turned over a number of our people to Asmodeus."

"Turned over? What could a demon lord do to a vampire who was already damned?"

She shuddered. "You do not want to know the answer to that."

The horror in her voice confirmed her words. I rubbed the goose bumps on my arms. "OK, so there's this guy named Adrian who sells out his own kind, and he's got it in for Saer. Why?"

If I didn't know better, I'd say Melissande was avoiding something. Her reluctance to speak was pretty obvious. "Saer believed it has to do with a ring, an object of great power which the Betrayer is hunting for."

"A 'one ring to rule them all' kind of ring?" I asked, peering in the side mirror to see if any wizards on white horses were following us.

"Decidedly not Tolkien, no," Melissande answered. "Saer believed the ring was once held by Asmodeus, and thus the immortal world would be put at risk if the Betrayer obtained it.

"Ah, *that* sort of ring." I pursed my lips. "I assume Saer is trying to stop this Betrayer guy from finding it, and that's why his son is being held hostage?"

"Damian is definitely being held hostage," she agreed.

"Poor kid," I said, guilt roiling within me. I'd seen what a demon lord's secondhand power bound into a curse could do; I couldn't even imagine what horrors a child, even an immortal child, would suffer in his control. "This is really an unpleasant question, but aside from being integrated into the demon lord, I assume Dark Ones like your brother can be killed?"

"Yes," she said, biting the word off. "As you might guess, Damian is as dear to me as a son. I don't see him as often as I'd like, but I will do anything to have him back safe and sound. I am his only close female relative here, you see. His mother lives in England, and he divides his time between her and the family here."

"Hmm." We had turned off the main road and were following a long, winding, dark road that bumped through what appeared to be a coniferous forest. Nearby mountains turned the darkness into something that felt close and smothering. I mused over what she had told me, interested despite my desire to steer clear of anything that

20

even remotely smelled of the supernatural. "So, is he . . . holy cats! Is that a castle?"

"Drahanska Castle. Didn't I tell you this is where we were going? What was I thinking?"

I glared at her for two seconds before craning my neck so I could look up at the battlements as Melissande brought the car to a halt before two very large doors. "I suspect you thought you could tempt me even further by dangling a real castle in front of my nose. How old is it, do you know? Who built it? And who owns it now?"

"I have no idea how old it is or who built it, but it is owned by a Dark One, a distant cousin. Come. It is from here that Saer called me and said he found the information about where Damian was being held."

"This castle belongs to your cousin?" I got out of the car, stretching after the long ride, trying to take in the monstrous structure before us, but failing miserably. It was just one of a very long list of things I'd been asked to accept, but my mind balked at the thought of it, so I let it go and decided to adopt a new "go with the flow" attitude that would hopefully keep me sane long enough to enjoy translating that exquisite breastplate. "Why don't you just ask him where your nephew is?"

"Christian is in London, or so Saer said." Melissande fiddled with the door for a moment, swinging it open. "I believe Saer was in the library when he called me. He said he'd seen some notes that Christian had made about the possible location of Asmodeus in London. The library is along the passage, first left, about halfway down the great hall. You can't miss it."

"I can't, huh? Well, we won't have to worry about that. You just point it out to me and I'll give you a hand searching the place, although honestly, if you don't need anything translated from fourteenth-century Italian, Flemish, or German, I'm probably more of a hindrance than a help." I held up my left arm. "I'm neither as fast nor as strong as I used to be."

"You possess many skills that compensate for any loss you might have suffered," she reassured me, waving me through the door. I walked in, marveling at the high arched stone walls, stopping about ten feet in when I realized she hadn't followed me. "Um . . . is there a problem?"

Melissande stood at the door, her face a beautiful mask of dismay and frustration. "I cannot come in."

"What? Why not?" I looked around me, wondering if she had tricked me. "Hey—you did say that your cousin gave you permission to look around his castle while he's away, right?"

Her eyes shifted slightly to look beyond my shoulder. "As to that, I don't believe I mentioned specifically that Christian gave his permission, but I know he would."

"Oh, lovely," I said, hands on my hips. "You set me up for a little breaking and entering while you get off scot-free? I don't think so."

I walked toward her, intending to leave, but she put a hand up to stop me at the door. Her eyes were swimming with tears. "Please, Nell, you have no idea how much I wish I could enter and look for something that would tell me where Damian and Saer are, but . . ."

"But what?" I asked, impatient. If she thought I was going to take the fall for her pathetic "pity me" act just so I could have a priceless, one-of-a-kind breastplate that would without a doubt ensure me tenure when the results of my studies were published, she could just think again.

Maybe.

Man, I wanted that breastplate.

"But I can't! The door is warded. Couldn't you feel it when you passed through it?"

"Warded?" I ignored the faint memories that struggled to come forth and walked through the door. "What are you talking about? I didn't feel anything. What warded?"

She made an impatient gesture with her hands. "How can you be a Charmer and not know anything about wards?"

"I told you, I'm not a Charmer."

"A ward is a device drawn by an individual. Most wards guard something like a door or window, keeping dark forces from entering. Wards can be drawn to protect or bind people, an object, or a building. As I told you earlier, you as a born Charmer have both the ability to draw and charm a ward just as you can draw and charm a curse—the unmaking process is basically the same, just reversed."

Her explanation teased my memory. "Oh. Those wards. I'd forgotten about them, to tell you the truth. A lot of what I learned before the tragedy was . . . er . . . for lack of a better word, erased from my memory. So you're saying this door is warded? Protected by magic to keep bad things out?"

She nodded. I walked through the door again, this time more slowly, experiencing only a slight tingle, but I had the worst feeling of an elusive something just out of the range of my vision. I eyed the door, but it looked completely normal ... until I looked away. A glint of gold hanging in midair caught my peripheral vision, flickering into nothingness when I focused on it. I gave a shrug. "OK, so why can I break it without doing any charmy-type things to it?"

I could tell she was fighting to hold on to her patience. "You haven't charmed the ward, Nell. You simply passed through it because it was not meant to keep you out. It is a protection ward to keep beings of the dark powers out."

"Like you?"

She nodded. "I am born of an unredeemed Dark One. Thus my blood is tainted. The ward will not let me pass. Now, if you are satisfied with the explanation, could you *please* go to the library and look for the notes regarding a house in London where Damian might be held? I will wait for you here."

"Not so fast, there's a little matter of breaking and entering—"

"I swear to you," she said hoarsely, yanking an amulet from under the mohair sweater she'd slipped on before the drive. "I swear to you on the Luna Crescens that you will not suffer for this. You will not be arrested for searching the house. If you do this for me, I will let you have the amulet as well as the armor."

Greed, I'm sure, flared up in my eyes for a few seconds while I fought with my better self to keep from snatching the hammered gold and silver piece from her hand. I'd heard stories of the fabled amulet worn by one of the Crusading knights who was said to have discovered the Holy Grail, but I never really thought such a thing had existed.

The same could be said for imps, vampires, and the Graven Plate.

"The breastplate is enough reward," I answered thickly, swallowing my desire. "But I'm going to hold you to that promise of no trouble. If your cousin suddenly walks in and finds me digging around in his library, I expect you to make things right."

"You can be sure I will. Thank you." She stood still and silent as a statue as I walked down the long, dimly lit hallway. Evidently the castle was built in a T-shape, and I had entered on one of the short ends. I turned left at a junction, wondering what I was going to say to anyone I encountered.

"Go with the flow, go with the flow," I repeated to myself as I walked into a huge entry hall.

My voice echoed back at me, sending a skitter of goose bumps down my arms and back. I rubbed my arms as I slipped through the hall.

"Boy, if I get through this without being tossed in jail, I'm definitely coming back here," I whispered to myself, sadly forced to give short shrift to the wonders in armor, art, and museum pieces that I was passing. "Hmm. This looks libraryish."

I opened one of twin bound oak doors, reaching inside to turn on a light.

My jaw hit the floor as lights flickered on down the length of a long, narrow, high-ceilinged room. "I have *got* to meet Cousin Christian!"

Tall mahogany bookcases lined three sides of the room, long glass cases filling the fourth wall. I drifted over to one of the cases, flipping on a light to illuminate what was within. Drool formed as I gazed at the frail illuminated parchment. "My God, that's a tenth-century psalter!" I did a bit of translating Latin on the fly and reached for my purse to take a few quick notes on what I was seeing. The feel of the tiny notebook in my hand reminded me of a more important task.

"Rats. The kid." Reluctantly I turned off the case light and bit my lip as I looked around the rest of the library. "If I were a scholarly vampire, where would I keep my notes about the possible location of a demon lord? Ah. Desk. Good choice, Nell."

The big rosewood desk was remarkably orderly, or perhaps it was that my own was particularly disorderly. I flipped through stacks of what were obviously bills, found a red-inked manuscript of what looked to be a romance book in the making, and discovered a cache of letters in one of the drawers. Most of them were in a language I couldn't read, although parts were oddly familiar. None of them contained the word "London" so I set them aside. I searched all of the drawers, finding nothing else that was even remotely like what I was looking for.

"Well, crap. Now what do I do?" I looked around the room again, searching for anything that was out of place or different. "Let's go about this in an orderly fashion. I'm going to assume that whatever notes Christian has are valuable. Thus he would not keep them in a drawer. That means he's got them hidden somewhere."

The sound of my voice echoed starkly in the high-ceilinged room. I glanced with dismay at all the book-cases. There had to be thousands of books in the library, each one a potential hiding place.

"Or it could be in a wall safe, or floor safe, or—hell"—I looked up at the high arched wooden ceiling—"the owner's a vampire. He can probably fly, so I wouldn't doubt that he's got a handy-dandy ceiling safe! It's hopeless!"

The word *safe* triggered something in my mind. I stood up, looking around the room again. If I were your average safety-conscious vampire, and I had something of value, I wouldn't just entrust it to a safe. "Not when I was the sort of guy who uses magic to guard a door," I mused, walking around the room with my hands stretched out, feeling a bit stupid as I tried to feel a tingle that might mean that something was warded against discovery. I found it on my third pass around the north wall.

"Hmm. Book. Tingly. A bit dusty. Title is . . . *Dark* . . . someone needs to tell the maids to dust on the bottom shelves . . . *Desire*. Sounds fun. Let's just see why this particular book has been picked out to be warded or what . . . whoa! This is interesting!"

The book seemed to be made of some slippery substance, or I suddenly had a whole handful of butterfingers (and not the chocolate kind), because I couldn't for the life of me seem to get a grip on it. It seemed to slither from my hands, falling with a solid "thunk" to the floor. I squatted down to give it a good, long look, and noticed if I glanced just beyond it, I could make out what appeared to be an intricate pattern sketched into the spine of the book, one with lots of swoops and curves that doubled back on themselves, like a Celtic knot design. It was almost as if someone had drawn a path of green luminous paint on the spine, then left the book exposed to the sun. The pattern was faded, but as I traced it with one finger, it seemed to dissolve. Was I *seeing* a ward?

A faint memory emerged from the dark corners of my mind: the face of a tiny Asian woman sketching symbols in the air. I thought I had lost or destroyed all memories of the woman as she'd instructed Beth and me, but there she was, saying something about the importance of wards. I shook my head to clear the sad thoughts, leaning forward to examine the pattern more closely. It shimmered and faded as I traced it, definitely of a suitably intricate nature as to qualify for my still extremely fuzzy memory of a ward.

The tip of my finger came to the end of the ward, and suddenly the book was in my hot little hands. "What the . . . ooh!" Pushing aside the question of why the book had decided to cooperate, I flipped it open to find a couple of torn-out sheets of scribbled notes, and what looked like a hoop earring pressed between them. It was made of some sort of shell, something like an opaque mother-of-pearl, rimmed with a thin band of gold.

"Houston, the eagle has landed," I said as I took the book, pages, and earring to the desk so I could examine them under a brighter light. "And what have we heeeaaaaargh!"

" 'Ello, you so very interesting lady," a spectral voice rolled out of the wall, quickly followed by a man with long brown curls, doublet, hose, and Elizabethan ruff. I backed toward the door, clutching the notes in one hand, the hoop earring with the other. The ghost—it *was* a ghost, my poor overworked mind admitted—swept a be-feathered hat from his head and made me a low, courtly bow. "I did not know we 'ad the company most fair. I am Antonio."

"Uh," I said, trying to wrap my mind around the fact that a handsome ghost was stalking me. I backed up a few more steps. I had to get out of there. "Right. I think this party is over. If these notes aren't good enough, then I'm just going to give up the breastplate, because honestly, I think at this point I'm going to need my sanity more than a career jump."

"You wish to talk about the breasts?" The ghostly Antonio shimmered forward as I backed up, his eyes locked on my chest. He twirled one end of a slight moustache as he ogled me. "I am most 'appy to do whatever will please my lady. Your breasts, they rise up off your chest like two plump pigeons just waiting to be plucked."

Oh, lucky me. I got a randy ghost.

"Um . . ." I felt behind me for the wall, not trusting the ghost enough to take my eyes off it to look for the door.

"What is your name, oh, beauteous lady of the pigeon breasts?"

"Er . . ." The fingertips on the hand waving behind me touched books. I took a couple of steps to the left, where the door I came in was located.

"You will permit me a slight squeeze? They are so at-tractive, your breasts. I 'ave seen many breasts in my time, but yours—ah, glorious one, yours are a banquet of breasts! I must feast at them."

"Eeek!" I squealed as Antonio's slightly translucent hand reached for my chest. I spun around intending to escape the library with my stolen items, but where the door used to be a brick wall had suddenly materialized.

A very warm brick wall.

One that had two piercing blue eyes, long reddish-black hair, and fangs bared in a soundless snarl.

Vampire!

Chapter Three

"I've heard of being caught between a rock and a hard place, but this is ridiculous." Behind me the ghostly Antonio was swearing at the vampire who blocked the door. "Hi!" I said to the vampire. "You must be Melissande's cousin. We weren't expecting you back. I'm ... uh ... she asked me to ... um ... you're probably wondering what I'm doing here, huh?"

"Beslubbered 'edgepig!" Antonio spat at the intruder, pulling a rapier from his side. "It is not enough that I must tolerate that other evil one putting 'is 'ands all over my beloved Allegra, now you come to claim my one true love! What is your name, my darling?" he asked in an aside to me.

"Uh ..."

"It is enough! I will not tolerate you claiming the most beautiful Uh and 'er glorious breasts! She is mine, all of 'er!"

31

The vampire Christian, who had been watching the ghost with an amused cock to one of his glossy chocolate eyebrows, transferred his gaze from Antonio to my breasts. Impudent hussies that they were, they tried to thrust themselves forward toward him. I wrapped my arms over my chest and glared at both Antonio and the vampire, mentally telling my body that no matter how handsome the vampire might be, the last thing I wanted was to get involved with someone who was technically undead. "Look, I know this seems weird, you catching me here digging around your library, but I have an explanation."

"You will go now, un'oly dead one, else I shall cut off your man'ood and feed it to you." Antonio floated between us and whipped his sword around in a manner that probably would have left us both dead if it had been real.

Christian closed his eyes for a second. "Just what I need, an antagonistic ghost," he said. "Go away. My business is not with you." He waved a hand through the middle of the ghost. Amazingly, Antonio started to disintegrate.

"I am not antagonistic! Me, I went to Mass every morning!" Antonio's sword flashed in an intricate move no doubt intended to geld the vampire. Evidently he noticed he was fading, because he stopped gelding and shook his fist instead. "Basta! I shall call the others. They are watching Angel DVDs, but they will leave their precious Spike for you, you 'ideous spew-specked . . ."

"There's a lot to be said for exorcisms," Christian muttered under his breath as Antonio faded away into nothing.

"I thought only people who were possessed with a demon could be exorcised?"

Bright blue eyes snapped to mine, narrowing as they examined me from toes to head. Nervously I stepped back a few paces, my hands behind my back as I tried to stuff the stolen notes and earring into my back pocket, hoping that if Christian caught a glimpse of them, he'd believe they belonged to me. I wasn't sure he wouldn't mind Melissande having them, but I'd leave that to the two of them to work out.

"Who are you?" Christian asked, his voice low and rough, but with an edge of something that sent a little shiver down my back.

"I'm . . . uh . . . your cousin Melissande hired me."

He took two steps forward until he was a hairbreadth away from me. "Melissande isn't my cousin, and do not make me repeat myself again."

As he spoke, fangs flashed white in his mouth. Out of the blue a thought struck me, one so startling that my brain processed it without giving overdue thought to just how precarious a position I was in. "You know, I always assumed that vampires' fangs retracted or something when they weren't using them. Kind of like a cobra's fangs— present and accounted for when you want to use them, and out of the way when you don't."

They do, in most Dark Ones. Christian's voice had an almost ethereal quality, such a physical presence that I felt it in my head as well as heard it.

"But not you?" I looked at the pattern of red that wrapped around his torso. Like the one on the book, it was almost so faded I couldn't see it, seeming to shimmer in and out of my vision, like a half-glimpsed shadow seen out of the corner of my eye. I knew what it was the minute

I saw it, though. Some things are just too horrible to ever forget, no matter how hard you try. "Does it have something to do with the curse that binds you?"

Christian stared at me for a moment, and I knew I'd gone too far. Just because Melissande had assured me that this vampire wouldn't hurt me didn't mean he couldn't if he was peeved enough. *What did you say?*

"Nothing," I said, moving to the side. "It's not important. You know, Melissande is just outside. Why don't we call her, and she can clear up this whole mess—"

"You heard me," he accused, grabbing my arm in a grip that was borderline painful.

"Ow," I said. His grip loosened a smidgen. "Yeah, I heard you. I'm standing right here."

You heard what I said about Dark Ones.

"Well, duh! I'm not deaf. I understand you're miffed about finding me here, but I promised Melissande—"

It is not possible. You are not Moravian. You are not a telepath. And yet you hear me. He pulled me up close to his body, the heat from his chest burning my arm. *You can see the curse?*

"Yeah, I can see it, but not clearly. If I look straight at it, it disappears. I have to kind of peek at it from the corner of my eye to see the patt . . . oh, my God. Your mouth didn't move just then. I was watching." The skin along my back and arms crawled as a horrible realization dawned upon me. "What's going on? Why can I hear you talk without your mouth moving? You're not like some sort of vampire ventriloquist, are you?"

He shook his head. "This is not happening."

"I know how you feel," I said on a sigh. "I've had that

feeling all evening, ever since the imp episode, but I've given up trying to make sense of it and am now going with the flow. Look, Christian—"

He frowned, his warm, strong fingers flexing into the soft pudge of my arm. "Why do you call me that? I am not Christian Dante."

I went still, very still, bunny-rabbit-spotted-by-a-dangerous-predator still. I didn't even chance breathing. "You're not?"

"No."

"But you're a vamp."

An annoyed look passed across his face. "Dark One. I am a Dark One."

"Whatever. What are you doing here if you're not Christian, the guy who owns the place?"

"The same might be asked of you. More, since I would like to know why you have the ability to hear my thoughts, and how it is you can see the curse that binds me."

"Yeah, but I asked first. Who are you, and what are you doing here?"

He eyed me for another minute, then released my arm and spun around to look around the library. "Melissande hired you. You are here, obviously seeking the same as I. You can hear my thoughts. You can see my curse." He stopped and pointed to a sea-green vase on a bookshelf. "What do you see there?"

"A vase?" He stalked toward me until I scurried in the opposite direction, which just happened to be toward the vase. "It's a green vase. Pretty. Looks like it's valuable."

"Look closer," he commanded, his eyes turning to an indigo color. I looked away, curious as to how he did the eye thing, but figured now was probably not the best time to question him about vampiric skills and abilities. Glancing at the vase again, idly I wondered if it was possible to knock out a vampire by cracking him on the head with a vase.

"It would take much more than a vase to render me unconscious. Do not even think of trying. Now look at it again and tell me what you see."

I bit back the words of surprise that he knew what I was thinking and toyed with the thought of refusing him outright, but the few steps he took toward me, menace all but pouring off him, had me changing my mind. I hurried to do as he commanded. "It's just a vase. About twelve inches high, with a gold rim and faint pattern etched into the sides."

"Describe the pattern," he demanded, his gaze boring into mine.

"Fish," I said desperately, just wanting to get the hell out of there, away from the frightening—and bossy— fanged mystery vampire. "It has fish on it. Looks Greek or something."

He half turned away, disappointment flashing across his face. A brief stab of guilt flared within me, as if I had let him down somehow. What on earth was I thinking? He was a vampire! Bad news no matter how you looked at it. It didn't matter that somehow, what I had said had not been what he'd hoped to hear. Except . . . somehow, it did matter. Sympathy rose within me as I caught another glimpse of the red curse binding him. I supposed even a vampire has a right to be crotchety if he's bound by a demon lord's curse.

I glanced back at the vase, keeping one eye on the vamp in case he should try to grab me and make me a late-night dinner. I might feel sorry for him, but I wasn't *completely* stupid. "The fish are swimming in a couple of schools. The waves they are swimming on are curvy, turning back upon themselves. Kind of like the pattern I saw on the book—" I clamped my mouth shut, horrified with both what I said, and what it meant.

The vampire spun around, pinning me back against the wall with the force of his gaze. "You can see the ward?"

"Uh . . . maybe."

"Melissande," he murmured as he glanced down at himself to where the curse flickered red. "She found a Charmer. I didn't think she'd find one who has the power to help."

"Well, she hasn't. That is," I said quickly when his blue-eyed gaze was back to goring me, "I would be more than happy to help, but I can't. Charm, that is. I never could. My Charming skills are stunted, you see. But I did promise to help her find her nephew by poking around Christian's library, and that's what I'm doing here. Now that I've spilled my info; it's your turn."

"Damian," he said, his eyes doing the indigo thing again. I was just about to throw caution to the wind and ask him how he did it, when he moved. I didn't even see it coming—one minute I was standing near a bookcase, the next I was slammed back against the wall, pinned by two arms of steel attached to one very large vampire. "You will relay everything to me, from the beginning. What did Melissande tell you?"

"I should warn you, I'm an expert on vampires. I've seen every episode made of Buffy, Angel, *and* Forever Knight, so don't think a little fang-flashing is going to scare me," I started to say, but an up-close look at those sharp white incisors sent my bravado flying out the window, leaving me babbling like a brook. Power and desperation rolled off him, swamping me with the knowledge that this man would kill to find out what he wanted to know. Had I any state secrets to hand over, I would have gladly given them. "She hired me to charm a curse, but I don't do that sort of thing, so she promised me a breastplate if I would break in here and find some notes her brother had found that told where Damian was, only I didn't know it was breaking in, because she said the castle belonged to a cousin vamp who evidently wouldn't mind, although he went and left the door warded so she couldn't enter the castle, and come to think of it, since you're a vamp too, shouldn't you be, you know, locked out? Ward-wise?"

"Only the doors and windows were warded. I entered through neither."

"Oh. So how did you get in?"

He ignored my question, his brows pulling together in another frown. My mind warred with my body at his nearness. I kept telling myself that he was a vampire, a man whose prey tendencies didn't stop at wanting a date. I could be his dinner, for Pete's sake! I tried pointing that out to my libido, but all it saw was one extremely dishy guy. He was tall, taller than me and I'm no slouch, with lovely broad shoulders and a chest that had my Inner Nell doing a girlish swoon. His hair, a thick, heavy auburn, brushed the top of his collar. Reddish stubble grazed his lower cheeks and chin, turning my girlish swoon into a full-fledged strumpet-attack. His eyes changed from a light sky blue to a blue-black that was almost indistinguishable from his pupils. But it was something else, something more profound, that kept me from fighting him or trying to escape. Somewhere deep within this man, this vampire, I sensed a need, a cry for help that struck an answering chord inside me. I looked into his beautiful eyes and for a moment, for a breathless moment of time between seconds, I glimpsed the true nature of the darkness within him.

Life as I knew it ceased to be.

"Take slow breaths and keep your head down."

The words, rough and abrasive, were oddly calming as awareness returned to me. I was sitting on the floor, my head between my knees. All I could see were two booted feet swimming in a nauseating spinning pattern until slowly they settled into unmoving solidity. I lifted my head and looked at the vampire. "You don't have a soul."

"No," he said dryly. "Are you better now?"

"Yeah. I've never fainted before. Then again, I've never looked into a man's eyes and seen nothing but hell, either, so I guess this is a first all around. Since I don't hurt anywhere, I take it you caught me when I passed out?"

"Yes. Can you stand?" He held out his hand for me to take.

I beat down the warm thought of what it must be like to be held in his arms, and got to my feet. "Yep. A little wobbly in the knee department, but other than that, everything is OK. Listen, I'm sorry about the soulless thing. I'm sure it's nothing you care to be reminded of."

"Come," was all he said to my apology, holding open the door to the library.

"Sure. Oh, just let me grab the notes. I think they say something about where her nephew is being held." The torn sheets of paper lay scattered on the floor. I had no idea how they had fallen out of my pocket, but my brain, jet-lagged and paranormaled within an inch of insanity, decided it wasn't important.

The vamp glanced at the window. Through a crack in the heavy curtain I could see that the sky was starting to lighten. "Leave them. I don't need the notes. I know where Damian is being kept."

"You do? Great! You can tell Melissande. She's outside, waiting for me. Uh . . . we're going the wrong way. Her car is behind the castle, by a big crypt thingy."

"We're not going to Melissande."

I put the brakes on. The vampire snared my wrist in one of his steely grips and tugged me forward. "Wait a minute! Melissande is desperately trying to find her nephew and her brother. If you know where Damian is, you have to tell her so she can rescue them."

"Saer needs no help." His eyes were ice blue now, so cold I felt as if I'd been burned where his gaze touched me. I tried fighting his hold on my wrist, but he pulled me through the empty hall like I were a sack of potatoes. I *hate* pushy vampires!

"You know Saer?"

"Yes. Stop fighting me. You cannot escape."

"Ha! Just watch me," I yelled, grabbing at a nearby suit of armor.

The vamp spun around and scooped me up in one

move. The breath slammed out of my lungs as he stalked off with me slung over his shoulder.

"Hey!" I yelled, dragging my gaze off the fascinating sight of his upside-down butt. I pounded my hand on his back. "Let me down! All the blood is rushing to my head!"

"Perhaps it'll do a little good there," he muttered as he flung open a wooden door, my body bouncing painfully as he raced down a long flight of stone stairs.

"I heard that! Now put me down and we can discuss this kidnapping plan you have."

"No. Stop struggling or I will be forced to subdue you."

"Subdue me?" I asked his butt, which, I'm ashamed to admit, I couldn't seem to stop ogling. Encased in snug-fitting black jeans, it was a thing of joy to behold as it moved. "Oh, right. Like what, you're going to bite my leg?"

He didn't even pause. One minute I was bouncing on his back as he trotted down the stairs, the next minute a sharp sting burned the back of my thigh.

I rose up as far as I could, shocked (and strangely thrilled) to my very core. "Oh, my God! You bit me on the leg! You drank my blood! *I am not an appetizer!*"

You are much more than an appetizer. You are a twelve-course banquet.

"Oh!" I yelled, pounding his back again. "Stop it! Stop it right now! Stop whispering into my mind, and stop biting my leg. Let me down!"

"No."

Without the least sign of gentleness or concern for me, he continued down the stairs. He didn't even pause when he reached the floor, he just headed straight into the inky-black abyss of what must have been a very large basement. Looming up in the faint light coming from the stairwell I could see stone statues, statues that seemed oddly lifelike in the shadows that embraced them.

Worry began to well up inside me. It was one thing to banter with a vampire, but if he had plans of dragging me into his crypt with him . . . my breath stuck in my throat at the thought of being buried alive. It was my worst nightmare. "You're squishing my stomach! I'm going to barf if you don't let me down."

That did the trick. He came to a halt, lowering me to the ground, his fingers encircling my wrist as I took my first full breath since he'd picked me up. "Whew! That's better. Now, about this—"

"We have no time to waste in conversation. The sun is rising. Come."

"You know, I can walk and talk at the same time. I bet if you put your vampy mind to it, you could do the same. Now, I know you've got some sort of a bee up your"— incredibly attractive—"butt, but I'm not leaving without letting Melissande know where her nephew is. She's worried sick about him."

"Regardless, you will not return to her," he said grimly, pulling me after him as he entered a narrow stone passage. There was a metallic *clink* as he flipped open a lighter, the blue flame set high. It did little to illuminate the tunnel, however. All I could tell was that it was damp, seemed to go on forever, and smelled earthy. As I was dragged down the passage after the vampire, the floor changed from rock to sand, then to root-riddled dirt.

My worry turned to anger as he dragged me deep into

the bowels of the castle. How dare he leave poor Melissande to worry and fret when a simple word from him could help? "You heartless bloodsucker! How can you be so selfish?"

"Selfish?" The vamp cast me a disdainful glance.

"Yes, selfish. I'm not an idiot, you know. I saw the way your ears pricked up when you found out I am a Charmer—not that I am, but Melissande thinks I am. You want me to unmake the curse I saw on you, don't you?" I asked, stumbling over a tree root that poked up out of the ground. He caught me, wrapping one arm around my waist. I ignored the voice inside me that was screaming to enjoy the embrace, realizing he was simply trying to keep me on my feet. "You think you can use me to charm away your troubles!"

"Yes."

The word was spoken with a coldness that left me shivering.

"Well, you can just think again. I can't charm anything. I'm just here to help Melissande . . . which is what you should be doing, as well. There's a boy's life at stake, and even if you aren't particularly kind or even polite, surely you're not so much of a monster that you don't care."

"How do you know I'm not a monster?"

Something flickered deep in his eyes, and once again I felt a warmth within me answering his silent call. "Don't be silly. If you were a monster, you would have ripped out my throat or made me your queen of eternal night or something like that. You're just a man, not monster. Yes, a man with really sharp pointy teeth and hands like a steel trap, but you're still a man, and because of that, you're bound by the constraints of humanity to help Melissande."

He marched onward, not even pausing at my plea. "She wouldn't welcome my help."

"But—"

"No!" The word was spoken with a finality that was just shy of chipped into stone. I glared at him and promised myself that the first chance I had, I'd pry the information from him about the kid, and pass it on to Melissande.

"This way." He veered off into a yawning black opening, releasing me in order to throw his weight against a root-bound stone door. It squealed its protest, a nasty stone-grinding-on-stone noise filling the small chamber as the vampire slowly pushed the door closed. I stumbled backward over a large rock, the dim flame of the lighter not doing much along illumination lines.

"Who are you?" As I spoke, a dull, solid rumble shook the room, stopping with a horribly final sound. The vampire turned from the now closed stone door. "Who are you, and where are we, and just exactly why have you kidnapped me?"

The vamp searched until he found an arm-sized piece of wood. It must have been dry, because it flamed pretty quickly when he applied the lighter to it. He held the burning wood high like a torch, his shadow massive as it flickered on the rough-hewn stone walls behind him.

"My name is Adrian Tomas, this is a small room off the tunnel leading from the castle's bolt hole, and I have taken you so that you will unmake a curse created by the demon lord Asmodeus."

"Adrian?" I whispered, my brain reeling. "Adrian the Betrayer? The one who turns his people over to Asmodeus for endless torture and horrible deaths? *That* Adrian?"

"Yes," the vampire answered, the light from the burning wood glinting on his fangs as he smiled a grim smile. "I am the Betrayer, and you, Charmer, are my prisoner."

Chapter Four

"You're going to kill me, aren't you?"

"What?" Adrian held the burning root high as he walked the perimeter of the dank hole he had thrust me into. It was approximately the size of my bedroom back home, two of the walls carved out of stone, the other two made of earth supported with aging wooden beams. Judging by the broken barrels heaped in one corner, at one time this room had probably been used as some sort of storeroom. "Why would I want to kill you?"

The root had burned down almost to his hand. Adrian came to a halt in front of me, evidently satisfied that no light could get into the room.

"*Why?* I'm trapped, caught, ensnared with a rogue vampire who spends his leisure hours tossing his fellow vamps to a demon lord. Why shouldn't I think I'm going to be dinner?"

He tossed the root onto the dirt floor where it sputtered

46

as the last few inches continued to burn. "I told you I wanted you to help me. I don't make a practice of eating people I need."

"Yeah? That would be a whole lot more convincing if you weren't licking your fangs while you said it." The light from the burning root dimmed. I pressed against one of the stone walls and wrapped my arms around myself. I hate the dark. I hate being closed into small places. Ever since that night ten years ago . . .

An odd sort of martyred expression came over his face, all hard planes and harsh lines in the dying light. "I wasn't licking my fangs. I never lick my fangs. I'm sorry they bother you, but there's nothing I can do about them."

"What," I asked, nervously watching the flame on the root go from blue to yellow to red as it consumed the last bit of fuel, "your fangs are stuck in landing-gear-down mode?"

He sighed. I don't know why, just the thought of a vampire having anything to sigh over struck me as funny. Obviously, the lack of oxygen in the room was making me delirious. "Something like that, yes. Why are you trying to climb the wall?"

"Don't you think you should build a fire before that bit of wood goes out entirely?" Behind me, the damp chill of the rough stone sank through my jacket and settled into my bones.

"A fire?" He looked at the almost dead root, then back to me. "You are afraid of the dark."

"Yeah. So a nice big bonfire would be really good right about now. Er. That root is dying. You should do something about it."

"What is your name?"

"What?" I moved forward cautiously, keeping one eye on him as I crept toward the barely burning root. "Is it some sort of vamp rule that you have to know the name of the person you're about to kill?"

I squatted next to the root and blew on it, trying to keep it burning while I found something else dry to feed it. Kindling, that's what I needed, something small and thin.

"It's not a rule, no, but I find it's always nice to know what to put on the headstone."

I scrambled around in the dirt and found a couple of slivers of wood which I tossed onto the root, blowing on it to keep the flame alive. It was almost completely black in the room, so dark I couldn't see Adrian anymore, but I could feel him. I could feel him and the darkness and the weight of the massive stone castle over our heads pressing down into me. "Nell," I gasped as the root glowed red, then faded. As the light died, panic, true panic, was born within me. "My name is Nell."

"Nell." His voice, as rough as the stone that imprisoned us, rubbed along my skin as if he were touching me. "That is a strangely old-fashioned name for such a modern woman."

I stood up, disoriented by the dark, panicked, my breath coming short because there wasn't enough air. It had been sucked away, and trapped as we were in this tomb of stone and earth, I had no way to get more.

His voice came from another direction, as if he were circling me. "Nell, why are you afraid of the dark?"

I spun around, my eyes blind, trying to see something . . . anything. "I'm not so afraid of the dark as afraid of who I'm trapped with. Stand still, will you?"

"You are afraid of the dark," he whispered behind me. "Your heart is beating so fast I can almost taste your fear."

I jumped and turned to face the direction the voice had come. "Stop doing that and let me have your lighter!"

"Why do you want my lighter? Do you intend to set me on fire?"

"That wasn't on my list, but I'll be happy to add it," I said grimly, reaching into the darkness for him. "I want a fire, OK? It's cold in here."

"If it's warmth you seek, I will be happy to oblige," he growled into my right ear. I shivered at the heat of his breath as it whispered along my skin.

"A fire would be better," I said, clearing my throat to try to ease the hoarseness. "I like fires."

"A fire would kill you." His voice came from in front of me now. I waved my hand in that direction, brushing against something warm and hard that melted away into the blackness. "There is no ventilation hole in this chamber. The smoke would asphyxiate you."

"So what?" I sobbed, the panic I'd been struggling to contain washing over me. I crumpled to the ground a pathetic blob of humanity, shaking with cowardice and fear as I panted, trying to ease the pressure that bore down from the weight of the stone above. "I'll be dead once you're done doing this cat-and-mouse thing with me anyway. Why not die where at least I can see my murderer? Are you breathing all the air? There's no air in here! I can't . . . there's not enough air to breathe!"

"Nell." Hands warm and strong pulled me to my feet. For a moment I thought of fighting him, fighting what I knew he was going to do, but the instinctual need to cling to another human being overwhelmed me. Adrian grunted as I threw myself on him, clutching him, wrapping my arms around him. He was warm and solid, and somehow with my face pressed into his neck, I could breathe easier. It was as if he alone kept the weight of the stone around us from crushing me into an insignificant little pulp. The panic that had washed over me began to ebb. "I'm sorry," he said. "I did not know you were claustrophobic. I would have found alternate shelter had I known."

"You have a heartbeat," I said against his neck, my lips having been pressed against his pulse point. Beneath my arms wrapped around him, his chest rose and fell in a slow, regular pattern. "You're breathing. I thought vampires were supposed to be the undead. You don't feel dead. You're not cold and clammy at all."

"We prefer the term Dark One," he answered, his voice starting deep in his chest. "It has less of the Count Dracula connotation to it."

"So you're not dead?" I asked, relaxing slightly as his hands came around me in a gentle embrace.

"No. I live as you do, but with a few differences."

"Like the fact that you're immortal, and you drink blood, and you burn up in the sunlight, and garlic repels you." I had half expected him to sink fangs in me, but instead he seemed content to allow me to cling to him, finding a shelter in his arms that I had never in my wildest dreams expected.

I felt him shrug, his hands skimming up my back in a manner that had me shivering—but not with cold. "I live until I am destroyed, yes. I need blood to survive, that is true. Sunlight is not especially healthy for me, although it will not burn me to ash as popular movies show."

"What about garlic?" I asked, perversely enjoying the discussion. Smooshed up against him as I was, I couldn't help but breathe in his scent, a masculine combination of man and something else, something woodsy and elemental, something that started a little thrum inside me that I didn't seem to be able to stop.

Nor was I sure I wanted to.

"Garlic doesn't bother me, although I admit to finding it a bit offensive when it's used too heavily in my food."

How sick was it that I was getting pleasure out of clinging to a man—no, not a man, a vampire—who thought nothing of betraying his own people?

What makes you believe I think nothing of it?

"Your food?" I gasped, trying to pretend his voice hadn't brushed my mind. "You mean people? That was a joke? You're talking about people with garlic breath?"

"Yes, it was a joke. If your panic has eased, I will get my lighter. I cannot light a fire, you understand, but if you will allow me to move over to that pile of wood, I will place my lighter there so you might have light as long as the fluid lasts."

I peeled myself off him with an effort, lured away from his warmth and solidity by the promise of light. He flicked his lighter a couple of times, cupping a hand around the flame to protect it as he walked over to a pile of discarded barrel bits. He cleared a small patch, setting

51

the lighter down carefully, lowering the level of the flame. The light from it didn't penetrate the darkness beyond a few feet, but it was better than nothing. I hurried toward it, drawn like a moth to the light that flickered and danced in the draft.

"Better?" he asked. I nodded, rubbing my arms against the chill of the room. Odd how I hadn't noticed how cold it was when I had been snuggled up to him. He kicked aside more wood, clearing a path to a wall a few feet away.

"Ryan," I said, watching as he sat down, his back against the wall.

"Adrian," he corrected, leaning back, his arms crossed, his eyes closed.

"Ryan is friendlier. Ryan all but oozes niceness. I like Ryan. A Ryan would never snack on someone's leg. Adrian sounds"—I made an expressive gesture with my hands—"cruel. Heartless. Savage."

"I am cruel, heartless, and savage. I am the Betrayer."

"Mmm. Ryan reeks of normalcy."

His eyes opened at that.

I made a face. "Maybe you're right. You're not exactly the Ryan type. Adrian it is."

I rubbed my arms again, glancing around for somewhere I could curl up and keep warm.

"No one has ever called me anything but Adrian the Betrayer." For a moment there was a look of surprised longing in his eyes; then it disappeared as he closed his eyes again.

"What are you doing?" I asked, shivering slightly. I hadn't seen any sign of them, but I couldn't help wondering if there were any rats trapped in the room with us. I bet if there were, none would bother Adrian. Weren't vampires supposed to be able to control the creatures of the night?

"I am trying to sleep. There are no rats."

"Stop reading my mind!" Annoyance at the way he dipped into my mind whenever he felt like it drove away the worry about rats and discomfort of the cold.

The corners of his lips quirked stiffly, as if he hadn't smiled in a long time. Even in partial shadow as he was, my inner squeal girl couldn't help but point out just how handsome he was. The faint glow of light picked up the red notes in his hair, kissing the hard planes of his face, the reddish whiskers softening an otherwise hard line of jaw. When his lips quirked upward at the corner, a hint of dimple showed on either cheek. His nose had a couple of small bumps down its length, indicating that he must have broken it once or twice. Eyelashes, thick and black, lay fanned on his cheeks, hiding those beautiful, haunted eyes.

He really was the most gorgeous man I'd ever seen.

The faint line of dimples on either cheek deepened.

Sexy as hell, too, but I expected he knew that.

One side of his mouth curled.

He probably didn't even have to go shopping for dinner. I bet the women were on him so thick, he had to shovel them off.

The other side of his mouth twitched. The dimples deepened.

He didn't do anything for me, though. Nothing at all. I was more sexually attracted to the burned root that lay on the floor than to him.

His eyes opened in surprise.

"Ha!" I told him, rubbing my arms. "That'll teach you to eavesdrop in people's private fanta . . . er . . . thoughts!"

"I assure you, it's not an ability I sought. In truth, the fact that we can read each other is more than a little disconcerting since it means . . ."

"What?" I asked, shivering with the damp and cold of the room.

"Nothing."

He closed his eyes again and appeared to go to sleep.

I kicked his foot. "You have dimples."

One of his eyebrows raised, but he didn't even bother to open his eyes.

"That's got to be against a law of nature. Everyone knows it's physically impossible for vampires to have dimples. Men who have dimples are cute and adorable, like little fluffy bunnies. Vampires are dark, brooding, and tortured. You can't be dark, brooding, and tortured if you could burst out into dimples at any moment."

His eyebrows lowered, but his arms remained crossed over his chest.

I kicked his foot again. "Men with dimples sing Broadway show tunes. *Upbeat* Broadway show tunes!"

"I don't have dimples." He crossed one ankle over the other just as I was going to kick his boot again.

"Yes, you do. I've seen them. You just don't know you have because you can't see your reflection in a mirror."

You shouldn't believe everything you read.

"You can see yourself in a mirror? Oh. Well, the next time you're near one, you'll have to smile at yourself and see your dimples."

His eyes opened for a few seconds to glare a steel-blue glare at me before closing again. *Do I look like the sort of man who goes about smiling at himself in mirrors?*

"You *look* like the sort of man who eats small children for breakfast," I answered. He said nothing to that, just went to sleep sitting on a hard, cold floor in a hard, cold room that somehow didn't seem to be quite as oppressive as it had a few minutes before. Dimples or not, I had to give him credit for calming the major panic attack I had been brewing. I stood for a few minutes shifting from foot to foot, finally saying in a whining voice that had me flinching in embarrassment, "I'm cold."

The martyred look was back on his face, but he opened his arms without saying anything. I didn't wait to debate the pros and cons of curling up next to a mind-reading vampire, I just threw myself onto him, apologized briefly for inadvertently jamming my knee into his groin, wrapped my arms around him, and buried my face into his neck. He was warm and strong and he smelled good. I relaxed into his body, his arms closing around me with a solidness that left me feeling safe and protected.

Which was ridiculous, considering he had just kidnapped me and wanted me to destroy myself in order to save him from a curse.

"Nell?" His voice was low and deep in my ear, his breath hot on my temple as he spoke.

"Hmm?"

"I've never once had to shovel women off me."

I chuckled into his neck, too warm and comfortable to protest the fact that he had been reading my mind.

"But it pleases me that you think I'm sexy."

I pinched a bit of flesh on his back exposed between his black cotton sweater and the waistband of his pants. "Bad vampire."

As I was falling asleep, a thought shimmered in my mind in a way that made me wonder if I had imagined it, or heard an echo of his thoughts.

There can be nothing between us. There is no hope for me. I must die, and you must live.

Chapter Five

"Ow. Stupid rock. My next kidnapper is going to have a Porsche."

Adrian said nothing, but the hand nearest me tightened into a fist, as if he wanted to strangle something. I had an uncomfortable feeling I knew what. Or rather, *who*. That worry didn't stop me from continuing, however. For some reason I didn't care to examine fully, I had gone from being terrified of Adrian to comfortable. Oddly comfortable. As in very, very strangely comfortable. And all because he was nice to me when he could have been cruel.

The fact that he didn't eat me for dinner also helped improve my overall impression of the Betrayer.

I shivered and trudged down the winding road that led from Drahanska Castle to the nearby town of Blansko, where I fervently prayed Adrian had a car stashed. "My next kidnapper is going to know how to kidnap a girl in style. He won't drag me off to a dirty, rat-infested hole, starve me, then make me walk miles and miles and miles after the sun has gone down. He'll kidnap me using his sports car with comfortable heated leather seats, complete with picnic basket filled with goodies. A *sexy red* sports car."

There was no response from Adrian other than his jaw tightening.

"A convertible!"

"For the love of God, woman, what do you want from me?" he burst out, his eyes flashing an irritated midnight blue. "I asked you if you wanted me to carry you, but you said you'd rather die first."

"Yeah, but I didn't mean it literally! Death by blisters, what an ignominious way to go." I rubbed my arms to keep the circulation going, wincing as I stepped on yet another rock.

"You have absolutely no respect for me, do you?" he asked, shooting me an annoyed look. "You have no idea how powerful and dangerous I can be. I am feared and loathed by all of my people, hunted like an animal by those who would destroy me, but you aren't the least bit in awe of me, are you? You should be terrified of me, and all you do is complain."

"Well, I'm a bit in awe of those fangs," I said, trying to make him feel better, although I honestly didn't know why I cared if his feelings were hurt or not. "Aren't they in the way like that? You must have to mumble a lot when you're in public, so people won't see them. And don't your lips get snagged on them? I had braces when I was in my teens, and I tore my lips on them something terrible.

I'd offer you some lip balm, but my purse was left behind when you abducted me. I hope the real Christian gives it back. All my money and my passport are in it."

"Dark Ones do *not* wear lip balm," he said in an outraged voice.

I shrugged and amused myself for a few minutes by trying to make the white puffs of breath that hung briefly in the air before me into a bat shape.

"No," Adrian said before I could ask the question. "I can't change into a bat."

I stopped in the middle of the road, a feeble moon casting light down upon us from between suitably dramatic wisps of cloud. "Stop. Reading. My. Mind!"

His fingers clamped around my wrist as he hauled my protesting feet forward. "I can't help it. You're projecting."

"Oh," I gasped, outraged. "I am not! I never project!"

"You are. You don't put up the slightest barrier to your thoughts. All I have to do is . . ." A warm presence touched my mind. I sucked in a deep breath of icy air at the feel of him merging with my thoughts. It was the most intimate touch I'd ever felt, far more intimate than just the joining of bodies.

Smug male satisfaction filled my mind.

"Stop it," I said, pushing him out of my mind. "It's not polite to wander around in someone's head without them knowing."

"You know," he grumbled. "You have to know. You also know you can read me just as easily as I can read you."

"Why would you think that?" I looked at the tall, dark figure next to me. "I've never been any good at guessing what people were thinking, let alone able to read minds."

"I've marked you," he said grimly. "It's the first step of Joining."

"Marked me? You haven't even touched me. I know you're the big bad wolf and all—"

"The Betrayer," he interrupted. "I am the Betrayer. I am hated and feared—"

"—by all your people, and hunted down like the dog you are, yadda yadda. Yeah, I know, you told me. I guess that's why I'm not afraid of you anymore, Adrian the Betrayer. You didn't hurt me when you could have."

"That's not the reason," he said shortly. I couldn't see his face because a cloud had drifted across the moon's face, but we were coming into town, which meant I should soon be able to see if his expression was as grim as his voice. "It's something much worse."

"Worse? What are you talking about?"

He refused to answer. Our conversation—sporadic at best—dried up into nothing as we started up a short hill into the town of Blansko.

"Nell," he said a little while later as we passed through a dark square. "You—"

"Oh, look, a train station! I bet you could hire a car there or something. And they probably have food, too. I'm starving. Come on."

"Nell." He grabbed my arm in his steel-fingered shackle grip and pulled me up so his mouth was next to my ear. To any of the few people driving through the square, we probably looked like lovers who couldn't wait to get home. "You will remember that you are my prisoner. You will keep uppermost in your mind at all times the fact that I'm a dangerous creature of darkness. I am a killer, a betrayer, a man without a soul who will not hesitate to destroy anyone who stands in his way."

I looked up at his face, visible in the bluish-white glow of a lamppost. A little ripple of fear skimmed down my back at the expression in his eyes. They were ice blue, and utterly hopeless. Without thinking of the folly of what I was doing, I turned so I faced him fully, gently touching the side of his face. Darkness, deep and all-consuming and endless, raged within him, a gaping hole inside him where his soul should have been. I wanted to fill the emptiness, to change the darkness to hope, and love, and happiness. I knew instinctively that I could lift the curse that bound him so tightly, easing the torment that had him within its twisted grip, but to do so would mean I had to open up that part of my mind that I had all but destroyed ten years ago.

The part of my mind that had killed an innocent woman.

"I'm sorry," I said, my voice a thin ribbon of sound on the cold night air as I lowered my hand. "I can't. I can't ever do that again."

His eyes went dark as I felt the soft brush of him against my mind. I turned away, as if that would keep him from seeing the truth about me. I had not thought for one moment that he hadn't noticed the slackness in the left side of my face, or the weakness in my left hand and leg, but he had not asked about it, and I hadn't offered an explanation.

"What do you hide from me?"

I stilled, clutching my guilt to myself. He turned me so I was facing him. Suspicion filled his face as he narrowed his eyes. "I cannot read what you hide. What secret do you have that fills you with so much horror?"

I took a deep breath, trying desperately to calm my suddenly racing heart. His thumb brushed over the pulse in my neck in a gesture so gentle, I almost melted at his feet. "You're not the only one who has betrayed people," I said finally.

"Who . . ." he started to say, then stopped abruptly, lifting his head as if scenting the night air. *"Do prdele!"*

I glanced around to see what had startled him, but saw nothing. We were in a dark square, the houses facing us dimly lit or dark already, even though it was only a little after nine at night. A few cars had zipped by us, but no walkers passed, and nothing nearby seemed to pose a threat.

"What's wrong?"

"Go." He shoved me forward. Beyond the square was a pink stone building that I recognized from the drive in with Melissande as the train station.

Melissande! I hadn't thought of her after wondering whether she would know I had been abducted. Surely she would count on my lust for the breastplate, at least, to keep me from walking out on her as it may have seemed I'd done. Had Melissande tracked us? Was I going to be rescued?

More importantly, why did I feel a distinct sadness at the thought of leaving Adrian?

"Quickly, go to the train station. Buy two tickets for Prague. The train leaves in less than twenty minutes. I will meet you at the platform."

"Wait a minute!" I grabbed at a lamppost as he pushed me down the sidewalk.

"You will do as I command," he snarled, spinning around to glare in the direction we had just come from.

I smacked him on the arm. "First of all, I don't take well to commands without an explanation. If you want me to do something, tell me why. And second of all . . ." I took a couple of steps back when he whirled toward me, his eyes all but spitting blue flames into the night. The words I'd been about to utter, telling him he could stuff his Mr. Macho attitude, died on my lips. "Uh . . . I don't have any money. You hustled me out of the library so fast, my purse was left with Melissande, remember?" I held up my empty hands.

He swore again in Czech, thrusting his hand in his inner jacket pocket before shoving a wad of bills at me. "Go!"

Before I could protest, he was off, slipping into the shadows as if he'd been made of them.

"Which," I said to myself as I peered down the length of the square trying to follow him, "is just about as apt a simile as I'll ever find. All right, Nell, what are you going to do?"

I looked down at the money in my hand. I could take it and buy myself a ticket to Prague, where I could throw myself on Melissande's mercy. I could hire a taxi to take me back to Drahanska Castle, where I could recover my purse. I could trot myself to the nearest police station and report my abduction (leaving out a few key insights into Adrian's dark nature).

"Or," I said on a sigh as I turned for the pink stone building, "I could buy two tickets to Prague, and spend the rest of the night figuring out why the hell I care the least bit about a bad boy vampire. Assuming he shows up from wherever he's gone off to, that is."

I bought two tickets. The ticket seller told me that the train was running a little late, but that it should arrive within the next half hour. Hunger gnawing at my stomach, my first act after paying for the tickets was to plug some change into a candy machine and consume three honey-chocolate bars in swift succession.

I think the sugar high must have done something to me, because by the time I was done licking the last of the chocolate from my fingertips, I was pacing the length of the sidewalk outside the train station, periodically pausing to consult the large clock in a minuscule waiting room.

"This is ridiculous. He's not coming. He's run off to find himself a quick dinner or something," I muttered, not believing it, but feeling better for saying it. "He's not going to make the train. You should be happy, Nell. You're free again. No more bossy vamp pushing you around. You can tell Melissande what happened, get your stuff, and go home."

Without the breastplate.

Without helping Melissande locate her nephew.

Without Adrian.

"Right, you can just stop thinking *that*, for one," I lectured myself, peering out into the darkness in hopes of seeing a large, vampire-shaped man running my way. "He might be nummy, and he might smell good, and he might

64

be filled with so much pain it hurts to even think about it, but he's a vampire. A night walker. A bloodsucker. And he betrays people, to boot. He's no good with a capital *NO*. Who cares if those other vamps he was talking about have found him? Who cares if they beat him up? Who cares if they . . . aw, hell!"

I ran down the sidewalk, following the path I had taken to get to the station. Try as I might, I couldn't deny that Adrian and I had some sort of connection, and I couldn't just stand around if he needed help. I told myself it was so I could worm out of him the information he knew about Damian—I owed it to Melissande to do what I could to help, since I wasn't going to do what she had brought me here to do—steadfastly ignoring the truth that it was Adrian I really wanted to help.

The square we'd stopped in was still dark. "Well, now what?" I asked myself as I spun around in a circle. I had no idea what threat he had seen, or even if it was a threat. Maybe I had been right—maybe he had gone off to dine on an unwary person walking their dog.

Or maybe the hunters had caught up to their prey?

I stood in a dim pool of light, wracked with frustration and indecision. Adrian had said I could read him as well as he could read my mind, but what would result if I tried to use my mental radar to pick up where he was? I started to turn back toward the train station, remembering all too well the horror of what had happened the first and only time I tried to use a part of my brain that lay dormant in most people. Would trying to make contact with him cause another stroke? What if something worse happened?

How could I try, knowing it might permanently damage me?

How could I ignore the fact that Adrian might need me?

"Fine," I snarled to the darkness, one hand on the cold metal of a lamppost as I closed my eyes. "But if I die from this, I'm coming back as a ghost to haunt him for the rest of his unnatural life."

I focused my thoughts on Adrian, what he looked like, smelled like, how he felt warm and solid when I was pressed against him, and the gentle touch of his mind on mine.

Nell? The word was soft in my head, filled with surprise and, strangely, anger. *What are you doing?*

Rescuing you, I answered grimly, my eyes snapping open as I marched off in the direction I suddenly knew Adrian to be.

His derisive snort filled my thoughts. *I am a Dark One. I am immortal, one of the most powerful beings of the ages. I do not need the help of a mortal, and certainly not a female mortal.*

Yeah? Well this female mortal isn't buying the macho act, so you can just—behind you!

I ran down the sidewalk, spinning around a corner and slipping on a patch of black ice as I raced toward the alley where I knew I'd find Adrian. Behind him I could sense another person, someone as powerful as he was.

Driven by heedless fear, I dashed across a street, right in front of a car that careened around the corner, its brakes squealing as I made an abortive attempt to avoid colliding with it. Pain burst across my left side as I bounced off the hood, hitting the frozen pavement with enough force to leave me breathless and stunned.

"Ow," I gasped, doing an inventory of my arms and legs to see if anything was seriously injured. I had just determined that I had nothing worse than a few bruises when a big shape loomed overhead for a second as it jerked me upright, slamming me backward into the car that sat running a few feet away.

"Where is he?" a man snarled into my face.

I blinked quickly to try to clear my vision. "What?"

The blond man holding me up by the collar of my coat twisted the material until I was choking. His face was filled with anger, lips drawn back to expose wicked-looking fangs. "The Betrayer. You reek of him. Where is he? Tell me or you die."

"I don't know," I said honestly, sure that Adrian must have left the alley I'd "seen" him in.

It wasn't an answer the man liked. He snarled something rude in French that I pretended I didn't understand, his eyes gleaming with fury as he tightened his grip on my coat. I choked, black spots starting to swim before my eyes.

"You lie!"

"I swear to you, I don't know where he is," I wheezed, trying desperately to get some air past the stranglehold he had on my neck.

"I will not leave you alive to help betray others," he hissed. Jerking me forward, he ripped my coat until my neck was bared. I gasped in pain when I sucked in much-needed air, the blackness that had been threatening to overwhelm me, blinding me to the fact that his head was descending toward my neck until I felt his breath on my skin.

Every atom in my body was repulsed by the thought of him touching me in such an intimate way. I tried to summon enough strength to fight off the vampire who intended on taking my life, but my arms and legs were strangely slow to respond.

Adrian! my mind screamed. I struggled feebly against the blond man as he jerked me closer, his breath hot on my skin, when suddenly he froze. He began to swear, leaving me positive I was going to die at that moment.

A rush of air, a familiar scent, and a deep, sexy voice snarling some inventive curses in German saved me. I sagged against the car, one hand massaging my aching throat as I gasped for air, my eyes on the two men who fought in the road. Adrian and the blond man were of the same size, but where the blond was wiry, Adrian was all solid strength. It wasn't limitless strength, I knew, and I could feel an echo from Adrian's mind that there was another Dark One nearby.

A train's warning horn sounded twice in the distance.

The blond threw a punch that would have decapitated a mortal man. Adrian's head snapped backed as he staggered sideways, and I knew I had to help him. He was too hungry, too tired from watching over me during the daylight hours, to beat two determined vampires. I looked around the empty road for something I could use as a weapon to disable the blond, but there was nothing.

Adrian lashed out at the vamp with his foot, slamming into the other man with enough force to send him flying.

Obviously, somewhere down the centuries Adrian had found time to study martial arts. I yanked open the car door in search of a gun, or stake, or whatever vamps used to kill each other with, but found nothing. Snatching the keys from the ignition, I jumped aside when the blond lunged past me, yelling something anatomically impossible as a knife suddenly appeared in his hand, glinting brightly in the light from a nearby building. A flick from his wrist and the knife was flying through the air. Adrian leaped to the side, but not quickly enough. The knife imbedded itself to the hilt in his chest.

"No!" I screamed, running toward him.

"Now you die, Betrayer," the blond man said, swaggering forward.

Adrian faced the vamp, his chest rising and falling quickly as he pulled out the knife. The black of his shirt grew even darker as a wet stain spread across it. I knew without touching his mind that he was quickly running out of strength, the wound coming perilously close to nicking his heart.

"You will die and our people will be safe at last," the blond vamp snarled.

Adrian raised his head, but it wasn't to glare at the vamp. His gaze touched mine, and I blinked in surprise to see in it regret mingled with sorrow. Within seconds those emotions were gone, and his eyes were brilliant ice-blue chips of determination.

"You have tried to destroy me before, Sebastian, and you failed. You will not succeed this time either."

Adrian was gathering himself for an attack, an action that I knew in my heart would leave him dead. Without thinking, I threw my hands out and drew the pattern that had been burned into my brain so many years ago, piercing with relative ease the shadow that had lain over part of my psyche.

Sebastian's eyes widened as my hands, remembering something my brain had long forgotten, sketched ancient symbols into the night air. The symbols twisted and curled upon themselves, glowing silver in the air for a moment before fading.

Immediately, pain sharp and deep slashed through my head. I clutched my temples, desperately trying to stay on my feet as Adrian stared in surprise for a moment at the glowing symbols. Sebastian cursed and swore as he tried to move, only then realizing what I had done.

The stab of pain melted into my brain, leaving me faintly dizzy and weak. Adrian grabbed my hand and jerked me past the impotent, snarling Sebastian.

"I will destroy you, Betrayer! You and your Beloved both will die for the crimes you have committed!"

"What the hell?" I asked, staring at my hands as Adrian dragged me down the road, forcing me into a limping gallop alongside him while he muttered about making the train. "Where did *that* come from?"

"You're a Charmer," he answered breathlessly. "You drew a ward to bind him." He glanced at me briefly as we approached the train station. "You said you could not charm, and yet you drew a powerful ward."

"Don't look at me, I have no idea how I did that," I replied, glancing behind us, the pain caused by drawing the ward thankfully a fast-dimming memory. "The other vamp is still out there."

A blast from beyond the station warned that the train was about to leave.

"It matters not. Come. We must hurry."

I raced up the steps, pausing at the top when Adrian almost doubled over, his hand to his chest.

"You're hurt badly, aren't you? We'll stop and—"

"No," he gasped, shoving me past him into the station, toward the platform. "We must leave now. I do not have the strength to fight the two of them together." *Too much blood has been lost. I must feed.*

His thought shimmered in my mind as we raced through the station. I jerked the tickets out of my pocket as we burst out onto the platform. The train tooted its horn a couple more times, slowly starting to move. Adrian lunged forward, jerking open one of the doors. I told my aching body it could rest if it got me on that train. Then I said a little prayer and jumped. I fell onto the floor inside, quickly pulling myself out of the way as Adrian threw himself beside me.

We lay panting and gasping for a few seconds before he got to his feet, helping me up. I waved the tickets at the conductor, who had given a mildly curious glance at our unorthodox entrance before we collapsed into a seat at the end of the car as my entire body screamed abuse at me, my mind numb with the events of the last twenty-four hours.

Adrian sat in the seat facing me, hunched over, his hand to his chest.

"Are you OK?" I asked. Stupidly. Of course he wasn't OK, he'd just been stabbed. Even a vampire had to feel a stabbing.

"Yes," he said, his breath shallow and fast. "Your head . . . I felt your pain. Is it better?"

I touched my temple. "All gone, but I don't think I'm going to try warding again."

The conductor wandered over to check our tickets. I gave them to him, scooting over to sit next to Adrian, casually leaning into him in a way that would hide the blood seeping out of his chest. I didn't want to think about at what point I'd gone from being captive to protector; I just wanted the conductor gone so I could see how badly Adrian was hurt.

After a few questions about where we were going, the man moved off to another car. I waited until a couple with two screaming kids passed us before turning to Adrian. "How bad is it?"

I pushed his shoulders until he was leaning back at a drunken angle, using my body to shield us in case anyone went down the aisle in the center of the car.

"It's healing. Leave it."

"I told you I don't take orders without a good reason." I brushed his hand aside and unbuttoned the black silk shirt that was glued to his chest, biting my lip at the deep slash in his pectoral muscle. The knife had barely missed hitting his nipple, and, going by my scanty knowledge of anatomy, probably had come very close to striking him in the heart. The wound was still bleeding, but sluggishly. "You can heal yourself?"

"Yes," he said, his head back. I gave the wound a long look, then stripped off my jacket and pulled my arms from the sweater I was wearing. Beneath it, I squirmed out of the thin cotton camisole, taking it off and redonning my sweater before turning to him. His face was still, his lashes thick slashes of black on cheeks gone pale with the loss of blood. Using my teeth, I tore a little hole in the bottom of the camisole, ripping off a couple of long strips before folding the remainder of the fabric over into a soft pad.

"This may hurt," I murmured as I glanced around the car before pressing the pad to the hole in his chest. His eyes opened to watch me as I slid my hands into his shirt and behind him, strapping the pad down with the strips of fabric. I tried my best to not notice the way the warm flesh of his naked back felt, but I couldn't resist spreading my fingers along the muscles before withdrawing my hands.

"Why are you doing this?" he asked, his eyes narrowing as I buttoned his shirt.

"I don't really know," I answered truthfully. "I was kind of hoping you'd be able to tell me."

His eyes closed again as his head sagged into the high back of the seat. "Every unredeemed Dark One has a Beloved, a woman who can save his soul."

"Yeah, Melissande told me about that."

"In order to be redeemed, the two must Join."

"You mean sex?" A warmth started in my belly, spreading out to the rest of my body as the wicked part of my mind indulged in some extremely detailed fantasies concerning him.

"No. Yes. Not wholly. A physical relationship is the fifth step, but there is more to a Joining than just lovemaking."

"So you think that because we can do the Vulcan mind meld, I'm your savior, and we're bound to end up having wild bunny sex together?"

He grimaced with pain.

"All right, I'll take back the wild bunny sex question since you're in no shape to even be thinking about that. Just tell me about this fifth step," I asked, leaning forward to brush a tendril of hair off the stubble on his cheek.

His eyes opened and caught me in a clear blue snare. I looked at his mouth, so near, so tempting. Normally held in a tight line, relaxed his mouth was sensual, the curve of his lower lip singing a sweet siren song that I couldn't resist. I kissed him gently, feathering light little kisses along his lips, watching in cross-eyed wonder as his eyes darkened to midnight.

"What was that?" he asked, his breath fanning my face. I shivered at the rough touch of his voice, my mind filled with erotic thoughts that I wasn't entirely certain were mine.

"A kiss. I think you're sexy, remember?"

"That wasn't a kiss," he said, his voice low, reverberating within me. "*This* is a kiss."

One hand tangled in my hair as his mouth claimed mine, the hot, sweet lure of his lips melting me into him as his tongue swept its way into my mouth, pushing aside any objections I might have wanted to make about the sinuous way it stroked me. I've never been one who found tongues overly stimulating, but the way Adrian tasted me, it was different, erotic. His tongue twined around mine, enticing mine to follow in a sensuous dance. Various and sundry parts of my body tightened and ached as I felt a need in him, a need in myself to taste him. I flicked my tongue over the corners of his mouth, tasting his skin before diving into unknown territory. His mouth was as hot as the rest of him, and oddly enough, just feeling his heat made me shiver. I slid my tongue around the glossy enamel of his teeth, pausing to stroke down the length of an elongated canine tooth.

Yeah. I know. How stupid is it to French kiss a vampire and not expect sharp teeth?

I jumped as the tip of the tooth pierced my tongue, blinking in surprise as Adrian stilled beneath me. Our mouths were still joined, but I knew I was bleeding. A roar of hunger swept through him, through me, screaming a demand that he couldn't deny. He suckled hard on my tongue, groaning deep in his throat as he sucked off the bead of blood.

I pulled my mouth from his, startled by the overwhelming desire that rocked him, feeling it as if it were my own. He stared at me, his eyes onyx now, and I knew what it was he wanted. *Needed.*

"You're hungry," I whispered, the background hum and clatter of the train all but obliterating the words. "You haven't . . . er . . ."

"Fed. No. There was no time before, and after, there was only you, and I couldn't . . ." He closed his eyes, his jaw tense. I was draped across him, careful not to put any pressure on his wound, the movement of the train rocking us together beneath the flimsy blanket made up of our coats. This close to him, I didn't have to open myself up to feel what he felt.

"Why couldn't you . . . er . . . feed off me?" I asked, turning my head so my lips brushed the bristled line of his jaw.

"We've already taken three steps of Joining." His voice

was so raw it sent a shiver of desire down my back. "Four, if you count this. You could have left me to the hunters, but you didn't."

He touched his chest.

"I don't quite follow you on this whole step thing, but I know you need blood. You've lost a lot, and if your tank wasn't full to begin with, then you're really running on empty."

Midnight-blue eyes looked at me, a question in their depths, almost hidden by hopelessness and despair. It wrung my heart, my throat closing with tears as I accepted the pain that howled within him, my body shaking as I took his darkness and fought to make it light.

"Take it," I whispered, pulling his head toward me. "Feed."

"Nell." His lips brushed against the skin of my throat. "You don't know what you're saying."

"I know what I'm doing," I lied, tilting my head back. "Feed on me, Adrian."

Beneath my hands, his shoulders shuddered as he fought the red wave of hunger that swept through him. I knew, in a distant part of my mind, that I should be horrified, sickened by what I was offering, by what I craved him to do, but the truth was, I ached to have him feed off me.

Not feed . . . feast. The words echoed in my head just before his teeth pierced my flesh. I gasped and arched back, my eyes open but blind with the overwhelmingly erotic sensation of his mouth moving on my neck, his mind bound so tightly with mine that I could taste my own blood as it slipped down his throat. Within him the endless night that howled so cruelly faded a little, the torment easing as I gave myself up to the moment, trusting that he wouldn't harm me, locked in an embrace more arousing than anything I'd ever known. My body seemed to catch on fire as his lips caressed my flesh beneath the cover of my coat, his hand spread wide over my breast before it slid down over my belly. The carnal images in his mind drove the fire higher, hotter, until I was sure I was going to explode with the heat.

"Adrian," I warned softly, his hair like cool satin as it brush my jaw. "You can't. *We* can't!"

We can do anything we want, he answered, his fingers undoing the button on my jeans, pushing the zipper down until his hand could delve inside. *Let me do this, Nell.*

"I . . . oh, my God, someone will see you," I gasped, my hips lurching as his fingers slid along the satin line of my underwear, sliding beneath the delicate material to cup the most intimate part of me.

Let me pleasure you, he begged.

You pleasure me any more and I may just die. My body moved against him, belying my words. Little flicks of fire touched me where his fingers delved. I tensed, unable to draw a breath, my mind caught between his hunger and my own need, which he was driving higher and higher within me.

Now, Beloved. One finger slid into me, triggering an explosion of white heat that seemed to consume the universe. I dug my fingers into his shoulders, trying to merge myself with him so that there would be no him and no me, only us.

"Oh, God," I gasped what seemed like eons later as he

pulled his head from my neck. His hand was withdrawing from me, zipping my jeans as I lay draped across him, my body quivering with little shocks of residual pleasure. "Now I know why women find vampires so sexy. You're the most amazing . . . that was the best . . . you are absolutely incredible!"

He said nothing, just pulled me down so I fit comfortably against his shoulder, but I felt his slow, sensual smile as it stole across my mind.

Chapter Six

"Get up, Nell."

"No. I am not getting off this train until you let me see your chest."

"I told you before that I do not like to repeat myself. I will this once because I understand you are American, and thus stubborn. My chest is healed. You will get up now and come with me."

I looked out the tinted window at the bright lights of the Prague central train station. I was tired, hungry, and a little dizzy from the amount of blood I'd donated.

We won't go into how my body seemed to hum every time Adrian was near.

"My stubborn American butt is not getting up off this seat until you bare your manly chest for me." I adopted the most innocent look I could muster.

He muttered to himself in a language I didn't understand, then yanked me to my feet, pulling me close with one hand while opening his shirt with the other.

"OK," I said, running a finger down the jagged raised white scar line that was all that remained of the wound. "You've impressed me. The next time you get a sucking chest wound, I won't worry at all. So now what do we do? And who was Sebastian? Why was he after you? Is it just a Betrayer thing, or did it have something to do with the reason you were in Christian's castle, which, incidentally, is something you've never explained. There's no time like the present, my mother always says!"

His hand clamped down on mine as I let my fingers do a little walking. "I can feel your hunger. You will get some food while I arrange for transportation."

"You think you can just ignore my questions and I'm going to let you get away with it, don't you?"

"Yes."

"You don't scare me," I told him as I followed him off the train, more than a little surprised to find that it was true. There was a bond between us that had me worried about him, heartsick because I knew that I couldn't give him what he wanted—freedom from the curse—but I wasn't frightened of him anymore. He might break my heart (where had *that* thought come from?), but he wouldn't ever harm me. Not intentionally.

"I am more powerful, more determined, and infinitely crueler than you. You should be terrified of me. Do as I say without questioning me further."

I thinned my lips in annoyance at his high-handed manner, blinking owlishly in the bright overhead station lights. "What makes you think I'm going to do what you want me to do? What makes you think I'm not going to run to the nearest police station? Or to Melissande? You know, it's really not fair, you running off without telling her where her nephew is. She's worried sick about him."

"You will not run from me because you know that wherever you hide, I will find you. As for the other— Melissande's feelings do not matter to me," he answered, tugging me toward the lobby of the train station where rows of shops and small food stands lined the walls. Overhead, steel-ribbed glass skylights mirrored the people meandering through the station. I grabbed Adrian's sleeve as he headed for the ticket windows.

"Hold on a minute, Sparky. You haven't answered any of my questions."

His frown was a thing of beauty to behold, magnificent in its black irritation. "Sparky? First Ryan and now Sparky?" He shook his head, his eyes a blue so icy I swore there were little icebergs floating around his irises. "I am centuries old. I have sent more people to their deaths than you can possibly comprehend. You will cease referring to me as *Sparky*."

I stood my ground. I knew if I let him get away with one single high-handed inch, he'd drag it out to a mile. "Answer my questions, and I might consider the request."

"I do not have to answer your questions. I am the Betrayer."

"You are also the Irritator, but that doesn't mean you can't be civil, as well."

He sighed the sigh of the truly martyred. "If I promise to answer your questions later, will you feed now?"

"Yes," I said, too aware of the growl of my stomach and

the mouthwatering scents of a nearby food booth to deny his offer. "But you have to promise to answer everything."

His eyes went even lighter.

I pointed a finger at his face. "And you can just add how you do that to the list of things about which you're going to spill. I'd love to be able to change my eye color."

"Feed," he growled before turning toward the ticket sellers.

"*Feed. Come. Do what I say.* We really are going to have to work at adding some words like 'please do this' and 'I would fawn at your feet in humble gratitude if you do that' to your vocabulary," I yelled after him.

His head shook again, indicating he heard me. I couldn't help smiling at him as he strode down the long lobby of the train station. Dressed entirely in black, his long wool duster flapping behind him, his hair sweeping down to his collar, he looked like a refugee from an artsy, atmospheric vampire movie.

"Someone's been reading *way* too many gothic novels," I mused as I lifted my chin to sniff the air, following the most enticing scent to a nearby sausage seller. I scraped together the remains of the money Adrian had given me and bought three sausage rolls.

I had consumed one by the time he found me and herded me toward a secluded waiting area.

"We have two hours before the next train," he said, pushing me onto a bench.

"You're always pulling me along somewhere or shoving me down onto something," I complained around a mouthful of sausage roll. "We really need to work on your people skills."

He sat down beside me, a familiar scowl settled firmly onto his manly brow. "I am a Dark One, not a person. I do not need people skills."

It was my turn to sigh. I held out the last sausage roll, which he eyed with malevolent suspicion.

"What's wrong, don't like sausage? Or can't you eat *food* food?"

"I can eat human food if I so desire, but it provides me with no sustenance."

"Well, that answers a question I'd always wondered about vamps—whether or not they were biologically the same as the non-bloodsuckers. I mean, why have the plumbing if you're not going to use it?"

"Plumbing?" he asked, his scowl deepening.

"Yeah, plumbing." I flicked a glance toward his crotch. "I know you have a belly button, and I figured that you have the usual genital accoutrements unless vamps do that differently, but from what I can tell, you're A-OK in that department—not that I've looked or anything—but then there's the back door, and, well, I've just always wondered. I mean, if you don't need it, why have it?"

He stared at me like I had suddenly sprouted buttocks on my head.

I gave a weak smile. "None of the vamp books I've read have ever addressed that issue, so I thought I'd go to the horse's mouth, so to speak."

His eyes lightened to the color of a robin's egg. "You are the strangest woman I have ever met."

"Strange in a good way, or strange as in ought to be locked up for her own safety?"

"I haven't decided yet," he answered, leaning back

against the wall, his gaze flickering around at the people nearest us.

I debated saving the last sausage roll versus making myself a pig in front of Adrian, but decided in the end that if I had to do the blood-donor thing again, I'd need all the nourishment I could get. While I ate I watched the man who in such a short amount of time had become increasingly fascinating to me. Although Adrian's body appeared relaxed, his hands resting open on his thighs, I could feel the tension in him. His eyes never rested as they constantly surveyed our surroundings. It struck me that although he'd fed from me, he had probably used most of the energy he'd gained from my blood to heal his wound. I knew he'd stayed awake while I slept on the train, and now here he was almost on point, he was so alert.

"Adrian," I said, putting my hand on his arm to get his attention. He cocked an eyebrow in question, his eyes going sapphire. I lifted my hand, about to ask him if he was going to be all right, but stopped when his eyes went sky blue. I blinked a couple of times, then put my hand back on his arm.

Twin irises of the purest sapphire regarded me with growing confusion.

"This is so cool! Your eyes change color when I touch you. Look!"

I lifted my hand again. Adrian rolled his (summer blue) eyes and started to turn away. I leaned forward and put my hand on his chest, over his heart. His eyes turned navy.

"Hoo! You're like a giant mood ring! I wonder if I can

make different colors show up depending where I touch you."

Adrian followed my speculative gaze to his fly, jumping up to stand in front of me in an aggressive pose, arms crossed over his chest, legs spread. "I am not a mood ring! I am not a toy! I am dangerous and feared by all! You are not to treat me in such a flip, irreverent manner—"

I put my hand on his thigh, close to his groin, but not actually touching naughty parts. His eyes turned a dark midnight blue.

"This is so fun!" I giggled, admittedly a bit less than sane after the very strange twenty-four hours I'd spent. "I could touch you all day! I wonder what would happen if I were to kiss you. . . ."

"There will be no more kissing," he answered on a growl. "Kissing leads to the fifth step, and I refuse to go any further."

"Why?" I asked, tipping my head to the side as I gave him a once-over, starting at the mid-calf-high black boots, moving up over the tightly fitting black jeans, the caress of silk across his stomach and chest, to the width of his shoulders as highlighted by the long black duster. I smiled into eyes as black and shiny as onyx. "You said that if I was this Beloved person, I would be able to save your soul. Considering I can't charm that curse that binds you, it seems to me that I'm pretty much your get-out-of-jail-free card. So why aren't you kissing my feet and begging me to save your soul?"

He sighed again and sat down next to me, silent for a few minutes before he said, "You aren't my Beloved. You can't be her. My Beloved does not exist."

Pain, disappointment, and something very much like regret fought for superiority within me. I put my hand on his, giving his fingers a gentle squeeze. "You mean she's dead? I'm so sorry, Adrian. I had no idea. You must have been devastated."

He looked down to where my fingers gently caressed his, not saying anything, but I saw the sorrow in his eyes. I looked away, but from my peripheral vision I examined the red pattern that twisted around his torso. Even if I wanted to charm the curse, I knew it would be beyond my embryonic skills, skills that had been stunted before they even had a chance to grow. There was no way I could do what he wanted, but now it seemed I didn't even have to make the choice about whether or not I wanted to bind myself to him in order to salvage his soul.

Which was a shame, because despite his fierce appearance and gruesome reputation, I was beginning to believe he was a man well worth saving.

"She did not die."

"I'm a little confused," I said slowly, still stroking his fingers. "She didn't die, but there is no one for you? I saw into you, really deep into you, remember, and you don't have a soul. If this woman didn't die, what happened to her?"

"Nothing," he said, his voice rough with emotion. His hand twisted under mine so that our fingers were twined. "My Beloved does not exist because I am not allowed to have one. To have a Beloved would imply that there is hope for me, and I can assure you from many centuries of experience, hope is one grace that has forsaken me."

"You can't say that," I said again, at a loss as to what I

86

could do to relieve the pain shadowing his beautiful eyes. How could I make him believe I was his hope when I myself wasn't sure I wanted to take on that role? "Adrian, I really wish I could help you, I honestly do. But as I told you back at the castle, I can't charm. You saw what happened when I drew that ward—something I truly didn't know I remembered—but it's pretty clear to me that my brain does not want me messing around with all that woo-woo stuff. I know you're hoping I'll lift the curse, but I can't. I wish I could, but I can't."

"You have the ability," he insisted, his fingers tightening on mine. "You have the power. I see it in you. You are frightened, but it is a foolish emotion. No," he said, forestalling me as I was about to protest his high-handed dictates. "There is nothing to debate—you *must* charm the curse. There is no other alternative."

"You can't make me charm the curse," I pointed out. "I don't remember much from the few times I chatted with my friend's Wiccan aunt who told me I was gifted with special abilities, but I do clearly remember her saying that I had to want to use my skills in order for them to work. You can't force me."

"I can, and I will. I do not wish to force you to do anything, but about this, I am immovable. It is too important." His grip on my fingers was painful, but the agony in his eyes made my heart bleed. Through the touch of our hands I could feel the need within him, the endless torment that filled him with blackness, a torment that he was confident I could end. I shivered at the silent desperation in his eyes, turning my head so I could look away.

"Tell me about what a Beloved does." I couldn't charm

the curse without destroying myself in the process, and quite likely him as well, but perhaps there was something I could do to help him. Maybe I could help relieve the suffering and anguish that gripped him so tightly. The time had come for a decision, and suddenly there was no choice to be made. I knew what I had to do—what I was meant to do. "And before you say it, yeah, I know, you don't think you're allowed to have one because you're the big bad Betrayer and all, but maybe, just maybe I've been given the nod to pinch hit for whoever your Beloved was supposed to be, but who isn't, because of the whole curse thing. If you understand what I mean."

I could feel him studying me as I watched people at the far end of the waiting area. We were seated in an isolated corner, tucked away from the hustle and bustle that made up life at the train station.

"Once a Beloved has Joined with her Dark One, his soul is redeemed. She becomes his lodestone, his reason for living. He cannot exist without her."

"You mean he's her love slave?" I couldn't help but smile at the thought of Adrian being wrapped around anyone's finger. "Sounds cool to me! Wanna give it a whirl?"

"He cannot exist, because to drink blood from anyone but his Beloved is poison," he answered with a heated look. "He is not a slave to her, but the two are bound together for eternity."

"So the Beloved becomes immortal as well?" A wistful desire filled me to be made whole, to be able to use my affected limbs as they were meant to be used, to never have to suffer the stares and quickly averted eyes when the weak muscles on the left side of my face were noticed. Surely such a gift would be worth regular blood donations. My eyes slid to Adrian, who was looking at our entwined fingers. It would certainly be no hardship to have him around me for eternity. I doubted I would ever get tired of looking at him, and the strange tension I felt around him, the promise of something profound, left me yearning for the completion I was sure we'd find together.

"Yes. She is made immortal once the final step of Joining is made."

"Hmm." The idea was starting to sound better and better with each passing moment. Adrian by my side for eternity, a body without weaknesses, all the time I needed to study the past . . . oh, yes, the thought of being his Beloved presented a glittering temptation.

"Nell, I will not allow you to become my Beloved."

"Maybe you don't have any choice in the matter," I teased, still mentally picturing myself saving his soul, then spending the rest of our lives together bound in peace and harmony.

"I do," he answered, his lips a grim line. "I refuse to bind you to me."

I pulled my hand from him, pushing down the pain of his rejection. So much for peace and harmony.

"It is not because I do not want you," he said stiffly, grabbing my hand and tightening his fingers around mine. I risked a glance at his eyes, and almost recoiled at the anger visible there until I realized it was an anger directed inward. "You have seen into my mind—you know that I desire you, that my body cries out for you. But I will not bind you to one with whom you can have no future."

Distraught as he was, I knew that this wasn't the time to press him for more information, or to argue my point. Besides, I wasn't absolutely sure I wanted to commit myself to him, especially since I couldn't give him what he so desperately wanted.

"I feel horribly guilty about running out on Melissande," I said, blithely changing the subject. I gently rubbed my thumb over the back of his hand in order to get him to loosen his grip. He dropped my hand like it was made of spiders, turning away to watch the people nearest us.

"You didn't run out on her. I abducted you."

"At first. But you can't really imagine I would be here now with you if I didn't want to be."

His outraged expression gave me the answer to that statement. Before he could go into his "me Betrayer, you Jane" routine, I added, "Yeah, I know, you're the big, bad wolf and all that, but the fact remains that I'm not a pushover, Adrian. I'm here because I want to be here. I want to help you—within the limits of what I can do. But that doesn't mean I feel any less guilty about the fact that I was hired to help Melissande find her nephew. And since you have information that she needs, I figured it'd be a fair trade if you gave me the info in exchange for my help."

He thought about that for a moment. "Melissande cannot help Damian."

"Why don't we let her be the judge of that?"

He grunted a disagreement, but didn't outright refuse to talk. "What do you want to know?"

I settled back on the bench, tucking my hands into my

coat sleeves to warm them. Funny how they never felt cold when Adrian was holding them. "Let's start at the beginning—what were you doing at Christian's castle?"

His jaw tightened, and for a minute I didn't think he was going to answer. With an annoyed grimace, he admitted, "Looking for the ring."

"Ah! The ring." I nibbled on my lower lip for a moment or two. "Um. What ring?"

"*What* ring? Melissande persuaded you to help her without mentioning the ring of Asmodeus?" He shook his head, a disgusted look on his face. "Foolish woman."

"She's not foolish, she's concerned. There's a difference. And yes, she mentioned a ring, but only briefly. I'm sure she would have gone into more detail if we'd had time. This ring—I assume, since you're looking for it, that it has some sort of power against Asmodeus?"

His hands clenched. "Yes. It channels his power. Without it, he is crippled, bound to his prison, unable to free himself."

"That tells me why he should be looking for it, but not who you . . . oh." Just as the words left my mouth I remembered what Melissande had told me: Adrian the Betrayer was bound to the demon lord Asmodeus. Which meant if his master wanted the ring but was too weak to go hunting for it himself, his tame vampire would be the likeliest person to send on a retrieval mission. "Asmodeus asked you to look for it?"

"Yes."

The word positively dripped ice cubes.

I mused for a moment over the fact that his eyes had gone a flat, dulled ice blue. "OK, got that, but what does this ring have to do with anyone else? Why did you say Melissande was foolish not to have discussed it with me? Wait—does this ring have power that can be used *against* Asmodeus as well as by him?"

"Yes."

The atmosphere surrounding Adrian was so cold, I wouldn't have been surprised to see a polar bear strolling by.

"Ah, gotcha. So if Melissande gets ahold of this ring, she can either trot up to the A-man and offer him a trade—the ring for her nephew—or use it against him and force him to free the kid?"

"To do either would be to sign both her and Damian's death warrants." His eyelids dropped to half-mast as he gave me a long look. "The ring is a conduit to great power. Whoever wields it has within his hands the ability to destroy the lord Asmodeus. It would be fatal for one unlearned in the ways of the dark powers to try to use the power against him. Melissande has neither the strength nor the ability to battle Asmodeus."

I pursed my lips, warmth flooding my belly with the way Adrian's gaze pounced on the movement. "I take it you didn't find this ring at the castle?"

"No. You did not happen to see it during your search of Dante's desk?"

"A ring?" I thought back to my scant few minutes in the wonderful library, dwelling for a moment on the warded book that yielded the notes and shell earring. Did Adrian know I had searched other places in the room than just the desk? He had recognized that the vase was warded, but perhaps he hadn't had time to look over the entire library and realize that a less obvious object had been warded as well. "No, I didn't see a ring in his desk. How did you know that vase was warded?"

One auburn eyebrow rose in question.

"The vase in the library, the one you tested me with to see if I could recognize the ward. How did you know it was warded? Can you draw them, too?"

He shrugged. "Anyone can draw a ward, but it takes a skilled Charmer or one learned in ward lore to unmake them."

"So you can see the ward as well?" I pressed, a growing suspicion making it important to know whether he had searched Christian's books. I slowly slid my right hand from my sleeve, along my hip to the back pocket on my pants, watching Adrian from the corner of my eye. He didn't seem to notice the movement.

"Not see them, but feel them. When I was near the vase, I felt that it was warded."

My fingers closed around the thin circle of the earring. "What . . . uh . . . what does this Asmodeus ring look like? Something big and garish? Gold Tolkien-ish band? Red-hot to the touch and leaving scorch marks on whoever touches it?"

He gave me a curious glance. I smiled and looked as innocent as I could.

"Your smile is lopsided," he said, apropos of nothing.

"I know." I kept my lips curved despite the almost over-whelming desire to grind my teeth at his comment. "Does the ring have spiders carved on it or something ghoulish like that? Does it leech blood? Is it connected in any way with a giant eye floating above a black tower?"

Adrian looked as if he wanted to roll his eyes, but managed to give me a weary look instead. "Nothing so dramatic. And you thought *I'd* been watching too much Buffy."

"Hey!" I said, about to protest the fact that he'd been in my mind again without my permission.

"The ring is about two centimeters in width, and consists of a thin circle of horn bound in gold."

"Horn?" I asked, my stomach doing a lurch as I ran my finger around the approximately two centimeter-wide circular earring in my pocket, the one I had assumed was made of shell. "What sort of horn?"

He looked away, once again scanning our surroundings. "Unicorn."

I laughed, the sound dying a cruel death on my lips as I realized he wasn't cracking a smile at his joke. "You're serious, aren't you? Unicorn?"

"Yes, I'm serious. Have you seen such a ring?"

I shook my head, the fingers of my right hand running around the object in my pocket, searching for a break that would indicate that it was an earring as I originally thought, and not a ring so powerful it could destroy a demon lord.

There was no break.

Adrian must have picked up on the sudden panic that filled me, because his eyes (medium blue) narrowed as they turned back to me. "Are you sure you have not seen it?"

I cleared my suddenly tight throat and eased my hand from my pocket. I couldn't know for certain just what the object I'd picked up was. I'd have to examine it fully at the first opportunity before making a determination about

94

whether it was a ring, or just a facsimile. "Sure I'm sure." When he stared at me a little longer, I added in all honesty, "If I'd seen a unicorn-horn ring, believe me, I'd have said something."

"Mmm." He watched me carefully for a few more seconds before returning to his scan of the immediate area.

"What . . . uh . . . what would this ring do to a person? It's not evil, is it? It wouldn't take them over and make them do bad things?"

"The ring itself is powerless—it is merely a conduit to the unbound power of Asmodeus. It is entirely up to the person wielding the ring whether or not the power is used for good or evil."

I slumped in relief against the wall and wondered just what I'd gotten myself into. In the span of slightly more than twenty-four hours I'd slept soundly on a vampire, fed him my blood, all but offered myself as his nooky queen for the rest of eternity, and discovered my back pocket was quite likely to be home to a demon lord's limitless power.

Some days it's just not worth the effort to stay sane.

Chapter Seven

"This is where you live?" I looked around the room. The word *squalid* immediately came to mind, but I squelched it as coming from a too middle-class background, and tried instead to see it as an unbiased visitor might. The drapes that hung in front of a grime-encrusted window didn't look the exact color of vomited Pepto Bismol, but they weren't off by much. A rickety desk to my left had one leg about two inches shorter than the others, while the veneer at the corners of the desk peeled upward. The bed next to the table had a distinct sag in the middle. Two flabby gray pillows and a mottled brown and green bed-spread topped it. Behind me a wardrobe missing one door appeared to have recently been the domicile of several families of incontinent mice. A cracked mirror above a rust-stained sink completed the room's accoutrements. "I'm sorry, I gave it my best shot, but I'm going to have to go with my initial impression, and that's god-awful."

"I don't live here," Adrian said, setting a beat-up black leather satchel on an obscenely overstuffed chair that was apparently upholstered with some sort of shiny bok choy. The satchel immediately slid to the ground. "I simply stay in this hotel when I'm in Cologne."

I crossed my arms over my chest, covertly rubbing my arms to warm them up. Evidently the Hotel Geh Shlafen didn't include a heat source in their rooms. "Which brings up the question of exactly why we're in Cologne. I thought you said we're going to England."

"We are." He unbuckled the straps on the satchel and dug out a small shaving kit. "But I prefer not to travel during the daylight hours, so we'll stay here until this evening."

"Here?" I looked around the room, ending at the saggy bed. He couldn't be thinking what I was thinking he was thinking. Could he? "Together? Us?"

"Here, together, us. You may sleep on the bed. I will use the chair." He pulled a straight-edge razor from the shaving kit and laid it on the sink.

"You're shaving?" I asked, intrigued as he lathered up a small shaving brush. "Wait a minute! You can't shave, you're a vampire! Everyone knows vamps don't have beards!"

"Everyone is wrong," he said carefully as he finished applying the lather to his face, the scrape of the razor along his left cheek sending odd little thrills down my back. I've always had a thing for men shaving—it was such an intimate act, one that hinted that Adrian was as comfortable with me as I was with him. Which, considering that we'd only known each other a day, gave credence to my growing belief that I was his own personal soul-saver. I shoved that thought aside and turned my attention to less confusing issues.

"Hey! You have clothes in here!" I pulled a black cotton pullover from the satchel. "What's the deal with that? I thought vamps could, you know, materialize their own clothes!"

He glared at me in the broken mirror as the straight-edge swept along his upper lip.

"First you have to shave, then you can't magic up your own clothes, and just what's this?" I shook a familiar object at him. "A toothbrush! Who ever heard of a vampire needing a toothbrush? You don't eat, for Pete's sake! And I have never, ever read a book where a vampire needed a toothbrush. Obviously, you need to get with the times, Adrian. How old are you, anyway?"

"Four hundred and eighty-one, not that my age has anything to do with me needing to shave or brush my teeth. I assure you that no Dark One I know can materialize clothing out of nothing. We are not magical sprites, Nell. We're damned, tortured men, children of the red abyss, nightwalkers bound to eternal torment, but that doesn't mean we have poor hygiene. We shave, we brush our teeth, and we bathe regularly. Does that answer all your questions?"

"Wow." I sat down on the bed, sliding backward into the dip, ignoring his rant to dwell on the weight of his age. "Four hundred and eighty-one. That means you were born in . . . uh—"

"1524."

"Wow," I said again, having a hard time wrapping my mind around that idea. Oh, I didn't have difficulty believing he was immortal, but the things he must have seen! The events he had lived through! The knowledge he had gained over four centuries! "You're a historian's dream come true! It makes me drool just thinking about what's in your head."

He washed off the last of the shaving soap, carefully drying his things before tucking them away, his eyes the color of a bright blue topaz. "You do not want to know what's in my head, Nell. Not even if you were my Beloved could you cope with the things I have done, the monster I have become. I was not named the Betrayer without reason."

"You know, you can't say something like that to me and not expect me to rise to the challenge." I suited words to action and got off the bed, stopping directly in front of him. "I'm still not convinced that I'm *not* this Beloved person, but I can assure you that I'm not going to push you into a relationship."

"That's good, because you're not—"

"I will, however, prove to you that you're not the scary monster you think you are. Oh, I know, you've done bad things, but come on, Adrian—you're cursed, seriously cursed! I might not be an expert on the subject of demon lords, but I'm willing to bet that bearing one of their curses doesn't mean you go around doing random acts of kindness. I also know that I wouldn't find you as nummy as I do if you were truly an evil person, so you can just stop frowning. You're not evil. You're not a monster. Don't forget I had a peek into your mind."

"You fainted after you did," he answered, his lips compressed into a grim line. It just made me want to grab him by the ears and kiss him until his eyes turned black.

"That was just the shock of finding out your soul had gone AWOL. It had nothing to do with who you are or what you've done. Want me to prove it?" I took a step forward until I was almost touching him. "Brace yourself, because Mr. Mind is about to have company. Now, let's see, what did I do before? Oh, yeah."

I stood very still, calmed my scattered thoughts, and held an image of him in my mind.

Nothing happened.

"What am I doing wrong?" I asked, opening my eyes. Adrian was standing before me, his arms crossed over his chest again. I gave the squealing, girlish part of my brain a few seconds to admire the way his silk shirt caressed his biceps, and how his rolled-up sleeves exposed the corded strength of his forearms. "When I did this before, whammo! I was in Adrian Central. But now it's not working."

"I do not choose to allow you in my mind," he said, his voice utterly dispassionate.

"Can you do that to your Beloved?" I was a bit taken aback by his refusal to allow me in, growing annoyed when I thought of the times he'd strolled into my head without my permission.

"If you were my true Beloved, no, I couldn't keep you out. There is nothing that can be kept secret between a Dark One and his Beloved, but as you are not . . ."

I put my hand over his heart and immediately sank into his consciousness, the howling emptiness within him filling me. I gasped with pain as it overwhelmed me, absorbing everything within me and leaving nothing but rage and agony. I fought to breathe, fought to keep my heart beating despite the ageless despair that consumed me.

Reality swirled away from me, time and place blending into an impenetrable miasma. Just as I began to fall into the heart of it, Adrian was there, holding me close, buffering the darkness so it didn't absorb me, his presence the lifeline I needed to survive. I clung tightly to him, struggling to control the emotions that were pouring into me, until slowly, atom by atom, I took the blackness and pain and torment, and held it trembling within me. I looked deep into Adrian's crystal-clear eyes, and knew what I wanted. I wanted his pain to be gone. I wanted his soul to fill the void that ached within him. I wanted the darkness to turn to light.

You've suffered long enough, Adrian. The words formed in my mind as his mouth descended upon mine, his heat fueling me as I transformed his darkness. For the pain, I gave him succor. For the emptiness, I gave him purpose. And for the black despair, I fed him hope.

You cannot do this. It is impossible. This is not happening. Denial was strong in him, but desire was stronger.

His lips burned on mine, his tongue a brand that scorched its way across my lips as it urged me to allow him into my mouth. I shivered with the sudden flood of erotic images that filled my mind, parting my lips to let him sink within.

I want you, Nell. I need you. My body cries out for you. But I cannot have you.

Why? I asked, running my hands down the planes of his back, tugging until I pulled the tail of his silk shirt free from his pants. *I'm willing. I'm more than willing, I'm just as desperate as you are. Why can't we do this?*

He groaned into my mouth as I sculpted my hands

along the hot skin of his back. I felt the struggle within him even before he managed to tear his mouth from mine.

"We cannot do this because I am doomed. We have no future together, Nell. We cannot be together. I will not damn another innocent soul because of my sins."

I grabbed both edges of the front of his shirt and ripped it open. I think he was as surprised at my action as I was, but I didn't let that stop me from yanking off the rest of the shirt. "Mmmrowr!" I purred, throwing myself on him.

"No! I will not let you do this!" he snarled . . . in between hot, fevered kisses that came close to melting the fillings in my teeth.

He spun us around so that I was caught between a cold, rough wall, and a hot, hard vampire. I sucked his lip into my mouth and used both hands to clutch his hair. "I'm your Beloved, dammit! You're going to let me save your soul, and like it!"

"You'll do nothing of the kind," he growled, whipping my sweater off over my head and staring with sizzling hot eyes at the swell of my breasts above my bra.

"Kiss me," I demanded, tugging his hair.

"No!" His lips possessed mine, his body hard and aggressive, slamming me back into the wall, his groin pressed suggestively against mine. I wiggled against him, mimicking the sinuous movement of his tongue as it bullied mine.

"Feed from me," I begged when his lips parted from mine only to trail kisses of fire down my neck to my chest. Almost five hundred years of experience weren't for naught—with a quick move he had my bra off and flung across the room, the steaming heat of his mouth making me stand on tippy-toe with delirium.

"I won't," he growled just before he took my breast in his mouth, the sharp sting of his canines as they scraped tender flesh soothed by the gentle caress of his tongue. I arched against him, aware but uncaring that he was tugging off my jeans with one hand, his other hand tangled in my hair, my mouth busy as I tasted the salt of his skin. I kissed a path up his neck to the spot behind his ear that I had been dying to nibble on, my hands skimming down the velvet steel of his arms.

"Need me," I moaned as he yanked my underwear off. I swirled my tongue around the curve of his ear, rubbing my now naked body against him, my senses overloading with the feel of his bare chest on mine, the soft hair teasing my breasts even as the rough texture of his jeans abraded more sensitive flesh. He dropped to his knees with a groan, his mouth suddenly possessing me in a way that left me gasping for air, my legs boneless as his tongue flicked and teased and tasted until I clutched his head to me and gave in to the passion he fired.

"Never!" He lifted my still trembling body and followed me down to the bed after shucking his jeans and boots. His body covered mine, all male strength and heat, but it was the sharp hunger within him that had me arching against him, my hands exploring the wonderful territory of his back and adorable behind.

I scraped my nails up his spine as he spread my legs. "Love me!"

"I cannot," he swore, his eyes a deep brilliant blue that burned deep into my soul a scant moment before his hips flexed. Like a brand he seared a path deep into my body, filling me, possessing me, completing me. The red hunger swelled in him, blending with his desire to join with me until it was a piercing white need that consumed me even as his mouth lowered to my shoulder. Pain sharp and hot faded into pleasure as his teeth sank into the base of my neck. The pleasure in the act of him taking life from me was almost as great as the orgasm I teetered on the brink of, his body moving against me with more and more force, our minds joined, his pleasure feeding mine until I honestly thought I would just simply die from the ecstasy of it all. In that moment, in that shining, brilliant moment of clarity I knew we were joined in a way more funda- mental than a mere joining of bodies. We were meant to be together, and nothing he could say would change that.

Tell me you didn't feel that. Tell me that wasn't the great- est thing you've ever experienced. Tell me I'm not your Beloved.

His tongue lapped at my neck as he rolled over, hold- ing me tight against him so we were still locked together intimately. Within him the pleasure faded, the blackness returning as sorrow and anguish banished the joy of our joining.

A cold chill clutched my heart. *Tell me, Adrian!*

His breath was harsh on my ears, his chest heaving be- neath me, the sweet, salty taste of him filling my mouth as I kissed his collarbone. I wanted to weep for him, weep for us both. *Please tell me.*

An agony of truth filled his mind, spilling over into mine. *I felt it. You are my life. You are my breath. You are the beat of my heart. You are my Beloved.*

I smiled into his neck and relaxed against him, my body still trembling with little aftershocks of pleasure. I didn't want to put a name to what I was feeling for him, I just wanted to enjoy it.

May God have mercy on you, Beloved, for you will find none in me.

"I'm not going to grow fangs now, am I?"

"No."

"Good." I traced a swirly pattern idly across the curse that bound Adrian's chest, admiring both the strength he possessed and the gentleness he'd shown me. "I don't think I could cope with a bloodlust, although I have to admit I find it incredibly sexy when you . . . you know . . . dine on me. But I can do without the fang issue. So, any guesses as to why yours suddenly went retractable?"

He opened one eye and gave me an outraged look.

"Oh, right. Recovery time. Sorry. I forgot that men don't like to chat right away. You rest. I'll just lay here snuggly warm and remember how wonderful it felt when we merged together."

He groaned as my hand slid down over his belly. "Is there any reason you feel the need to draw wards on me?"

I propped myself up on my elbow and looked at his chest and stomach in growing horror. "I didn't . . . I mean, I don't remember how . . . I've never really drawn wards before."

"You drew a binding ward on Sebastian," he answered, both eyes open now, his irises a speculative light blue. Glimmering faintly in the dim gray light that seeped in through the curtains, an intricate pattern of green spread across his chest and down over his stomach. Beneath the swirls and curves and dips of the pattern, the harsh, sharp lines of the curse glowed red. "It takes a strong ward to hold a Dark One."

"I know I did it, but I don't know how! It just happened!"

His disbelief was strong in my mind. I shook out the mental welcome mat and allowed him in to see the truth for himself. "You must have had some sort of training. People do not just draw powerful binding wards by accident."

"It's kind of odd having you in my head," I mused, running my finger along one silky auburn eyebrow, smoothing out the frown that had formed. "I'm not quite sure I like it. Except when we . . . you know. Then it's really fabulous. And before you say what I know you're going to say, no, I haven't forgotten any Charmer training. I was never trained. Not formally. I met with a Wiccan a couple of times, that's all."

"But something happened to you, something so horrible you will not allow me access to the memory." His fingers touched my left cheek. *What happened to you, Hasi? What happened, to leave the left side of your body weak, and a dark place of sorrow in your heart?*

I looked away, biting my lip against the unexpectedness of his endearment (*Hasi*, a literal translation of "bunny," is a German term often used by lovers), and needing to pull away from his questions.

"I'm not allowed to ask?" His voice was a deep velvet rumble along my skin that had me shivering in sensual delight.

"No, you can ask. It's only fair, since you've put up with me asking you all sorts of personal questions." I took a deep breath, reminded myself that I'd been more intimate with him than with any other person, and looked him dead in the eye. "I killed my best friend when I was twenty. I had a stroke after that."

He stared at me, plainly waiting for more. I curled up on his chest, hiding myself so his cerulean eyes couldn't see into my soul.

"That is all you are going to say? That is all the explanation you are going to give me?"

"The stroke is why my smile is crooked, and why my left side isn't as strong as the right," I said to his nipple. Beneath my cheek, his chest rose and fell, warm and strong and alive, and I wondered how anyone could think of a Dark One as the undead.

It is a matter of some misconception, the silky voice whispered through my mind. *Why did you kill your friend?*

I heaved a mental sigh and knew I wasn't going to get away with not explaining the whole of my painful past. I stroked along his chest, feeling the slight tingle of the curse as my fingers crossed the path of its pattern. "I told you I couldn't charm the curse that binds you. That's not only because I don't exactly know how to charm, but because the one time I did try, my roommate ended up dead, and I spent three months in the hospital after having fried my brain."

Adrian's mind curled itself around mine as memory of that horrible night filled me, images dancing before my mind's eye of Beth's smiling face as she urged me to try to untangle the curse woven into an altar cloth said to have been owned by Tomás de Torquemada, the infamous Spanish inquisitor.

"Come on, Nellie," Beth had said with a hushed giggle that night so long ago as she unlocked the door to the antiquities room in the university museum where she did her work-study time. "Aunt Li said the curse is right up your alley. All you have to do is unmake it like a ward."

"And I'll say the same thing I said to your aunt, Beth: I don't know a thing about wards and curses. It's all Greek to me. Just because she thinks I'm adorable—"

"A Charmer, not adorable, you idiot," she replied fondly, flipping on her flashlight before hurrying to a tall locked cabinet on the far side of the room. "And Aunt Li should know."

"So she's a big noise in the Chinese Wiccan society—that doesn't mean she knows everything, Beth. She was remarkably vague when it came to explaining to me just why she felt I was going to be able to undo a curse. And as for those wards, she only showed me a couple. I can't even remember what they were for."

Beth sorted through a collection of keys on a ring as big as my wrist, selecting one to open the cabinet. "Well, you're really good with getting knots untied. How hard can a curse be?"

I laughed softly as she pulled a small wooden box from the cabinet, opening it to reveal a soiled, tattered piece of blue wool material. Beth seemed oddly reluctant to touch the cloth, instead shoving the box at me, gesturing for me to sit on the floor. I touched a finger to a rent in the material, noticing that despite its age, the gold embroidery on the cloth was remarkably preserved. "So this is it? The famous cursed altar cloth?"

"That's what Dr. Avery says. What do you think?"

I examined the material, trying to remember everything I'd learned thus far in my European history classes. "Mmm. It's old."

She rolled her eyes as she dropped down next to me, watching as I pulled the cloth from the box. "Duh! I meant, what do you think about the curse? Can you uncurse it?"

"No. I didn't understand anything that your aunt rattled off about curses, and how they were supposed to look like patterns or something. It just doesn't make sense! How can a curse look like a pat . . ." My voice came to a halt as I realized that my fingers, of their own accord, had been tracing an intricate, curved path along the altar cloth. I squinted at it, noticing for the first time the odd pattern of weft that had been woven into the rough cloth. It swooped and swirled, sometimes spiraling back on itself into tight coils, a detailed and beautiful maze of pattern. I'd always loved mazes, taking no little pride in my ability to solve even the most complex maze in a fraction of the time it took others. "Wow. Someone really had some skill. Look what's woven into the material."

"What?" Beth leaned her dark head close to mine to peer at the pattern my finger traced.

"That. See the red thread? It's very fine—probably silk or something—but it's woven into the cloth."

"Maybe it's the curse," she suggested, her voice strangely hushed. A joking response to such a silly suggestion died on my lips as a little shiver went down my back at the strained note in her voice. For a moment I was very aware that we were the only two people in the administration section of the museum, alone in the dense darkness. Just my best friend, a strange piece of cloth that reputedly witnessed some of the most horrific atrocities of the Spanish Inquisition, and me.

I tried to ignore the sense of foreboding that seemed to seep into my bones, shivering as I shook out the cloth to examine the pattern. "If it is a curse, then it will be a piece of cake to uncurse. It's nothing more than a really complex maze."

"That's what Aunt Li said about the wards she showed us earlier—that they were nothing more than intention and a pattern."

"Mmm." I spread the cloth out on the carpeted floor, crawling on my knees around it, directing Beth's flashlight as I tried to find the starting point of the strange pattern of red thread. "I think this is it. What did your aunt say I had to do?"

"I don't know! You were the one who was supposed to be listening."

"You're the Wiccan-in-training—you should have paid attention!"

"Wiccan, not Charmer." Beth's face loomed pale in the darkness. "I think she just said you had to unravel the curse to destroy it."

"OK." I took a deep breath, curving my lips into what I hoped was a confident smile. "Here goes nothing!"

I put my finger on a tiny knot of the thin red silk, tracing the intricate design, following the complex trail as it worked from the left center of the cloth outward.

"It's glowing," Beth said, her voice high and excited. "Look, Nellie! Where you touch it, it glows bright red, like it's neon or something."

A chill shivered down my spine. The thin red thread of the pattern I had already traced was indeed glowing softly in the darkness of the room, as if my touch gave it energy, the light from it growing brighter as my finger curved and swooped along the cloth.

The frigid foreboding that had been within me ever since we stepped into the room grew so great that it was almost a tangible thing weighing me down.

"Something's wrong," I said, my teeth chattering, my heart pounding faster and faster as my finger followed the red thread unerringly along its labyrinthine weave. "I think I should stop."

"This is so cool!" Beth leaned over the cloth, her nose a few inches away as my finger swept past. "My God, the glow really is coming from your touch. I've never seen anything so amazing."

"No," I said, trying to quell the dread that suddenly roiled in my stomach. "This is wrong. Something is not right with this. I'm going to stop."

Beth glanced up at me, her eyes bright with excitement. "What's wrong, Nell? You look like you're going to be sick or something."

"It's this cloth," I said, horror crawling up my back as I struggled to pull my finger from the material. "I can't . . . I can't . . . dammit, Beth, I can't stop following the thread!"

"What?" She looked down to where my finger was swirling through a series of complex loops. "What you do you mean, you can't stop following it?"

"I mean I can't stop!" I gritted my teeth, grabbing my wrist with my left hand, trying to physically pull my arm back. I was so cold, my fingers had gone numb. "It's like I'm locked to the horrible thing! Help me stop it!"

"Maybe you are supposed to destroy it," she suggested, sitting back on her heels, seemingly oblivious to my distress. Despite the iciness that filled me, sweat beaded on my forehead, my skin all but twitching with growing fear. "Maybe that's why you can't stop," she said. "Oh, wow! Look at that! It's sparking!"

My finger dragged over to trace out the pattern as it moved to the right corner. Behind me, the part of the material I had traced over was not just glowing red, now little flecks of yellow light were starting to drift upward from the cloth like a burst of embers spat out of a bonfire on a cold winter's night. "Help . . . me . . . stop . . ." I ground out through my teeth, throwing my entire body behind the attempt to pull myself from the cloth.

"It's so beautiful," Beth breathed, running her hand across the glitter of yellow floating upward. "I've never seen anything so amazing in my life. It's like little fireflies! Don't stop, Nell, don't stop!"

"I have to," I yelled, the blood pounding in my ears making her voice distant and thin. I swear my eyeballs started to frost up. "This isn't right, Beth. Something's seriously wrong here. Please, help me stop it!"

"So beautiful," she cooed, her face a mask of pleasure as she fluttered both hands through the yellow sparks.

I watched with horror as my finger approached the center of the cloth, knowing instinctively that the heart of the curse lay there, a heart that I was suddenly sure was just as alive as the organ pounding wildly in my chest. As if drawn inexorably on, my finger swirled tighter and tighter toward the center, my soul filling with a blackness I knew would consume me. A voice whimpered pathetically, "Beth, please—"

As my finger touched the heart of the curse, Beth screamed, her voice cutting through my body as a blinding light burst inside my head. Before me rose the image of a creature so terrible, just to look on it tore bits from my soul. It held Beth in its arms, her body twisted and mutilated as she screamed and fought against it. The monster, the thing, the atrocity against nature, turned its attention to me, and for a moment I knew I could save my friend if I sacrificed myself.

The light and the monster—demon, devil, I had no idea what it was other than it was made up of the purest form of evil—slid into blissful nothingness as my mind made the decision I was too cowardly to consciously make, shutting itself off, leaving me floating senseless down into a bottomless abyss of sorrow.

Tears streaked my face as slow awareness brought me back to the present. I lay sobbing in Adrian's arms, comforted by his warmth and strength despite the guilt that wracked me, my body shaking with the remembered horror of my foolish arrogance in tampering with something I knew nothing about, torn with the knowledge that I had failed my friend when she needed me.

Adrian's embrace never lessened, his body cradling mine as I cried, clutching him, soundlessly begging for understanding, the gentle, warm touch of his mind more comforting even than the solid body that protected me.

Chapter Eight

"Nell. You must wake up now. It is time to leave."

I burrowed deeper into the thin linens of the bed, burying my face in the pillow Adrian had used, breathing in the faint scent of him.

"Nell, you must come. We have little time."

I pulled the blankets over my head, the full memory of the time we had passed together coming back to me with amazing clarity. I had told him my secret, bared my soul to him—how could I ever face him now that he knew what I was? A murderer, a weak, pathetic woman who had chosen to sacrifice her friend rather than herself.

You are not to blame for your friend's death, Hasi. His voice was soft with comfort in my head. *The monster you inadvertently challenged was Asmodeus, one of the seven princes of hell. Even the most experienced of Charmers would hesitate to confront him.*

I could have saved her, I wailed silently. *If I had done something, he would have let her go, released her and taken me instead.*

Cold air hit my back as the blanket was peeled off me, the bed lurching to the side with Adrian's weight. His hand stroked up my spine, causing shivers that had nothing to do with the chill of the room. *There was nothing you could do, Nell. You had not the knowledge nor the power to save your friend from Asmodeus. It is a miracle you saved yourself. Lesser Charmers would not have been able to do even that.*

I pulled my face from the pillow and turned to look at the man who sat at my side. He was dressed once again in black, his hair loose around his shoulders, his eyes a bright ice blue. "It's my fault Beth died. If I hadn't agreed to try to unmake that curse, I wouldn't have drawn Asmodeus's attention, and she wouldn't have been caught."

He nodded gravely. "That is true. If you had not attempted to charm the curse, your friend would not have died, and you would not have had the stroke. I have not the ability to see the future to know which of my actions I will later regret, but I do not punish myself for that lack."

"Yeah, but how many people have died as a result of your lack of foresight?" I muttered to the bed, forgetting for a moment to whom I was speaking.

His fingers were warm on my chin as he lifted it. *You have seen into me, Hasi. You know that I am damned by those I have destroyed. You know that I am just as much a monster as the demon lord who struck you down.*

"No," I snarled, throwing myself on him, pushing him

115

back onto the bed so I loomed over him, my lips brushing against his as I sank effortlessly into his mind. The raging emptiness inside him whirled around me, sucking me in, threatening to tear me apart in its fury. "You are not a monster! You are not like Asmodeus! You are bound by a curse, Adrian, that's all."

"That doesn't excuse what I have done. I have ruined lives, Hasi. I have handed my own people over to Asmodeus knowing they would not survive. You do not see clearly when you look at me. You see only what you want to see."

"Do I?" I touched his cheek, his words sharp little shards of agony that pierced my soul. "I think that I see clearer than you. Tell me, Adrian—what would have happened if you had not turned other Dark Ones over to Asmodeus?"

His eyes were as pale as frost. For a moment, he struggled with himself. "He would have wreaked vengeance."

"What sort of vengeance? Would he have been mad at you? Others?"

"Others. My people."

"How?"

Pain roiled through him. He tried to turn his face away, but I wouldn't let him. "How, Adrian?"

"He would have called upon his legions to destroy the Dark Ones."

"All of you? Every one of you?"

"He would have tried to destroy all, yes. He does not have that power, but . . ."

I brushed my lips against his. "But he'd have enough to wipe out a bunch of you?"

"Yes." His eyes closed, but his pain was seeping from him, swamping me. I pushed it away, not wanting to accept it.

"So rather than risk global extermination of your people, you satisfied the demon lord by handing over a couple of your fellow vamps."

He lay still beneath me, this man who had suffered so much. I had touched the depth of his agony, and I knew he had felt the full enormity of his actions. He was trapped, caught between a vengeful demon lord and his people, with no way to save either himself or the innocents he was forced to sacrifice. And yet, how many lives had he saved by having to do just that?

"It wasn't by your choice, Adrian. None of it was your choice." I pressed my lips to the pulse in his throat, opening myself up to his pain, allowing it to merge with me, accepting it into my soul, returning it with acceptance and understanding and something I shied away from putting a name to.

And if the acts have been my choice? he asked, his fingers sliding into my hair as I nibbled around his lips. *Would you condemn me? Would you damn me as the others have? Would you leave me?*

Never, I said into his mind, my mouth caressing his. I nibbled his lips until they parted, allowing me in, the taste of him filling me with so many emotions I couldn't untangle them. *You are not evil, Adrian. I could never fall in love with a man who was truly evil. You did the best you could, saved as many people as you could.*

His fingers dug hard into my hips for a moment as I

117

plundered the silk of his mouth; then roughly he pushed me aside, leaping up from the bed, his back to me as he spoke. "You are too inexperienced to see the truth in me, Nell. I am no better than Asmodeus himself."

My heart ached at the self-loathing in his voice. It was an emotion I was very familiar with, but one that Adrian was unjustly embracing. I also knew how destructive it could be unless it was nipped in the bud. I pushed myself off the bed, grabbing my clothes, jerking them on quickly. "Will you stop with the pity party? I can't cope with my own wallow in self-pity and yours as well."

His shoulders twitched as if I had stung him, but he didn't turn around to face me.

I sighed and pulled on my socks and shoes. "You're not evil, you're not a monster, you're a man who's been cursed, that's all. That gives you a get-out-of-jail-free card as far as guilt goes."

Dark Ones may not be able to conjure up things out of nothing, but they can move fast when they want to. One second I was standing glaring at Adrian's back, the next I was slammed up against the wall, his body hard and aggressive on mine as his eyes spat blue fire at me.

"I had choices," he said slowly, his words as hard as granite. "The deaths I caused, the Dark Ones I destroyed—I chose to do so."

"Because of the curse," I said gently, sliding my arms around him, holding him tight against me. He was filled with pain, a veritable whirlpool of anger and guilt and agony all tied in upon itself. I wanted to show him that the choices he made, the things he'd done, were not because he was a monster. A tremor went through his body as I melted into his mind, my lips pressed against the pulse point of his throat.

How can you have such faith in me when you have none in yourself?

I smiled into his neck as the torment within him receded until it was a dull throb. *Call it womanly intuition. I just know I couldn't be falling in love with a man who took pleasure in others' pain. You might not realize that I can see it in you, but I know what price you've had to pay for being Asmodeus's servant. I know also that in each situation, you chose the lesser of two evils. A few Dark Ones died, yes, but how many* didn't *die because you were strong enough to do what had to be done?*

He said nothing verbally or mentally, but I sensed that behind the remaining anguish a deep well of sorrow kept him in check. Warm lips caressed my ear for a moment; then he pulled back and collected his satchel. "The toilet is at the end of the hall. I will meet you downstairs in five minutes."

He left the room without a backward glance.

"About this ring of Asmodeus's that you were looking for at Christian's castle . . ." I began.

Adrian glanced at me, the hand resting on my waist tightening with a possessiveness that thrilled me to my toenails as we made our way through the darkening streets of Cologne, past the magnificent cathedral toward the main train station. "Why do you ask about the ring? You said you did not see it."

Actually, I hadn't said anything of the kind, but only because I still wasn't exactly sure what the item I'd found at the castle was . . . and Adrian hadn't left me alone long enough to examine it. I wasn't sure it *wasn't* an earring, but it sure seemed like it could be the ring Adrian had been looking for. My best bet was to get a little more information so I could make a decision about it. "I'm curious about something that holds so much potential power against Asmodeus. Why didn't you continue searching for it after we ran into each other?"

He shrugged, pulling me tighter against him to avoid a group of laughing Japanese tourists who spilled out onto the sidewalk as they posed in front of the steps of the cathedral taking each others' pictures. "The ring was not there."

"How do you know that? I was there before you, so I know you didn't do any searching—"

"I know because I could not feel its presence."

Hmm. Maybe it was just a strange horn earring after all?

"Would you have felt its presence if something else had been there to distract you?" I asked slowly, blindly feeling a path through a confusing morass of speculation.

He slid a suspicious glance my way, and I felt the soft touch of his mind. I did my best to arrange my mind into images of innocence, hiding the one thought I didn't want him to read. It must have worked, because he merely shrugged again, hurrying me across a rain-slicked street toward the glass structure of the Hauptbahnhof Köln. "I might not, if the distraction was strong enough. What are you referring to?"

He stopped outside the front entrance, and I gave him my best naive look. "Well, you knew that vase was warded. I was wondering if that could mess up your supernatural radar, so to speak."

"No, it would have to be something much more distracting than that to hide the presence of the ring."

Something like the appearance of his long-lost Beloved? I wondered. I followed as he tugged me up the steps toward the entrance.

"If you had this ring, could you use it to break Asmodeus's curse?"

"I could not, but others might." He gave me a sharp, questioning glance.

"You can't use the ring?"

"Not against Asmodeus. I could wield it in other circumstances, but not against the dark lord to whom I am bound."

"Oh, yeah, I forgot he was the one who pulled the nasty on you. Say you found the ring and gave it to me," I said slowly as we hurried into the train station. "Using it, could I blow the curse away without doing any Charmer stuff?" If I could, there was I chance I could help him and Melissande's nephew both without burning out any more of my brain.

"Yes."

"Really?" Hope swelled within me. Maybe things weren't as dire as they seemed. All I needed to do was use the ring against Asmodeus to free Melissande's nephew and break the curse on Adrian. Then he and I could live happily ever after. . . . What was I thinking? Use the ring against Asmodeus? Just the memory of that hideous monster left me faintly nauseous. How on earth could I rally enough strength to face him again?

"If you had the training to master a demon lord, or access to someone with that information, yes. But as you have neither that nor the ring, the point is moot."

Before I could grill him further about the ring, he hustled me to the main floor, pointing at a seating section. "I will get the tickets. You wait over there for me."

"Um." I gnawed my lip, looking around at all the flashy shops that edged the waiting area. "I assume the reason we're taking the train rather than flying to London is because you don't want to be trapped on an airplane in case something happens and you'd be stuck, possibly exposed to the sun?"

"No," he answered, giving the area a quick once-over, obviously looking for anything threatening. It gave me a warm, fuzzy feeling inside to be on the receiving end of his protective manner. Some women might find it stifling to have a man constantly be concerned about her well-being. I found it endearing. "We travel by train because that is all I can afford."

"What?" I all but shrieked, grabbing the back of his duster as he started away. "What do you mean, that's all you can afford? You're a vampire! You're four hundred and eighty-two years old!"

He turned back with an annoyed look. "Four hundred and eighty-one."

I smacked him on the arm. "Old enough to have put aside considerable wealth so you can keep your Beloved in the fashion she means to be kept in! You can't be poor! Everyone knows vampires have oodles of money lying around!"

"Would these be the same people who expect Dark

Ones to be able to change themselves into bats, and to materialize objects just by the will of their mind?"

I made a face, my eyes dropping before his midnight-blue ones. "Maybe. Are you telling me you're broke? I'm going to spend eternity broke?"

"No." He gave me a grim look. "I will see to your future, have no worries about that."

"Yeah, but what about—"

"Stay here." His voice was rough and hard, but I slipped into his head long enough to know it hid a regret so deep I could not fathom it. Gently he pushed me out of his mind. "I will return as soon as I have the tickets."

I thought about pouting over his putting up the no-trespassing sign, but decided I was bigger than that. Slowly I window-shopped my way down the main hall, wondering how I was going to tell him that I held the key to his salvation nestled firmly against my right butt cheek.

A woman wearing dark glasses limped by me as I stood peering into a bookstore, wishing I had my purse so I could buy us a couple of books or magazines for the long trip to London. She stopped near me, arguing in a soft American voice. I turned at the unexpected sound of English, my eyebrows shooting up as she stuffed a snow globe into a bulging canvas bag. Who was she talking to, I wondered.

"Next time, you're all finding something smaller to bind yourselves to. One snow globe is fine, but seven is heavy."

Was she talking to her show globes? And what the heck was binding? One thing was certain, this American wasn't all there upstairs.

My eyebrows shot up as she glanced toward me, giving me a weak smile. "I . . . uh . . . they're snow globes."

"Uh-huh," I said, moving away slowly. You never knew where you were going to find crazy people. "Seven of them."

"Yes, seven," she said with another tense smile, turning to mutter into the bag's opening.

"You don't . . . uh . . . have names for them, do you?" I couldn't help but ask.

She turned back quickly, the bright lights of the station shining on her impenetrable black glasses. "Names?"

"Yeah, you know, like Dopey, Sleepy, Snowy, Icy . . ." I stopped when her lips made a thin line, slowly moving down to the far window. From the corner of my eye I watched as a tall man in a black leather coat strolled over and put his arm around the crazy lady. The man was handsome, very handsome, movie-star handsome with black eyes and long black hair pulled back in a ponytail.

"Now, that's how a real vampire should look. Sexy, well-dressed, and loaded," I muttered as I watched the reflection in the shop window. The woman gestured toward the shop, and the man pulled out a wad of cash big enough to choke a water buffalo, peeling off a number of bills and giving them to her. I was just about to turn away when another man joined them. A blond man. A blond man who looked all too horribly familiar.

The blond man who had tried to kill Adrian, voicing his intentions to do away with me as well.

"Sebastian," I hissed, remembering what Adrian had called him. Another vampire, one that evidently made it his job to rid the world of the Betrayer. I had to warn Adrian and fast, but without drawing undue attention from Sebastian and his friends.

Adrian!

Both Sebastian and the dark-haired man turned as I reached out to touch Adrian's mind. I leaned into the shop window, my head craned as if I was trying to read something farther in the shop. Sebastian took a step toward me.

What is it, Nell?

I pulled up my coat collar, rubbing my arms and hunching my head down as I pretended to be cold. Obviously the dark-haired man was a vamp, and both he and Sebastian had some sort of mind-meld radar that I'd inadvertently set off. I hated to give them something to ping from, but if I didn't answer him, Adrian would run straight into my arms. I had to keep that from happening. *Nothing. Just making sure you didn't run into the pointy end of a stake or something.*

His sigh rippled across my brain. *Have patience, Hasi. I will be with you in a moment or two.*

I sidled down the length of the shop window, being careful to keep as much of my back as possible to the two vamps. In the window I saw the reflection of Sebastian as he took another step toward me, his eyes scanning back and forth across the stream of people passing. I felt his touch for a moment as if it were barbed with fire, fighting to keep from reacting to it before it moved on. The dark-haired man said something, calling him back. I breathed a sigh of relief as Sebastian's attention was withdrawn, not risking a glance back as I walked away from them as quickly as I could. I whipped around a corner, heading for a sign pointing toward the ticket counters.

Adrian strolled toward me, a sinfully handsome, sexy figure in black.

I ran to him, struggling to push aside the heavy material of my jacket in order to reach my hip pocket. "What happened to your coat? Never mind, it doesn't matter. Here, take this." I pressed the ring into his hand, ignoring his startled look as I tugged him over against the wall behind a big pillar. "It's Asmodeus's ring. Don't ask me how I found it, there's no time to explain now. There are two vamps just around the corner, and one of them is that Sebastian guy who stabbed you."

The frown of puzzlement wrinkled Adrian's brow as he looked from the ring resting in his hand to me.

"You said you couldn't use the ring against Asmodeus, right?"

One glossy auburn eyebrow raised, his eyes a stormy blue. "That is correct."

"But you can use it against other Dark Ones?"

"Yes," he said, giving me an odd look.

"OK, well, you go take care of those two bully-boys, and I'll take over when it's time to lift that curse Asmodeus bound around you."

His eyes darkened until his pupils absorbed all the color in his irises. "You wish for me to use the ring?"

"Yes, yes, go on," I said, shoving him toward the way I had come. "Then we can go to London and I'll use the ring to rescue Melissande's nephew, save you, and we'll all live happily ever after. Go!"

Adrian didn't wait for me to tell him twice. He strode off in the direction of the bookstore. I leaned against the wall, suddenly tired with the strain of the last few days. It took about thirty seconds before I realized that I had sent Adrian into battle without knowing how much power the ring would give him. What if it wasn't enough? What if the two vamps overpowered him and hurt him?

"Stupid, stupid Nell," I groaned, jumping out from behind the pillar, intent on following the man with whom I was falling deeper and deeper into love with each passing heartbeat.

Desperate as I was, I didn't notice the person standing on the other side of the pillar until I'd run into her.

"*Verzeihung*," I apologized in German, moving around the person.

"Nell?"

I spun around at the soft voice, blinking in surprise at the sight of Melissande.

Her smile was filled with relief as she squeezed my hand. "It is you! Oh, I'm so glad to know you're safe! Sebastian said you were with Adrian, but I knew that must be a mistake. He had to have kidnapped you, forced you to go with him. Are you all right? Has the Betrayer hurt you?"

"No!" I said, startled by the mention of Sebastian. "No, Sebastian—he's got it all wrong. Adrian isn't your en . . . em . . . y. *What the hell?*"

Behind Melissande, Adrian approached, a familiar scowl on his face as he saw me speaking to someone. He was back in the clothes he had been wearing ever since I met him: his long black duster, jeans, a leather satchel slung over one shoulder.

Melissande turned to see what I was staring at, and gasped. "The Betrayer!"

127

Behind me, male shouts echoed angrily down the hall. Sebastian and the dark-haired vamp were sprinting toward us, dodging and weaving through the crowd, knocking down a few people who didn't get out of their way fast enough. Adrian froze for a moment, his face blank.

"Run!" I yelled at him as I jerked myself away from Melissande. Adrian's confusion, indecision, and anger were so palpable I could taste them. "Run, you foolish man!"

I threw myself on the dark-haired vampire as he streaked past, bringing him down to the cement floor with a fierce shriek. Adrian, rather than running like any sane man would do, roared something in a dialect of Czech I didn't understand, lunging forward. I grappled with the dark-haired man, desperately trying to draw the one ward I was able to pull forth from my crippled memory.

The man swore in Italian, flinging me from him, only partially restrained by my unfinished ward. Behind me, Sebastian tackled Adrian, both men snarling oaths. Adrian tried to shuck off Sebastian in order to reach me, but the blond vamp just slammed him against the wall and started fighting in earnest.

I crawled back to the struggling dark-haired vampire, trying to finish the binding ward. As I started to draw the last symbol, someone grabbed my hair and jerked me backward. I swung to the side, kicking at my assailant's legs. To my surprise, it was the crazy snow-globe lady who crashed down on me, her bag of snow globes slamming into my jaw hard enough to leave me stunned for a few seconds.

Adrian, you must go. They don't want me, but they will kill you if you stay.

I will not leave you, Hasi.

I shook my head to clear my vision, pushing the woman's body off me. She clawed at me, but I avoided her hands, crawling to the nearest pillar. *I know you want to protect me. I know it kills you to leave me, but, Adrian, you must escape. These people won't do anything to me, and I swear to you I will find you.*

I will not leave you.

My eyes stung with tears from where the crazy woman had pulled my hair. Inch by painful inch I hauled myself up the pillar until I was on my feet. I stood to one side of a ring of passersby who now made up a fascinated audience, urging on the two men locked in immortal combat. The dark-haired vamp had just about broken through my binding ward, the crazy woman trying to tug him up from where he writhed on the ground. With menacing determination I stalked forward and drew the last of the symbols, the ward glowing silver for a moment before dissolving into nothing.

"Why are you doing this?" the woman asked, her face streaked with tears.

"I'm keeping him away from the man I love," I snarled, turning to run to Adrian's aid.

Melissande blocked my path. "Nell, you must stop! You don't know what you're doing! He's brainwashed you—"

"Get out of my way," I growled, prepared to knock her down if she thought she could keep me from helping Adrian.

She grabbed my arm and tried to drag me backward, away from where Sebastian and Adrian were fighting near a bay of lockers, Sebastian lunging with his knife,

Adrian using his body as a weapon. "You must not fall under his thrall—"

I drew a binding ward on Melissande to stop her, spinning away to help Adrian. Before I could take three steps, I was jerked backward.

"You will stay here, Charmer," the dark-haired vamp hissed, his fingers hard on my neck.

I spent a moment being astonished that he could have worked his way out of my ward so quickly, then began to struggle in earnest.

"Watch her left hand, Christian!" the crazy lady called as she limped toward us. "She's trying to draw another ward."

Christian? The dark-haired vamp was Melissande's cousin Christian? The man with the delicious library?

Good academic taste or not, he was a threat to Adrian, and that meant he was going down. Rather than struggle to get away from him, I threw myself forward, slamming my fist into his face at the same time as I kneed him. I didn't hit ground zero, but came close enough that he doubled over, one hand still clutching my coat.

"Nell," Melissande said, grabbing my arm as I tried desperately to unbutton my coat. Adrian and Sebastian had knocked down the row of lockers and moved their battle into a nearby office. Five policemen poured into the hall through the far door, yelling, blowing whistles, and shoving aside the people clustered around the office.

"Stop!" Melissande pleaded with me. "I beg of you, stop. You do not know what you are doing."

"I know what I'm doing. It's you people who have it all wrong!"

She wouldn't listen to me. None of them would. Melissande and the crazy woman both held my arms as I fought to escape Christian's clutch, but it was no good. I sobbed with frustration, worried sick about what that blond devil was doing to Adrian. The policemen who had finally forced their way through the crowd had been thrown one by one out of the small room behind the lockers. Crashes, the sound of breaking glass, and the shouts and yells of the onlookers as they followed Adrian and Sebastian told me they were still at it, but I was helpless to do anything, helpless to give Adrian the assistance I knew he needed.

Unless I tried to tap into that power that I'd done so much to forget.

I closed my mind against the shriek of agony that thought had spawned, ignoring Melissande before me as she pleaded with me to listen to reason, ignoring the crazy woman as she simultaneously helped Christian to his feet, and threatened to bean me with one of her snow globes, ignoring the distant sounds of madness as Adrian fought for his life.

"Come on brain," I whispered as I looked deep within myself to the black spot on my soul. "I'm not asking for much, just a little something, just enough to give Adrian the escape he needs."

Melissande's beautiful face faded as my sight turned inward. Christian had a hard grip on both my wrists—in order to keep me from drawing a ward, I presumed. His mouth moved as he spoke, but his words never reached my ears. I closed my eyes, concentrating, focusing on remembering something I hadn't known I had learned.

"Air, I invoke: sky and wind, storm and mist."

A breeze brushed past my face as I spoke the words that Beth's aunt had chanted so long ago.

"Water, I invoke: stream and cloud, ocean and pool."

The words came from me slowly, sounding distant, as if coming from someone a long way away. I opened my eyes, aware of but not paying attention to the shocked look on Melissande's face.

"Fire, I invoke: flame and spark, blaze and flicker."

Christian leaped back from me, looking at his hands in surprise. Within me, power grew hot as I spoke the words of an ancient ward. A white flame ignited in my head, but I ignored the panicked part of my brain that was shrieking at me to stop before I went too far.

"Earth, I invoke: stone and mountain, rock and sand."

Beneath my feet, the ground rumbled.

"By the air, I hold your spirit."

The white flame grew until it filled my mind. I struggled to keep it controlled, to not let it overwhelm me as it had done ten years before.

"By the water, I hold your life."

Melissande began backing away from me, her look of surprise changing to horror. She said something, but I couldn't hear her over the roar of the light filling me.

"By the fire, I hold your strength," I yelled, needle-pointed bits of the light starting to pierce my brain, the pain building until it held me so tight I couldn't draw a breath.

"By the earth, I hold your courage!"

The light filled me, shards of it digging deep into my body as it ate through my brain. I fought the light, fought the need to let it go in order to save myself, fought the knowledge that I was just a hairbreadth away from another stroke. Above the screaming in my head, Adrian's voice protested, but I couldn't release my concentration to listen to him. I had to speak the last words.

I spread my arms wide, fighting the light within me with every last ounce of strength I had. "By these powers, I banish thee!"

The light exploded within me, pain so sharp it tasted of the blood that sang in my veins as I slipped away, my heart and soul and mind consumed by the light until there was nothing left of me but ash.

Chapter Nine

It was a woman's voice that spoke first. "I say we dump her in the river."

"We cannot do that, Beloved," a man's voice answered, humor lacing his voice.

"No? Then we'll find a lake and dump her. A *deep* lake." The woman's voice was American and vaguely familiar. That thought startled me, not because I found her voice familiar, but because I found *anything* familiar. It meant I wasn't dead, or a mental vegetable.

"Allie, you're not being very charitable. It's not Nell's fault she did what she did, although I truly did not know she had that much power. She swore to me that she was *not* a Charmer, and yet she managed a banishing ward by merely speaking words. I was not aware that was possible."

I cracked an eye open at the words. Melissande was speaking, shaking her head sadly as stood looking out a window.

"Oh, she knew what she was doing! Did you see what she did to Christian's hands? It took him an hour to heal those burns! A whole hour!"

I rolled my opened eye to the side and watched the crazy woman—evidently named Allie—who sat on Christian's lap. A faint smile touched my lips. Although I've always prided myself on being a fairly peaceful, nonaggressive person, I was not averse to causing a little grief to a vampire who was trying to harm the man of my dreams.

Adrian! Oh, my God, how could I have forgotten him! What happened after I cast the banish charm? Had he escaped? Where was he? Immediately I tried to stretch out with my mind to reach him, but a sudden blinding pain pierced my brain, causing me to waver on the edge of unconsciousness.

"Christian, have you ever heard of a Charmer who could speak a ward?" Melissande turned to address the dark-haired vamp.

The pain ebbed slowly, enough so I could catch my breath. With tentative, careful movements I tried moving my left arm and leg a tiny fraction, praying with a wordless prayer that they'd respond to my commands. I couldn't stand finding myself a prisoner of my body again. Not now, not when my life had taken on new meaning.

Christian looked thoughtful. "Two or three centuries ago I met a Charmer who could verbalize a ward. But she was a very powerful Charmer, and I do not get the same sense of power from this one." A languid hand waved my way, stopping in midair as he noticed the movement of my left foot. "Ah. I believe she has returned to us."

I clenched the fingers of my left hand into a fist, relieved almost to the point of tears that my body did what I asked of it. I had stopped in time. I hadn't been consumed by the white light of my mind failing me—I had charmed and still lived whole and complete. Or as whole and complete as I was when I started this little adventure.

Adrian. What had happened to him? Oh, God—what if I had killed him as I had killed Beth? "Adrian," I said, my voice coming out a panic-filled croak. "Where is Adrian?"

"She's awake? Good. Let me go look up where the nearest lake is."

I turned away from the angry Allie as she slid off Christian's lap, looking at Melissande. She seemed to be the most sympathetic person in the room. "Where is he? Where is Adrian?" I asked.

Melissande's hands fluttered helplessly as she cast a glance at the vampire who approached the bed where I lay covered with an eiderdown. It was Christian who answered. "The Betrayer is in confinement, Charmer."

Confinement. That could be good or bad. If I hadn't killed him with my attempt to charm, his jailers could have. "Did you hurt him?" I asked, my fingers curling as I pictured Adrian lying somewhere hurt or dead.

"He is"—Christian paused, and I knew that whatever he was about to say would be a lie—"unharmed. What we would like to know is, what is the exact nature of your connection to him?"

Unharmed. I didn't believe that for a moment, but at least I was reassured that he wasn't dead. They would have been celebrating had that been the case.

"Nell, what did the Betrayer do to you? How did he turn

you?" Melissande sat on the edge of the bed, smoothing a hand over my forehead in a motherly gesture that confused me. She was a vampire . . . or at least, a female of the species. Christian was a vamp, a powerful one if the aura of menace that cloaked him was anything to go by. Couldn't they tell that I was Adrian's Beloved? Maybe other vamps didn't know.

"Turn me?" Until I knew where he was, and how I could help him, I would play stupid—an act I suspected wouldn't be too hard to pull off.

"He fed off you, didn't he?" Melissande asked, her face filled with sympathy. "Sebastian said you carried the Betrayer's scent. He thought you had somehow joined forces with the Betrayer, but I told him that could not be so. No woman, mortal or Moravian, could bear to be bound to him."

My gaze slid from her to where Christian loomed over the foot of the bed, an angry Allie next to him. She wasn't wearing dark glasses now, but I could see why she had worn them in public—her eyes were the strangest I had ever seen, one a pale, washed-out gray, the other a mottled brown.

"You seem concerned about the Betrayer," Christian said, his dark eyes unreadable. "Did he feed on you?"

I looked them all over as I thought of how to answer the question. If I told them I was Adrian's Beloved, that he wasn't the monster they had all painted him, would they believe me and release him? Or would they confine me, too, their hatred of him spilling over onto me?

Stupidity has its uses, I decided. Despite my reticence to lie to Melissande—whom I truly liked, even though she was all wrong about Adrian—it was clear to me that here was a situation where less than the whole truth would be wise.

"Yes, he fed off me. After some blond bloodsucker named Sebastian gutted him. I'm concerned about where he is because"—my mind, newly awakened from what I guessed had been a protective slumber, reasoned with awkward slowness—"because I seem to be under some compulsion to help him."

There. Let them interpret that as they would.

"You poor dear," Melissande cooed, gently touching my cheek. "I knew he was capable of the most horrific of crimes, but to turn an innocent, to enthrall a mortal, is the worst sort of sin to my people."

"Really?" I asked, not bothering to correct the impression I had hoped she would leap to. "I thought making human slaves was what vamps did best?"

"Only in fiction," Melissande said with a smile, glancing at her cousin. "Moravians do their best to blend into mortal society, not draw attention to themselves."

"There are many questions we must ask you," Christian said smoothly, but I wasn't fooled by the softness of his voice. He was trouble with a capital T.

I closed my eyes as if I was too weary to keep them open, allowing my voice to crack. "I will do my best to answer them."

"Later," Melissande said, patting my arm. "She needs rest now. She suffered tremendously in her attempt to banish the Betrayer. She must rest and regain her strength."

Banish the Betrayer? Hmm. What I wanted to know was

what happened to Adrian. My brain refused to review in detail the events at the train station, leaving me with no idea if the power I summoned had been enough to expel Sebastian from the train station, and now did not seem a good time to inquire. I opened my eyes halfway, sounding as pathetic as I could when I asked, "Adrian? He is safely confined?"

"For the present," Christian said, his eyes narrowing.

"Have no fears," Melissande soothed. "He is in a secure place and cannot escape."

"I still say we should find a lake," Allie mumbled, giving me a dirty look as Christian escorted her out the door. His dark head tipped toward hers as he murmured in her ear, the door whispering softly as it closed behind them.

Melissande fussed with the eiderdown for a moment, asking me if there was anything I wanted, pointing out the bathroom behind an adjacent door.

"You'll feel better after you . . . oh, there you are. As you can see, she's recovered from her traumatic experience."

I almost came off the bed with surprise when the last man I expected to see walked through the door. "Adrian!" I shoved the cover back and swung my legs off the bed, about to throw myself protectively across him lest Melissande try to attack him.

"No, Nell, it's not the Betrayer! There is no need to run. This is Saer, my brother." Melissande hurried forward to stop me. "You remember I told you about him? Saer is organizing the rescue of Damian. He was in England, tracking Asmodeus when he received word that I had found you."

"As my darling sister says, there is no need for you to

run from me," the Adrian lookalike said, his voice carrying more than an edge of mocking amusement.

"Brother? You're her . . . her . . ." My voice crawled to a stop as I stared open-mouthed at him. He was dressed the same way I had seen him in the train station, in a black pullover and pants. His hair was pulled back, but it was Adrian's dark auburn hair, Adrian's nose and jaw and adorable lips. Even his eyes were the same changeable blue, although, on looking closely, I saw a hardness to Saer's eyes that was lacking in Adrian's. Other than that, they were carbon copies of each other. Which meant it was to *him* I had given Asmodeus's ring in the train station. My heart tightened as I realized that not only did he have the ring I needed to release Adrian and Damian from their captivity, but he knew the truth about my relationship with Adrian.

No wonder he was so amused with Melissande's assumption that I was trying to escape the Betrayer.

"Brother, yes. And Adrian's twin, if you hadn't guessed." Saer finished my sentence, and I shivered at Adrian's voice coming from his mouth. His lips quirked in a catlike smile, his eyes filled with secret laughter. "Identical twins, as you have no doubt noticed."

"Twins." I absorbed that information, turning my gaze to Melissande. "But that means Adrian is your brother."

She looked away. "That is our burden, yes."

"But . . . but you're trying to kill him! Your own brother?"

"He is the Betrayer," Melissande said, still not meeting my eyes. "He would think nothing of destroying Saer or me. Family bonds mean nothing to him, as he has demonstrated to us over and over."

I didn't believe that. Not for one moment did I believe that. Everyone else might believe that Adrian was a cold-hearted, cruel killer, but I knew the truth. The curse that bound him to the demon lord was responsible for his actions, not his desire to hurt people.

"Adrian is responsible for many things," Saer said as if he had read my thoughts. I panicked for a moment, wondering if being Adrian's twin meant he could dip into my head as easily as his brother. "Including Damian's present tragic situation."

I dragged my mind from the worry about brain-invasion to what Saer was saying. My mind skittered around the thought, unwilling to even think such a horrible thing. "Adrian handed Damian over to Asmodeus? Are you sure?"

Melissande nodded, her head down as she obviously blinked back tears.

Saer's jaw tightened, his eyes going black as he said, "I swear I will save him. I will not let Adrian destroy the one being I love more than life itself."

Oh, God. Adrian had handed over Saer's son to a demon lord. Even accursed, how could he do that? "No," I said, shaking my head. "There must be a mistake. Adrian wouldn't do that. I know he's the Betrayer and all, but I cannot believe he would do something so inhuman as to hand a child over to Asmodeus."

"Inhumanity is an apt description of my brother's character. You sound strangely as if you were protecting him, Charmer."

I met the laughing eyes of Saer, and wondered how I could ever have confused him with his brother. "It sounds that way, doesn't it? But then, as you've so clearly proven, appearances are misleading."

He made a slight bow, a faintly exotic move that I knew would be dashing if performed by Adrian, but was merely yet another form of mockery as done by his twin.

"You have something of mine, Saer," I said softly, getting to my feet. Melissande was still by the window, obviously too wrapped up in her grief to pay us much attention. "I'd like it back, please."

He smiled, an awful parody of Adrian's smile that made the hair on the back of my neck stand on end. "I would be happy to oblige, but the return of such a unique object would naturally raise many questions . . ." His voice dropped to a whisper that wrapped itself around me. I gritted my teeth against the sensation. "Questions which I assumed you would prefer not be discussed. Am I wrong? Would you care to explain not only how you came by the object, but how it fell into my hands?"

"Why are you doing this?" I asked just as softly, glancing nervously toward Melissande. "Aren't we both on the same side? I will be happy to use the ring to release your son from his unholy bondage."

"You do not have the skill needed to harness the power of the ring. I, however, will be able to use it to the fullest of its abilities."

"But what about Adrian?"

Saer reached out to touch a strand of hair that lay on my cheek. I recoiled, not wanting him to touch me. Melissande turned at my movement, mopping up the last of her tears and smiling a sad, brave smile at me as she moved to her brother's side. "I am sorry to be so weak, but I fear so for Damian." She put her hand over Saer's heart, her eyes liquid. "We will save him, my brother. We will find him, and save him, and destroy the one responsible for his torture."

"Asmodeus," I said, my stomach balling as Saer wrapped an arm around his sister.

"The Betrayer," she hissed, turning her face into his shoulder. His eyes met mine, and I read his intentions in them.

He would save his son, but not his brother.

No matter how nicely Melissande phrased her words to me, explaining that everyone was concerned about how weak and near death I had been after the banish charm, the plain fact was that I was a prisoner.

"I have rested," I said tersely as I paced past the small table where my jailer had deposited a tray of food. "I have recovered. I am fine, I swear to you—absolutely, perfectly fine. Why can't I leave the room?"

"The others feel you might risk harming yourself if you were to leave now," Melissande said with suspect complacency.

I toyed for a moment with the idea of binding her to the room and making my escape, but alienating her would do neither Adrian nor me any good. Obviously, I was going to have to find another way out. I sat down at the table and poked at the food. "So, where exactly are we? This doesn't look like your cousin Christian's castle."

She smiled and brushed back a long, flowing curtain. "No, we're still in Cologne, in a house that belongs to one of Christian's friends. It is a very old house, a historic structure, actually."

"Really?" I looked around the room. It was your normal European bedroom—if your idea of normal included molded gilt-touched ceilings, linen paneling, and an antique rug probably worth more than I made in an entire year. "I assume this historic house includes a handy dungeon for storing unwanted guests?"

"You're speaking of the Betrayer." She looked out the window, her face unreadable. "There is no dungeon, but I assure you he is safely confined."

"Where?" I asked, desperate to know. She frowned. I hurried on before she could ask why I was so interested. "Adrian can be very persuasive when he wants to be. Once I'm given the thumbs up health-wise, I'd like to know where he is . . . so I can avoid him, naturally."

"Naturally," she answered, her voice as smooth as silk. "I will tell you so you will be easier in your mind, but truly, there is no need for you to worry. Saer has most effectively bound the Betrayer, and Allie—she is Christian's Beloved—has warded all the exits in the room so he cannot possibly escape."

"Room?" I asked, feigning horror as I looked around. "A bedroom? Near me?"

"No, no, a storage room in the basement," she answered quickly. "As long as you do not venture there, you will be perfectly safe."

I hated to deliberately mislead Melissande, I really did, but I had no choice. "And Saer? Is he staying here as well?"

Her eyebrows rose as she gave me a speculative look. "He's very handsome, is he not?"

"Uh . . ." For some insane reason, I felt myself blushing. "Yes, he is. I'd like to talk to him when he has a free moment."

"I'm sure he would enjoy speaking with you, but unfortunately, he's returning to London. He interrogated the Betrayer while you were sleeping, and he believes he has the information he needs to find Damian."

Damn! He'd gone to save his son. I suppose that was only to be expected—if it were my child whose welfare was at stake, I would have left the second I had the ring. "Ah. Well, I'm sure he won't have any trouble rescuing Damian now that he has the ring. Will he come back here, or does he live somewhere else?"

"Saer has homes in Berlin and Prague," she answered, her frown back. "But what ring are you speaking of?"

"The ring—Asmodeus's ring. The one Adrian was looking for in Christian's castle—"

"Saer has no such ring," she interrupted before I could explain that I had found it. "He would have told me if he did. I'm not entirely sure there is such a ring. You of all people know how easily superstition and speculation over the centuries can make something that doesn't exist seem real."

"Saer doesn't have the ring," I repeated slowly. Why wouldn't he tell his sister he had it? She was obviously terribly distraught when it came to Damian—why wouldn't Saer put her out of her misery by telling her he had a surefire way to save his son? Perhaps it wasn't as surefire as I assumed it was. "Well, I hope he frees your nephew. I know you're worried."

"Yes." She bit her lip and hesitated for a moment before speaking. "Nell, I want you to know that I appreciate you had a reason for insisting you were not a Charmer, but now more than ever I need your help. Assuming Saer locates Damian, we will need you to charm the curse binding him to Asmodeus. I would not insult you by offering you more money to help us, but I am not too proud to beg you for your help if that's what it will take."

"You don't have to beg, but, Melissande . . ." It was my turn to do a little lip-gnawing. "I didn't lie to you when I told you I wasn't a Charmer. I'm not."

She gave me a sad, disappointed look.

"Well, obviously, *now* I am," I allowed, trying to think of a way to explain the situation without exposing my true relationship with Adrian. "I told you that I had an accident ten years ago. That accident resulted in the death of a very good friend, and caused me to have a stroke that took me months to recover from."

Her eyes widened.

"My actions, my attempt to charm a curse, caused my friend's death. My own destruction aside, you can see why I was so hesitant to offer to charm the curse that binds your nephew—I could very well kill him in the attempt."

"Of course I understand," she said sympathetically, her hand giving mine a little squeeze. "But that's all in the past! You warded earlier this morning, and although you swooned afterward, you do not seem to have seriously harmed yourself."

"What . . . uh . . . what happened to Sebastian?" I asked, suddenly worried that maybe I had killed him.

She grimaced. "I'm afraid your banishment charm wasn't as successful as you would have liked."

146

Oh, God, I did kill him! Now I had *two* deaths on my soul!

"Rather than Adrian being banished from the building, it was Sebastian who was removed."

"He's alive? Not hurt?" I asked, almost afraid to hope.

"Oh, no, not hurt at all. He is here, as a matter of fact. I'm sure you're distressed that your ward went awry, but I have every hope that you will succeed with Damian's curse."

Pride that I had successfully cast a ward, which had been growing as she spoke, suddenly took a nosedive to despair. "But . . . but, Melissande! There's a big difference between casting a banishment ward and trying to un-make a demon lord's curse!"

"I am confident you will succeed," she said, an obstinate look on her face. "You have to. There is no one else."

There might not be anyone else to charm the curse, but sure as shooting there was a big ole magic ring that could do the job.

"I can't," I said as firmly as I could without being obnoxious. "The curse I tried to lift when I caused my friend's death and my stroke was cast by Asmodeus. It is very clear to me that when it comes to besting a demon lord, I'm out of my league—dramatically and fatally out of my league. And while I would be willing to risk my own soul, I will not risk another's."

Her gray eyes were stormy as I spread my hands. "Please, Melissande, you must understand. I have already taken one life—I will not be responsible for taking another."

Her gaze dropped. "Then he is lost to us."

I struggled with the desire to swear I would do what she asked, knowing full well that the only chance I had of saving Damian involved using Asmodeus's ring. "I swear I will do everything within my power to help him. I swear it."

She left after murmuring a hope that it would be enough. I stayed put just long enough to have a quick wash and bundle up the sandwiches and fruit she'd brought me, pausing to look out the window at the rain-washed streets of Cologne. It was about an hour to sunset, but I felt driven by a strange need to get Adrian out of there. I didn't want to risk disabling myself by trying to contact him via our mental phone line, which meant I couldn't reassure myself that he was not harmed and in no danger.

The door wasn't locked, a fact that surprised me. As I strolled down the corridor and turned to a grand sweeping staircase, I saw why. A big musclebound man sat in a wing-backed chair reading a German magazine.

"Hi," I said with my friendliest smile, holding behind my back the small metal statue of Pan that I'd snatched up from a hall table. "Can you answer a question for me?"

Mr. Muscles towered over me when he stood up. He had a hard, suspicious look about him, as if he were a professional bodyguard. "You are woman American?" he asked in a heavy German accent. "You should not be out from room. What is question?"

"What's the difference between a bird and a tractor?"

He blinked at me. I smiled as I swung the statue down on his head. "They can both fly . . . except for the tractor."

Chapter Ten

The big guy crumpled up without a sound. I dropped the statue and crouched next to him, feeling for a pulse. It was steady and fairly strong.

"Sorry I had to do that, but it was necessary." After peering over the banister to the floor below to make sure it was empty, I hurried down the stairs, pausing frequently whenever the house made a noise. Breathing a sigh of relief that no one was around, I ran silently down a hall that seemed to stretch the length of the building, listening at doors for conversation or sounds of habitation. Melissande's voice was audible at one of the doors, along with the low rumble of a male voice. I picked up my pace upon hearing them, stopping only when I reached the back of the house. Another stairway faced me; this one had obviously been meant for servants in the days when people could afford such luxuries.

"Down means basement," I whispered as I descended

the bare wooden stairs as quietly and quickly as possible, stopping to bend over the railing midway down to see if anyone was standing around below. No one was on guard.

The basement was laid out in old compartment style— one room leading to another, which led to another, and so on the length of the big house. I had no trouble finding the door to the room Adrian was kept in, not just because it was the only door available, but because the wood of the door glowed gold with a confusion of numerous interlocking three-dimensional symbols that made it look as if someone had read too many books on how to create a Celtic knot.

"Let's see if I can unward this thing without blowing out any more circuits in my head," I said softly, looking at the door, allowing my vision to slip into a soft focus that let me visualize the pattern of the wards without subjecting them to intense scrutiny. It didn't take long before the mishmash of curves, lines, and curlicues doubling back on themselves separated into distinct symbols. I breathed a silent prayer as I reached out to the brightest symbol, tracing it in reverse. The ward flared for a moment when I reached the end of it, then dissolved in a shower of silver. Relief trembled in my voice as I touched the next ward. "One down, five to go."

Only the last one gave me any grief, and that was because it was a powerfully drawn ward that did not take kindly to me unmaking it. It was a circle-shaped ward, and as I undrew one line, the rest of the pattern shifted, knotting itself up again. My hand was shaking with strain by the time I finally wrestled the ward into nothingness, but I thought little of that as I threw open the door to Adrian's prison.

I didn't get two steps into the unlit room before I was thrown backward onto the dirt floor by an enraged, furious vampire. A flash of fang was all I saw before he was at my neck, his teeth sinking deeply, pain hot and sharp mingling with my fear that he had been somehow pushed too far.

"Adrian! It's me!" My voice was a thin whimper, but it was enough. Adrian pulled his mouth from my neck, his lips crimson with my blood.

"Nell?" His eyes were a cold, flat onyx. "You're alive."

"As are you. I wasn't sure you were, for a while," I said on a sob of happiness. I clutched him tight, reveling in the feel of him in my arms again. "I thought at first I'd killed you. You're all right? You're not hurt? Sebastian and Saer didn't harm you?"

"They tried," he growled, his lips lowering to mine. I tipped my head back to welcome him, but he stopped before he touched me. "Why didn't you answer me when I called you? Why did you ignore me?"

"I didn't know you were trying to reach me," I wailed, relief at finding him whole and safe making me weepy. "I burned out my intercom when I spoke that banish ward. I tried to find you, but . . ."

I rubbed my forehead. Adrian's lips followed the path my fingers took. "Do not distress yourself, Hasi. It will come back to you."

"I'm sorry you were worried." I tucked a strand of his hair behind his ear. "I guess I was so focused on finding you, I didn't think you'd be trying to contact me."

His face darkened as he pulled back, hauling me to my

feet and dusting off my backside. "Saer told me you had turned from me, that you were cleaving to him."

"Oh! I would never cleave to him!" I threw myself in Adrian's arms, kissing him for all I was worth, leaving my lips on his as I added, "You're the only cleave-worthy man in my life."

He didn't answer that statement with words, but by the time he had made it clear that he too was in business for some cleaving, we were both breathless.

"Saer is a great big poop, and you shouldn't listen to anything he says," I said, panting just a little.

His lips twisted into a wry smile as he grabbed up his satchel. "I realize that now. What he said could not be."

"Right."

I checked the room, creeping to the outer door to listen for sounds from above. It was silent.

"Obviously, he was trying to demoralize me."

"Men who are poops demoralize people all the time," I agreed as Adrian pulled me aside, forcing me behind him as we made our way to the next room.

"If I had been thinking correctly, I would have known that what he was saying could not be true. He told me you had given him Asmodeus's ring, and I know you would never do anything so foolish."

I froze as Adrian paused in the doorway, his nostrils flared as if seeking the scent of danger. Satisfied there was none, he gestured me forward, silently making his way through the dimly lit room, noticing only when he reached the door to the next room that I wasn't with him.

"Nell? Come. We must escape now, before they discover you are missing."

I gnawed my lip for a few seconds. Adrian made an ex-asperated noise, walking back through the room to stand in front of me. "You can't be afraid of the dark—you came through this room on your own."

"No, it's not that. Uh . . . about the ring . . ."

He brushed my jaw with his thumb. "What is wrong, Hasi? I cannot read your thoughts, but I can sense your emotions. Why are you feeling fear?"

I didn't have to tell him. I could just continue to play dumb and not tell him. He'd never have to know.

I sighed. I couldn't lie to him, not to Adrian. "I did give Saer Asmodeus's ring."

Adrian stared at me in disbelief.

"I didn't betray you," I said softly, putting my hand on his chest, my heart crumpling at the pain that flashed in his eyes. "I thought he was you. No one—including you, I'd like to point out—bothered to mention that you have an identical twin running around. So when I saw Sebast-ian and Christian in the train station, I gave you the ring to use against them. Only it wasn't you."

His jaw tightened. His hands fisted. His body language screamed so much anger, I took a step back, even though I didn't really think he would harm me. "You had the ring and didn't tell me?"

"I didn't know it was the ring until . . ." The explanation dried up on my lips. I wanted to sink into the ground, sick with what I'd done even though my motives had been good. "I was going to tell you. I was going to—"

"Allow him to use the ring to destroy us, perhaps?" came a voice from the doorway.

Adrian turned around slowly to face the blond man

who lounged in the doorway with deceptive nonchalance. Adrian moved to block me with his body. I stepped to the side to look around him.

"Sebastian." Adrian's voice was soft, but filled with so much menace it made the hairs on my arms stand on end. "So you still live."

Sebastian made a courtly bow. "As you see, Betrayer. Alas that the same will not be said of you come the dawn."

"The dawn?" I asked. Adrian promptly moved in front of me again. I pinched his butt and stepped to his opposite side. "What do you mean, the dawn? You guys don't like dawn."

"Your woman is not very intelligent, is she?" Sebastian said, looking bored.

"Hey!"

"You will leave Nell out of this," Adrian said in a macho he-man sort of way that simultaneously warmed my heart and made me want to crack him over the head with the Pan statue. "She has nothing to do with this."

I elbowed Adrian, and slapped his hand when he tried to pull me behind him. "Like hell I don't. I'm in this up to my armpits. Now, what exactly did your vague threat mean, Sebastian? What do you guys think you're going to do to Adrian?"

Adrian growled deep in his chest as Sebastian strolled into the room. "A camarilla has been formed. The decision to destroy the Betrayer once and for all has been agreed upon."

"Destroy?" I asked, horror growing at his words. They

were going to toss Adrian out in the sunlight? Over my cold, dead body! "You guys are insane! Utterly and completely—erk!"

Sebastian pulled a wickedly curved knife from his boot, casually gesturing with it.

"Stay back, Nell," Adrian said, moving forward to answer the wordless invitation Sebastian offered.

"And let you get gored again? No, thank you." I grabbed Adrian and hung on. "Look, this has gone too far. Obviously, Sebastian holds some sort of grudge—"

"Grudge?" the blond vamp snarled. "He betrayed me, tricked me, helped bleed me dry until the only thing that stood between death and me was my desire for revenge. He did all that for the glory of his master."

I looked back at Adrian. His eyes were indigo, intent on Sebastian. Although he stood as still as a statue, I knew he was poised to attack the other man. "You did all that to him?"

"Yes," Adrian answered, his eyes meeting mine for a moment, his gaze unabashed and offering no explanation.

"Oh." I turned back to Sebastian. "Well, I'm sure Adrian must have had a good reason to do it. He's not mean normally."

"A good reason?" Sebastian asked a bit wildly.

"Do you think it's easy being cursed by a demon lord?" I asked, hands on my hips. "Do you think he's had fun being the Betrayer?"

"Nell—"

"No, Adrian, I want to know. I want Sebastian to tell me what he thinks it's like to be bound body and soul to a demon lord, forced to destroy your own people. I want to hear from his own lips just how much entertainment he thinks you got from all this."

"Nell, it does not matter—"

"I want to hear how enjoyable he thinks it is for you to ruin everything and everyone you love. Go ahead, Sebastian. Tell me all about it."

Sebastian stared at me in disbelief for a moment before looking at Adrian. "*This* is the woman you would choose?"

Adrian's lips twisted in a wry parody of a smile. "She does not always see things as we do."

I smacked him on the chest. "Thank you both so very much! Can we get back to the attempts to kill each other and stop talking about me like I'm not standing right here?" The second the words left my lips I regretted them. I held up my hand as Sebastian started forward. "Wait! I didn't mean that. We can talk this out, I'm sure we can. It's just a matter of finding a common ground—"

"She will die after your withered corpse has turned to dust and been scattered to the wind," Sebastian told Adrian with an evil flick of his knife in my direction.

Adrian growled and thrust me aside.

"What makes you think you can beat us both?" I yelled, clutching the back of Adrian's shirt in my attempt to keep him from throwing himself onto the blond vamp. Adrian twisted and turned, trying to dislodge me, but I held on. There was no way I could stop them from trying to kill each other once the fight began, so I had to stop them before they started. "You've gone up against us before, Sebastian, and lost both times. All I have to do is draw a binding ward on you and—"

In hindsight, I realize that belittling Sebastian's abilities and threatening him with a binding ward wasn't the smartest move, but I was on the verge of exhaustion, both mental and physical, so allowances have to be made.

Adrian didn't see it that way, though. When Sebastian switched his target and lunged for me, the wicked blade of his knife gleaming in the bare bulb hanging drunkenly overhead, Adrian sent me flying as he thrust his body between me and Sebastian. I cracked my head on the stone wall, seeing stars for a few seconds. By the time I cleared my head and got to my feet, Adrian—in better shape than the last time he'd met Sebastian—had the blond vamp pinned to the wall by the knife at his throat.

"You dare attack my Beloved?" Adrian snarled, his hand on the knife's hilt, ready to rip it across Sebastian's neck. Although Sebastian could survive the neck wound, not even a vampire with excellent regenerative healing skills could repair a severed head.

"Adrian," I said softly, holding out my hand as I would to an animal in pain while I slowly approached him. His breath came ragged and hard, his eyes ice blue, so pale they were almost white. "I know you are thinking it's a good idea to kill Sebastian, but it isn't. You can't do this."

A low growling noise emerged from Adrian's chest. I touched him gently on the arm, slowly moving closer so that my body pressed against his. Sebastian evidently realized how close Adrian was to killing him; rather than striking out, which would have meant his immediate death, he stood still, watching us. Blood snaked out of the wound in his neck, soaking the front of his shirt. I eyed it worriedly. He was losing too much blood too quickly.

"Sebastian is not your enemy, not really. He is just as much a victim of Asmodeus as you are," I said slowly, brushing my fingers through Adrian's hair in a gentle caress. "I know you were forced to betray him. I know you had no choice then, but you have one now, Adrian. If you kill Sebastian, it will stain your soul forever. His death will haunt you for the remainder of your endless years."

Pale blue eyes turned to look at me. I leaned forward, brushing my lips against his. As I did, his emotions swamped me, all his fury and anguish, a sort of madness at the thought that Sebastian would try to harm me. "His death would haunt me as well. Do not do this, my love. Do not throw away the soul you have struggled for so long to regain."

A great shudder went through him as I pressed my lips to his in a kiss that pleaded more eloquently than words. The madness receded with my touch, the fury that gripped him lessening.

"He would kill you if he could." Adrian's voice was low and rough, as if he hadn't spoken in years, his breath brushing hotly on my lips.

"The acts you were forced to carry out have given him reason to hate us," I whispered into his mouth, allowing his emotions to fill me. Behind the rage, guilt lay thick and black. "But that does not mean you must hate as well. Every crime you have committed has been enacted against your will. Do not now commit one out of anger. Please, Adrian, show him mercy where none has been shown to you."

He sucked in a deep breath, his eyes closing for a moment, and when they opened, they were clear again, a deep blue that signaled a return to sanity. He turned to Sebastian, the planes of his face stark. "When you next think to kill my Beloved, remember that it was she who saved you."

Sebastian had time only to respond in a squawk as Adrian yanked the knife from his throat, tossing the blond vampire's body across the room. I ran to follow him as he dragged Sebastian to the room in which he had been held captive.

"There is no lock. You must ward the door," Adrian said as he slammed the door, leaving Sebastian lying on a ragged cot within.

Panic rose. "I don't know how to ward a door!"

He frowned. "Now is not the time for false modesty, Hasi. You drew a binding ward when you claimed you knew no wards. You spoke a banishment charm. I know you do not wish to use the part of your brain that controls your powers, but you must ward this door."

I wrung my hands. "I'm not being modest. I don't know how to ward doors. You saw my memories—I was only taught a couple of wards, and those I barely remember. But"—I stopped wringing and gave the portal a squinty-eyed look—"I think I remember how the wards were drawn that I unmade. At least I remember the really hard one."

It took me three tries: one incomplete ward that luckily held the door when Sebastian rallied enough strength to try to escape; a quarter-drawn ward that was so bungled, it tied itself into a knot and froze the doorknob; and then at last I completed a full ward.

"That's it," I said, breathing easier as Sebastian threw himself in vain against the door. "Let's get out of here."

We made it out of the basement, up the stairs, and out the back door that led into a dark alley without anyone the wiser, although I knew it wouldn't be long before the unconscious muscle-man and the missing Sebastian were noticed.

"So, we're off to London, right?" I asked as we stood crammed together in a phone booth a few blocks away from the house from which we'd just escaped. "We go find your brother and get back the ring?"

Adrian pulled a black notebook from his satchel, rifling through it. "Reach in my pocket and find some coins small enough for the phone. We are going after Saer, but first we must seek assistance."

I dug around in the pocket of his wool duster as he found the phone number he was looking for in his book. "Assistance? What kind of assistance? Shouldn't we be hot on Saer's heels? He's had a couple of hours' head start on us—"

"I have no money," Adrian reminded me. "I cannot get us to London without money. I have a friend here in Cologne who will help me. Once we have the necessary funds, then we will fly to London."

"Yeah, but that's going to take time," I pointed out, driven by some inner need to hunt down Saer and get back the ring that I knew would save Adrian.

"I wish to leave as much as you do," he suddenly exploded, his eyes furious. "Every molecule in my body is screaming for vengeance, but I cannot give in to it. You seem to think I am the paranormal equivalent of Superman, but I am just a man, Nell. Immortal, yes, but I cannot breach the boundaries of time and space, nor can I manufacture something out of nothing. As much as it galls me to be beholden to another, I must seek assistance in order to continue."

Mortified, I wrapped my arms around him and kissed the wild pulse behind his ear. "I'm sorry. I have been expecting you to work miracles, haven't I? Blame it on Buffy. That show has done some serious misleading about vampires."

"Dark Ones," he corrected, his voice gruff now, but gruff with a warmer emotion as he tipped my head up to kiss me.

"I think my brain is recovering. I can feel what you're feeling when I touch you," I said just before his lips claimed mine. His mouth teased and tasted, his moan captured between us as I gave in to his demands and parted my lips, allowing his tongue to slip into my mouth, tormenting me with its sweet touch. He was surrounded by a thick veil of desire that had me squirming with a matching fire. I couldn't merge with him fully, but pressed against him as I was, his tongue invading my mouth, I knew he was as aroused and full of need as I was.

A man in an overcoat, huddled under an umbrella that streamed silver by the light of the blue-tinted streetlight, rapped impatiently on the glass door of the phone booth. I sucked Adrian's bottom lip for a moment, then released it. "I don't suppose this friend of yours has a room we could use for a little bit?"

An odd look flickered across his face as he turned to the phone, dropping in the coins I handed him. "As a matter of fact, she does."

He spoke briefly into the phone in German so rapid I had a hard time keeping up with it.

"OK, I got that your friend has opened her door to us, but what was that about Brussels? Where exactly does she live?" I asked as we vacated the phone booth.

Adrian wrapped his arm around my waist, hauling me up close as we hurried through the dark, wet streets of Cologne.

"Gigli lives on Brüsseler Platz in the Belgische Viertel, the Belgian Quarter. We can take the tram."

Cuddled up against him, I could feel both his distraction and concern as he constantly scanned the people passing, no doubt watching for Sebastian or Christian. No one tried to stop us as we boarded the train that led to an area of town filled with historic old buildings and expensive apartments.

"So, exactly who is this Gigli woman?"

"She's not a woman, she's a knocker."

"She has *what*?" I asked, my voice filled with outrage as I stopped dead on the cobblestone street. Vampires don't use words like knockers! Everyone knows that!

Adrian tugged me forward. "Not what, who. Gigli is a knocker."

"And what's a knocker when she's at home?"

"Knockers are Welsh spirits. They used to inhabit mines."

I stopped again, but Adrian was ready for me and hauled me up tight, urging me forward over the slick cobblestones. "A spirit? You're taking me to see a spirit? A Welsh spirit?"

"Yes."

"Spirit as in ghost? You have ghost friends?"

"Spirit as in an incorporeal being now inhabiting a human form."

"Oh." I contemplated that during the time it took for us

to turn the corner toward a small square. "What is a Welsh spirit doing in Germany?"

Adrian shrugged. "She likes the beer."

I ground my teeth. "Just when I thought I was getting a handle on this whole Dark One/demon lord/imp thing, you go and throw knockers into the mix. I'm going to have to request that you stop, Adrian. I'm about at my limit of how many impossible things I can believe before breakfast."

He flashed a heart-stoppingly roguish grin at me, his dimples just about bringing me to my knees. "Your middle name wouldn't be Alice, would it?" he asked.

"No, it's Diane, and you're no White Rabbit, so let's just stop pretending we're in Wonderland, OK?"

He laughed and pointed across the tiny square at our destination. I watched him for a moment, seeing a glimpse of the charming, charismatic man he must have been before the demon lord cursed him and leeched away all the softer emotions.

Chapter Eleven

Haus Glietgel. I frowned at the discreet blue metal sign posted above a buzzer on the bright pink house. Part of a block of connected buildings, each house was painted either yellow or pink, with glossy black highlights picked out around the windows and doors. The windows were all adorned with flower boxes that were now empty, but I was willing to bet that in the summer they overflowed with the ubiquitous red flowers in Germany. "I know my German is mostly academic in nature, but doesn't that mean House of Lubricating Jelly?"

"Yes," Adrian answered, pushing me past him as the door hummed its willingness to allow us entrance. I had only a quick glance at the shop that filled the lower floor of the house before Adrian hustled me upstairs. At the top, a wrinkled old woman in a shapeless black dress stood waiting for us.

Adrian bowed politely. "Jada. It has been many years."

"Betrayer," the old lady answered in a sing-song voice so dry I swear bits of the words were flaking off into dust. Her face was a morass of wrinkles, her flesh sunken and loose, as if it were only just holding on to the bones beneath. Her hair, scraped back from her head and pulled tight in a minuscule lump on the back of her head, was white with a few thick black hairs mixed in. Her eyes were also white, clouded with cataracts, and although I knew she must be blind, the way she turned her attention on me had me squirming as if she could see deep into my soul. "So you have found her at last?"

"This is Nell. Jada is Gigli's"—Adrian stopped, unable to find the proper word—"sentinel."

"Sentinel?" I looked at the old woman. She was blind, frail, wrinkled within an inch of her life, and looked to be older than the building we stood in.

"Bouncer," the old lady corrected Adrian, cackling at my air of disbelief. "It is an American word, but it carries much power."

"Uh . . . OK. You're a bouncer." Right. And I was Alice after all.

"You are a Charmer," she answered, a whip-crack of steel in her dusty voice that had me taking back a little of my disbelief in her claim. She raised her hand, and one bent, gnarled finger touched the side of my head. The touch sent icy shivers down my back and arms. "You have light in your head, the white light of oblivion, but your fear is what will destroy you, not the light."

Goose bumps marched up and down my arms at her words. I had never told anyone but Adrian how the stroke had manifested itself as a white light, and he certainly had had no time to tell her about it . . . not that I thought he would discuss something so private.

"It wasn't my fear that destroyed part of my brain ten years ago," I said softly as I moved closer to Adrian. His arm came around me, comfortingly solid.

The old woman cackled again and waved us in. "That is one very strange woman," I said in a low undertone as Adrian walked behind me down a dark, narrow passage. "Who on earth would hire someone blind and feeble to be a bouncer, of all things?"

"Jada is a Kohan." I looked my question at him over my shoulder. "Kohan is Farsi for ancient."

"Well, she's certainly all that," I agreed, opening the door at the end of the passage.

It was like opening the door to Wonderland. I looked around the big room pulsing with lights and soft music, walls filled with erotic pictures and paintings, the red and black carpeted floor all but invisible in the sea of bodies that moved and swayed in time with the music. Along the walls little alcoves had been built, shielded with long red velvet drapery, most of which were closed. But some had been left open, and the bodies within the alcoves were entwined and writhing together in a manner that left nothing to the imagination. I finally understood what sort of business Adrian's friend Gigli was running in her house.

"This is a brothel, isn't it? Some sort of weirdo German sex club?"

Adrian just shot me a look that warned me against making a scene, his hand warm and steady on the small of my back as he pushed me into the room. The music

swept over us as we entered, and I realized that something must have been added to it, some sort of subliminal
message leaving the listener with a strong compulsion to
join the throng and dance the night away.

"Dance with me," I said, whirling around to face
Adrian, anticipation pooling in my stomach at the
thought of his body pressed hard against mine as we
moved to the music. "I want to dance with you."

"You must resist the glamour," he answered, pushing
me backward through the crowd. "It is meant for the others. We have much to do tonight, Nell."

"Yes, much," I purred, rubbing myself against him, feeling wickedly sensual. An overpowering swell of emotion
rose within me, a need to touch him, to hold him deep inside me.

His eyes went sapphire at my words, but he held me off
his chest when I would have wrapped myself around him.
"Business first, Hasi. Later I will allow you to perform all
those wicked acts you are imagining."

"I can imagine a lot of wicked acts," I warned, quivering
with the need to touch him, to possess him. My body was
sensitized with a heightened awareness that left the very
touch of clothing against my flesh an intolerable irritation. The only thing I wanted touching me was Adrian. I
tugged at buttons on my jacket, throwing it to the floor as
Adrian backed me through the seemingly solid mass of
dancers. Others brushed against me, but it was only
Adrian's touch I wanted, only his body that mine craved. I
ran my hands over my belly, up to my breasts, imagining
they were his hands stroking me as I ripped off my
sweater.

Adrian paused long enough to pluck both my sweater and jacket off the floor. "Hasi, look at me. You must fight the glamour. It is making you feel things you will later regret."

"I want you, Adrian. I want you right now. I could never regret that. Make love to me, my darling. Make love to me now!"

He swore under his breath as he pushed me through the crowd until another door stood before us, this one painted red with a sign marked *Private*. He knocked while I wrapped my arms around him, nuzzling his neck and rubbing my hips against him in blatant invitation. "I want to feel you inside me, Adrian. I want to feel you hard and hot and deep inside me. I want to feel every inch of you pressed against me, our flesh sliding together, your body pumping into mine."

My hand slid down his chest to the fly of his jeans. The cloth was tight, bulging with the strain of holding him in, his body shaking with the effort to restrain himself. His hand covered mine, intending to remove it from his groin, but at the touch of his fingers I felt his desire and need as I caressed the hard, thick length of him. Passion rose within him along with a terrible hunger, the blackness that still remained in him gone red with arousal.

"Love me," I breathed, tugging his hair until his mouth descended toward mine.

He scooped me up in his arms, his lips hot on mine as he kissed me.

"Has it been so long that you did not remember to ward yourself before entering the lounge?" a voice asked behind Adrian. His body stiffened as his lips parted from mine, but before I could protest the action, we were in a small room, the sound of the door closing behind us cutting through the red wave of need as effectively as if someone had thrown ice water on me.

Adrian set me down, silently handing me my sweater and jacket.

"Crap!" I squealed, grabbing both and pulling them on without meeting anyone's eyes. I vaguely remembered that a glamour was some sort of magical compulsion that could be bound to something audible or visible—like a piece of art or music—but I had no idea that it could be such a powerful thing, even away from its direct influence. My body tingled with the remainder of the glamour-induced lust.

"This must be your Beloved. You are welcome in my house, Nell."

I buttoned the last button on my jacket and forced myself to look at the woman who ushered us into the room. I don't know what I had expected a Welsh spirit to look like, but she looked as normal as any other red-headed, freckled, buxom woman in a tight scarlet dress that exactly matched the color of the door. She smiled a bit wryly, gesturing with a languid hand toward the room beyond. "I'm sorry Adrian didn't prepare you for that. It is a little bit of silliness, but the locals seem to enjoy it."

I gritted out a smile and a brief apology for my little striptease before glaring at Adrian.

"It has never affected me before," he shrugged, peeling off his coat and setting his satchel on a nearby black and red chair. "I did not think precautions were needed."

Gigli smiled, and I warmed up to her despite my embarrassment over almost ravishing Adrian in public. "You did not feel it before because you had not found your Beloved. Your emotions for her are what leave you vulnerable to the glamour. Please, sit down and tell me how I can be of help."

I sat in a black leather chair. Adrian stood behind me, his body language expressing unease and discomfort. "I have nothing to offer you in payment for your help, Gigli."

Her smile turned rueful. "You have done much to help me in the past without demanding payment, Adrian. I am happy I will be able to pay off my debt to you, although I must warn you, I do not have much cash. My clientele demands only the best, and just last week I had to fly in an entirely new group of sylphs after the last girls decided to form a union and start their own house." She snorted disgustedly. "After all I did for them, that was how they repaid me!"

Adrian frowned. "I'm sorry about your labor problems, Gigli, but—"

"Ungrateful, selfish sylphs," Gigli stormed. "You would think they'd have felt some loyalty to me, but no, they stayed long enough to learn what it takes to entertain a poltergeist, then poof! Off they went to start a rival house."

"Poltergeists?" I asked, my eyebrows shooting upward as I looked at Adrian.

"They took their costumes, too. Do you have any idea how expensive it is to clothe sylphs? It's all sheer silk this and gossamer lace that."

"Gigli's clientele," Adrian answered my question, a black frown settled on his brow.

"*And* they took my spectral whips. The price of those have positively skyrocketed ever since the poltergeists learned they served as an aphrodisiac."

"Really?" I slid a glance toward the door, the memory of the entwined bodies still fresh in my mind. "Those were poltergeists out there? Huh. They didn't look ghostly at all."

"That's because they aren't. Gigli uses the lounge as a cover for her real clients."

"The poltergeists," I said, trying to look as if there were nothing out of the ordinary in the idea of a whorehouse for ghosts.

"Exactly."

"They pay extremely well," Gigli added, evidently having worked out her tirade on the mutinous sylphs. "Not in money, of course, because everyone knows poltergeists have no head for any form of treasure, but they are expert kobold catchers. The market here for tamed kobolds is incredible."

"Kobolds?" I asked, trying not to look too stupid.

"A form of house imp," Adrian answered. "If we can get back to the point—"

"Very popular amongst the affluent set," Gigli said in a confidential tone. "A fully matured kobold can fetch anywhere from four thousand euros up. You can see why it pays to keep the poltergeists happy."

"Of course I can," I agreed, wondering if now was the point where my head exploded from all the strange things I had seen or heard about in the last seventy-two hours. "It makes perfect sense. You have to buy sylphs so the poltergeists can get it on with them, thereby obligating them into hunting kobolds for you. What's not to understand?"

Adrian's hand descended upon my shoulder, squeezing it gently. "Gigli, you're frightening Nell."

"I'm not frightened. Disturbed, yes, I'm disturbed within a hairbreadth of going stark raving mad, but I'm not frightened."

"We need two tickets to London," Adrian said, ignoring both the rising note in my voice and Gigli's attempt to smother laughter. "If you can provide us with them, I will consider your debt to me paid."

"Done," she said, lifting a black phone from the black glass desk that sat diagonally in a corner. She punched a few numbers, covering the mouthpiece to add, "I will need your passport numbers."

I looked at Adrian. He looked at Gigli.

"What?" she asked, her red brows pulling together slightly. "Don't tell me you don't have your passport!"

"I have mine," Adrian said slowly, his gaze dipping to where I sat.

"But mine got left behind in Christian's castle."

Gigli set the phone back on its cradle, her gray eyes suddenly hard and assessing as she looked me over carefully before turning to Adrian. "Christian? C.J. Dante?"

He nodded sharply.

"If you don't have your passport, how did you cross from the Czech Republic into Germany?"

"Adrian used me to do a mind push on the conductor on the train, which worked great, even though I had no idea how to make someone do what I wanted them to do just by giving them a mental shove, but . . ." I gnawed on my lower lip and slid him a quick glance. His face was frozen, his eyes locked on Gigli. "But I had a bit of an accident in the Cologne train station, and we can't do that again."

"Can you not have Dante send you the passport?"

"Are you kidding?" My lips curled into a jaded smile as Adrian's fingers tightened on my shoulder. "Christian wants to see us dead. I don't think he's going to help us escape Germany."

She sucked in her breath, her eyes huge as she turned them on Adrian. "You did not mention that Dante is the Dark One pursuing you."

Pain radiated from under Adrian's grip. I touched his fingers, wordlessly asking him to loosen his hold. He did so immediately, rubbing the sore spot as he answered Gigli. "Does it matter who is trying to find us? We still need to get to London."

"But this changes everything. Dante is"—she spread her hands wide in a gesture of helplessness—"very resourceful. You know that as well as I. The airport will be the first place he looks for you. This is not merely a matter of booking you on a flight to London. If you insist on flying, you must have new identities, and I cannot help you with that."

I stood up, twining my fingers through Adrian's. Frustration raged in an angry swirl around him, wrapping me in its embrace until I thought I would scream at the obstructions that seemed to block our every move. "Look, I realize we're asking a lot, and I don't have much I can offer in return, but I can withdraw some money from my retirement fund—"

"Money," she said, snorting at the idea. "What good is money? It is used only in the mortal world, and I keep my contacts with that to a minimum."

"A big bucket of cash sure would come in handy right

about now," I snarled, immediately ashamed that my bad mood had caused me to lash out at someone who was trying to help us. "I'm sorry. I didn't mean that. It's just that it's important that we get to London. Very important. And we'll do almost anything to get there, so whatever it will take—money, information, kobolds, *whatever*—we'll get it just so long as we're on a plane in the next couple of hours."

Adrian disentangled his fingers from mine, wrapping both his arms around me as he pulled me back against his chest. "Who do you know who can make us new identities?"

Gigli had pursed her lips at my outburst, softening the look to a thoughtful moue as I'd pleaded with her. Her lips relaxed into their normal full lines now as she eyed us. "Seal."

I leaned back against Adrian, exhausted and too over-whelmed to cope anymore. "Trained or harbor?" I asked.

"The man who can help you is named Seal," she answered, looking away quickly. "He will be able to make you both new passports."

"At what cost?" Adrian asked, his voice rumbling deep in his chest.

She wouldn't meet his eyes. "That is between you and him. I cannot help you there. Once you have the passport numbers, I will arrange for you to be on the next flight to London."

I had a bad feeling about this guy Seal, but didn't see that we had much choice. Adrian's frustration was still spilling onto me, joining with my own impatience and leaving me edgy and more than a little jumpy. Gigli wrote down the directions to Seal's apartment while I rubbed my arms, trying to quell the sense of disaster that seemed to grow stronger with each second that we were stuck in Germany.

Before we left, Gigli gave me an odd look, then unlocked a steel filing cabinet, pulling out a small green book which she offered to me.

"What's this?" I asked, flipping through it. It was in Latin, filled with diagrams and brief explanations along with what appeared to be very bad poetry. I translated a few sentences, surprised when I realized they weren't poems . . . they were spells.

"It is a book of charms. As you can see, it's not very old, and thus not worth much on the resale market. I thought you might like to have it, as you are a Charmer."

I smiled and handed the book back to her. "Thanks, but no thanks. I know that no one but Adrian believes me, but my Charming skills are pretty much limited to a couple of wards."

"How do you know what you can do until you have tried?" she asked, her lips curving in a smile.

Unbidden, the image of Beth's bleak grave rose in my mind. I grimaced and looked away. "Trust me, I know."

Chapter Twelve

"Do you know this guy Seal?" I asked as Adrian and I hurried toward the nearest intersection, where we stood a better chance of finding a taxi.

"I have heard of him," he answered. His voice was flat, but as soon as I slid my fingers around his wrist I could feel what he had been trying to hide—intense, profound worry. "He is a forger of some repute, a mortal, but one who has dealings with immortals."

A taxi zoomed to a stop as if it had read Adrian's mind. I slid into the back seat, waiting until Adrian had given the address before snuggling up to him, asking softly, "Why did I hear an unspoken *but* in that last sentence?"

His arm tightened around me. "When I heard of him last, he was mixed up with the Eisenfaust, an offshoot of the German Mafia."

"He sounds like a delightful individual." I gave his ear a quick kiss, just because it deserved it. "But if it comes down to you against him, my money's on you."

"I am not concerned with beating him in a fight," Adrian said, his eyes a bright cerulean that promised so much. "I am worried about what payment he will ask."

"Well, I've told you how much I can raise. If he asks for more than that, just flash a little fang. I bet that'll knock a couple of grand off his price."

Seal turned out to be an emaciated man whose skin—the color of very milky coffee—was stretched tightly across his bony frame, making me think of him as sort of an animated skeleton. The entire five minutes we were in his apartment, the skin under one eye ticked constantly, but it was the jittery, slightly unfocused look in his muddy eyes that screamed *serious drug addict*.

"What do you want?" he asked in impolite German through the barely opened door after Adrian had pounded on it for three minutes.

"Gigli sent us. She said you could help us."

The eye peeping out at us narrowed as it examined first Adrian, then me. "A Dark One and a human. What sort of help do you want?"

"I prefer to not discuss my business in public," Adrian said. I nodded, holding firmly onto his arm while giving the hallway behind me a suspicious glare. I swore I saw something small and rodentlike move under one of the many piles of garbage that had been scattered down the dirty passage.

Seal's shadow moved behind the door as it closed, the sounds of several chains scraping across it as he unlocked it. His head popped out to peer around us.

"Come in, come in," he said quickly, pulling us through

the door before he slammed it shut, locking in fast succession three dead bolts, four chains, and a metal brace designed to keep a door from being kicked in. "Now you will tell me what business you want of me."

Adrian frowned as he glanced around the room. It, like our host, was threadbare and shabby, hinting of days of glory long past. Dingy wallpaper peeled off the walls, bits of it drooping onto a sad, shapeless armchair. Two and a half plastic chairs sat around a small linoleum table that held an extensive array of printing equipment—probably worth more than the entire apartment building. No wonder Seal was serious about keeping people out of his digs.

Adrian pulled out one of the plastic chairs for me, removing the plate of furry French fries and a half-eaten burger so I could sit. "We need to get to London without anyone knowing our identities. How quickly can you make us passports?"

"How quickly do you need to be there?" Seal spoke in clipped German, almost as fast as Adrian. I lumbered along behind them both linguistically, German not being a language with which I'm very familiar, trying to follow the conversation without getting too lost.

"Before dawn."

Seal shook his head without even glancing at the cracked and broken clock that clung drunkenly to the wall over the table. "Impossible. It takes at least three days to make a passport that can get through international security."

"We don't have three days. We need to leave tonight." The muscles in Adrian's jaw tensed. I touched his arm, more as a way to remind him not to lose his temper with the forger than to assess how angry he was.

"That is no concern of mine. I'm telling you how long it will take me to make the passports."

"Do you have any idea who I am?" Adrian snarled, his fangs flashing wickedly sharp as he grabbed a handful of the stained T-shirt that drooped off Seal's chest, lifting him up and slamming him against a wall. A tendril of wallpaper drifted down at the impact, following in the path of a piece of disattached plaster.

"Yes, you're a Dark One," Seal squeaked, his arms and legs flopping around helplessly as Adrian held him a good foot off the ground. "A very big Dark One."

"I am the Betrayer," Adrian answered, his voice a low hiss that promised retribution if he was crossed. "I do not have three days."

"I might be able to do it in one," Seal gasped as Adrian lifted him higher against the wall. "Tonight! I could have it for you tonight! Twelve hours, that's the fastest I can make them."

Adrian snarled and let go of the man, who promptly fell in a whimpering heap. "To delay an extra day does not please me."

"Twelve hours is the fastest." Seal dragged himself to his feet, dusting off already filthy pants and unbunching his dirty tee with an odd sort of dignity. "It's not just a matter of putting pictures on existing documents. First I must find the names of people who've died recently, in order for the computers to register a history. Then I must create the holograms, and those take time. Twelve hours is

179

barely enough time to do the background research, but as you are in such a hurry, I will make an exception for you."

Adrian grunted an acceptance.

"Now, shall we talk reimbursement for my services?" Seal asked, rubbing his large hands together.

"I have money," Adrian said stiffly, lying through his fangs as he took up a protective stance next to me. I leaned against his leg and tried to look wealthy.

Seal smiled. It was an awful thing, that smile, filled with black and yellow broken teeth, but the worst part was what the smile did to his eyes. He might not be one of the weirdo immortal beings who hung around Cologne, but the avarice that flashed in his eyes sent shivers down my back. "The lady, she is your Beloved?"

"The lady is none of your concern beyond making her a passport," Adrian growled.

Seal's smile grew broader until it was like looking at a grinning death's-head. "So she is your Beloved. The Betrayer has found his Beloved. And if I am not mistaken, she is a Charmer as well. How very interesting." He held up his hand quickly as Adrian took a menacing step forward. "I meant no disrespect, of course. My price, ah, yes, my price. For this special rush job, for the exacting nature of the work you demand, my price is naturally higher than a lesser job."

"Naturally," Adrian said dryly.

Seal transferred his grin to me. My creepy shivers went into overtime. "You would not want me to provide your Beloved with a product that would not pass the scrutiny at the airports."

"Get to the point," Adrian snapped, moving closer to me.

"My point, Betrayer, is that my time, my expertise, and my resources do not come cheap. My price is not payment in coin, but payment in service."

"Service?" I asked, my German sounding thick and awkward in the strained atmosphere of the apartment. I cleared my throat. "What sort of service do you want? I can't charm anything, and my ward drawing is limited to a slippery containment ward and a binding ward."

Seal's smile dimmed significantly. He glanced quickly at Adrian before looking back at me. Leaning against Adrian's leg as I was, I knew the minute he picked up the scent of fear that Seal was exuding. "I find myself in the unenviable position of having attracted the attention of a member of the Eisenfaust. A most unwelcome attention, caused by a minor financial transaction gone awry."

"I told you I have money," Adrian said.

Seal's gaze slid away from Adrian as his large hands waved expressively. "The nature of the man in question has driven me to take drastic actions. He will no longer be satisfied with a mere repayment of the amount I owe him. He must be destroyed."

"Destroyed?" I asked suspiciously. "Financially, you mean?"

"Destroyed as in destroyed," he told me, his murky brown eyes meeting mine for a moment. The avarice still glowed behind their depths, mingling with a cruel satisfaction that had me even more worried.

"Killed," I said.

"Destroyed," he repeated, emphasizing the word. He glanced at Adrian again. "Killed would lead directly back to me. The rest of the Eisenfaust would come after me. The trail must not lead to me. He must be turned."

"Turned? What's that?" I didn't like the way Seal was looking at us any more than I liked the way Adrian moved away a step so I wasn't touching him. The fact that he didn't want me to feel his emotions was suspicious in itself.

"I agree to your price," Adrian said. "You will give me the man's address now, then you will begin work on the passports immediately."

"You will not get them until I have proof that the matter has been taken care of," Seal warned, scurrying around Adrian to unlock the many locks on the door.

"I will attend to it by sunset tonight," Adrian agreed, his voice as grim as the flat blue of his eyes.

I held my tongue, not wanting to grill Adrian in front of the creepy Seal, but the second the door closed I turned on him, clutching the arm of his coat. "OK, dish. What's this turning business?"

A glossy eyebrow cocked. "I'm surprised, Hasi. You seem to be so knowledgeable about vampire lore, I assumed you would know what it meant to turn a person."

"You're a Dark One, not a vampire," I said, poking him in the chest. He captured my hand in his, his fingers stroking mine. "And, as has been pointed out, I can no longer rely on Buffy to keep me *au courant* with matters vampiric."

He shooed me down the hallway. I skirted the pile of garbage that rustled ominously, racing down the stairs to the next floor before I added, "If you mean turning the way I think you mean turning, the answer is no. I won't let you make someone else a vampire."

"Dark One."

"Whatever. I won't let you do that. It'll screw up the whole soul-retrieval thing we have going on. Besides, I thought you told me Dark Ones could only be created by a demon lord or born to an unredeemed vamp."

"That is so."

"Then how does Seal expect you to turn someone?"

Adrian gave me a short, piercing glance. "I will turn the man over to a demon lord."

"Absolutely not!" I said quickly, giving him a fulminating glare. "Not on your coffin, you won't!"

He sighed. "I don't have a coffin, Nell."

"Well, thank heavens for small favors."

Adrian stopped on the landing to the floor below, taking my arm and turning me so I faced him in the dim light of the bulb overhead. "Hasi, we do not have a choice. I do not like this bargain any more than you do, but it is a price I can pay. We must have those passports. To delay will bring disaster upon our heads."

I touched the tip of his nose, smiling determinedly into his midnight-blue eyes. "I know that, and believe me, I'm just as anxious as you are to get my hands on your tricky brother, but there has got to be a way to pay Seal without damning yourself any further."

"Other than the fact it must involve a demon lord, you do not even know what a turning is comprised of," he answered, following me as I trotted down the remaining stairs to the street.

183

"Ungrammatical, but true. However, I can guess most of it, and I don't like the answer." I wrapped my arms around myself against the cold, sticking close to Adrian as he stalked down the street. We were in the bad part of Cologne, the part the tourists seldom see. The streets here were dark and narrow, the buildings all wearing a decrepit, abandoned air, the people on the street either brazenly soliciting, offering illicit substances, or scurrying by with heads down, trying to avoid catching anyone's attention. It was thoroughly depressing, and I said nothing more to Adrian until he found us a taxi.

Before he could give the driver the address Seal had given him, I told the driver where I wanted to go, then sat back against the shiny plastic upholstery to find Adrian glaring at me.

"Hasi, you heard Gigli. She cannot help me with the price I must pay Seal. To return to her house now is to delay the inevitable, and we do not have the time to spare."

"She said she couldn't help you, but she said nothing about me—"

"This is ridiculous," Adrian interrupted. "I know you do not approve of what I must do, but we have no choice. It must be done." He leaned forward to tap on the glass between the driver and us. I yanked him back.

"No, it mustn't. I mean, it shouldn't. You shouldn't."

"I am the Betrayer—"

"Which has nothing to do with why you're doing this," I interrupted him this time, my fingers skimming over his face so I could feel his emotions. "You're doing this because you think we have no other way to pay Seal, but we do."

I smoothed the frown that pulled his brows down. "Seal said he did not want money. What do we have to pay him with if not that?"

"Me." I smiled as I kissed his chin. "And you can stop looking so indignant, I don't mean sexually."

He looked even more outraged. "My Beloved would never even consider being with another man, for any reason!"

"Think so?" I choked back a gurgle of laughter at the fury that flashed in his eyes, and kissed him properly, my lips caressing his as I added, "You're absolutely right, I would never consider being with anyone but you. I was just teasing you, Adrian. A little touch of jealousy always looks good on a man, I think."

"I do not like to be teased. You will not do it again."

"No, I won't," I soothed. "At least, not until we catch up with Saer. Then all bets are off."

"If you are finished joking about the circumstance we find ourselves in, we will proceed to the German's house."

"I wasn't joking," I said, pulling him back again, this time draping myself across his front to keep him from leaning forward. "I would never joke about your redemption, Adrian. I'm very serious when I say that I think we can fulfill Seal's request without putting any more black marks on your soul."

"I do not have a soul."

I nuzzled the area where his jaw met his ear. "I could never love a man who had no soul. Yours is almost within reach, but it's at risk of being torn away if we step out of line. So rather than have you tempt fate, why don't we do this the easy way?"

"Nothing is ever easy where you are concerned," he mumbled against my hair, but I could feel his resistance fading with each nibble on his ear. "How do you think you can pay Seal?"

"That book Gigli offered me, the Charmer book. When I was flipping through it I saw something about how to charm a curse that changes someone temporarily into a toad. It looked like it had drawings and complete details about how to unmake the curse, so all I have to do is reverse everything to cast the curse. Considering that what Seal wants is the Iron Fist guy out of his hair but not killed—something I wholeheartedly agree with—what better way to do it than to curse him into toadhood?"

Adrian's kiss was sweet, so sweet it brought tears to my eyes. "There is a big difference between charming and casting a curse, Hasi, and you yourself have said you are not a Charmer. While you may ward with impunity, charming exacts too heavy a price. Can you imagine what a curse would cost you? I will not have you risking yourself on my behalf."

"I'm totally with you on the not wanting to blow out any more of my brain circuits, but I don't think this is going to be a problem. After all, I've got you. I'm immortal now, aren't I?"

Adrian gave me a long look. "No, you are not."

"I'm not? Why aren't I? Haven't we done that Joining thing?"

His eyes, always a barometer to his feelings, darkened to midnight. "There is still the seventh step, the final step."

"Which is?"

"A blood exchange."

186

"Oh." I looked at his neck, at the spot where his pulse beat slow and true. "I get to do the vamp thing to you, huh? OK. I can do that. It . . . uh . . . doesn't have to be a lot of blood, does it? I'm not sure if I'd like that."

"No, it does not have to be a lot of blood. One drop will do, but that point is moot. We will not conduct the final step of Joining."

I goggled at him. "We won't? Why won't we?"

He tried to turn his head, but I grabbed his ears and made it stay put. Pain flickered in his eyes, swelling within him, mingling with regret and guilt that he had drawn me so far along the path of Joining.

"You don't think you're going to survive Saer," I said, reading the echo of his thoughts even though he struggled to keep them from me. "You think he's going to destroy you, and you don't want to leave me unprotected, a Beloved without her Dark One. Why, Adrian? Why would you think your brother would try to destroy you?"

He pulled my hands off his ears, gently pushing me back onto the seat. "You do realize what casting a curse involves, don't you?"

"Other than invoking ill will on someone, no, and don't change the subject. Why do you think Saer is going to mash you into vampire pulp? And why don't you think you can beat the pants off him if he tries?"

"To conjure a curse, you must first call a demon. It is through the demon that the curse is cast."

"Why do you think Saer is . . . a demon?" I stared at Adrian in growing horror. "You mean a *demon* demon? The kind demon lords have, those sorts of demons? The

187

icky, nasty, mean things that rain terror and horror upon mankind? The habitants of hell?"

"Yes," he said, opening the door as the taxi stopped in front of the pink part of Gigli's house.

I scurried out after him, waiting until he paid the driver to ask, "I don't suppose there are any good demons, are there?"

"A good demon?"

"Yeah, you know, kind of how you're like a good vampire. I was hoping maybe there is a lesser sort of demon that isn't too bad that I could work with."

He looked at me like I was crazy. "No. There are no good demons."

"Oh." I thought that over as we made our way upstairs, Adrian nodding to Jada as she tossed a drunken patron down the stairs. I looked after the man in surprise. He had to be at least a foot and a half taller and fifty pounds heavier than Jada, and yet she tossed him down the stairs like it was nothing.

"Strength spell. Not even the biggest of the lot can fight it," she told me, her blind eyes on me for a moment before turning to Adrian. "Gigli is expecting you. Don't forget to ward yourselves this time."

Adrian swore under his breath as Jada cackled her dry, ancient crone cackle, dusting off her gnarled hands with satisfaction before reclaiming a comfortable-looking rocking chair next to the door. "You must draw the ward, Hasi," he said.

"Why? If you know how to do it, it makes more sense for you to do it than me. I'm not sure how much warding charge I have in my mental batteries."

188

"I cannot ward." Adrian pulled me toward the door at the end of the short hallway, behind which I could hear the dull throb of music. I shivered, remembering how that music had seemed to burn into my blood, pushing my need for Adrian to the forefront of my mind.

"Really? Dark Ones can't draw wards?"

"Others can, I cannot. I am cursed, bound to a demon lord, which leaves me without the resources to ward. The glamour ward is drawn thusly . . ."

It took me five minutes of practicing before I could draw the ward to his satisfaction.

"I hope that does it," I said as I finished drawing the ward over him. It glowed weakly for a moment, then evaporated into the air, leaving behind a faint pattern I could see only when I wasn't looking directly at it.

Adrian took my wrist as I reached for the door. "No. You must be certain that you drew the ward correctly. The power of a ward comes from your belief in the ability to draw it. If you do not believe, the ward will offer no protection."

"It won't? No one ever told me that before." I bit my lower lip. "Maybe we should ask Jada or someone to ward us? I'm not sure that my ward will hold up—"

"I believe it will," he answered, rubbing this thumb over my abused lip. "I have confidence in your abilities, Hasi. You have great power that you have not yet touched."

I opened my mouth to protest, but the look of pride in his sapphire eyes brought a warmth to my heart that I hadn't known was missing. I touched his cheek and knew he was telling the truth—he really did have faith in me. He believed I could do anything I tried. That knowledge glowed inside me, reinforcing the wards I had drawn on us both. They flared gold for a moment, then shimmered into the air.

"Right," I said, my hand on the doorknob, feeling reckless and invincible, as if we were starring in a high-budget action flick. "Come on, Vampbo, let's get this over with, so we can go find your brother and get that ring back."

"Vampbo?" Adrian sighed as I threw open the door and marched into the room, my head held high, pushing my way through the small, crowded dance floor. "Never has anyone treated me like you do. I am feared and shunned by all. I am never mocked or teased. I am the Betrayer—"

"And I"—I elbowed my way through the crowd, tossing a smile over my shoulder at Adrian—"am your Beloved, which makes me the Charminator! Out of my way, dancing humanoid! The Betrayer and I have important business to attend to."

I heard Adrian sigh again, but paid his faux regret no attention. I knew from touching him just how much he cherished the fact that I wasn't afraid of him, that I would fight for him, that I had chosen him over freedom.

Now we just had to see about salvaging that soul of his. . . .

Chapter Thirteen

"Do I have the word *Charmer* tattooed on my forehead or something?"

"What?" Adrian's whisper was no louder than mine, but the touch of his breath on my ear sent shivers of delight down my arms.

I leaned closer to Adrian, so we wouldn't interrupt Gigli from chastising a recalcitrant sylph. "Why is it that everyone we meet seems to know I'm a Charmer just by looking at me? Is there some sort of mark on me that I've never seen before? How do they know?"

"Members of the immortal world see things differently than mortals," he answered, his lips brushing the curve of my ear.

I fought the need to turn my head and kiss him until his fangs dropped, contenting myself with nibbling on his earlobe as I mumbled, "Yeah, but Seal isn't an immortal."

"He has submerged himself in our world long enough

that he sees things as we do," Gigli answered, having shooed the flighty sylph out a door. It didn't close all the way, the pulsing throb of the music drifting in to wrap around us. A shock of electricity zapped through me at the sound, sending my heart racing as my libido shifted into overdrive.

Gigli gave us the eye. "If you two would like a room, I would be happy to oblige. Other than that and the plane tickets, there is little more I can do for you."

The alacrity with which both Adrian and I stood up at her offer, not to mention the wave of desire that washed over me as his scent teased my nose, gave ample evidence to the fact that although Adrian might have every confidence in my ward-drawing skills, I had a long way to go yet.

"Ward's fading. Need charm book," I gasped, never taking my eyes off the blazing blue of Adrian's eyes. I clutched the small green book when it was placed in my hand, following him when he grabbed my wrist and dragged me toward a side door.

"Room?" he asked Gigli.

"Seventeen is free, or if you'd prefer, I can let you have the presidential suite. It has a hot tub."

"We'll take it," Adrian yelled as he hauled me out the door into another hall, Gigli's laughter trailing behind us.

This hallway was different from the other; the walls here were lined with what looked on first inspection to be your standard erotic photography, but as I stood before one picture while Adrian opened a door marked *Präsidentensuite*, I realized that the three participants in the picture were transparent, and one seemed to have an extra set of arms.

"Is that what a poltergeiiiiiiii—"

The door to the presidential suite slammed closed behind me as Adrian literally tossed me onto the huge bed that dominated the room.

"Are you ready for me? Tell me you're ready, Hasi," Adrian demanded, his voice rough and deep as he tossed his satchel and coat onto a nearby chair, quickly pulling off his boots and sweater.

I ripped my jacket and sweater over my head in one move, frantically squirming my way out of my jeans and shoes as he peeled off his pants. "I was ready hours ago. Come to me now, my wild stallion!"

"Stallion, eh?" he asked, falling into my waiting arms, his body hot and hard and wildly aroused. He slid to the side, his hands skimming down my breasts and belly. "You think me a stud now?"

"Oh, yes, you're a wonderful stud, a manly stud, *my* stud," I cried, wrapping my arms around him and trying to pull him back onto me where I wanted him.

"If I am to play stallion to your mare, we must do this properly," he growled, winding an arm around my waist.

His mind filled mine with images of what he intended to do, stirring my desire to a fevered pitch as he flipped me over, pulling me up onto my knees.

"You don't think you're going to . . . oh my God, you are!"

Adrian spread my legs, positioned himself, and thrust hard into me, all in one swift move. I hadn't lied, I was more than ready for him, but the force of his invasion coupled with the unusual angle, and the arousal he felt that spilled into me, sent me spiraling into an immediate orgasm. I was aware of his fingers biting hard into my hips as he pounded into me, acknowledged and matched the blast of need and desire that swept through him, but it was all I could do to stay on my knees and not collapse with the strength of the pleasure that his touch brought.

"Is this what you wanted?" he growled, leaning over my back to nip my ear, his voice as erotic a touch on my skin as his heated flesh.

"I want you," I gasped, my body humming like a top. Within him, the darkness was chased away by the brilliant warmth of our joining. Wave after wave of ecstasy swept him, catching me in its wake, merging me with him until we were caught together, unable to separate. "I don't care how we do this, I just want you. I will always want you."

His shout of exultation rang in my ears as he pulsed deep within my still quivering flesh. I collapsed under his weight, sated within an inch of my life, and yet already wanting him again. Despite the wonder of the moment, despite the overwhelming joy we had shared, something seemed to be missing, something hadn't been right. "You didn't bite me! You didn't feed off me!"

He pulled himself from my body, leaving me more than just bereft over his withdrawal—my heart threatened to shatter at the fact that he no longer wanted to bond with me in the most elemental way a Dark One could.

"Hasi, Hasi," he murmured, pulling me into his arms as he stood. "Do you really believe I no longer need you? You are my life, my breath, the blood that runs in my veins. I could not exist without you."

"Then why . . ." I started to ask, feeling the truth in what he said, but confused by his actions.

"What we did only took the edge off our hunger. Now begins the main course." He laid me down on a thick white pelt that served as a carpet before a small fireplace. I glanced around the room as he knelt to make a fire with wood stacked neatly nearby. Skylights showed the moon and stars flickering between occasional clouds, the room itself lit by candles scattered on several small tables. The bed and a long couch were the only other furniture in the room.

I turned my attention to the wonderful play of muscles in Adrian's bare back as he lit the fire, smiling as I realized his mind was filled with a wicked intent that I wholeheartedly endorsed. "The main course, hmmm? I'm positively famished, so I think you should let me go first."

"I believe that can be negotiated," he answered, turning to me with a smile that made my heart lurch. The firelight gilded the smooth, warm brown of his skin, kissing his hair until it glowed more red than brown. His eyes were dark, so dark I couldn't tell their color, but even without touching him, I could feel the passion in him, the depth of emotion that he felt for me.

"I love you," I said without thinking.

He blinked.

"And what's more, you love me."

His nostrils flared . . . in an adorable way.

I smiled. "I can feel your emotions, and I'm not even touching you. Looks like you were right about my brain healing itself bit by bit."

195

"Hasi," he said, then stopped. I didn't need to open myself to him to recognize the regret in his eyes.

"No," I said, pushing him onto his back. "I don't want to hear anything about you not surviving your encounter with Saer. I don't want you being noble and selfless. I want you to love me as much as I love you, Adrian."

Despair lapped at the lingering arousal that still filled him. He closed his eyes against the pain, and I kissed him, part of my heart contracting with the knowledge that he sincerely believed we had no future. The need to force an admission of love from him warred with the desire to show him just what it meant to love someone. In the end, I decided to accept what he was willing to give me, and leave the worry about our future for another time.

I slid down his body to his feet, parting his legs, trailing my fingers along the top of one foot to his ankle. His leg twitched.

"Are you ticklish?" I asked.

"Evidently," he answered, opening his eyes. They were indigo, dark with passion and arousal. I smiled a wicked smile, one that had suddenly entered my repertoire after I'd met him. "Who knew vampires could be ticklish? I'm definitely going to be straightening out the Buffy people about a few things."

He sucked in his breath when I bent over his ankle to flick my tongue along the bone.

"Tell me what you like," I murmured against the curve of his calf as I nibbled and licked my way up his leg.

"Everything. I like everything," he said, a tad desperately, to my ears. I slanted a glance upward, studying the long length of his body, pausing for a moment to admire the thickening source of so much pleasure. His hands were clutching the rug on either side of his hips, the tendons on his neck standing out with strain. He groaned, his Adam's apple bobbing with the effort needed to swallow.

"Good. Because I like everything about you." I turned my attention to his other leg, kissing and nibbling my way up it, gently scraping my nails up the sensitive inner flesh of his thighs.

He trembled beneath me as I slid upwards, rubbing my cheek against his thoroughly aroused penis. "Do you, perhaps, like this?" I asked just before I lathed my tongue across the fleshy sack beneath it.

His hips shot upward. *Christus, Hasi! How can you ask me that? Your touch sets me afire.*

I smiled at his straining nether bits, pulling away for a moment when I realized what had happened. *Adrian? I heard you! In my head I heard you!*

There was no answer, no feel of him sharing my thoughts again. He opened his eyes and looked down his chest at me. "What's wrong, Nell?"

I looked down at him. His legs were spread wide to accommodate me romping between them. No part of him was touching me. I spread my fingers on his belly. *Adrian?*

What is it, Hasi? Why are you so shocked?

My lips curved as they pressed against the firm flesh of his stomach. *I can hear you again, but only when I'm touching you. I just guess that means I'll have to touch you. A lot.*

The groan of utter pleasure echoed in my head as his eyes rolled back when I took the rampant part of him in my mouth. My tongue went wild swirling, savoring the taste and feel of him, the power he held in strict check as I did my best to drive him beyond wild into uncontrolled.

You always make me lose control, Hasi. The touch of his mind was so pleasurable, it made me aware of how much I had missed it. *You make me desire things I cannot have. You make me hope.*

I shifted upward, bending to kiss him deeply. *Taste yourself on my lips, my sweet Adrian. Taste my love for you.*

He groaned again as I sank slowly down upon him, my body accepting his intrusion with a cry of pleasure so profound it filled me and spilled onto him, mingling with the hunger that was quickly rising in my mind. It was his hunger, but I shared in it, reveled in it, celebrated it in the only way I knew how.

His hands were on my breasts, teasing them until I was overwhelmed with the need to feel his mouth on them. *Nell, my beautiful, wondrous Nell. I need you so much, my glorious one. I need everything you have, Beloved. I need all of you.*

My movement against him, which had been measured and controlled in my determination to make this precious time we had together last as long as possible, changed as he sat upright, his mouth on my breast, his tongue and teeth taking over the sweet torment that never seemed to end.

I will always be yours, my love. Every last bit of me. I will never leave you. His fingers were clasped on my behind as he urged me to a faster pace. The hunger rose between us, blotting out everything but his need for blood, and my desire to give it to him. *Take it, Adrian. Take from me what only you can.*

His teeth sank into the swell of my breast, the pain sharp enough to startle me for a second before it melted into a pleasure so intense, I swore we left our bodies. He drank, the rapture he felt from feeding mingling with the sharp pleasure of another orgasm. As it burst upon me, I was consumed with the desire to share myself with him fully, irrevocably, eternally. It was right. We were right. We were meant for this.

Hasi, no! he shouted in my mind as I sucked his earlobe into my mouth, biting it with my canine. *You must not take my blood! You must not Join with me!*

It was hot and sweet, unlike the occasional rusty tastes of blood I'd had from a bitten tongue or lost tooth. I swirled my tongue over his abused earlobe, sucking it to get another precious drop. Adrian exploded beneath me, his ecstasy as I took his blood pushing him over the edge. Coming on the heels of my own orgasm, sharing his feelings as he pumped life into me at the same moment he took it was enough to send me spinning again, my body clenching hard around his, my fingernails scraping the flesh of his back as we were locked into a seemingly endless spiral of pure joy.

What have you done? His voice drifted lazily through my head as we collapsed onto the soft rug, lying together, our bodies still bound as our hearts beat the same frantic rhythm. One of his hands stroked gently down my back, the other held me tight to his heaving chest. *You do not understand what you have done, Hasi.*

I understand that you're the man I want to spend the rest of my life with. I understand that you need me. And I understand that without you, I won't have a life.

199

He closed me out of his mind, gently but firmly pushing me back so that I could still feel his emotions but not read his thoughts. I didn't need to read them, though—the regret and sadness that stained the happiness of our Joining were enough to tell me that he still believed he would not survive the next meeting with his brother.

"Hey! I thought we Joined?"

Adrian stirred as I prodded him with my toe. I refused to allow myself to be distracted by his sheer masculine beauty as he slept before the now-dimmed fire, the light of the candles casting a golden glow over his skin. He slept on his back, one hand on his chest, his face relaxed and so handsome it all but stole my breath. The dark smudges of lashes parted, and a cool, icy blue regarded me standing before him wrapped in a peach-colored towel.

"You took a bath without me?"

I smiled to myself at the accusation in his voice. "The sun is going to go down in an hour. We have a lot to do, and you were sleeping so soundly, I figured you needed the rest more than you needed to frolic in a soapy tub. Besides, we have to have something to look forward to."

His eyes went dark as he propped himself up on one elbow, his hand caressing my bare calf in a way that had me shivering with want. "Do you honestly believe that we need to save such treats against potential boredom?"

"No," I said, dropping the towel to kneel beside him. "I don't think there's enough time in all eternity to get bored with you. I have a feeling you're going to be infinitely interesting."

"Mmm," he agreed, pulling me down across his chest, his mouth moving over my breast with a warm, wet heat that immediately drew answering fire in other, more secretive parts of my body.

"Adrian, my love, we don't have time," I protested, albeit weakly, as I tried not to melt onto him. My hands ignored my commands to stay put and stroked a path down the thick ropes of muscle on his arms. His teeth grazed my nipple before he turned his attention to the other one, his mind and body humming with simultaneous satisfaction and unfulfilled need.

"To hell with the time," I murmured, giving in to our shared desire.

My feelings exactly, he thought, his mouth moving lower on me as he positioned me beneath him. His hair trailed like black skeins of silk down my belly as he parted my legs, my entire body tingling as his stubbled cheeks brushed against my sensitive flesh. I gave up trying to hold on to a thought, and allowed my being to merge with his.

"Why did you ask if we Joined?" he questioned my shoulder an eon or two later. "You made the choice to take my blood despite my pleas for you not to. Your regret now—"

"I don't regret it," I interrupted as he levered himself upward to peer down at me with suspicion. "Not one bit. I might be a reluctant newcomer to your world, but you truly are everything I've ever wanted in a man. Other than that whole eternally damned thing, that is, and I'm fairly certain we'll be able to work that out somehow."

"Then why did you ask me if we were Joined?"

I kissed the furrow between his brows, and accepted his hand when he got to his feet. "Because," I answered, wrapping the towel around me. Adrian didn't seem to feel the least bit self-conscious as he stood before me starkly male, his body all hard lines and muscle, but I was much less perfectly made than he. "I looked while I was in the bathroom, and nothing seems to be changed. In me. Does it take a while before the effect is seen?"

"Effect? What effect?"

"The Beloved effect. Or whatever you want to call it. Look." I smiled and pointed to the left side of my face. "See? It's still lopsided. And my leg and arm feel the same, too."

His frown deepened until enlightenment suddenly dawned in his eyes. Then his face went stiff, as if a mask had dropped into place. "You believed you would be made perfect when you Joined with me."

"Well, yeah! Isn't that part of being immortal?"

"No." His voice was a harsh whisper that disturbed the silence of the room, but it was his eyes, his expressive eyes, that haunted me. Shuttered and flat, they were empty of all emotion. "In the case of a Dark One and his Beloved, immortality merely refers to an inability to die of natural causes. It does not mean that physical imperfections are eliminated."

"Well, hell!" I stormed, my hands on my hips as I glared at him. "Why didn't you tell me that?"

His entire body went still as I tossed my hands into the air and marched toward the bathroom. "I mean, shoot, you could have mentioned that! Here I was hoping that I'd be fixed up when we finally Joined, and now what do I have to look forward to? An eternity of having a weak arm and leg, and a face that isn't quite symmetrical. Lovely. Just lovely."

It wasn't until I was in the bathroom that I realized something was seriously wrong.

"Adrian?" I poked my head out the bathroom door and looked at him. He stood where I had left him, just as if he was a life-sized statue of an ancient Greek god. "Since you got me all dirty again, I thought it's only fair if you clean me up."

He said nothing, staring at the space I had formerly inhabited.

"I'll clean you up, too. There's bubble bath! Adrian? What's the matter—oh, my God!" I walked toward him, vaguely wondering what was wrong with him, but as soon as I came within a few feet, his pain swamped me, almost bringing me to my knees.

I realized then the mistake I had made.

"Adrian, touch me." I stood in front of him, feeling the full weight of his anguish. Without waiting for him to comply, I leaned against him, wrapping my arms around his waist, nuzzling the sweet spot behind his ear. *Feel me. Feel how much I love you. Feel the truth, my sweet Adrian. I didn't just Join with you so I would be made whole—I did it because you are now my life. I can't possibly be happy without you.*

The brush of his mind against mine was tentative, fleeting, as if he were afraid to merge with me. I smiled into his neck and welcomed him as his velvet touch filled me with such contentment, I couldn't begin to express it with mere words. Instead, I laid my soul open to him, allowed him to feel for himself the depth of my emotions.

You want to be made whole, his thought filled my head, a whisper of regret trailing the words.

Yes. I'd also like to be twenty pounds thinner, have longer legs, and get rid of that annoying birthmark on my back, but if it's not to be, it's not to be. I'm sorry you misunderstood me, Adrian. I was just a little disappointed to find out how things work, but in the end, what's important is that we are together.

His arms went around me as he accepted the truth, his body hard against mine. He held me tight for a moment, his mind closed to me as he fought with his inner demons. I didn't press him, just held him in return, and prayed like mad that I would find a way to prove him wrong about his lack of belief in our future.

Our bath, by necessity, was quick.

"We must be off," Adrian said as he dressed in fresh clothes from his satchel.

"Do you have anything but black clothes in there?" I asked, unable to keep from watching him as he pulled on yet another pair of black jeans. "It looks really good on you, but I'd kind of like to see you in something blue—a blue silk shirt, maybe. I bet it would set off your eyes."

"I am the Betrayer," he answered. "I do not wear colors. Black symbolizes the absence of my soul. It indicates the stark nature of my being, and signals to all that I am outcast, an exile."

"You are the ex-Betrayer, and you have a Beloved. That means you are getting your soul back, so you can wear whatever you like," I pointed out, dragging my gaze from him to the clothes Gigli had left for me, along with a tray of bread, cheese, and white wine. I plucked a pair of undies from the bed and pulled the tag off before donning them. "We won't even go into the fact that black is very stylish and makes you look incredibly masculine. Thank heaven Gigli bought me a new pair. Hand-me-down underwear is just too icky for words."

Adrian made no comment, but his eyes followed my hands as I slid into the ankle-length silk chiffon skirt and matching beaded crochet sweater.

Ten minutes later I had brushed my teeth (silently blessing Gigli for thinking of that necessity), combed my hair, and sat down to consult the book of charms she had given me earlier.

"This is ridiculous," Adrian fumed as he paced by the couch where I sat. "It will not work. You will cease this immediately and let me do what I must. We have no time to waste on such foolishness."

"It's not foolish. You're on the brink of reclaiming your soul—we're not going to risk losing it now." I turned the page, nibbling on my lower lip as I scanned the Latin text for something that looked like it would serve us. "Let's see . . . killing someone. Nope. Way too evil. Um . . . dismemberment. Ick. Turning victim into a wraith. What's a wraith? Is it bad?"

Adrian nodded.

"*Bad* bad, or just semi-bad?"

"A wraith is a spirit that has been sent into limbo for eternity."

"Ouch. OK, no go on the wraith curse. Hmm. Here's a charm to lift a curse that leaves the victim with the head of a dog and the body of a snake."

I looked at Adrian. He rolled his eyes.

"Right, that one's out as well. Oooh, here's something: a

charm for lifting a curse that renders its victim helpless. Hmm. Doesn't sound like the person cursed is injured, just made helpless against the person who orders the curse. I bet that would work."

I looked up as Adrian stopped in front of me, his hands on his hips. "Even if I agreed to allow you to use your power against the Eisenfaust member—which I have not—the fact remains that you cannot curse someone without invoking a servant of a demon lord, and I doubt if you have the strength or ability to control a demon."

"I'm sure I don't," I said with a smile. "But you do! You can call up a demon for me, and I'll use it to curse the Eisenfaust guy."

He shook his head before I finished the last sentence. "Dark Ones cannot summon demons."

"They can't?" My hopes fell. I knew he was right, knew I didn't have what it took to summon a demon. If we didn't have a demon, I wouldn't be able to cast a curse, and that meant Adrian would end up putting himself at risk by having to turn a mortal. "Damn! Why not?"

"Our bond to the demon lord is too great. Servants cannot summon other servants."

I frowned, on the verge of throwing down the book and giving in to a good old-fashioned hissy fit when his words filtered through my frustration and disappointment. I leaped up from the couch, kissing the tip of his nose. "You're a genius!"

He stepped back as I snatched the book in one hand and his satchel with the other. "Nell—"

"Don't you see?" I stopped at the door to grab my coat. "You said yourself that I needed to have a servant of a demon lord to cast a curse. We both assumed that meant a demon, but until we lift that curse from you, *you're* a servant of a demon lord! I can use you instead of a demon. Come on, the sun's down. Let's go find this Eisenfaust bully and turn him into a helpless blob of German Mafia jelly."

Chapter Fourteen

"You know, if I couldn't see for myself that it wasn't true, I'd say I was cursed."

Adrian shook his head at the flight attendant's offer of a beverage and cocked an eyebrow at me when she moved off.

"That whole nothing-turning-out-as-planned thing," I answered his silently questioning eyebrow. "First there was you—well, OK, I'm willing to admit that turned out better than I imagined."

The grin that never failed to make my heart do backflips curled his lips for a moment before he resumed his scan of the passengers on the British Air plane en route to London.

"But then there was the cursing in Cologne." At Adrian's look of warning, I pushed up the armrest between us and slid my hand onto the hard muscle of his thigh. Two could play at the possessive game. *Not that I'm blaming you, of course. You did your part perfectly, and I'm strangely pleased to know that, should the need ever arise to curse someone again, we're set, but that whole experience of Herr Baxton growing a third eye has given me the willies. You're sure it will go away?*

Adrian's hand covered mine, almost as warm and reassuring as his voice in my mind. *I am certain that both the extra eye and the tail that were the result of your curse will disappear with time. The curse you cast was not a strong one, Hasi. It will dissipate in a few weeks.*

Good. I'd hate to think Herr Baxton would have to get a whole new wardrobe just because my cursing skills aren't terribly accurate.

His laughter rumbled in my head as I snuggled into his side. The flight itself was uneventful despite a storm that followed us as we flew toward England. Adrian didn't seem to be much in the mood for conversation, his attention focused on making sure that no one had slipped past his guard. I understood he was worried about Sebastian and Christian finding us, but I wasn't overly concerned. Gigli had sent one of her henchmen along with us to the airport, and both he and Adrian had kept their eyes peeled for any vampires, but neither one spotted anyone suspicious. None of the travelers had paid any attention to us as we collected our tickets and waited to board the plane. The passports Seal had given us had been works of forged art, so perfect that not even the overly conscientious Cologne security had given them a second glance. I had to admit being a bit disappointed that we had no

209

need for the hastily conceived cover story I prepared about who we were and why we were going to London, a story that involved a coffee pot left plugged in, a litter of newly born kittens, and a priceless Picasso, but the realization that we were, at long last, on our way soothed that minor irritation.

"So, what now?" I whispered to Adrian less than an hour later when a tired flight attendant asked us to make sure our trays and seat backs were upright. Beyond the tiny airplane window, the lights of the London suburbs flashed beneath us. "We find Asmodeus, and we'll find Saer, right? Since you're working for him, you must know where Asmodeus is."

Adrian's eyes went cold. "Yes. I know where he is."

"Good. This is going to sound kind of odd, but where exactly does a demon lord stay when he's in London?"

The plane dropped into its final descent, bouncing slightly when the wheels hit the tarmac. A few minutes later, everyone leaped to their feet and began tugging luggage from under seats and out of the overhead bins. Adrian leaned toward me to avoid being beaned by a woman with a large stuffed panda.

"Since losing his source of power, Asmodeus has been bound to an ivory figure currently in storage at the British Museum."

My mouth dropped open. "He's *what*?".

Adrian's fingers closed around mine. *You must be quiet, Hasi. For anyone to realize we are in England is a danger to us both.*

I scooted out of my seat as Adrian stood, his satchel slung over one shoulder as he waited for me to precede him. I hurried off the plane, smiling at the flight attendant as we left, pausing in the disembarkment area until Adrian caught up with me. "I'm sorry, I didn't mean to shout, but, Adrian, the British Museum?"

He shushed me and nodded, hurrying us up the long corridor to the customs area.

I grabbed his arm. *There is a* demon lord *in the British Museum?*

Yes.

Doesn't anyone notice?

He slid an irritated glance my way. *He is bound to a figurine, powerless until the ring is returned to him. No, no one has noticed he is there.*

Oh. I showed my passport, chatted briefly with the passport control lady, and waited until Adrian did the same and joined me again before I asked, "What sort of figurine? One of those china shepherdesses with all the pink frou-frou and stuff?"

"Hardly," he answered, his voice dry as we followed the signs to the train station beneath Heathrow. "This figure is ivory, from Toprakkale, in Urartu."

"Urartu," I said, frowning as I dug around in my historian's memory.

"Ancient Rusahinili. Eastern Anatolia." Adrian plopped a couple of coins in a machine and grabbed the two train tickets that emerged.

"Oh, that's Turkey! Gotcha."

"The statue is of a griffin-headed demon, one of the figures used in an altar devoted to Asmodeus. Because of its nearness and the fact it had been consecrated in his name, he was bound to it when his ring was lost."

"Huh. So he's stuck in the British Museum, powerless. Where's Saer, then?"

"I suspect with his Beloved," Adrian answered as he shoved me toward a train that had just arrived.

I was getting a little tired of being astonished by what he said, so I didn't stop and demand an immediate explanation. No, I held my tongue until we were settled in the back of the last car, then I asked in a casual, barely interested voice, "Your brother has a Beloved?"

"He's found her, but they haven't yet Joined. At least they hadn't when I last heard of Saer." Adrian sat stiffly next to me, his eyes constantly moving around at the people filling the car. It was just before dawn, a fact that seemed to worry me more than Adrian, but he was focused on the occupants of the car. Most of the people were commuters clutching travel cups of coffee, blinking with bleary eyes at the morning paper.

I put my hand on Adrian's and gave it a squeeze. "Angelpants, I know you're just doing the protection thing, but I really don't think you have anything to worry about here. No one knows we're in England, and quite frankly, I don't think anyone on this train gives a hoot about us."

An eyebrow cocked as he slowly turned to look at me, his lips thinned. *"Angel . . . pants?"*

I sighed and raised my hands in surrender. "I'm trying to find an endearment for you, but nothing seems to fit. Do you have any idea how hard it is to find a love name for a vampire? You guys thrive on names like Betrayer and Spike and Vlad the Decapitator, none of which lend themselves to cute, adorable cuddle names."

Adrian's eyebrow arched even higher. "I believe you are

referring to Vlad the Impaler, the man later known as Dracula."

"Whatever. My problem is that *honey* is too bland, and I don't like *darling*, and *sweetie* really is not you, so that leaves me with *babycakes*, *angelpants*, and *love*."

"I choose *love*," he answered, trying to look stern and unbending, like a man feared for centuries as the Betrayer, but I saw the corners of his mouth quirk.

"You know, the more you do that, the easier it'll get," I teased, leaning over to kiss the curved corners of his mouth.

"I have not had much in my life to smile about," he admitted, his eyes starting to go dark with desire. Mindful of the passengers around us I moved my kisses to the safer region of his stubbly cheek.

"I know you haven't, but that's going to change. You've got me now, and all my friends say I'm a wacky girl. I'm just what you need."

He looked for a moment like he was going to argue that point, but stopped before he said anything. I leaned into his side, content to be there with him, the feel of him warm and solid next to me bringing me a sense of fulfillment and completeness I'd had no idea was missing from my life.

So, was Vlad one of you guys?

A Dark One? No.

What was he, then? And why did Bram Stoker think he was a vamp?

Dracula was a strigoi, a member of a rare blood clan. Strigoi ingest blood as sustenance by choice.

Whereas you guys have to have it?

Adrian's thumb brushed along my jaw in a tender gesture that melted my heart. *Dark Ones cannot manufacture blood. We must absorb it from other sources, but we do not ingest it. The blood I take from you joins with my own to give me life.*

A little erotic shiver ran down my spine, but whether it was from the soft touch of his mind or the remembrance of just how exciting I found it to feed him, I didn't know. I *did* know that I had to stop thinking about it, or the early-morning commuters on the train to Oxford were going to get the show of a lifetime.

"Let's back up a minute to your brother. Why would he not Join with his Beloved?"

An interesting mixture of regret, pain, and something that looked very much like embarrassment passed over his face before he turned his head to look out the window. "Saer has always been determined to wield great power. I have done what I could to deny him the power he seeks, but I fear my reign of influence is at an end."

I looked at him, for a minute confused. His jaw was tight, and his hands fisted, both indicators that he was revealing another facet of his character that he felt would show him in a bad light. I knew better—I'd seen into his heart, and I knew he was not a vindictive man.

"You've done bad things in your time, Adrian," I said softly, just loud enough for him to hear. His body tensed as he slowly turned to look at me. I smiled, allowing him to see the love in my eyes. "But you are not responsible for them. You did not ask to be cursed by a demon lord. You do not take pleasure in the acts he's forced you to do in his name. You are not an evil man, so I know that you must have had a good reason for putting the stymie on your brother."

He stared at me in disbelief for a moment, his eyes bright with astounded wonder that darkened into sadness. "You are the only person who has ever believed in me, Hasi. You are the only one who has not feared me. I swear by all the saints, if I could change the inevitable outcome of what must happen, I would. I would give the soul you have all but reclaimed for me in order to change my future, but it is not to be."

I leaned forward to kiss him, changed my angle of attack, and flicked my tongue across the tip of his nose instead. He looked startled by the gesture, just as I intended. "You know, I've never been one to buy into that whole fate thing. I've always believed that life is what you make it, and as I fully intend to spend the rest of mine with you, I'd appreciate it if you weren't quite so doom-and-gloom and 'I am the Betrayer, I must perish!' and start thinking about ways to beat your brother, because I'm not giving up on you. On us. So let's talk about Saer and what his weak spots are. I understand that he wants power, and heaven knows he certainly has that with Asmodeus's ring, but what does his Beloved have to do with it? And why wouldn't he Join with her if it would give him back his soul?"

Adrian sighed a long, put-upon sigh, one that had me smiling to myself. I knew how hard he struggled to maintain his bad-boy image, but I also knew that his Betrayer days were over. It was time he realized that he'd been dealt a bad hand, but now the deck had been reshuffled and I was dealing. "For a Dark One to Join with a Beloved means his life is bound with hers. Their souls are entwined and cannot be separated."

I ignored the pointed look he gave me and nodded.

"Thus any decisions he made would affect her, and vice versa. The type of power Saer seeks would require him to forfeit not only his soul, but that of his Beloved as well."

"And he doesn't want to damn an innocent woman that way," I said, nodding again.

Adrian shook his head. "I would like to believe that Saer could not hand over his Beloved, even without having Joined with her, but the truth is simply that only she can make the decision to submit to a demon lord. Saer, on his own, cannot force her."

"Oh." I thought about that for a few minutes as the train stopped at a station, a couple of people leaving, but more getting on. Adrian peered at each person intently, relaxing only when everyone settled into their seats. "So he hasn't Joined with her because she won't give herself up to a demon lord, and Saer needs to be able to do that to get the power he wants. Got that. But why is he trotting off to see her now?"

"He has the ring," Adrian answered grimly, glancing out the window. There wasn't any sun to be seen, it being a typical rainy English day, but the gray outside was lightening significantly. "He will Join with Belinda, then use the ring against her to force her into compliance with his plans. It is the only way he can do so."

My heart sank. Not only had I screwed up royally in failing to rescue Adrian's nephew, now my stupidity had damned an innocent woman to an eternity as a demon lord's slave? "Crap!"

"Exactly," he agreed, watching as the next station's advance warning signs flashed by. "We will get off here. I cannot risk being caught out in the full light of day."

"Do you know Saer's Beloved?" I asked, more to distract myself from wallowing in guilt than because I really wanted to know. I followed Adrian off the train and through the small suburban station.

He shot me an odd look as he pulled up the collar of his coat.

"You called her Belinda," I pointed out. "I wondered if that meant you know her."

"Yes, I know her. She is . . . she was . . . I mated with her. You will please go ask that taxi if he is free. If he is, I will join you and we will go to Belinda's pub. If we hurry, the light should not harm me."

I grabbed his arm and shoved him into a corner of the room, out of earshot of the few people trickling in and out of the station. "You *mated* with her?"

He frowned, just as I knew he would, but at that moment I wasn't overly concerned about his emotions. "Yes. Did you think I was a virgin?"

"No, of course not, but you don't just blurt out something like that. And especially you don't use the word *mated*. It sounds so . . . so . . . animalistic."

"It was animalistic," he answered, still frowning. "I thought at first she was my Beloved, but as soon as I merged with her"—I ground my teeth, pushing down hard on the need to rail at his cavalier manner of flaunt-

217

ing his ex-lovers at me—"I realized she was not. We engaged in sex for a few months. That's all there was to it."

"New rule," I said, releasing his arm to shake my finger at him. "No introducing lovers without warning. No using the word 'mating' in a sentence mentioning said lover. And absolutely, positively no warm remembrances of your fun time in the sack with her!"

"You are overreacting," Adrian said. "You were not a virgin, and yet I did not demand to know everything about the two men you were with before you gave yourself to me."

"How do you know it was just two men?" I asked, momentarily distracted from my diatribe.

His eyebrows rose.

"Dammit, you poked around in my brain without asking if you could look in my former-boyfriend folder!" I took a deep breath and reminded myself that wasn't the issue at hand. There were much more important things to do right now than harry him over a few poorly chosen words. "Right. Your relationships before we met are no more my business than my past relationships are to you, but I would appreciate it if we could exclude mentions of sex when referring to Belinda."

Adrian tipped his head toward the door.

"Fine. I'll go see if a taxi is free. But no more sex-with-Belinda talk! I'm serious, Adrian! There's only so much a girl can take before she goes totally and completely insane."

"You are jealous," he said, satisfaction rife in his voice.

"You bet your boots I'm jealous! And green isn't a good color on me, so stop looking so smug."

Three minutes later we were zipping through the streets of High Wycombe. It had been raining, but it looked as if the clouds were clearing as the sun started to rise. Adrian had pulled a soft wool fedora from his bag, and with that on his head and the collar of his duster turned up, he didn't seem to be suffering any undue effects.

He slid his hand along my arm until his fingers encountered the bare flesh of my wrist. *Why are you staring at me so avidly, Hasi?*

I'm just watching for smoke, I answered, sliding a quick assessing glance out the window. *It's almost fully daylight. I don't want you to start burning up.*

A warm blanket of gratitude fell softly over me. *No one has ever worried about me. No one has ever cared if I suffered, but I will not have you concerned unduly, Hasi. Although I cannot help but wish you had not done it, our Joining has given me a slight tolerance of weakened sunlight. As long as I remain covered and out of the direct light, I will not be damaged.*

"Good," I said as he removed his hand from my wrist. He answered the taxi driver's question about which pub we were going to, ignoring the driver's comment that the pub wouldn't be open at this time of the morning.

My curiosity got the better of me. "So . . . um . . . this Belinda. You said you thought for a little bit that she was"—I glanced in the driver's rearview mirror—"right for you, but she wasn't, she was meant for Saer. Does he know that you and she were an item at one time?"

"Yes," he answered, his face and voice grim. "We were never close, but my history with Belinda drove him into a fury of hatred that left him swearing vengeance on me. For the last ten years, he has attempted by all means possible to destroy me, hiding his true reason for wishing me dead behind the fact that I am the Betrayer."

"What a bastard," I growled, thinking of a couple of particularly juicy curses mentioned in the charm book. "Just let me have five minutes alone with him, and I'll take care of him."

Adrian didn't bother to tell me the obvious—that as long as Saer had the ring, there was nothing either of us could do that would seriously harm him. "I will admit that at the time I thought he was overreacting to the situation with Belinda, but now . . ." He brushed a strand of hair off my face. "Now I understand the feelings that I must have stirred in him when he found me with his Beloved."

"Wait a minute," I said softly, ignoring the spurt of jealousy that rose every time I thought of Adrian with another woman. "You said you two were never close. I know you're the B-man and all, but Saer's your twin! How can you *not* have ever been close to him?"

Adrian's eyes were the color of underwater icebergs. "I was bound into service to Asmodeus when I was less than two years old. My father bartered me in exchange for the power to mesmerize women."

I stared at him in horror, fully aware but uncaring that my mouth hung open for a few seconds while I tried to get my stunned brain to function again. "Your father gave you to a demon lord? When you were just a baby? That's how you were cursed?"

He laid a finger across my lips, shushing me.

Your own father, the man whose loins you sprang from gave you to a demon lord? He just said, "Here, take my baby and give me the power to get laid?" Your father did that?

It is a long time in the past, Hasi. I appreciate the anger and outrage you feel on my behalf, but I assure you that I have long since accepted my fate.

Well, I haven't! I lunged across him, framing his face between my hands as I looked deep into his being, mourning for what had been ripped from him. *You're not the Betrayer, Adrian, you're the betrayed. Is your father still alive?*

A smile curved his lips as he moved my hands so he could kiss my palms before releasing them. "No. He ended his life many years ago when he tired of the shallow nature of his existence."

Impossible as it seemed considering the fury I felt on his behalf, that just made me angrier. "He sold you for sex, then killed himself when he wasn't getting his jollies anymore?"

"I doubt it was quite that simple."

"What about Saer? Did your father give him up, too?"

"No." Adrian's eyes would not meet mine, but I didn't need to touch him to feel the swift stab of pain that lanced through him. "Saer is the oldest son. My father did not feel he was expendable as I was."

"Like father, like son," I muttered to myself, but Adrian heard me. "Saer is a chip off the old block."

"Here you are," the cabby called back to us, pulling up

221

before an old building done in faux half-timbering, a sign next to the door depicting a churchman in full regalia presenting his hindquarters as he looked over his shoulder at a saucy-looking woman who held a switch. "The Flogged Bishop. That'll be six pounds ten."

I stared long and hard at the sign as Adrian tossed some money at the driver, following slowly as he entered a small unmarked door at the side of the pub. "I have just one question—this is a real pub, isn't it? It's not another place like Gigli's?"

His dimples deepened as a grin flashed briefly while he knocked on a door at the top of a short flight of stairs. "You didn't mind me knowing Gigli, so why would you mind Belinda running a brothel?"

"Because Gigli said the only non-mortal beings she serves are poltergeists, which means I didn't have to worry about you having tasted forbidden pleasures there. This"—I waved at the blank wall that stood between us and the pub—"is an entirely different situation!"

The door opened before he had time to respond, the woman standing in the doorway clearly having just gotten up. I eyed her carefully, this woman who Adrian had once briefly thought was his salvation. She was pretty, much prettier than what I expected a pub owner to be, standing a few inches shorter than me, with short curly brown hair and soft brown eyes. "Adrian!" she said in blatant surprise. Her expression quickly changed to one of mingled hope and sorrow. "Have you heard anything? Have you found Damian? Saer said a demon lord has him. Is it true? Is he lost forever?"

"Damian?" I asked, at first a little surprised by her primary concern, then reminding myself that if she was Saer's Beloved, she would no doubt be worried about his son.

"Belinda is Damian's mother," Adrian explained before turning back to the woman. "Is Saer here?"

"No," she answered, stepping back and gesturing us through the door into a small apartment above the pub.

The nervous energy surrounding Adrian lessened a smidgen at her words. I heaved a mental sigh of relief as well. "Thank God he hasn't been here. We've been worried sick that you Joined with him."

The door closed with a hushed click as she turned to face us. "I'm sorry, you don't understand. Saer isn't here now, but he was earlier, and we *are* Joined. Saer insisted we take the final steps last night, before he left to call up his army."

"Army?" I asked weakly, groping blindly behind me for a chair. My legs gave out as the implications of Saer's actions became very clear in my mind.

"Yes," she nodded, bustling past us to a tiny kitchen. "He's gone to raise an army to defeat his enemy and rescue Damian. He's quite confident that no one will be able to withstand his force now. He's got a special ring, you see, and evidently with it, he's quite invincible. He told me that no one, not even the demon lord himself, can stand against him now." She paused, glancing from Adrian's still form to me, a cheery smile lighting her face as if she hadn't just spelled out the doom of everyone in the room. "Would you like tea or coffee?"

Chapter Fifteen

"How are you feeling now, Nell?"

I pushed the cold washcloth aside and peered up at Belinda where she hovered over me. "A bit sick to my stomach at my carelessness. Not to mention the guilt over my stupidity in not recognizing that Saer wasn't Adrian, which means you will suffer for the rest of your now unnatural life. I'm furious that your son is caught up in this. And lastly, I want to throttle Adrian's and Saer's father, but he's dead, so all I can do is think really nasty thoughts about him."

Belinda looked a bit nonplussed at my exhaustive answer. "I meant how is your head? Is the headache gone?"

I sighed and sat up, folding the washcloth neatly and handing it to her before dredging up a smile. It was pitiful, but it was a smile, and I held on to it for all I was worth. "It's much better now. Thank you for the aspirin."

"My pleasure. Do you like your coffee white or black?"

"Black, thank you."

She nodded before heading to the kitchen, not even glancing at the man who stood with his hands clasped behind his back and looking out a window with carefully angled blinds. I felt no such reticence, and stared at Adrian until he felt the touch of my gaze and turned to face me.

"It is hopeless, Hasi. He is Joined, he has the ring, and he is raising an army to defeat both Asmodeus and me."

"Mmm. I'm reserving judgment on the 'hopeless' verdict, and you don't know that the army Saer is raising is meant for you."

"I do not have the luxury of your doubt. He will come for me just as surely as he will attempt to overthrow Asmodeus. Saer is absolutely correct—with the ring, he is all but invincible. I cannot withstand an attack by him, and with Belinda Joined to him, he will have the strength he needs to overthrow Asmodeus and destroy me."

I frowned as I glanced toward the entrance to the kitchen. Belinda was humming happily as she puttered around fixing breakfast, the cheerful sounds of the radio drifting out to us. "Now I really am confused. You said that Saer would use the ring to force her to forfeit her soul on his behalf. I can see why he Joined with her once he got his grubby mitts on the ring, but not how that gives him more power, not when you yourself said that being bound to her would hold him back."

Adrian looked out the window again, his face as hard as chiseled marble. "A Beloved's soul carries much value. By its very nature it is pure, one of the purest examples of selfless love ever to exist. To those who seek and use the dark powers, it offers an almost unlimited endowment."

"So he gains power just by virtue of being Joined with her, because her soul is so pure?"

"Something like that."

I rubbed my forehead. I was exhausted, and could feel both Adrian's hunger and fatigue. It seemed like we'd been up for days without sleep. "Where does Damian fit into all this? Surely Saer won't sacrifice him too?"

"No, he won't sacrifice him. At least . . . no. Not even Saer would seek power in that way." Adrian sounded as tired as I felt. His eyes were clouded with pain and defeat. It was an expression that left me wanting to simultaneously sob in despair and instigate a plan of attack. I decided the latter was the only way we were going to get out of the horrible situation.

"That's a relief, but even if Damian is safe, Saer is a monster to use Belinda as you described. We have to stop him. We can't let him sacrifice her too, not even for Damian."

Adrian ran a hand through his hair, dark smudges bruising the skin beneath his eyes. "It's too late, Hasi. Saer is invincible now."

"Maybe he can't be killed, but that was never my intention." I stood up and went to him, wrapping my arms around his waist and breathing in his wonderful scent a moment or two before pressing a little kiss to his adorable lips. "But I still have Gigli's charm book, and I'm more than happy to try a curse or two in order to give us an edge. I think a tail would look good on Saer, don't you?"

Adrian refused to be jollied out of his glum mood. "This is not a subject for levity, Nell."

"I'm in deadly earnest, loveykins." He flinched. I smiled. "Sorry, I'm still searching for the perfect love name."

"Keep trying."

I kissed his chin. "I won't give up if you won't."

A familiar frown settled on his brow. "Why do you insist on maintaining the deception that there is any way I can stop Saer? I have told you three times that so long as he holds Asmodeus's ring, it is impossible for me—or you— to gain control."

"Oh, Saer doesn't have the ring with him," Belinda said as she set down on a small round table a pot of coffee, two mugs, and a plate of toast. She fussed over setting the breakfast things out, evidently not in the least aware of the stunned silence that stretched between Adrian and me. Eventually we managed to gather our tired wits.

"He doesn't?" I asked at the same time as Adrian demanded to be told the ring's whereabouts.

Belinda looked up from the table, blinking in surprise at both of us. "No, he doesn't have it. He said it was too risky to use the ring to summon minions, so he left it with me."

I stared at her for five seconds, a sudden giddy happiness threatening to burst out of me as Adrian grabbed Belinda by both arms, shaking her in his impatience to get the answer. "Where is it? Where exactly is it?"

"I have it," she said, her teeth chattering a little as she reached up to her neck, pulling on a gold chain that was looped beneath her bathrobe. She tugged it up until a familiar horn-and-gold ring emerged.

"My ring!" I yelled, tears of relief pricking my eyes.

"*Your* ring?" she asked, the ring dangling before us.

227

Adrian's eyes glowed hot as he watched it, his fingers twitching as if he wanted to take it. "Saer said it was his."

"Yes, well, I'm the one who originally borrowed it," I said. "I gave it to Saer thinking he was Adrian. If you don't mind, I'd like it back."

Her fingers closed around the ring as I reached for it, a mulish, hard expression on her face. "As it is, I do mind. Saer said this ring will free Damian. I can't give it to you until my son is safe."

"Nell is a Charmer," Adrian said, his voice rough and harsh as if he were fighting for control of himself. "She stole the ring to save Damian."

"I did not steal it!" I glared at Adrian, mouthing that I was going to get him when we were alone. "I simply borrowed it. I have every intention of returning it to Christian just as soon as I'm done with it."

"Nell has sworn to help Damian," Adrian said. I nodded. "She is the only hope of freeing him without releasing a power greater than any of us can imagine. You know Saer. You know what he is capable of. You must trust us."

"Please, Belinda." I touched her arm. "Adrian is right. I've sworn to do everything within my abilities to release your son from his bondage, but I must have the ring to do so."

"Saer is a little . . . confused, I freely admit that. He's changed the last few years, become a stranger, but even so, I know he would never harm Damian—" she started to protest.

"It is not for Damian's sake he desires the ring," Adrian said softly.

I sent a puzzled frown his way, then remembered that Saer was evidently willing to sacrifice Belinda in order to gain power. Such a monster as I was coming to realize he was wouldn't even blink about leaving his son in the hands of a demon lord.

Belinda looked from me to Adrian, indecision clearly visible behind the tears that filled her eyes. "I don't know what to think. Saer said he would free Damian, and now you say Nell is the only hope. But I don't know her. I don't know that she will do what she says she will do, that she will save Damian. He is only a child!"

"She will save him. She is my Beloved—she cannot do otherwise," Adrian said, his voice smooth with persuasion.

Belinda looked back at me. I tried to look like someone who went up against demon lords every day of the week without batting an eyelash. Finally she nodded, and pulled the chain over her head, dropping it and the ring into my waiting hand. "If you truly are Adrian's Beloved, then I will trust you."

"You won't regret it," I promised, clutching the ring tightly in my hand. It was warm from being next to her skin, but it seemed to glow hot for a moment as I held it. I flashed Adrian a triumphant smile, slipping the chain over my head before I shoved my arms into my coat. "Come on, sweetcakes, we have a demon lord to crush!"

Adrian grabbed me by the back of my coat as I rushed past him. He nodded toward the window. "Loath as I am to waste any time, I cannot go out in that."

"Damn," I swore, glaring at the fading gray. Blue sky was showing before rapidly dispersing clouds. "Why is it that just when you want a nice overcast day, the sun insists on coming out?"

"I wouldn't allow you to go now even if it was midnight," Adrian said as he took my hand in his. "You are too tired. It would be the sheerest folly to charm when you are so tired you can hardly stand. We will rest until the sun goes down."

"But—" I started to protest.

"Damian—" Belinda said at the same time.

Adrian raised his free hand, silencing both of us. "Asmodeus will not harm Damian until he has the ring. Damian will be safe until tonight when Nell will free him. But she needs rest to do that. We had little sleep yesterday and none last night. I hate to impose on your goodwill—"

"You're welcome to stay here," Belinda interrupted quickly. I could tell she didn't like to wait any more than I did, but she saw the sense in what Adrian said. As did I, although I hated to admit that he was right about me being exhausted, and I noticed he didn't include himself in that statement despite the fact that I could feel him weakened by both hunger and lack of sleep.

He shook his head. "If Saer was to come back unexpectedly, he could harm Nell. Do you still have a cot in your office behind the pub?"

"Yes," she answered, eyeing him in a familiar way that sent my hackles up, hostess or no hostess. "But it is meant for one person, and you're rather large—"

I stepped closer to him and gave her a firm look. "A cot will be lovely, thank you. Adrian can sleep on the cot, and I'll sleep on him."

She had the grace to look away, her cheeks slightly rosy as she hurried off to the next room. "I will get the key to the pub."

"Nell," Adrian said. I watched in amazement as his eyes

changed from deep sapphire to a light steel-blue. "I know what you're thinking."

I raised my eyebrows in faux horror. "You know I am planning on jumping your bones the second I get you alone?"

"I know you are planning to slip out once I'm asleep. I know you intend to free Damian without me."

My eyebrows dropped back to their normal position as I slipped into the most innocent look I could muster. "I never once thought that."

"No?"

I couldn't meet those knowing eyes. I glanced down, picking at a piece of invisible lint on my sleeve. "No. Not seriously. The idea might have flitted through my brain, but I didn't consider it. Not for long."

"Good. It is an idea that goes beyond foolish. To attempt to best Asmodeus without me to help you would be suicide, and that"—his fingers caressed my chin as they tilted my face upward—"I could never allow. You are too important to me."

"Face it," I said, rubbing the tip of my nose on his. "You're madly in love with me. You'd be lost without me. I'm your earth and sun and everything in between."

I held my breath as I waited for his response to my half-joking statement. I knew he desired me, knew he needed my blood, knew we were bound together in ways I couldn't begin to understand, but I had no idea whether or not his feelings for me were more than physiological.

His lips parted to speak.

"I found the key for you. It would probably be best if you two entered the pub via the back way, so no one will see you."

Adrian turned away as Belinda entered the room. I swore to myself, cursing her bad timing. What had he been about to say to me? His eyes were shuttered, giving me no clue, and now I wouldn't know.

I would just have to find out once we were alone. Adrian gave Belinda instructions to wake us a few hours before sunset, so we would have time to prepare for the ritual I'd be conducting—or trying to—that evening. I accepted the package of food she'd made up for me, and waited by the door attempting to hide my impatience, praying Adrian would finish talking so we could make our escape to the office below. Tired as I was, I had plans for him . . . plans which included not only a little therapeutic lovemaking, but the consumption of breakfast as well.

"You know, I have a very good feeling about this," I said over my shoulder to Adrian as I marched down the stairs from Belinda's apartment to the outside door. He was a shadow on the dark stairs, being clad in his coat and hat, with a black scarf that Belinda had dug out of a closet wrapped around the lower part of his face. "We've been dealt a few blows, but we're still on top. It's all going to be downhill from here, just you wait and see!"

I reached for the doorknob, jumping away as it suddenly swung open toward me.

A man in a black overcoat and hat loomed in the doorway. Behind him, a woman in sunglasses limped toward the door.

Christian stared at me in surprise—probably the same amount of surprise that was visible on my face.

Only I was quicker. I lunged forward, shoving him backward through the door, slamming it shut and twisting the deadbolt closed as I quickly traced the binding ward on the door.

"They found us!" I hissed over my shoulder to Adrian. He didn't need any further explanation. He grabbed my wrist and started dragging me back up the stairs to Belinda's apartment.

I grabbed the newel post to stop my ascent, my gaze riveted on the door. I watched with amazement as the ward I had drawn began to unravel, the green ward dissolving bit by bit. Right before my eyes!

"What the hell?" I pulled myself free from Adrian and ran the few steps to the door, touching the unraveled end of the ward, quickly redrawing it into the pattern of binding.

The ward glowed green for a second, started to fade, then glowed again as it once more began to unravel.

"Nell, leave it! There is a back way out of Belinda's flat!"

I touched the ward with the tip of my finger, gritting my teeth as it fought my touch. "You go," I said, focused on the recalcitrant ward. "I'll stay here and hold the door."

"I am not going to leave you," he snarled, jumping down the stairs to grab me.

"It's that Allie woman," I said, fighting with the ward to keep it from undrawing any more. "She's trying to unmake it on the other side of the door."

"Nell, leave it. We must escape now."

I twisted the unraveled edge of the ward back onto itself, tying it in a knot, watching it for a second to make sure Allie wasn't going to be able to undo it quickly. The ward quivered and strained, but held.

"I don't think so," I said, facing Adrian. "No, listen to me, I think we should split up. They don't want me, they want you. You go up to Belinda's and slip out the back. I'll keep Little Miss Wardypants busy here so they can't get in until you've gotten safely away."

"I will not leave you," he growled as he grabbed me. I allowed myself to droop against him for a moment, brushing my mouth against his.

I appreciate the macho he-man protective instincts, Adrian, but this time you're going to have to conquer them. You know as well as I do that Christian and Allie won't harm me. I'm in no danger, so you can stop bristling with indignation over the thought of us splitting up.

I will not leave you. I will not throw you to their mercies.

My lips drifted over to his jaw. *It wasn't Christian who wanted to kill me, it was Sebastian. I swear to you, I will be safe. Now that I went to all the trouble of believing six impossible things before breakfast, White Rabbit, I don't intend on losing you.*

Hasi—

Go. I will meet you later, at the British Museum.

Where will you go? He was weakening. His need to protect me warred with the realization that what I said was true, but it was touch and go there as to whether or not his heart or his head would win out.

The one place a vampire can't go—a church.

His sigh brushed my mind as he pulled away from me. "Dark Ones can enter churches, Hasi. We are damned, but not demons."

"Oh." I glanced at the ward. It was beginning to fray at the opposite end as Allie worked to unmake it. I had a few seconds, nothing more. "I'll go to the US Embassy, OK?

That's got to be the most secure place in London. I'll meet you at the British Museum just after sunset."

"Nell, if we separate, we won't be able to merge."

That stopped me for a few seconds. I have never thought of myself as an overly clingy person, but since meeting Adrian, I felt any separation greatly. It was almost as if a part of my consciousness were missing. If I felt that way just by being in a different room from him, what would it be like with the entire city between us?

The door behind me shook with a blow. I had no choice.

"Go!" I shoved him up the first couple of stairs, leaping back to the door to wrestle with the ward. The knot I had tied slipped free. Reluctantly Adrian stared up the stairs. "Adrian?"

He paused at the top, swathed in so much black he almost faded into the shadows.

"I love you."

His head jerked, but whether in acknowledgement or disagreement I'll never know. The ward slipped through my hands and almost completely unraveled. I grabbed the end of it, holding tight as Adrian pounded on Belinda's door. It opened, and he disappeared at the same moment the door in front of me bucked with the force of a hard blow. The ward twisted and squirmed in my hand, the sound of a large, angry vampire attacking the other side clearly audible. I held on to the ward as long as I could, trying to knot it again, but Allie had much more experience with wards than I. The entire ward melted in my hands as wood splintered. I leaped back out of the way as Christian threw himself at the door again, the wood giving way completely without the ward to hold it shut. I leaned against the wall, my arms crossed, with what I hoped was an insouciant look on my face. "Fancy meeting you here."

Christian snarled something in a vaguely familiar language as he rushed past me.

"Get a little too much sun?" I called after him, waggling a finger toward one side of his face where the skin of his neck and cheek were red. "You'd better watch that. Skin cancer, you know."

He ignored me. I looked past Allie as she marched in. "What, no Sebastian?"

She paused at the bottom of the stairs, pulling off her dark glasses to glare at me. "He can't tolerate the light at all. And if you had made my husband stay out in that sun one second longer, I would have decked you!"

I lifted my chin, refusing to allow her to intimidate me. "You could try."

She snorted before limping up the stairs after Christian. "Don't tempt me."

I waited until Belinda answered the pounding knocks Christian was delivering to her door before turning and slowly walking out the now destroyed front door into the cheerful light of a rare sunny day.

Chapter Sixteen

With the morning came the usual London hustle and bustle—cars, buses, and people all hurried up and down the streets, everyone moving with purpose and a sense of belonging. The scent of diesel mingled with more enticing odors drifting from a nearby bakery. My stomach rumbled as I clutched tighter the paper bag of food Belinda had pressed on me. There would be time to eat it once I found a safe place to hole up in. I wandered around to the back of the block-long building in which the pub was located just in case Adrian had hung around waiting for me, but he wasn't there.

"Whoa!" I jumped back in surprise as Christian landed suddenly on the ground in front of me, having leaped, I assumed, from the second-story balcony outside Belinda's apartment.

He jerked his coat up around his neck, pulling low over his head an Indiana Jones-ish hat as he glanced upward. "You stay here, Allegra. I will follow the trail of the Betrayer."

I looked up as well. Allie leaned over the balcony and yelled down, "He's not worth it, Christian! I know your tolerance of the sunlight is growing, but it's not strong enough for you to go haring around London!"

"Perhaps I won't need to chase him. Perhaps this one will tell me where he is hiding." His head turned to look at me. Before I could do so much as blink, he had my neck in a painful grip, his face near mine, his black eyes narrowed. Suddenly he stopped, sniffing the air a couple of times.

"You have Joined with the Betrayer?" he asked, releasing my neck.

I stepped back, rubbing my bruised skin. "Not that it's any of your business, but, yes, I have. And I'd appreciate it if you'd stop trying to kill him. He's mine, and I don't intend to let you or Sebastian or anyone else who thinks he has a grudge do anything to him. So why don't you and Ward Girl there leave us alone!"

"I'm a Summoner, not a Ward Girl," Allie corrected me. "Christian, come out of the sun. Your chin is turning pink."

Christian's eyes narrowed on me as if he were seeking proof I was lying. A strange pressure invaded my head, a touch that wasn't Adrian's.

"Stop that!" I yelled at Christian, backing up. "No one is allowed in my head but Adrian!"

"What do you hide?" he asked, stalking forward.

I stopped retreating and raised a hand. "I know a curse

that will strip you stark naked where you stand. If you don't stop trying to get into my brain, you'll be barbecue."

That stopped him.

"Oh!" Allie cried, firing a glare at me that all but spat fury. "You wouldn't dare! Don't you move, either of you! I'm coming right down!"

Christian gave me a considering look from under the shadow of his hat brim.

I raised my eyebrows. "Don't think I won't do it! I'm leaving now. I don't know how you found us here, but it won't do you any good to follow me, because I'm not going to where Adrian is. As a matter of fact, I don't even know where he is. So good-bye, so long, hasta la vista."

My hands fisted as I walked past him, half expecting him to grab me, but he didn't reach for me. Instead he waited until I was halfway down the alley before calling after me, "We didn't follow you here. We were seeking Saer. What confuses me is why the Betrayer would seek him as well."

"Maybe if you asked yourself who is the real villain of this piece, it might make more sense," I said over my shoulder. "You'll have to do it on your own, because I don't have time to straighten you out. Thanks to you, I don't get to spend the day with Adrian on a nice comfy cot."

When I glanced back as I turned the corner at the end of the alley, Christian was being tugged into a yawning black doorway by Allie. I gave a mental shrug, figuring that I might have given Christian enough to chew on so he'd leave us alone.

There was always the possibility that he didn't believe me, though. And it was for that reason that I made my way to the nearest tube station, and dug through the coins I had filched from Adrian earlier in search of something I could use in a phone. I managed to round up enough for a three-minute overseas call to my friend and next-door neighbor Sabrina.

"Hulluh?"

I peered through the morning throng to a distant clock and did some quick mental arithmetic. "Ooops, sorry, Sabrina. I didn't realize it was one A.M. there."

"Nell?" Her voice was thick and fuzzy with sleep.

"Yeah, it's me, and don't ask questions. I only have two and a half minutes left. I need you to call a hotel in London . . . uh . . . sec . . ." I flipped open the phone book and turned to the hotel pages, picking out the first name I saw. "I want you to call the Dorchester Hotel."

"Hotel? Nell? London?"

"Yes, it's me, and I'm in London. I want you to book me a room in the Dorchester Hotel for a couple of days. Use your credit card to pay for the room. I'll pay you back later, OK?"

"London? I thought you were in Prague?"

"I was, but now I'm in London. Here's the number. Make the reservation under the name Diane Hall." I read the number off to Sabrina, repeating it a couple of times until she seemed to have it.

"Who is Diane Hall?"

I signed, watching the seconds count down on the phone screen. "Me. It's way too long a story to tell now. I'll fill you in when I get home. Just call the hotel now and pretend you're my secretary or something, and pay for a room for a couple of days."

She yawned. "You're going to owe me more than just money for this, Nelly."

"Bottle of wine and a box of Godivas, I promise. Gotta go, time's gone. Thanks a million!"

The phone clicked off in the middle of her response. I hung up the receiver, consulted with the big station clock, and went to find out just how long a walk I had to the Dorchester Hotel.

I'd like to think that being bound spiritually to a vampire meant I had all sorts of superpowers, but I didn't seem any different than before when I flopped down on the hotel bed. My body was sore and tired from the long hike, my mind was exhausted, and the toe blister born on the walk from Christian's castle had blossomed into adulthood.

"The least Adrian could have done was give me some sort of extra resilience or wonderful pain-blocking techniques," I grumbled as I hauled myself into the bathroom, dredging up enough strength to run a bath. "There's not a lot I'm getting out of this deal. Eternity with a weak left side, crooked smile, and blisters. Oy."

I fell asleep in the tub, but managed not to drown myself. By the time I dried myself off, crawled into bed, ate one of the two sandwiches and an orange Belinda packed for me, I was at the end of my strength. I roused myself enough to make sure that no dark-eyed vamps were lurking at the end of the hotel hallway, staggering back to bed to collapse into the soft pillows. Worry about

Adrian was uppermost in my mind, worry that made me feel ill and restless despite the exhaustion, but I comforted myself that he had taken care of himself for several centuries—surely he would be all right on his own for a few hours.

I missed him. I missed the touch of his mind on mine, the warm security of his body. I missed the way his eyebrows arched when I said something outrageous. I missed the way his eyes darkened when he was aroused, the heat he fired within me with just a flick of his eyelashes, the joy we shared when we merged bodies and minds. But most of all I missed the piece of me that he had taken with him.

It's hard to sleep when your heart is off somewhere else.

Six hours later I limped (the blister still hurt, despite the three band-aids I had begged from hotel housekeeping), up the front steps to the British Museum. The sun hadn't set yet, but I had gotten little sleep despite my body's fatigue. I figured I might as well start looking around the British Museum. It certainly couldn't hurt to scope out the area, just in case Christian or Sebastian were out looking for us.

I stopped in the Great Court at one of the information desks and inquired about the location of an ivory griffin-headed figure. "It's from Toprakkale," I added as the information woman entered keywords to search the BM's collection.

She looked up. "How do you spell that?"

I told her.

"I'm afraid that item is being held in a conservational storeroom in the basement. It is not open to the public."

I heaved an inner sigh of relief. My memories of the cursed cloth that had resulted in Beth's death were enough to convince me that any article that had come in contact with a demon lord posed a hazard to unwary observers. "That's all right, I don't mind going off the beaten path, so to speak. If you'll just tell me where it is—"

"I'm sorry, but it is museum policy to limit access to such items to approved students and visiting scholars."

"Perfect! I'm an assistant professor at the University of Washington. That makes me a visiting scholar."

"Oh," she said, brightening. "Do you have your credentials?"

My hopeful look dimmed. "Um. As a matter of fact, no. I ... er ... left them behind. In my hotel. And I don't have much time, so I'd really like to see the figure this afternoon."

"We must see credentials," the woman said firmly. "Do you have anything with your university affiliation on it?"

"No," I said, biting my lip. I was familiar enough with museum security to know it would be no easy task to break my way into a storeroom. I much preferred just walking in. "Oh! I know. The UW website. My page has my picture on it. Would that suffice?"

"Well—"

"You can look it up. Start at the UW main page and work your way back to the antiquities. You'll find me in Medieval History."

"I'm not sure—"

I smiled my most winsome smile, trying to remember

exactly what Adrian had done when he used my power to give a customs official on the train from the Czech Republic to Germany a brain push.

"I would really appreciate it," I said, sending the feelings of trust and agreement to the woman. "It would mean a great deal to my research if I could view the figure."

"Very well," she agreed, blinking a couple of times before she started zipping through websites to find the appropriate faculty page. I thanked my stars that the university had seen fit to put our pictures on the page, and after agreeing with the woman that identity photos were never flattering, I toddled off clutching a temporary ID badge marking me as a visiting scholar—a passport to most of the restricted areas in the museum.

A map of the museum in hand, I wandered through the Great Court to the north stairs, pausing now and then to hold up the map and scan the room, as if trying to find my bearings. No one appeared to be interested in me, nor did I spy either Christian or Sebastian, although if what Allie had said—which meshed with Adrian's announcement that he could tolerate weak sunlight now that we were Joined—I didn't expect Sebastian would be up and about yet.

Once downstairs I showed my badge at three different security points before being allowed into the part of the museum which had been recently remodeled into storerooms. I passed a conservation workshop, a room devoted to the storage of Japanese ceramics, and several rooms filled with armor that I positively salivated to examine, but the thought of Adrian kept my feet on course for the farthest room, where the information woman had said Asmodeus's figure was kept.

As I passed a steel door to a stairwell, an arm snaked out and clapped a hand over my mouth, tugging me backward into the dim stairs. My shriek of surprise was muffled by the hand, but just as I was baring my lips to bite the fingers covering my mouth, a soft chuckle filled my mind.

I do not object to you biting me, Hasi, but I can think of many other places I'd prefer it than my hand.

"Adrian!" I squealed beneath his hand and spun around, throwing myself on the shadowed figure. He grunted as the force of my body slammed him back against a wall, but he didn't complain before claiming my mouth. The taste of him was hot and wonderful and so Adrian, I smiled into his kiss.

His tongue swirled around mine, dominating my mouth in a way that never failed to make my knees go weak. I pressed myself tighter against him, wanting nothing more than to merge body and soul into him. His arms were hard around me, and even through the thick wool of his coat and the clothes he wore beneath, I could feel his heat. Passion rippled around us in waves, licking against me until all I could think of was my physical need for him.

"You're hungry," I said when I managed to pull my lips from his. "I can feel it gnawing at you. I'm hungry too. . . ."

I let him see in my eyes the form my hunger took. His turned indigo in response. "Hasi, nothing would delight me more than to take you right here, against this wall, but we must restrain ourselves. Our encounter this morning with Dante means he is working with Saer. No doubt both will arrive with reinforcements. I have located the room in which Damian is being kept. It would be best to free him and escape before the sun fully sets."

"All right, I won't rip your clothes off and have my wicked way with you right here on the stairs, but you can at least feed. That won't take but a minute or two, and I have a feeling I'm going to need you running on all four thrusters when I go to use Asmodeus's ring."

His gaze caressed me as I tilted my head back, baring my throat, his lips soft on my flesh as he murmured German endearments against me. I held myself still, my hands limp at my sides, my back pressed against the cold brick wall. Every last ounce of my being clenched in anticipation for that exquisite moment of pain when his teeth would sink deep. His tongue swirled fire over my skin; then the sharp, hot sting of pain melted into a euphoric sensation so unlike anything I'd experienced before Adrian, I didn't think there were words to describe it.

As he sated one form of hunger, another rose within him, matching mine, the two twining together into something that outstripped simple need and formed an elemental drive that almost overwhelmed me. Adrian stood close to me, his body shielding me, almost touching, but not. His hands were fisted against the wall on either side of my head, his mouth providing the only bridge between us. The sensation of his lips on my throat joined with the bone-deep satisfaction he felt in possessing me, changing into something so erotic that just the brush of his hair against my face, his indefineable scent, and the feel of his mouth on my neck pushed me to the point where I thought I would burst into an orgasm.

I was seriously contemplating just how long it would take for me to tear off all his clothing and make love to him when his mouth caressed me one last time, reluctantly parting from me.

"You are my life, Hasi," he said simply as he brushed his thumb over the still-sensitive pinpricks on my neck, but I felt the profound sense of gratitude in him.

"Just see that you remember that when you're talking about giving in to Saer," I answered, my voice almost as shaky as my legs. The act of his feeding had left me trembling on the verge of a climax, unfulfilled and unsatisfied, my body tight as a bowstring as it screamed for a finish to the torment.

Adrian's brows pulled together as his thumb feathered over the pulse point he had fed from. Even without the ability to merge himself into me, I knew he could feel my heart racing. "Nell—"

"No," I said, pushing myself away from him, struggling to regain control of both my mind and body. "You're right, now is not the time. But, oh, baby, am I going to make your fangs rattle when I get you alone!"

His boyish grin flashed at me as he swept a hand toward the stairs that led downward. "I will hold you to that promise, Hasi. Damian is in a sub-basement."

"How did you get in?" I asked, hurrying down the stark metal stairs. "I don't see a visitor's badge on you. Did you turn invisible, or sneak in without anyone seeing you?"

I could feel his mock regret even without seeing him shake his head. "How you come up with these ridiculous

247

ideas about Dark Ones is beyond me. I cannot turn myself invisible, Hasi. I merely borrowed an employee's badge."

"Oh. That's so anticlimactic. I liked the thought of you going invisible. How about bun hair? Can you turn yourself into an old man with a big white bun hairdo like the guy in the Dracula movie?"

He reached around me to open a heavy steel door marked *Arts and Antiquities: Storerooms*, his lips twitching despite his attempts to not respond to my teasing. "I will be glad to discuss my bun ability with you at a later date, Hasi. But for now, we must focus on Damian and the task that is to be done."

"You know," I mused as I trotted after him down a brightly lit hallway. One or two people gave us curious glances as we passed, but I adopted the same businesslike expression that graced Adrian's face, making sure to keep my badge clearly visible. "There are some phrases that are just wrong for a vampire to say. *Bun ability* is one of them. It's way too surfer boy."

Adrian stopped in front of a door, glancing quickly around before opening it and waving me in. I hesitated for a couple of seconds, trying to steel myself to what I'd see inside. Despite the passing of time, the memory of the tragedy so many years ago was still fresh in my mind. I really didn't want to face anything like that again.

"Hasi," Adrian said softly, his fingers stroking the back of my neck. Regret was strong in him, but hope was stronger.

I nodded. "OK, let's do this."

The room was dark, but Adrian flicked on the lights before I was a step or two into the room. I looked around as he dragged a wooden crate to the door.

"Can't you lock the door?" I asked, rubbing my arms through my coat. The room was chilly, the air having a slight refrigerated feel. I don't know quite what I was expecting, but the room was exactly what the sign said—a storeroom. The walls were lined with big open metal shelves containing boxes and wooden crates, all marked with identifications of the contents, dates, and acquisition numbers. In the far corner, a long wooden crate leaned drunkenly against a wall, three smaller square crates stacked beneath the angle it made. Nowhere was there a small boy.

"I had to break the lock to get in. Can you ward the door?"

I continued to rub my arms, glancing back at the long crate. I took a couple of steps toward it, then stopped. The cold seemed to be emanating from it. There was also something else it emanated—a familiar sense of dread and horror.

"I don't think so," I said, wanting to back away from the crate, wanting to grab Adrian and leave the whole damned museum. "Damian's in there, isn't he?"

"Yes." Adrian's voice was so devoid of emotion, I dragged my eyes off the crate and turned to look at him.

His eyes were as pale as the new moon.

"Is he dead?"

"No. He is in what you might call suspended animation. He does not live, but he is not dead."

I shivered as I faced the crate. "Is that something vamps can do, or is it something Asmodeus did?"

"Both. You must help him, Hasi. You are his only hope."

"I know," I said, starting to sweat despite the cold. "And I'm going to, Adrian. I'm going to do everything I can to help your nephew. But it's difficult." He started to say something, but I interrupted, needing him to understand that I wasn't wimping out. Not completely. "The room reeks of Asmodeus. It makes me sick. It's just like that night when I tried to charm the cursed altar cloth and Asmodeus rose and took Beth. I'm afraid I'm going to screw this up, too. I don't want Damian to die. And . . . I don't want to kill myself either, or turn into a vegetable."

"Damian will not die, because you will not fail." Adrian's arms slid around me, his body warm and solid behind me, his mind open to me so I could feel the confidence he had in me. He poured strength of purpose into me, bolstering my flagging nerve. "I would not allow you to harm yourself. The ring will protect you. It has many powers, and it will keep you from harming yourself or others while you charm the curse. You can do this, Hasi. It is what you were meant to do."

I leaned back against him for a moment, soaking up his heat and determination and strength, warming myself in his confidence. Then I nodded and stepped out of his embrace, pulling up the ring from where it hung under my sweater.

It was warm again, far warmer than it should have been from just my body heat. I slipped the ring over my thumb and faced the crate. Adrian moved around to stand next to it. I nodded. He jerked the lid off, revealing the body of a small boy packed in straw. The boy's eyes were closed, his skin waxy. If Adrian hadn't said he was alive, I would have sworn he was dead. My feet wanted to turn and run from the room. I forced them to step forward until I stood next to the crate, my body wracked with nonstop tremors as the cold wrapped itself around me, sinking into my bones, slowing my blood, slowing my heart . . .

"Hasi!"

I roused myself at Adrian's sharp bark, realizing that what I was feeling were tendrils of the suspended animation snaking out to me. It was so cold it hurt, making my joints grind as I moved, little spikes of pain shooting through my body. I ignored the pain and leaned closer, examining the red pattern of the curse that had been bound over the boy.

"Book." Without looking at Adrian, I held out my hand for the charm book he had stashed in his satchel. The cool leather-bound book was placed in my hand. I turned to the page I had noted earlier, one concerning the confinement curse of a demon lord. The ring grew tight on my thumb as I spoke the words of the charm, sketching the symbols of purification over the curse. "Blessed be thou who lie bound. By my art, thou will be changed. By my blood, thou will be freed. By my soul, thou will rise. I wrap thee in softness; I bind thee with love; protection surrounds thee, below and above."

The ring grew tight on my thumb as the words hung in the air for a moment. I felt Adrian move behind me as I leaned closer to the boy, unsure if it was just my imagination or if his flesh really was beginning to lose its waxy appearance.

"The brightest of blessings fill thee this eve," I murmured as my hand swept above the curse. It glowed hot for a moment, darkening until it was a rich purple. The ring was heavy, dragging my hand down until it touched an angled corner of the curse pattern. I jumped at the cold that flowed up my arm from the curse, fighting the voice of self-preservation that screamed in my head. Adrian was counting on me to save his nephew. I couldn't turn craven now. Biting back a moan of pain, I grabbed the beginning of the curse, and drew my finger along its intricate path. As my finger unmade the curse, it glowed black, then dissolved into the air. Pain stung my arm, creeping upward with frigid claws until my body shook so hard, my finger wavered on the curse. I struggled to unmake the curse, half expecting the brilliant white pain to lance through my head at any moment. It didn't, but that could be simply because my body was coping with as much pain as it could tolerate without passing out.

I continued to untrace the curse, the charm book clutched in my left hand, my eyes blurring with tears of pain that I blinked away madly in an attempt to see. I was almost blind with the combination of cold and tears, but the ring seemed to guide my hand, not needing my sight to unmake the curse. As more and more of the curse dissipated, the cold intensified until I felt as if I were standing naked in the Arctic. Gritting my teeth, I spoke the last words to the curse itself. "Thy power is dispersed. Thy desire is undone. Thy darkness is revealed. All who were bound to you, heed only my voice."

The last little curl of the curse glowed black, then burst into a white flare that threw me backward with the force of its unmaking, slamming me into Adrian. Light dazzled my already blinded eyes, filling my head, filling my soul, filling the entire room with one moment of absolute joy.

"What was that?" I heard my incredulous voice ask, my body still tingling with the residue of the wonderful feeling.

Adrian gently propped me up against the side of a metal shelving unit, quickly returning to the crate.

"It was the ring," he answered as he pulled the body of the boy out of the crate.

I rubbed my left hand over my eyes, surprised to note that, for once, it was the stronger of my two arms. My right arm hung cold and heavy at my side, apparently lifeless. "Did it work? Is he alive? Is the curse unmade?"

My vision cleared enough to see the boy standing on his feet, engulfed in a bear hug, Adrian's tender kisses being pressed onto his head.

I sniffed with happiness at the sight. It was worth a little pain and frostbite to see such a loving reunion. If only Saer could witness his son being greeted with such love.

The boy pulled back slightly, turning to look at me. He was dark-haired and blue-eyed like his father, and even had the family frown. "Papa, who's that?"

My jaw dropped at his words. *"Papa?"*

Chapter Seventeen

"She smells bad." Damian's nose wrinkled as he examined me with disdain evident in his reproduction Adrian eyes.

"Papa?" I asked again, figuring part of my brain must have been frozen in the curse-lifting. I hoped it would thaw out quickly, because I was definitely at a loss without it. "Papa as in father? Does he think you're Saer?"

"Damian is my son, not Saer's," Adrian said quickly, his hand on the boy's shoulder as he shoved him toward the door. He held his hand out for me. "Come, Hasi, we must leave. No doubt every immortal within a five-mile radius felt the force of you unmaking the curse. We must be gone from the area before Saer and Dante find us."

"Your son?" I parroted, feeling more than usually stupid. I ignored his hand to stare deep into his eyes. They held impatience and worry, and a warm look of gratitude that I badly wanted to explore, but I knew he was right.

That feeling of extreme joy the ring blasted out was something that I knew instinctively others would feel. "But he's Belinda's son, so that means . . ."

"We will discuss this later." He grabbed my wrist in a painless but nonetheless iron grip and pulled me from the room, shoving Damian ahead with his other hand.

"You called her Hasi," the boy said, looking back at us as Adrian hustled us down the corridor. "She's not your *girlfriend*, is she?"

The horror he imparted to the word made it sound like I was only slightly less detestable than the plague.

"We'll talk about that later, too," Adrian ground through his teeth. He totally ignored the couple of people who emerged from the stairwell, holding the door open so Damian and I could precede him.

"She stinks," the boy said with a sneer that would have done Beau Brummell proud.

"You'd think someone who was deader than a doornail a few minutes ago would have a little more gratitude toward the person who saved him," I snapped back, wondering what sort of nightmare my life had turned into. Damian was Adrian's son? I was going to be a stepmother to a rude, obnoxious little boy who thought I stank? I shook my head, hoping to clear the cold-induced confusion. It was the stress of being cursed and then freed that was making Damian so surly. I'm sure once he recovered from the trauma, he'd—

"She's not going home with us, is she, Papa?" Damian asked over his shoulder as we trotted up the stairs. "If she stays with us, I'm going to be sick."

—continue to be the little monster he obviously was. I

bared my teeth at him as we burst out to the basement. "You wouldn't happen to have seen *The Omen*, would you?"

"Quickly, to the stairs," Adrian ordered, ignoring us both in order to shove us down the hallway. I bit back a retort, picking up his sense of unease and worry. I could feel something in the air, myself, something . . . not right.

We dashed up the stairs into the Great Court, the covered courtyard at the center of the British Museum.

Straight into pandemonium.

People ran screaming like madmen through the big hall, their shrieks echoing off the high glass ceiling, magnifying the noise until it seemed as if we were trapped in one long, endless scream.

"What the hell—" The words froze on my lips as I got a good look at what everyone was running from. "Good God, are those . . . those . . ."

"Mummies," Adrian said with a weary sigh. "I feared as much. I hoped that your power would not reach them, being so many floors below us, but evidently you are stronger than either of us allowed for."

"Mummies?" I said, my voice rising an octave.

Adrian shushed me, shoving Damian and me to the left. "There is an exit beyond that statue. Quickly, before the—"

"Mummies!" I yelled, it finally sinking into my thawing brain just what I was seeing. The people who were screaming and fleeing the Great Court were normal people—living people. The people-shaped things moving with apparently no particular goal trailed suitably theatrical bits of gauze, their bodies gaunt and brown as they milled blindly around the hall. "Those are mummies! Real mummies!"

"Nell! Do not speak!" Adrian said at the same time as Damian started toward them, saying, "Cool!"

The volume of noise in the room died down as most of the people made their escape. Only a few security guards and museum employees remained, the former taking up positions behind the statues in the hall, the latter huddled in a small clutch as they watched three mummies wander around like so many ducklings who'd lost their mother.

"Is one of them Imhotep? Is he going to suck the life out of everyone? Can I watch when he does?" Damian asked eagerly.

"You are a bloodthirsty little vampire," I said without thinking, still staring at the amazing sight before us. The second the words left my lips, I realized just how stupid a statement that was. Damian lifted a mocking lip at me. The mummy nearest us turned its head toward me, the movement resulting in horrible crackling noises that had me flinching in anticipation of his head breaking off.

"Nell, you must remain silent," Adrian said in my ear.

"What?" I asked, distracted by the sight of Damian boldly walking up to the creaking mummy. Its head weaved back and forth, as if it were trying to see but couldn't, a soft little distressed call issuing from its mummified mouth. Unlike in the movies, these mummies didn't seem to want to kill anyone. They looked more pathetic than frightening, to be honest. One of the mummies, one with bright ginger-colored hair clinging to the dark brown of his head, walked crablike across the floor, his body doubled up and evidently unable to straighten himself. "Damian, leave it alone! Mummies are very fragile. If you touch one, it could break—"

Adrian groaned as my shout echoed throughout the courtyard. The mummies, to a man (or woman—it was hard to tell gender in the shriveled, withered bodies), turned toward me, all three of them making mewing noises as they started toward us.

"By the saints, woman, when will you listen to me?" Adrian growled as he grabbed the back of Damian's shirt as well as my wrist, hauling us both to the side entrance.

"What? What did I do? And why are they following us?" I asked as he hustled us down a short passage to an emergency exit. Looking over my shoulder, I could see the mummies lumbering, staggering, and crab-walking their way after us.

"You raised them," Adrian answered grimly.

"I did not!"

"You did. Normally you would not possess the means to lift more than one curse at a time, but with the power of the ring, you effectively lifted the curse of everything in the museum, including the mummies."

"The mummies were cursed?" The cool evening air blasted around us as Adrian kicked the emergency door open, a flashing blue light going off along with a siren. I glanced back. The mummies were still coming toward us; behind them trailed a cadre of museum employees and security guards, keeping well back but with guns drawn and radios held to their mouths as they gave orders.

"Some are. Not all. Those three you raised obviously were. Move quickly—the guards will have the police surrounding the building in less than a minute."

"Why can't I see one of the mummies?" Damian complained as we ran out the door. It was full dark now, and the streets around the museum were busy with commuter traffic, both on foot and in cars. We emerged into a small parking lot containing a number of official museum vehicles, mostly small cars.

"I understand what you're saying about me charming the mummies' curses, but why are they following us?" I asked as Adrian ran to the nearest car, yanking at the door and swearing profoundly when it proved to be locked.

"They follow the sound of your voice," he growled as he stepped back, lifting his boot to slam it into the car window. The window cracked but didn't break. "It's part of the ritual you used to unmake the curse."

I remembered the words contained in the charm book. The last thing I had said was spoken directly to the purpose of the curse: *Thy power is dispersed. Thy desire is undone. Thy darkness is revealed. All who were bound to you, heed only my voice.*

"Oh, great," I sighed as Adrian kicked the window again, wincing as the glass shattered all over the interior of the car. "I'm the only girl in the whole of England who ever voice-activated mummies."

"Get in the back," Adrian told Damian as he unlocked a side door. I hurried around to the passenger seat, waiting as Adrian ducked into the car to sweep bits of broken glass off the seat.

"I want to ride in the front," Damian whined.

I smirked. "Hey, is Damian affected the same way the mummies are? Does he have to follow my voice too? Does he have to do whatever I order him to do?"

"Not likely!" Damian snorted.

"No, he's not affected. He's a sentient being. The mummies aren't sentient any longer." Adrian swore colorfully in German as the emergency exit to the museum creaked open and three battered mummies staggered out into the night air. "Get in the car!"

Their blind eyes were turned toward me, the soft little noises they made halfway between a moan and a plea. I hesitated at the opened car door, torn between the desire to get away and the need to protect the helpless mummies.

"Nell!"

I waved my hand at the mummies. "Look at them, Adrian! They're helpless, and it's all my fault. What do you think the museum people are going to do with them? They'll torture them trying to figure out what's going on! I've got to put them back to their inanimate state."

"There's no time. Get in the car."

I looked around the parking lot. The first security guard had reached the emergency exit, poking first his gun, then his head around the doorway to peer out at us. Beyond the high stone perimeter fence that lined the museum lot, police sirens wailed. A guard stood outside a manned guard gate at the entrance of the parking area, his mouth hanging open as he beheld the mummies creeping toward him.

I spied a big white paneled van near the gate. It was empty. I spun around, slamming the car door as I sprinted toward the van, calling back to Adrian, "We'll take them with us! I can't leave them to be tortured, not when it's my fault they're walking around."

The mummies turned in my direction, the pitch of their

nonstop mewling growing higher and more desperate as I raced away from them. I reached the side of the van, praying for a miracle.

It was locked.

"Damn," I swore, jerking the charm book out of my pocket.

Adrian and Damian reached me just as I found the unlocking charm and opened the door.

"Nell, what the hell are you doing?" Adrian demanded, shoving me to the side as a bullet whined past. "Why are you attempting to get us killed for a few mummies?"

"You can't be killed, remember? And the mummies are my responsibility, so I can't leave them." I lifted my voice so it could be heard above the sound of sirens, now multiplying in alarming numbers, joined by shouts from the museum guards and occasional bullets that zinged off nearby cars. *"Mummies! Heed My Voice!"*

They moved a lot faster now, and by the time I jerked the rear door open, they rounded the back of the van. "In!" I commanded, jumping in and hoping they'd follow me.

Adrian, smart man that he is, knew when he'd been outmaneuvered, and with only a quick fulminating glare at me, he tossed Damian into the van, scrambling over the kid to get into the driver's seat. Luck favored him better than me, because a set of keys was hidden under the seat and he quickly found them.

The mummies may not have been sentient, but they were smart enough to figure out that if I was in the van, they needed to be in the van, too.

Unfortunately, they all tried to cram into the same seat with me.

"Ack!" I yelled as Ginger lunged onto my lap. Another mummy, one bound totally in gauze, fell onto my shoulder, his face pushed into mine, the horrible mewling noise coming from lips that were dried and lifeless, and he smelled strongly of resin and age. I pulled away from his unintentional embrace, trying not to notice the black holes that were his empty eye sockets.

Adrian gunned the motor, looking over his shoulder as the last mummy, a bit more regal with its cartouches of a long-dead pharaoh painted on his wrappings, lunged toward the back seat, struggling to lift his withered legs high enough to get into the van. Adrian jumped out, grabbed a handful of gauze wrappings, and threw the mummy into the van, slamming the door behind him.

"Argh! What is this, pig-pile-on-Nell day? Get off!" I was covered with mummies. They moved feebly against me as I tried to push them off, but the force of the turn Adrian took as he swung the van into motion threw us all against the side of the van, me beneath the mummies.

Buried as I was, I didn't see the escape Adrian enacted to get us out of the museum parking lot, but if the amount of swearing under his breath and sounds of gunfire were any indicator, it was more than a little hair-raising.

"Police, Papa!" Damian said helpfully as I removed a withered elbow from my mouth, gently shoving a mummy aside enough so I could peer out through tangled bodies.

The police had indeed arrived, their cars pulling up outside the parking area.

"Get down!" Adrian ordered as his foot slammed down on the gas pedal. Damian crouched as we swung around, fishtailing madly, the rear of the heavy van slamming into a small police car blocking the street outside the parking lot. The mummies and I went flying to the floor in a heap, their cries taking on a happy, cooing sound as three pairs of ancient hands stroked the nearest of my body parts.

"I'm glad you guys are happy to find me, really I am, but this is too weird for words," I told them as I struggled out of the pile of mummies, pulling myself to my knees behind Damian's seat. Adrian had used the impact of the van to clear away one of the obstacles, the force of the van reversing at a high speed doing the rest of the job. He slammed on the brakes, yanked hard on the steering wheel, and jammed his foot down on the gas, effectively spinning the van around clear of the blockade. We burst out into traffic with a squeal of tires on asphalt, the mummies flying backward with the acceleration. I clung to the back of Damian's seat, damn near jumping out of my skin when a black shadow at the edge of the road threw itself onto the passenger-side front window.

Adrian's face was plastered up against the window, his eyes almost white with fury.

"Onkel Saer!" Damian gasped, lapsing into German as he flung himself back in his seat, one hand thrown up protectively as if to ward off a blow.

Adrian snarled a curse, yanking the steering wheel to the side in an attempt to dislodge Saer. We spun through a red light, barely missing a big lorry, the sounds of crumpling metal and breaking glass that trailed us through the intersection giving testament that others weren't so lucky. I sent up a little prayer that no one was hurt as I scrambled under the van seat until my hand closed around a familiar-shaped object. I opened the leather-bound volume, squinting in the dim light provided by the streetlamps to find the charm meant to stop an ejection curse. I found the pertinent words, grabbing Adrian's shoulder to tap into the blackness inside him.

"Adulterinus succenturio!" I yelled, throwing every ounce of purpose I had into the demand that Saer be displaced. I had forgotten that I still wore the ring. Adrian was right about its powers—not only had it protected me earlier so I felt not even the slightest sense of strain when charming Damian's curse, now it took a simple ejection curse and added the equivalent of a nuclear-powered wallop to it. One moment Saer was slamming his fist through the windshield, grabbing for a screaming Damian, the next he was flung to the side, splatting against a wall of the museum.

Adrian looked back at where I knelt on my pile of mummies, the charm book clutched in my hands. "Remind me never to make you angry while you're wearing that ring," he said.

I started to smile at him, but saw through the cracked windshield another familiar figure as it stepped into the street before us. "Adrian!" I shrieked, pointing.

His eyes narrowed as he beheld the figure of Christian, standing in the middle of the street holding up a hand in a command for us to stop. The van jumped forward as Adrian stomped on the accelerator, clearly intending to run down the other vampire.

"No, you can't!" I yelled, jerking on his shoulder. "Don't kill him!"

"Why not?" Adrian growled, his fingers tense on the

steering wheel as the van hurtled directly toward Christian. The stupid man just stood there, inviting Adrian to run him over, but I couldn't stand that. Not that I cherished any warm feelings for him—he'd done his worst to try to kill Adrian—but when we were so close to regaining Adrian's soul, I wasn't about to let him blow it on a hasty act of revenge.

"Because you don't have your soul yet!"

"I told you—that was because Asmodeus's curse continues to bind me. If that was removed, I could reclaim my soul."

"Not if you go around . . ." I glanced over to where Damian was crouched against the back of his seat. His eyes were wide with horror as he watched Christian loom up before us. "Not if you kill someone without just cause. You can't run him down, Adrian. Please, don't do this. Don't risk everything for a fleeting moment of pleasure."

"Papa?" Damian asked, his face a mask of worry as the van approached Christian.

The vampire just stood there, as if he were giving Adrian the choice to kill him or not.

"Verdammt noch mal!" Adrian spat in German, jerking on the steering wheel at the very last second. The van's tires, not used to such driving, screamed on the asphalt as we spun around in almost a 180-degree turn. Inside the van, both Damian and I screamed, the mummies' high-pitched shrieks cut off as the van sideswiped three parked cars with a great crashing and squealing of metal upon metal. The engine coughed, sputtered, then died in a glorious silence.

A silence that was quickly filled by the sound of sirens racing toward us.

"Quickly, you must come with me!"

I pushed off the mummified body that lay across my head and looked in utter disbelief at the man who yanked open Damian's door and pulled the boy out of the wreckage.

"What—" I started to ask as Adrian lunged across the seat—the driver's side of the van was crumpled in, effectively locking the door—and threw himself on Christian with a snarl of rage so intense it raised the hairs on the back of my head. "Adrian, don't you dare kill Christian! I forbid it! Dammit, Ginger, stop hugging my legs. I need them. Let go of me, all of you!"

The mummies protested with distressed little noises my climbing over them to the passenger-side front door. I ignored them, half falling from the van to stagger over to where Adrian held Christian by the neck.

"Let go of him, Adrian," I said, watching as the blue lights down the road grew brighter. "We can't fight everyone."

"Nor do you have to," Christian said, his voice just a smidge hoarse. I had to give the vamp credit—I doubt that anyone else could have been throttled by Adrian and still be able to talk. "I am not your enemy. I am here to help you."

"I don't believe you," Adrian hissed. "You lie."

I shook my head at him, tugging on his arm. Damian stood behind the protection of his father, watching us all with bright, interested eyes. He didn't look afraid of Christian as he had Saer. "It doesn't matter if he's lying or not," I said. "We have to run. That traffic jam you left at the last intersection isn't going to stop the police for long."

Christian held up his hand. "I know now that it is Saer

266

who is responsible for your son being held by Asmodeus, and that is the reason you sought the ring. I offer you my protection against your brother."

The mummies made it out of the van in one piece, hurrying toward us with happy little cries. An approaching car caught the weird trio in its headlights. The terrified driver slammed on the brakes, immediately shifted into reverse, and backed down the road until it crashed into an oncoming truck.

"Why would you offer to help us now when you have tried to kill me so many times in the past?" Adrian asked, his face hard with anger.

"It is your Beloved who made me realize the truth."

"She's your Beloved? Oh, no, now we're *never* going to get rid of her," Damian moaned.

I jerked Adrian's arm, ignoring the warning growl that resulted, shoving myself between the two men until I had Adrian's attention. "Look, it doesn't matter why he's had a change of heart, he has. So let's take advantage of it, because those guys"— I pointed down the street to where a phalanx of police cars was trying to circumnavigate the multi-car pile-up that blocked the intersection—"aren't going to take long before they go around the block! We've got to get out of here or we'll spend the rest of our unnatural lives in jail for antiquities theft."

"There is a threat much greater than the police," Christian added. His black eyes met Adrian's. "Your brother has raised an army, and is joined by Sebastian. Together they seek to destroy you, your Beloved, and your son."

Adrian hesitated. I put my hand on his chin and turned his face so he was looking at me. I was pinned between the two men, Adrian still holding Christian in a death grip. "We have no choice, love. We've run out of options. We have to trust him."

"You ask me to trust the man who just a few days ago planned to execute me? The man who would see you dead without a single regret? Why do you ask this of me?"

"I give you my word that I will not harm any of you," Christian said quietly.

I ignored him as I leaned forward to brush a kiss against Adrian's lips. Damian made gagging noises. "Why do I trust him? Simple, lambykins. He's the only man who's shown the good sense to believe what I tell him."

Chapter Eighteen

"I don't like this."

"I know you don't, my little spaetzel. But I am too worn out to run from both the police and your murderous twin, and Damian's looking peaky, plus Christian *did* apologize for trying to kill us earlier."

"I wasn't talking about that. It's your lamentable habit of using completely unsuitable love names for me that gives me grief," Adrian groused. "I am not a lambypie, nor am I a spaetzel."

"I believe it is a habit common to Americans." Christian, who was escorting us down a hallway toward the bedrooms of his house in a classy section of London, cocked an eyebrow at Adrian. "Has she called you snugglebunny yet? It is a particularly loathsome appellation, and yet American women seem to find it strangely charming. My own Beloved uses it frequently."

"Snugglebunny!" Adrian shot an outraged glare over his

shoulder at me, silencing my giggles. "She would not dare. I am the Betrayer!"

Christian paused before a door, sweeping it open with a grand gesture for me to enter. "To set matters correct, I would never have killed you, Charmer. It was only the Betrayer's death we sought. I trust you will be comfortable in here."

I looked around the large bedroom, too tired to care even if we were back at Belinda's back room with the narrow cot. I rallied a smile, poking Adrian in the side with my elbow. "Thank you, it looks wonderful. Doesn't it look wonderful, honey pants?"

Christian rolled his eyes. Adrian scowled. "The room is tolerable."

"Mister Gratitude," I said under my breath as I turned to Christian. "Please excuse Adrian. He really is a nice man beneath that harsh exterior."

"I am the Betrayer. I am not nice."

Christian looked as if he wanted to smile but didn't dare.

"He's just not used to having anyone do anything for him," I told him.

"Dark Ones fear my very name!"

"Nor is he used to accepting help," I explained, feeling it necessary that Christian understand just how isolated Adrian had been all these long centuries. "Being bound to a demon lord really did a number on his ability to trust, but he's getting better."

"Death and destruction follow in my wake!" Adrian yelled, indignation filling his eyes. I kissed the tip of his nose until his irises darkened to a clear sapphire.

Christian burst into laughter.

"You see what I must tolerate?" Adrian demanded of Christian. "This woman, this Beloved who is bound to me body and soul, she who is everything to me, does not admit to the power and terror I wield."

"Used to wield," I pointed out, wrapping my arms around him and kissing his chin. "Now that we've got the ring, we're going to take care of that curse, so it'll be bye-bye, Betrayer, hello, happy Adrian."

"She treats me as if I am a mortal man," Adrian continued. "Me! One who has seen darkness that would kill a mere mortal!"

Christian's laughter faded as his eyes narrowed on me. "It is like that also with my Beloved. She has no respect for what it is to be a Dark One. They do not understand, these Americans, just how dangerous we can be. When angry, Allegra refers to me as *Fang Boy*."

They both looked at me, Christian with speculation, Adrian with outrage, as if I were to blame for Allie's choice of words. "Hey," I said, holding up my hands. "I'm innocent."

"See that you stay that way," Adrian said softly as Allie, Damian, and the mummies came into the room.

"They can stay in Christian's study," Allie was saying. "It has a TV. My ghosts love it, so I think your stepmother's mummies would like it, too."

"She's not my stepmother!"

"No?" Allie looked from me to Adrian. "I thought you two were Joined?"

"We are," I said, extracting myself from the group hug with which the mummies felt it necessary to greet me after a prolonged absence of roughly thirty seconds. "But neither Damian nor I were expecting each other, so we've got some issues to work out."

"She stinks," the annoying little snot said. I made mean eyes at him.

Allie, who had started moving toward her husband, stopped at the look he gave her. "What's wrong?"

"Snugglebunny," Christian answered.

"Do not forget Fang Boy," Adrian added helpfully, glaring at the nearest mummy as he wrapped his arm around me and hauled me to his side. "My Beloved would never be so discourteous as to refer to me in such a flippant manner."

"Not so long as you watch your step, my little love potato," I answered.

Allie rolled her mismatched eyes when her husband gave her a pointed look. "Oh, for God's sake . . . come on, Dracula. Let's leave the happy family to themselves."

"You are determined to drive me insane, are you not, woman?" Christian asked as he followed her to the door.

"Where is *she* going to sleep?" Damian demanded, hands on his hips as he stared pointedly at a big bed. "There's only one bed, and I can't sleep with that awful smell in the room."

"We have a very nice room across the hall," Allie said, limping back into the room to steer Damian out the door. "You will be close to your father, and Nell's . . . uh . . . odor won't bother you there."

Damian shot me a disbelieving look, but allowed himself to be escorted to the opposite room.

"What is it with that kid?" I asked Adrian as the door closed, trying not to look as if I cared what the little monster said about me. "I took a bath! I do not—Ginger, off! I can't talk with you humping my leg like that."

The mummy wasn't actually trying to get busy with my leg, but in his crouched, doubled-over position, his attempts to hug me ended up in a somewhat X-rated move on my leg. I pointed to the door and told him to leave, more than a little startled when he complied.

Adrian gave me a long-suffering look as he began to unpack his satchel.

I looked at the other mummies. "Leave!" I ordered in a dramatic voice.

They left, cooing a sad little lament about their banishment.

"I could *so* get used to this," I said, turning back to face Adrian. His frown said it all. I smiled and hurriedly added, "Not that we're going to keep them. I'll put them back to their original condition just as soon as I figure out how to recurse them."

"I fervently hope you do. The next few hours will be difficult enough without your mummies getting in the way." Damian stuffed a few articles of clothing into the top drawer of a dresser.

"Yeah, well, the same could be said for your son. Why didn't you tell me Damian was your son? And why is he going on about me stinking?"

"You said you had spoken to Melissande, so I assumed you knew he was my son. As for the other, you smell different to Damian. The blood of a Beloved is poison to all

273

but the Dark One she is Joined with. That is what Damian is reacting to."

I stared in open-mouthed surprise as Adrian tucked his satchel behind a chair and peeled off his duster. "Are you saying that to every Dark One I smell funny?"

He nodded.

"Does Allie smell funny to you?"

"Yes."

"Like what?"

"Something rancid."

"She does? Are you sure? Oh! That means I smell the same way to Christian! I do not smell rancid!" I whapped Adrian across the arm. He just looked at me. "Rancid? Really? Like what? Old milk? Stale bread?"

"More like something dead that has lain in the street for several weeks."

I goggled at him as he pulled his sweater off. "I smell like *road kill*?"

He looked up at the rising note of hysteria that I was all to aware streaked my voice. "Only to others, Hasi. To me you smell . . ."

"What?" I asked as he struggled to find the right words. "Sludge? Bloated whale carcass? A sewage plant?"

Like the sun warming a field of wildflowers. Like the rarest and most exotic of spices, tantalizing and teasing my senses until you threaten to overwhelm me. Like a costly wine aged and mellowed such that it warms the blood and lifts the spirit. You smell of hope and love and life, Hasi, and I do not want to spend even a minute of my life without you.

Oh, Adrian! I sniffled as I threw myself into his open

274

arms. *That's the nicest thing anyone has ever said to me. You're going to make me . . . hey! I heard you before I was touching you! My mind is back to normal!*

He scooped me up and carried me over to the bed, his eyes indigo with desire as he set me down in the center, pausing only long enough to strip off his remaining clothing before he lay next to me. *I knew your powers would return, Hasi. But I am glad you are no longer worried about it. Now perhaps I will have your full attention as I prove to you that I am not to be taken lightly.*

I squirmed out of my shoes, socks, and pants as his hands swept under my sweater, pushing it up, tugging it off with one hand while using the other to caress one of my breasts. I shivered with the feeling of his hot breath as it teased the other. "I never, ever doubted your skills at that. Where lovemaking is concerned, you're top of the heap. If I had the power, I'd formally crown you King of Hoocheewawa."

And you, my beloved Hasi, are the Queen of Seduction. He licked the underside of my breast with long, sweeping strokes of his tongue. I shivered again, the cold air on my wet breast mingling with the fire of need that he generated with the simplest of touches. I read with perfect clarity his dark, erotic intentions, and despite my body's instantaneous approval of said intentions, I felt obliged by the responsibilities thrust upon us to offer a token protest.

"Christian said he'd be waiting for us in his library so we could make plans about Saer and Sebastian," I said on a gasp as his mouth closed briefly over a taut nipple that wanted badly for him to do just that. My back arched as he paid his respects to the other breast before he kissed a hot, wet path southward. "Shouldn't we . . . shouldn't we . . . oh, good Lord, Adrian, that's got to be illegal!"

No, it is not illegal, he said, his mind filled with arousal and need and hunger that boiled into me until it swept me up as well. I accepted it and returned it with all the love I had, reveling in our joining. His tongue flicked over the tender flesh that protected my secrets, sending me spiraling toward heaven. He turned his head slightly so his lips caressed the pulse of my femoral artery, his stubbly cheek pressed against me in such a way that it provided a wonderful abrasion that picked up where his mouth had left off. *But this is, Hasi.*

His teeth pierced the flesh of my inner thigh, the momentary pain making me gasp as it melted into a profound pleasure that joined with the erotic feel of his whisker stubble brushing back and forth on my sensitive parts as he drank deeply of my blood.

It was too much for me. My sense of the satisfaction and pleasure he felt with the taking of my blood, his heightened arousal, and the stimulation of manly stubble to my womanly parts drove me over the edge. The orgasm swelled over me in a wave of elation that had every part of my body celebrating. It was a high, and I rode it joyously, giving myself up to it, aware that Adrian was with me even when I soared. Eventually, I slowly drifted back to conscious awareness of my body and immediate surroundings.

Adrian's head lay on my belly, his fingers spread over me in blatant possession, sadness and regret covering us like a soft blanket of melancholy.

You're not going to die, I said firmly into his head, gently sweeping his hair off his brow. *I know you are rattled by the things that Christian told us on the ride here, but it's no longer just you against Saer and his army, Adrian. I'm here, and Christian is willing to help us, too. He's not nearly as bad as I thought he was, and I have to admit he's got a lot of strength. I doubt that many other vamps could have stood you throttling them and not had a permanent kink in their necks.*

His lips pressed a sweet kiss to my belly. *I would have liked to see our children, Hasi.*

Tears snaked down the sides of my face as his sorrow filled me. I slid down, pushing him on his back, angrily brushing away the tears as I crawled off the bed. "I refuse to give up, and you know what? I'm damned tired of you giving in so easily. We are Joined. We're a family—you, Damian, and me. And I do not let my family sacrifice themselves, so you can just stop telling yourself that the only way to save Damian and me is to hand yourself over to Saer."

He looked startled for a moment. Clearly he had thought his intentions were hidden from me, but in that, he'd underestimated me. "Hasi—"

"No!" I said, grabbing his duster, slipping into it and buttoning it down to my knees. "There is no excuse. We're going to see this through, all of us. And when it's finished, you're going to be apologizing for doubting me for a very, very long time." I marched to the door.

Adrian propped himself up on an elbow, the air filled with his mingled outrage and confusion. "Where are you going?"

"To see if Allie will lend me something. Stay right there. I'll be back in a minute."

"What—" he started to say, but I closed the door on his question. He read me better than I read him; he could just trust me.

Ten minutes later I returned with a warm bowl, a small pastry brush, and a renewed sense of purpose. Adrian was still lying on the bed, naked, his arms behind his head as he glared up at the ceiling.

"That was more than a minute," he pointed out as I shucked his duster. "That was exactly eleven and three-quarter minutes. What were you doing?"

"Dancing the cancan with the mummies and Christian." I nudged his hip with my knee. He gave me a sour look, but scooted over to the middle of the bed. I couldn't help noticing that he was no longer aroused. I smiled to myself. That wasn't going to be a problem.

"What do you have?" he asked, suspicion lightening his eyes until they were the color of a rain-washed morning sky. He sniffed. "Chocolate?"

"Yes, chocolate," I answered, stirring the melted chocolate with the brush. "Milk chocolate, to be exact, since I don't like semisweet."

His brows pulled together. "I do not like chocolate."

I swirled the brush around the silky brown confection. "Have you ever tried it?"

"You know I do not eat." I fought to keep from smiling at his petulant tone.

"If you haven't tried it, you can't say you don't like it." I lifted the brush and allowed it to drizzle a few drops of melted chocolate onto his belly. His breath sucked in as I lowered my head to lick up the chocolate, my tongue chasing all the little chocolate splatters. His muscles contracted with each dab of my tongue until he was stiff as a board.

Everywhere.

"See? You do like chocolate," I purred, stirring the brush in the chocolate again.

His eyes widened as I painted a chocolate protection ward over his heart. The ward, despite being drawn with melted chocolate and a pastry brush, glowed gold for a moment before fading into a lovely swirl of chocolate. Adrian twitched.

"Something the matter?" I asked as I leaned over his chest, my tongue flicking at the beginning of the ward.

"It . . . burns."

I sat back, concerned for a second that I'd inadvertently harmed him. Using the cloth that had cradled the warm bowl, I wiped off the chocolate ward, worried that what I had intended as an erotic experience might have turned pleasure into pain. With the chocolate gone, I could see a faint red mark where the ward had lain on his skin. As I watched, the redness faded to nothing. "I'm so sorry, Adrian. The chocolate isn't that hot. I tested it on my wrist first. I didn't think it was anything but pleasantly warm—"

"Do it again," he said, his voice hoarse, his eyes almost black.

"But if it's burning you—"

It's a good burn. Do it again, Hasi. Feel what I feel.

My worry dissipated at his command. Obediently I merged into his mind, feeling his reaction as I stirred the chocolate, painting another ward on his sternum. His body clenched as the warm chocolate touched his flesh, but it was the act of tracing the ward that left a little tingle on his skin. He was right. It was a good burn. It was just hot enough that it left his skin sensitive, but not so hot that it hurt. I smiled my most wicked smile, and lolled across him to retrace the ward with my tongue.

He bucked beneath me, an erotic pleasure skittering between us as the protection ward sizzled to life. *Hasi, if you knew what you do to me . . .*

What makes you think I don't know? I asked, painting another ward on his hipbone, sucking it off as soon as it glowed gold. Next to my head, his arousal was standing at attention, all hard unabashed maleness. I sucked the last bit of chocolate from his hip, turning my head to consider it. *I'm thinking I need to ward Vlad the Impaler here.*

His eyebrows rose as I got to my knees, stirring the brush in the cooling chocolate. *It has never been at risk before. What exactly do you intend that you must draw a protection ward on that part of me?*

I leaned forward and dragged my tongue along the sensitive underside. Adrian almost rose off the bed. *Who said anything about a protection ward? Allie showed me something while the chocolate was melting. I'm going to ward this puppy for stamina.*

Adrian groaned as I painted the strength symbols on his penis, his hands clutching the bedspread convulsively as the soft brush swirled around his shaft, curling around the head before swooping back down to the base. Admittedly, it was an overly elaborate version of a strength ward, but the rapturous anticipation that Adrian felt with each stroke of the brush made it worth a little extra effort.

"Is it burning?" I asked as I set the bowl and brush down, glancing up to his face.

His eyes had rolled back in his head.

"Yes," he said in a half groan, half gasp.

"Good." I nudged his knees aside and crawled between his legs, looking with no little pride at his chocolate-covered arousal. Warded as it was, it could probably bring down a few trees should Adrian wish to put it to that use.

I, however, had other plans for him.

His hips shot up as my tongue began to trace the ward, his fingers tangling in my hair as I moved up and down, around and around, retracing the ward's elaborately detailed design. By the time I reached the end of the ward, his body was as tightly strung as I had been in the museum, his jaw clenched with strain. I dipped into his mind and felt the enormous restraint he'd clamped down on the surge of need and want and desire that filled him, just so that I'd be able to complete my love play. His body and mind told me what I'd suspected—the flicks of my tongue had fired him to the point of spontaneous combustion, but it hadn't satisfied his true need.

"Dessert was fun, but now I'm hungry for the main course," I whispered as I straddled his hips, guiding his now slick length to where my body was crying for him, mentally querying him as to whether he was ready.

"Christus, Hasi, yes! Take me inside you now!"

I sank down upon him, reveling in the sensation of him

invading my body, his velvet-covered steel shaft stretching me anew, burrowing deeper until it seemed as if he had touched the very center of me. Adrian groaned as I sat still for a moment, cherishing the feeling of his heartbeat so deep within me.

As you are within me, Hasi. You are life itself. I could not exist without you. You are everything. He sat up, his hands on my hips to guide my movements as his lips nuzzled my collarbone, slipping down to where my breast ached for him. I arched back, my breasts thrust forward as I heeded his direction, setting a pace that left me breathless with elation as I rode him. His bliss folded into mine, sending us both spiraling. A warm touch on my breast had me jerking in surprise.

You are right, his voice rubbed inside my head with the sinuous grace of a cat. *I should not say I dislike chocolate before I try it.*

My breath caught in my throat as his mouth descended to my nipple, now covered with warm chocolate. My breast ached, positively ached for his touch, and when it came, first the soft wetness of his tongue, then the gentle tugging of his teeth, finally a hard suckling, I almost exploded with rapture.

My orgasm caught me by surprise, but even in the middle of it I realized that Adrian wanted more.

Take it, my love. Take what you need from me, I coaxed, pulling his head tighter to me as my body burst into a shower of euphoric sparks, lighting up us both. He didn't hesitate, his teeth piercing the soft flesh of my breast. I knew from the need within him that, after feeding earlier, he sought my blood not as a form of sustenance, but to satisfy the primal need in him to bind us together in all ways, body and soul, life to life. As my blood mingled with his, he poured life into me, his climax so elemental that it seemed to rock our world, ripping a scream of pleasure from me that flew straight to the heavens.

Minutes, hours, days later I pulled myself from where I was plastered against his chest, my body weak and shaking with the effects of our lovemaking.

"You think anyone heard that?" I summoned enough strength to ask.

Adrian lay exhausted, his eyes closed, his body still. The only sign I had that he was alive was the chest that heaved with ragged breathing beneath me. He spoke without opening his eyes, as if he were too tired to even manage that. I was strangely pleased by that. "Hasi, I believe everyone in greater London heard your scream of completion."

I propped an elbow on his slick chest, frowning down on him. His stubborn jaw and lower cheeks were shadowed with reddish brown whiskers, the black slash of his eyelashes suddenly parting, framing eyes of the purest indigo. I leaned forward until my lips teased him. "I love you, Adrian. I don't know how we're going to defeat Saer, but I promise you, I will never let you go."

His fingers tightened on my hips. *We may have no choice.*

There are always choices, I answered, sucking his lower lip into my mouth. *We just need to find them.*

A sudden burst of emotion swept over me, originating in Adrian as his arms wrapped like steel bands behind me, crushing me to his chest. His mouth moved on mine, ceasing my teasing touches, his tongue sweeping inside in a move of blatant possession. *I will fight to the death for you, Hasi. You are light and love and life. You saw good in me when no one else did. Do not believe I would give you up so easily. I love you with all the passion I possess. I love you with every beat of my heart. I love you with every atom of my being.*

My tears mingled with his as I lay clinging to him, seeking reassurance and offering everything I had. We were bound together by a love too strong to be destroyed.

Or so I prayed.

Chapter Nineteen

"We have got to get rid of Saer," I announced as I preceded Adrian and my cadre of mummies into the long, L-shaped room that a housekeeper had pointed out as Christian's library. It had nothing on the library in his castle, but was interesting enough that I paused to eye an incomplete suit of armor before facing Christian and Allie. "Adrian and I are madly in love, and I'm not going to stand for Saer trying to destroy him. Something's got to give, and I intend to see that it's Saer."

Melissande and Belinda looked up from where Allie was pouring tea.

"Oh," I said, stopping in the doorway. The mummies squawked. Adrian gave me a gentle shove into the room.

"Melissande." He nodded to his sister as he stood next to me. "You look well."

Her hand twitched, sending the tea in her cup splashing over the side. "Thank you, Adrian." Her eyes skittered to me before returning reluctantly to him. "As do you. I . . . er . . . congratulate you on your betrothal."

We're betrothed? I asked him.

It is customary for Dark Ones to marry their Beloveds. A dark suspicion flitted to life within him. *Unless there is some reason you do not wish—*

"Thank you, we're delighted, as you might expect. We hope to be married just as soon as your other brother is pounded into a pulp," I told Melissande. "We'd love to have you at the wedding, although I have no idea when it's going to be, or where it will be held, or even where we're going to live—"

"We will live in my home," Adrian said, wrapping his arm around me and hauling me against his side. It was a gesture that I'd abhor in anyone else, but it made me go all warm and fuzzy every time he felt the need to be possessive.

You have a home?

I do not live under a rock, if that is what you are asking, Hasi.

I smiled brightly as Allie invited us to sit. "Do you have some newspapers or something?" I asked.

Allie looked puzzled.

"For the mummies. Oh, they're housebroken—at least I think they are—but little bits and pieces of them tend to break off, and it's less messy if they stay on a newspaper."

She blinked a couple of times, but pointed to a neat stack of papers.

Hasi, they are not puppies, Adrian said as I spread out several sheets.

Of course they're not puppies. I never said they were puppies. Puppies are cute and adorable and have big eyes.

My mummies are only cute and have no eyes. But they are former people, and thus they deserve the respect and reverence due to any deceased individual. We owe them that much, Adrian. "Sit," I ordered the mummies, pointing to the paper. They sat.

Belinda looked tired but not at all surprised to see us, but Melissande . . . she was clearly not comfortable with the change in Adrian's status from the feared and hated Betrayer to a lovable—and much loved—man.

I perched on the edge of a love seat, Adrian sitting next to me. Allie handed me a cup of tea and a plate of goodies, her mismatched eyes twinkling as she said, "I'm sure you need this after your . . . uh . . . nap."

A blush heated my cheeks at her unspoken amusement. Melissande's lips tightened as she mopped up the spilled tea. Belinda smiled benevolently at us, while Christian sent Adrian a glance filled with some male knowledge that I did not want to examine closely.

"Damian is sleeping," Melissande said, breaking the silence.

"Yes, I know," Adrian answered.

"You are still cursed, are you not?" she asked, one eyebrow lifting. "Does that not prohibit you from merging with anyone but your Beloved?"

"Yes, I am, and yes, it does."

She frowned, clearly puzzled. "Then how—"

"We looked in on Damian on the way downstairs," I answered for Adrian, hating this awkwardness between them but powerless to fix things until we got rid of Saer. I winced at that thought, knowing that Melissande was fond of her brother. "Melissande . . . about Saer . . ."

"He must be defeated," Christian said, his voice tired. Allie curled up next to him on a long leather couch, her hand resting on his leg. From the corner of my eye, I could see the faint pattern of wards drawn over his chest and head. I wondered if Allie had been worried about his meeting Adrian. That was probably one of the reasons he survived Adrian's attempt to snap his neck. "I am sorry, Melissande, but Saer's act in raising an army goes too far. Although his intentions are hidden from us, they cannot mean good."

"His intentions are not hidden from me," Adrian said quietly, his fingers warm on the back of my neck as he toyed with a strand of hair.

"Really?" Christian gave Adrian a considering look. "Enlighten us, please."

"I am not comfortable with us discussing Saer in this manner," Melissande interrupted, getting up to move restlessly around the room. "He has always been a devoted brother and loving uncle. I admit that his actions defy explanation, but we have not yet heard his side of recent happenings. It may well be that he is innocent and we are putting an incorrect interpretation to his actions." She shot a quick, unreadable look toward Adrian.

Adrian ignored her. "Saer plans to topple Asmodeus from power," he told Christian.

"There, you see?" Melissande started to say.

"By means of sacrificing Belinda, at which time he will claim Asmodeus's throne for himself," Adrian finished.

The only sound was that of one of the mummies sucking contentedly on the toe of my shoe.

"Well, I guess that takes care of the issue of Saer's innocence," I said softly, watching Melissande. Her face was pale, but she had an obstinate mulish set to her jaw that was extremely familiar to me. Heaven knew I'd seen the masculine version often enough.

"You cannot know for certain that he will do as you surmise," she said.

"I do know," Adrian answered, the pain that swirled within him so strong it made my heart tighten. I leaned into him, offering him unconditional love and acceptance. His fingers tightened on my neck. "Who do you think arranged for Damian's capture?"

Melissande stared at him in open-mouthed horror. "You can't mean . . . you're not saying that Saer . . . that he would turn over his own nephew . . . he is my brother! You cannot expect me to believe that he would do something so inhuman!"

"And yet, sister, you have no difficulty believing that *I* would," Adrian said, his pale eyes light with a mocking glint.

"That's different," she snapped, her nostrils flaring as she stopped in front of Adrian. "You are the Betrayer. Such unthinkable actions are commonplace for you."

"OK, time out!" I jumped up so unexpectedly, Melissande had to back up a couple of steps. "First of all, Adrian is no longer the Betrayer. Second, you guys, all of you, seem to think that he took pleasure in the things he did!"

"Hasi, do not bother. It doesn't matter what they think—"

"It may not to you, but it does to me," I said, my Irish temper flaring as I glared at everyone in the room. Even

Belinda, the most innocent of all of them, couldn't meet my eyes. "Adrian is cursed. Do you understand what that means? A demon lord, this Asmodeus that Saer intends to overthrow, has bound Adrian body and soul. He had no choice but to obey his master's bidding. No choice. Death isn't even an option, because as long as the curse binds him, Adrian cannot be killed."

"He had a choice!" Melissande shrieked, surprising all of us with her sudden explosion. She pointed a shaking finger at Adrian. "He offered himself in service to Asmodeus in exchange for dark powers."

"Bullshit!" I bellowed, without a care that my language wasn't at all polite.

"Nell—"

"No," I said, shrugging off the restraining hand Adrian had placed on my arm. He stood, obviously intending to stop me, but I had had enough. "They don't understand, none of them do, and it's about time someone told them a thing or two." I turned to Melissande, my arms crossed over my chest, my chin lifted so I could look her in the eye. "Do you know why Adrian was cursed? He didn't have anything to do with it. Your father turned him over in exchange for sexual powers. When he was nothing more than a baby, your father took his son, flesh of his flesh, blood of his blood, and handed him over to a demon lord without so much as a backward glance. He was sold into bondage, Melissande, sold by the very man who should have been protecting him."

Hasi—

Melissande stared at me, her face a picture of denial.

"No. I do not believe—it cannot be—he made the choice—"

"He was two years old! Tell me how he had a choice! Because of his father's betrayal, he has been made an outcast," I yelled, swiping at the tears that suddenly seemed to appear out of nowhere. The mummies, evidently sensing my upset, started wailing in eerie, high-pitched voices. "He has been hated and scorned and hunted because of acts he was forced to commit, acts he regretted with every beat of his heart, but did any of you take the time to ask why he did what he did? No, you just condemned and vilified and denounced him without ever bothering to find out why he was cursed. Your self-righteous purity makes me sick! Adrian has been alone for five centuries, tormented and tortured, without even one hand extended to him in friendship!"

The mummies, still obeying my command to sit, pawed at my legs in distress. I gently pushed them away sniffing back my tears, unashamed of my outburst but wishing I had conducted it with better control over myself.

Adrian pressed a warm kiss to the back of my neck.

Thank you, Hasi. No one has ever stood up for me before, especially not with such an eloquent tongue.

I accepted the handkerchief he held in front of me and angrily wiped my eyes, absently patting the mummies' heads to calm them down. *They deserve it,* I thought about the objects of my diatribe. *They all deserve it.*

Melissande had sunk into a chair by the time my tirade was finished, her hand held to her mouth as if to contain a scream.

Christian stood, looking awkward for a moment before he offered his hand to Adrian. "I am ashamed that I did not question the origins of your role as Betrayer. It is a small payment, but I offer you my help now."

A few more tears snaked down my face as Adrian gravely shook Christian's hand, allowing himself to be pulled into a brief hug. Allie sniffled and reached for a napkin. Belinda smiled, saying nothing, but her eyes were filled with sadness. I realized then what my outburst had cost her. I had been so focused on making Melissande understand how evil Saer was, I'd given no mind to the pain the truth would cause Belinda. Whether or not she knew the depths he would go to, she was his Beloved. They had a bond which I knew went far beyond mere emotions.

"I'm so sorry, Belinda, I spoke without thinking." I disengaged the mummies from my legs and leaned down to give her a penitent hug. "That was cruel of me to speak about Saer in front of you, but you have to understand that part of Adrian's and my concern has been for you."

She shook her head, giving us all a sad smile. "You don't have to sugar-coat the truth for me. I knew when Saer returned a few days ago desperate to Join after years of refusing to do so that something was up. I'm not blind to his faults, you know. I've always known he was the ambitious sort, and knew that someday he would resort to using me to get what he wanted."

"We'll protect you from him," I said firmly, reaching for Adrian. His fingers were warm and solid as they held mine. "We won't let him use you again."

She nodded, her eyes full of tears. I turned away to give

her a little privacy, returning to the love seat next to the mummies. They cooed with happiness, stroking my leg as they raised their eyeless faces in adoration.

"You really have to return them to their inanimate state," Adrian said, his voice dry. "In the very immediate future."

I twirled the ring I still wore on my thumb. "You're just jealous because they don't fawn all over you."

"It is the power of the ring, Hasi, not your personal magnetism."

I pinched his wrist in retribution. "That's as good an opening as any, so I'll take it. With all due apologies to Belinda and Melissande, let's talk about what we're going to do with Saer. I assume that the ring wields enough power to do a number on him? Do we want to just hobble him, or . . . uh . . . fix him permanently?"

Christian, who had reseated himself, rubbed his chin as he glanced toward Melissande. She had remained in her chair, her face an expressionless mask, her gaze lowered to her hands. "I suspect that any action less than a full defeat would only delay the inevitable." He looked a question at Adrian.

To everyone's surprise (but mine), Adrian didn't jump in with an agreement. Instead he sat with his arm around me, his hand stroking my hair as he worked out what he wanted to say. I knew how loath he was to destroy his brother. Even though Saer and Melissande clearly felt no bonds of loyalty to him, he regarded his familial ties in a different light. "Saer will use his army to destroy me. He cannot defeat Asmodeus with the ring in my possession, or that of my Beloved. Thus he will strike at me first. If we can weaken him sufficiently, he will be effectively destroyed without it being necessary to take his life and put Belinda at risk."

Could she survive Saer's death? I asked. *I know you claim you can't live without me, but is the same true for Beloveds? Will she go mad or fade away if he was to die?*

An echo of sadness brushed my mind. *A Dark One cannot survive the loss of his Beloved, but she can survive his.*

I don't care what you say about other women, but I know for a fact that this *Beloved couldn't.*

He didn't answer that, although I knew he wanted to deny it.

"I have always felt it necessary to remain separated from Saer because of Damian," Belinda said quietly, her voice clogged with unshed tears. Her eyes met mine, and an unspoken promise was asked and granted. "But now Damian has another mother, so perhaps it would be best—"

"Right," I interrupted rudely, holding up my hand to stop her from finishing her sentence. "New house rule. No one gets to sacrifice themselves, OK? Not Adrian, not Belinda, no one. We can do this without anyone having to become a martyr."

Allie smiled at me. "At last, someone with common sense. I forgive you for trying to burn Christian in the sunlight."

"Thank you," I said. "I nominate myself as leader of this shindig. Any objections?"

"Yes!" Adrian and Christian yelled together.

"No!" Allie and Belinda answered.

Melissande remained mute. She was apparently finally

coming to grips with the idea that the brother she had long believed to be a traitor wasn't, while the one she loved was. She deserved some time to get it all straight in her head. I looked at the mummies. "What do you guys say?"

"Aeeeeiiiii," they crooned in unison.

"That's five for me and two against. I win. So, let's talk about the power of this ring." I stared for a few seconds at the band of gold and horn on my thumb before turning to Adrian. "Why is it the ring doesn't feel cold to me? Everything else to do with Asmodeus feels cold, frigid really, but this ring is warm. And the sensation of joy when I charmed the curse on Damian—surely a demon lord's ring shouldn't bring people happiness?"

"The ring was stolen by Asmodeus many centuries ago," Adrian answered, his thumb stroking gently over a pulse point behind my jaw. "It was not fashioned for him, but was created by a powerful mage. The ring is made from a unicorn's horn, chased in gold transmuted by one of the greatest alchemists in history."

"Oh, that's right, it's a unicorn's horn," I said, giving him a look that let him know I didn't appreciate having my leg pulled.

He nodded, his face serious. I glanced over to Christian. He nodded as well. "Allegra herself removed the ring from Asmodeus's hand. She would not have been able to do that if the ring had originated with the demon lord. We lost the ring temporarily, but it was found and returned to us by Sebastian. Naturally, he recognized the ring for what it was. We decided that Allegra and I would keep it safe until such time as it could be wielded. When we found out about Melissande's quest to save Damian, I recommended the ring be used. That is what we were doing in Cologne—returning home to collect the ring."

"That's all understandable, everything but the part about the ring being made from the horn of a unicorn. You can't seriously expect me to believe that unicorns . . ." I stopped. Everyone was looking at me as if I were the crazy one. I decided that I could just let that go without exploring it further, and moved on. "That explains where the ring came from, but what can it do to stop Saer?"

"I will use it against him, Hasi."

I frowned at Adrian. "Wait a sec, you said before that you couldn't use it to rescue Damian."

"That is because Damian was being bound by Asmodeus's curse. The servant of a demon lord cannot harm another servant, or one who is bound to the lord. Thus you were able to free Damian when I could not."

"Thank you," Belinda said softly.

"Any time," I said, a little uncomfortable with her gratitude.

"I will use the ring and confront Saer," Adrian said firmly. "With the ring in my hands, he will not be able to defeat me."

"Mmm. That takes care of the how, but not the when or where." I looked at Belinda. "Do you know where Saer is staying?"

Christian shook his head, answering before Belinda could respond. "It does not matter. He will come to us."

Adrian's eyes narrowed, his irises turning robin's-egg-blue as he pinned back the other vampire with his frown. "You believe he will attack here?"

"We've already been through the lower part of the house, warding everything wardable," Allie said. "Christian expects Saer and his Aryans will track you here before dawn." She glanced at the clock. "That's a little less than three hours away."

"Aryans?" I asked, thinking I must have heard the word incorrectly.

Christian and Allie nodded.

"Aryans as in white supremacist, those sorts of Aryans?"

"Yes," Christian said.

"Neo-Nazis?" My mind was having a hard time grasping the idea of a power-hungry vampire leading an army of Hitler's Youth. "Skinheads and their ilk?"

"Hasi, what is it you find so unbelievable?" Adrian asked, a smile in his voice.

"Oh, I don't know. I guess I just expected that any army Saer raised would be . . . you know . . . the evil undead." Everyone just looked at me. "Oh, yeah, I guess you're right. Neo-Nazis are more or less the evil undead. Right. So we have Saer about to attack at any moment with a bunch of goose-stepping Nazis. Great. Anyone here do a really good Winston Churchill impression?"

Chapter Twenty

We discovered that Belinda was missing about five minutes before Saer and his army of Nazis descended upon Christian's house.

"What do you mean, she's gone?" I asked Allie as she hurried past me on the way to the basement. "Gone where?"

"Christian didn't say. Antonio checked the house—he says Belinda is nowhere to be found."

"Oh, great," I moaned, pausing in the middle of drawing a complicated strengthening ward on a window. "Where's Adrian?"

"On the roof with Christian setting traps. I want to ward the basement windows again, just to be sure." The words trailed behind her as she trotted down a flight of stairs to the basement, the dark-eyed ghost I had met in Christian's castle following on her heels. He paused to waggle his eyebrows suggestively at me.

"I'm sorry," I said, waving a hand at the flock that stood hopefully behind me. "I already have mummies."

"Eh," he said with a dismissive shrug, then floated down the stairs after Allie.

I finished the ward on the window, mentally dividing my brain power between it, a review of my checklist of tasks to be accomplished before Hurricane Saer hit us, and trying to think where Belinda might have gone. Surely she knew that Saer was a danger to her? Surely she must know he was going to try to use her? She had to know that the only way both she and Damian would be safe would be to keep as far away from Saer as possible . . .

"Hell!" I spun around, suddenly sure of where she had gone, and why. I ran straight into the mummies, scattering their emaciated forms throughout the hall. "Sorry! Stay here. I'll be back in a minute."

I raced up the stairs as fast as my weak leg would allow me, sprinting down the hall that ran the length of the house until I reached the end, yelling, "Belinda's missing! I think she went out to try to stop Saer by destroying herself. We have to get to her before she does anything stupid!"

Melissande was on the second floor, carefully scattering bits of broken glass before the windows. There wasn't enough time to ward all the windows in Christian's eleven-bedroom mansion, so Allie and I had concentrated on protecting all the doors and windows on the ground floor and basement, while Melissande was in charge of prohibitive measures for the second floor. She sprinkled broken glass on the floor before the window, pausing to frown over her shoulder at me as she straightened up, absently dusting her glass-encrusted leather gloves together. "What did you say about Belinda? What's the matter with her?"

I skidded to a stop, avoiding the glass scattered in front of a nearby window. "She's gone. She's being all noble and self-sacrificing and martyring herself to bring down Saer. Dammit, I knew something was wrong when she hugged me before she went to check on Damian. No one hugs like that when all they're going to do is check on a child!"

"Belinda wishes to destroy Saer?" Melissande gasped, throwing down the metal can that held the shards of broken glass. I spun around and headed back down the hall, Melissande on my heels.

We ran down the stairs, coming to an abrupt stop at the front door. "Can you open it?" she asked.

"Sure. It's warded to keep things from coming in, not from letting us out." I opened the door a crack, peering outside to make sure no army of white supremacists stood outside. The street was empty and quiet, a few forlorn brown leaves scuttling quietly down the gutters in the predawn breeze. "All clear."

We slipped out the door, shivering as we looked around. Christian's house was detached, a red-brick former ambassador's residence set back slightly from the rest of the residences, with a minuscule garden to the side, garage to the rear, and wrought-iron-fenced area to the front. The traffic in this part of London was at a minimum at four in the morning, so we had the street to ourselves as we trotted down the empty sidewalk.

"Where are we going?" Melissande asked, her voice hushed as she wrapped her arms around herself. "Are you sure that Belinda has gone to destroy herself? She is Saer's

Beloved—she knows that to destroy herself would mean his end as well."

"Oh, she knows what she's doing. Or she thinks she does." I stopped in the middle of the street to look back at Christian's house. Silhouetted against the black sky, blacker figures moved around on the roof, setting up quickly rigged sensors that would alert us to anyone who tried to get in via the top floor. "First Adrian, now Belinda . . . I don't know why everyone thinks the only solution to the problem of your brother is to martyr themselves. Why don't we split up? You go down that way to the intersection. I'll go this way."

"But she's had at least ten minutes! We'll never catch up to her—"

"She doesn't have a car, there are no buses or trains running at this hour, and heaven knows there are never any taxis when you need them, so she must be going to Saer on foot. I'm assuming that he is fairly close, as she probably knows. I know when Adrian is around."

Melissande stilled, closing her eyes as she held her breath for a few heartbeats. "He is near. Very near." Her eyes opened again, and even in the dim light from the streetlamp I could see her fear. "Oh, Nell, what are we going to do? If Saer knows that Belinda intends on stopping him"—she choked for a moment—"I have been so stupid, so blind, but I see it all now. Forgive me, Nell—"

We didn't have time for her to unburden herself about either her treatment of Adrian or her unquestioning acceptance of whatever Saer told her. I gave her arm a squeeze before gently shoving her in the direction of the intersection. "You can don your hair shirt later, after we find Belinda and stop her."

She didn't say anything, and I didn't stay around to give her another chance to vent. I jogged down the road, trying to open myself to possible movement ahead, but the only thing I sensed was a sudden rush of anger that washed over me at the same time a voice barked in my head.

Hasi! By Christ's bones, what are you doing, woman? Are you out of your senses?

I turned in mid-jog and waved at the dark figure that blended into a gable on the roof of Christian's house. *Not quite, although I'm seriously starting to wonder if I wouldn't prefer life as a boring old history professor rather than a dashing, adventuresome Beloved to a nummy blue-eyed vampire. Belinda's gone. I think she's planning to kill herself in front of Saer in an attempt to destroy him, too. Melissande and I are trying to find her, scouting around the neighborhood for signs of either of them.*

Swearing of the most profound sort filled my mind, quickly replaced with a familiar arrogant voice. *You will do nothing of the kind! It is dangerous to be outside the safety of the house! Not even for Belinda will I have you risking yourself. You must return immediately. I will find her.*

Don't worry, we know how to protect ourselves, I told him with a whole lot more confidence than I was feeling.

Hasi, I insist that you return at once! You do not know the danger you are in!

Sorry, I must be going out of range of my receiver. You're breaking up. All I can hear is static.

You can hear me with perfect clarity, Nell. Distance is no barrier to us. Do not move one more step! I am coming down.

You can't. You have to stay there. You're the one with the ring. If you go, Damian will be unprotected.

More swearing echoed in my head. *I will give it to Christian. Do not move.*

I stopped at the end of the street. Although I was too far away to see anything, I knew Adrian was making his way through the house. It was imperative that he stay there to protect Damian. If Saer got his hands on the boy . . . just the thought of it made my stomach roil. *Adrian, my love, I know you want to protect me. I know you want to save Belinda, too. But you must stay there and keep Damian safe. Saer will use him to bring us all to our knees if he is left unprotected.*

Hasi—

I think I see something. It looks like a woman running down the middle of the street. I'll let you know if it's Belinda.

Nell, I command you—

Roger wilco, over and out!

I closed my mind to Adrian's increasingly incensed orders, focusing my energy on making my weak leg carry me down the road without collapsing. "Immortal my ass. What I'd give for a good bionic leg," I grumbled as I ordered my body to put on a bit of speed. "I just hope being immortal means you can't die of a heart attack . . . Belinda! Hey, Belinda! Stop! It's me, Nell!"

Needless to say, it was Belinda who was pelting down the street. She disappeared down one side street, only to return and cross the road to another street. Obviously, she too had been searching the neighborhood for Saer, but surprisingly, she hadn't found him. He must not have been as near as Melissande thought. "Belinda!"

She stopped as my bellow echoed down a row of semi-

303

detached houses, turning to face me as I huffed and puffed my way up to her. "Thank . . . God . . . I . . . found . . . you before . . . too . . . late . . . man, I'm . . . out . . . of . . . shape."

"Nell," she said, clasping her hands together and looking just like you'd expect someone to look when martyring themselves for a deranged power-crazy vampire. "Don't try to talk me out of this. It's the only way to stop him. I'm his Beloved—I'm the only one who can do this."

I doubled over, clutching my knees to keep from keeling over. "What is it with you people? It's all or nothing, do or die to you guys. Well, that's not the American way, dammit, and I'm not going to stand by while you commit suicide in the name of honor and all that other crap. Damian needs you. *I* need you. I assume you've got some sort of time-share arrangement, or whatever you call it, worked out with Adrian, and that means I'm going to have to be a stepmom to that monster, and I'll be damned if I'll do it without you helping me!"

She looked indignant for a moment over my reference to Damian as a "monster" then her eyes puddled and she threw herself on me, engulfing me in a hug. "Oh, Nell, you're the sweetest person! I'm so glad Adrian has you. He's needed someone for so long. I knew that when we were together. After we'd have sex, he'd have the most heart-wrenching, lost look in his eyes." I pulled myself free, holding up a hand. She stopped, hiccupping twice. "Too much sharing?"

"Way too much. I would greatly appreciate it if you could expunge from your mental filing cabinet any and all intimate memories of Adrian. I can cope with you and him having a child together, but I'd really rather ignore what went into making that child."

She gave an odd little laugh, brushing away the tears that had rolled down her cheeks. "I will expunge."

"Thanks mucho. Now, if you're done with the Saint Belinda routine, can we get back to the house? Adrian's probably having a hissy fit to end all hissy fits, and he really is a lot easier to deal with when he's allowed to have his own way."

"But Saer—"

"We'll deal. Remember, we have the ring, and all he has are a bunch of hatemongers."

"Yes, but—"

"No buts. Come on, we're short of time." I tugged her the way I'd just come. She resisted for a moment, then gave in and trotted next to me.

"You do not know how angry Saer will be to find that you and Adrian have joined forces with Christian. He was counting on Christian's assistance to destroy Adrian."

"Tough noogies. Christian's on Team Nell now." I slid her a glance. Her lips twitched. "I mean Team Adrian. So Saer can just suck on that fact."

She laughed as we picked up the pace. The back of my neck was beginning to tingle, as if there were a lot of static electricity in the air. "You've learned quickly about Dark Ones and their need to always be dominant."

"I had a crash course in it from a master in the art. Hey, do you feel something—"

The words died on my lips as Adrian merged himself with me, not just his mind, but his whole being, his frustration and white-hot fury boiling into me until it obliterated everything I was. *Hear me, Beloved. Do not return to the house! Belinda has betrayed us. Saer is here in the house, allowed in by her treachery. Christian has smuggled out Damian and will guard him with his life. I will use the ring against Saer, but, Hasi, I must know that you are safe before I do so. And whatever you do, do not attempt to find Belinda! She will lead you directly to Saer.*

I stumbled so hard that I went down on my knees, sick with the dread that had leeched into my mind from Adrian's. Belinda had betrayed us? Her niceness and concern and willingness to help us were all a trick? She had sided herself with Saer against us? She was his Beloved, yes, but did that mean she could turn on us?

"Nell? Are you all right? Let me help you up."

I looked at the hand held in front of me, aware but strangely uncaring that I was on my knees in the middle of a damp street, and the woman who threatened the love of my life was offering her hand to me. For one wild moment I saw red, my hands itching to draw something—ward or curse, I didn't know—my brain picking through the memorized charms from the book Gigli had given me to find something to destroy Belinda. All my rage and anger and fury that she would threaten the man I loved were channeled into one brilliant focus, and for a moment power was mine, filling me, snapping like stray bits of current from my fingertips as I looked up at her, the words of a destructive curse on my lips. Belinda's eyes widened as she stepped backward. I pulled on Adrian's darkness, the connection to a demon lord that I needed in order to draw a curse, sucking power out of the very surroundings until the streetlamp nearest us flickered and started to fade. The power within me took shape as I started to direct it at her, but at that moment pain blasted into my head, cutting through bone and tissue with ease, piercing every atom with the familiar white agony, a warning that I was about to seriously overload my brain.

Both the power and pain faded as I fell forward onto the street, sobbing with frustration and anger. Without the ring to guard my brain, I could wield no powers. I was helpless, useless to Adrian, just one more responsibility for him, one more reason for him to sacrifice himself.

And I had been about to destroy someone I had thought was my friend.

"Nell, what's wrong? Are you all right? You seemed to have some sort of fit. Are you epileptic? Should I get a doctor?" I sensed her hovering near me, but I couldn't bring myself to face her. I was shaken by the extent of my reaction to Adrian's fury. It was as if it had possessed me, consumed me. I lay on the street and thanked God that my brain had stopped me from killing a second time. "I'll get Adrian," Belinda said.

"No!" I yelled, prying myself off the wet street. She was there immediately, helping me up with solicitation and concern. The remnants of Adrian's anger fought with my own disbelief that she would turn on us. I struggled with the conflicting desires, but his emotions were still pouring into me. The anger won.

"Nell—"

I grabbed her arms, shaking her a little as I fought to regain control over myself. "Did you betray us?"

"What?" We stood in the blue-white pool of light from

307

the now steady streetlight. The light washed all the color out of the surroundings, leaving Belinda's gray eyes black, her skin a deathless white. "Did I what?"

"Betray us? Did you lure me away from the house, separating me from Adrian so he'd be weaker? Did you do that? Did you betray us to your Dark One?"

"No!" she gasped, her teeth chattering in response to the shaking. "I swear to you, I haven't done anything like that! I would never endanger Damian that way!"

I dropped my hands, the exhaustion that always followed one of my brain fits crashing over me like a fifty-ton weight, mingling with my regret that I had put Adrian's anger into words against Belinda. Sanity prevailed once again, and I believed her. Everything about her, everything in her eyes and voice, protested her innocence. She loved Damian—I knew that without a doubt, just as I knew she realized that to Saer, the boy was nothing more than a prize to be offered to any demon lord who would favor him. As much as it tore her up to leave Saer, she would not risk Damian's life by rejoining Saer.

"Come on," I said, turning wearily and starting toward the street where Christian's house was. "Saer managed to find a way into the house through our defenses. Christian has taken Damian off somewhere safe, but we have to help Adrian. I have a feeling that even with the ring, he's going to need us. I don't trust Saer any further than I can long jump, and if Sebastian is helping him, that makes it two against one."

"More, with the Aryans."

We ran around the corner to Christian's street, and

stopped, shocked for a moment by what we saw. The house was crawling with Nazis, at least twenty cars parked haphazardly up and down the street, acting as barricades to keep anyone from traversing the street. Every car bore red banners with the white and black Wolfsangel symbol the white supremacists favored. On the car nearest us, a hand-painted sign hung in the back, declaring "WAR—WHITE ARMY REVOLUTION—HAS BEEN DECLARED!" Beyond the cars, a handful of guys wandered around in front of the house, some holding baseball bats and other large, hard objects. Lights blazed from the house, and in the gap in one of the ground-floor curtains, I could see figures moving around inside.

From a distance, the wail of a police siren cut through the night; apparently, someone in the neighborhood had seen Saer's army descend upon Christian's house.

"Aren't they a happy little army?" I asked under my breath as we started toward them, my fingers itching to draw all sorts of horrible things upon them.

"Nell, wait!" Belinda cried, grabbing my arm and stopping me before I made it more than a few steps toward the Nazis.

I shook off her hand. "Wait? I don't think so. That's my vamp in there going up against those guys all by his one-sie. He needs me. I'm going."

She grabbed my arm again, this time shoving me into the darkened doorway of a nearby house. The Nazis hadn't seen us, but I didn't really mind if they were alerted to our presence. They were road hash as far as I cared. "We can't just walk up to the house!" Belinda said.

"We have to have a plan. We have to figure out some way to distract those men so we can sneak inside and do what we can to defeat Saer and Sebastian."

"Plan schman," I sneered, my lip curling with scorn as I pulled away from her and started toward Christian's house. "We're immortal now, remember? They can't kill us. You can stay here if you want, but I'm going in to kick some serious Nazi butt. And then it's Saer's turn."

"Nell—"

The distress in her voice was evident, but I didn't have time to reassure her. I charged forward, my hands fisted as I tried to decide which of the two curses mentioned in the charm book would be the worst—turning the Nazis into voles, or impotent. I decided that while the latter might keep them from breeding, the former was the way to go.

"We can be killed, you know," Belinda said, deathly white with fear. "If our heads are cut off, that's it."

"Piece of cake. Voles aren't known for their tendencies to gnaw off human heads."

"Voles?" Belinda asked, jogging to keep up with me. One of the Nazis, evidently on patrol around the perimeter of the grounds, spotted us and yelled to his buddies.

I waved at them as they took up protective stances.

"Water voles, to be exact. That's the only curse I can think of that won't actually kill them." I slowed my trot to a walk, slapping a confident look on my face.

"You can't turn those men into water voles," Belinda said, clearly shocked by my intention.

I stopped for a moment and gave her a long look. "If I do not change them into water voles, it will take us much longer to get inside the house, and while I'm willing to bet that we won't actually be killed if they beat us up, it will probably hurt. A lot. Not to mention delaying us helping Adrian. Besides, there's something much worse for you to consider than watching me turn a few lowlifes into voles."

"There is?" she asked, blinking a couple of times.

"Yeah. If they win, you'll be Beloved to the head Nazi."

She grimaced. "It's not that I don't want to help, but . . . they have terribly large sticks."

I paused, watching men bolt out of the house in response to a warning call. The Aryans stood in a line, each armed with some form of weapon—several baseball bats, one cricket bat, and a couple of tire irons with spikes welded to the end to form a mace—all of them hurling taunts at us. Belinda had a point. I like to think I'm not a coward, but there was no sense in getting smacked around before I could turn them into voles.

"Turn around," I ordered her, raising my hand to draw a ward. I kept her turning until I had drawn protective wards all around her, repeating the action on myself.

"Will this work?" she asked in a nervous whisper as we marched toward the line of Nazis that filled Christian's driveway.

"Of course it will. I'm a ward drawer from way back," I lied, praying the wards might actually hold out if she believed in them.

"What do you two think you're doing?" one of the Nazis stepped forward to ask with a sneer. He slapped his bat against his gloved hand and raked us both with a look so foul it left me craving a bath to wash off the residue.

I stopped and smiled, Belinda bravely beside me. The words of the curse were on my tongue as I took a deep breath, then tapped into the darkness that Adrian carried within him, the darkness that bound him to Asmodeus. I pointed my finger at the lead Nazi, saying in my best Gothic voice of doom, " 'The guardians of the four quarters lay open their minds, filled they are with blood, guilt, and fear. Within you, loathsome beast most blind, thy tongue shall taste of . . . er . . . shall taste of . . . ' " Crap! I'd forgotten the words of the curse. Desperately I tried to visualize the charm book, now sitting on a shelf in Christian's library.

"What's the matter? Why have you stopped?" Belinda asked me in a worried whisper, one eye on the Nazis as they moved restlessly.

"We have us a witch, lads," the head Nazi snarled, brandishing his bat. "And what do we do to these filthy women?"

"Kill them!" the gang yelled, raising their weapons to pump them in the air.

"I can't remember the rest of the curse," I mumbled to Belinda, running back over the curse in my mind. " 'Within you, loathsome beast most blind, thy tongue shall taste' . . . hell! It's gone! I just can't remember what comes after that."

"Beer?" Belinda suggested, stumbling backward as the men started toward us.

I shrugged. "Works for me. I'll just wing the rest. Halt!" I held up my hand and gestured dramatically. The men ignored me, moving faster now that they smelled fear. I spoke quickly, drawing once again on Adrian's darkness, sketching the symbols of the curse that bound the words to the victims. " 'The guardians of the four quarters lay open their minds, filled they are with blood, guilt, and fear. Within you, loathsome beast most blind, thy tongue shall taste of stale beer!' "

The men stopped, looking puzzled. I held my breath, waiting for them to turn into small, furry brown ratlike creatures. Although a couple of them twitched, and one started batting at his ears, they were all still human.

Well, as human as neo-Nazis could be.

"Is that it?" Belinda asked, peering around me at the men. "Is there supposed to be more to the curse? Aren't they supposed to change, or are they more mental voles than actual voles?"

"I think there's more, but I can't remember it. Um. OK, how about this. 'Nazi, Nazi, go away. Become a vole to-day, I say!' "

Thunder rumbled overhead, a cold breeze whipping around us. Long-dead leaves were caught up in a maelstrom, a veritable tornado of spinning fury. Belinda cried out as she ducked behind me. I covered my face to keep from being struck by the wild leaves. In the center of the windstorm, the Nazis all fell to the ground, covering their heads.

The leaves were so thick, and the wind and cold so intense, that I turned away for a moment. When I turned back, the sudden wind had died. Leaves drifted slowly to the ground in a spiral pattern on the flagstones of the courtyard. Collected in the middle of them was a group of small, squishy brown things.

"Did it work?" Belinda asked, spreading her fingers to peek through them.

"Kind of," I said, prodding one of the small objects with the toe of my boot.

"Those aren't voles," she commented helpfully.

"No, they're not." I sighed, stepping around the slimy mass. "I'm two for two on curses. I guess that's a sign I should give them up, although I think there's a certain amount of poetic justice in this."

"Really? You think so?" she asked, confused as she followed me up the front steps.

I smiled. "Who better to be a slug than a Nazi?"

Chapter Twenty-one

The house was strangely quiet as we entered, not a sound penetrating what seemed to be an icy, dense thickness that filled the building.

Squish.

"Ew! Well, there's one Nazi slug less," I muttered as I scraped my shoe on a carton containing several cases of beer. I paused on point like a retriever, trying to open myself up to the house.

"Can you feel Adrian?" Belinda asked in a whisper, her words emphasized by the sight of her breath on the cold air. It was evident by the number of slugs that slid their way along the hardwood floors or down the carpeted stairs that my curse had been all-encompassing, so there was really no reason for us to be whispering, but I felt just as creeped-out as she did. The house was too still. I imagined that with Adrian, Saer, and Sebastian all locked in battle, the house would shake to its foundations, but as we slowly made our way through the hall, peering into the rooms whose doors had been flung open, the house was utterly quiet, as if holding its breath, bracing itself for a blow.

"No, I don't feel him. Can you feel Saer?"

We reached the bottom of the staircase. She shook her head, her face pinched and white.

"Maybe you should try to do the mind-meld thingy with him," I suggested, rubbing the goose bumps on my arms as I looked around. It was freezing in the house, seeming colder than outside. The Nazis hadn't been in possession of Christian's house very long, but long enough for them to spray-paint red supremacist logos all over the lovely mahogany paneling. Nothing but the slugs moved.

She shook her head again. "I can't."

I glanced at her, one foot on the bottom stair. "What do you mean, you can't? You can't because you don't want Saer to know you're here?"

"No, I mean I can't. I could before we were Joined, but afterward"—she looked away for a minute—"I couldn't. Something seemed to go wrong."

"Odd. Well, there's nothing for it—we're going to have to search the house to find them." I added a silent prayer that we would find Adrian alive. I was more than a little shaken by the fact that I couldn't feel Adrian's presence. I knew instinctively that he would break off mental contact with me when Saer was around, no doubt feeling he was protecting me somehow, but even when I'd blocked him from speaking to me earlier, I could feel him. Now there was nothing.

We found Melissande in the basement, bound and gagged, her long blond hair a curtain around her face as she slumped in a chair to which she was tied.

"Melissande!" Belinda jumped forward and knelt before the woman. I moved behind the chair, frowning at the cloth that had been used to bind her hands. I touched it, my frown deepening as the tactile memory of sliding my hands over that shirt came back to me. "What happened to you? Are you all right? Poor Melissande! Who did this?"

I untied Melissande's hands as Belinda carefully unknotted the matching black scrap of cloth that had been used to gag her. As Melissande lifted her head, Belinda gasped and fell back, staring in horror at her.

I moved around to look, rubbing my thumb over the warm silk. Why had Adrian ripped up a shirt to bind her? The questions that trembled on my lips died when I got a look at what had so horrified Belinda.

The symbol that had been burnt into Melissande's left cheek was one I was all too familiar with, the mere sight of it sending a cold wave skittering down my back that ended in a sick feeling of dread in the pit of my stomach. "Asmodeus."

Her eyes closed, tears slipping from beneath the closed lids. Faint silvery trails were left as the tears traveled a path down beautiful porcelain skin until it reached the red, angry swelling that marked the brand.

"Asmodeus the demon lord?"

I waved my hand toward Melissande's feet, feeling sick, feeling worse than sick. Now I knew why the house was so cold. Someone had invoked the power of Asmodeus, and, given the fact that Belinda and I had searched every square foot of it and found no sign of Adrian, Saer, or Sebastian, the odds were that Adrian had come to some sort of grief using the ring. "I fervently pray there's only one of him. Who did this to you, Melissande?"

I stood in front of her, confused by the anger visible in her gray eyes as she lifted her face to me. "My brother."

I turned away, unwilling to believe her, but driven to defend his cruel action. "Adrian has been—"

"Not Adrian," she interrupted, her voice throbbing with anguish. "Saer. He did this to me. He did this after I agreed to arrange a safe passage into the house for him. He marked me with the symbol of the power he's claimed after he promised to keep Damian safe."

"Safe," I snarled, whirling around to face her. My hands were clenched with the need to grab her and shake her as I'd done to Belinda, but I couldn't, not with the blood still fresh on the brand that marked her lovely cheek. "Safe from what, his own father? Don't you understand that Adrian loves Damian? Don't you see that he's sacrificed everything to save the boy? Are you so blinded by prejudice that you can't get it through your head that Saer is the one who means Damian harm, not Adrian?"

She stood, slowly lifting a hand. Her fingers were clenched tight in a fist, unfurling stiffly to reveal a small white and gold object lying in her palm. "I know that now. I am more sorry than I can ever express that I didn't recognize the truth."

I looked from Asmodeus's ring to her tear-stained face, confused. "Did Saer give you that to hold for him?"

"No." Her eyes were filled with pain similar to what I'd so often seen in Adrian. "Saer doesn't know I have it. Adrian gave it to me to give to you."

"Adrian gave you the ring? Why—"

"They took him," she said, shoving the ring at me. Of their own volition, my fingers plucked the ring from her palm, the familiar warm weight of it a comfort as it slid onto my thumb. "Saer and Sebastian took Adrian. He tried to save me despite what I had done, but it was no use. Saer threatened to kill me outright if Adrian did not cooperate. Sebastian went after Christian, but Saer remained. He made Adrian watch as he marked me, and then he tied me here, leaving me to face death alone."

"Death—" Belinda said. We both turned to look at the wall opposite. Melissande's chair was carefully placed so that as the sun rose in the morning, light from the unshuttered window would creep slowly across the tile floor until eventually it would consume her—but not before she had a few hours to anticipate her end.

"I don't understand," I said, turning away from the window as I fought my own battle with a rising sense of panic. "Why didn't Adrian use the ring against Saer?"

"He could not," Melissande answered, her voice breaking as she slumped back into the wooden chair. "Saer too has been bound to Asmodeus. The ring was useless to Adrian, but he knew that in the right hands—your hands—it could wield the power needed to free him. Please, Nell, please free my brother. Save Adrian. Don't let Saer destroy him."

"Oh, don't worry, I won't," I said, marching determinedly toward the stairs up to the main floor, pausing when I realized I had no idea where I was going. "Uh—where exactly has Saer taken Adrian?"

"The British Museum. Adrian told Saer that the ring is hidden there. He did not admit it, but I know his intention is to summon Asmodeus before Saer can make the sacrifice. When Asmodeus finds out that Saer is trying to usurp him, Adrian will destroy them both."

My shoulders slumped. Alice and her six impossible things had *nothing* on me. "I really am going to have to have a talk with Adrian about his obsession with martyring himself. What sacrifice does Saer plan on making?"

"Damian," she said, sliding a guilty glance toward Belinda. "The only way Saer can gain power over Asmodeus without the ring is to offer the sacrifice of an innocent."

Belinda stiffened.

"OK. So we just have to get there and put a cap on Saer before either Adrian can summon his demon master to wipe out everyone, or Sebastian finds Christian, whom he'll have to kill to get Damian, which means Allie will probably die too, thus making the death toll three even before he drags Damian in to be turned into a sacrificial offering. And I thought Americans were violent! Belinda?"

She stared at Melissande for a few moments, then shook her head. "Saer is lost to me. I can't do any good if I go with you. He would only use me as a hostage, and I couldn't stand being the cause of any more of this horribleness."

"You're not the cause of any of this," I said, running back to give her a quick hug. "You're the most innocent of all of us—you and Damian. You're just caught up in a war between siblings."

I looked at Melissande, part of me wanting to blame her for Adrian's capture, but a more benevolent side of me pointing out that she had had her comeuppance, and had paid the price for her misguided loyalty. I summoned as much of a smile as I could manage (which admittedly wasn't much). "I won't let the bad guys win."

"Thank you," she said simply.

"I'll stay with her here," Belinda said, getting to her feet as I headed back to the stairs. "In case someone needs to know what's going on." She bit her lip for a moment, her eyes shadowed. "You're sure that Christian—"

"Absolutely. That's one tough vamp. I know, I've tried to take him down a couple of times. Damian will be as safe with him as he would be with Adrian."

"Good luck," she said, her chin lifting as she tried to put a brave front on her worries. "May God go with you."

"Thanks. I'm going to need all the help I can get."

It wasn't until I hit the first floor that something struck me: My mummies were gone.

"Well, hell!" I swore, looking around the hall in case someone had dumped them in a corner. "Sorry, guys, wherever you are. I'll deal with you once Adrian and I have taken care of the baddies."

It's amazing what a ring of power will do for you when it comes to escaping a forming police cordon. I had figured that there was no way I'd be able to slip out of Christian's house without being stopped and grilled by the cops, but either London's police force had been warned about coming between a Beloved and her vamp in need, or the ring had some sort of invisibility mojo going on that allowed me to walk out in plain sight of the police who had gathered beyond the rim of Nazimobiles. Blue lights flashed, sirens wailed, and occasional staccato bursts on bullhorns demanded that the supremacists surrender.

I walked down the sidewalk past two sharpshooters hiding behind a rhododendron bush. The men's eyes shifted to look at me, but neither gave me more than a glance as I walked by.

"Cool!" I whispered to myself, twisting the ring like it was some sort of talisman. The other police, everyone from a guy in a yellow jacket who was trying to convince the neighbors to go back into their houses to the incident officer in charge of the bullhorn, all clearly saw me, but I didn't seem to register on their psyches.

Which was perfectly fine with me.

I took the ring off after I figured out that its protective powers went so far as to make me insignificant to the taxi drivers gathered around a train station a half-mile down the road. By the time I found a cab and was whisked through the oddly empty streets toward the British Museum, enough time had passed for all sorts of horrible, torturous, life-ending, apocalyptic things to have happened to Adrian.

And each and every one of them paraded through my mind in glorious Technicolor and Dolby digital surround sound as we drove.

I expected there to be more guards than normal at the museum, given the events of a few hours past, but I hadn't expected to find a veritable army camped around the museum.

"Sorry, love, but this is as close as I can get you," the taxi driver said as he pulled up a block away from the museum. He nodded toward the two big black police vehicles that blocked the road. "Must be a terrorist threat or something."

"Something like that," I agreed, handing him a couple of pound coins I had bummed off Belinda. I slipped on the ring as soon as the taxi made a U-turn, smiling and nodding pleasantly at the various police stationed at checkpoints that led to the museum.

I approached the museum bold as could be, secure in the power of the ring. Police and the British Special Forces guys in ultratechy skin-tight black body armor and armed with enough firepower to blow a small country off the face of the planet filled the forecourt of the museum. Small mobile dispatch centers, command posts, and a couple of official police chemical toilets (even SWAT team members have to go sometime) stood like black monoliths amidst a sea of police on the paving stones that led to the museum front doors.

I weaved my way through the maze of vehicles and people, pausing to listen to a radioed message from a couple of guys who I gathered were crawling their way up the glass roof of the Great Court, reporting no signs of movement via their thermal night vision goggles, but picking up an odd keening sound from the ultrasensitive microphone taped to the glass dome.

The man who was listening to the report on the radio glanced toward me. I smiled at him and walked toward the front doors. When I looked back, he was frowning at the spot in which I had been standing, as if he was puzzled by something.

"I could definitely get used to this," I said aloud as I walked up the stone steps to the doors. With my fingers crossed that they would be unlocked, I strolled past a small terrier-sized camera-mounted security robot that was crawling toward the door. Obligingly, I held the door open for it to enter, following without a backward glance.

The second I entered the museum I was swamped by anger, anger so intense that it almost sent me running. Adrian's anger.

"Well, at least you're alive," I said, trying to make my feet move when Adrian was pouring wave after wave of resistance into my head. I knew he was trying to protect me, but it didn't make it any easier to ignore the compulsion that pummeled me with every struggling step forward.

By the time I made it to the center of the Great Court I was covered in sweat, my heart pounding so loudly I couldn't hear anything else, my breath as labored as if I'd run a hundred times the distance. I stopped, trying to calm my heart, doing my best to shut out the almost palpable waves of anger swamping me, but it was no good. I weighed my options, and decided that with my brand-spanking-new immortality—and a stylish ring of power—there wasn't much that Saer or Sebastian could do to me personally, so it wouldn't hurt to make my presence known.

"I get the picture, Adrian," I bellowed, needlessly cupping my hands to amplify the volume since my voice echoed eerily off the glass ceiling, rebounding off the walls, and flitting along the stairwells. "I appreciate it, but it's not necessary. The cavalry is here!"

A red pinpoint laser light skittered along my face for a moment. I looked up and saw a man's shape silhouetted against the glass roof, his laser-gun sight pausing on me for a few seconds, then moving on in a steady sweep along the floor.

Adrian's obstructionary measures ceased. I smiled ruefully to myself, knowing he was going to be one very tetchy vampire when I found him, but also well aware there was no way we were going to come out of this with our skins intact unless he allowed me to help.

"You left me the ring," I muttered as I hurried across the rest of the Great Court, heading for the stairs that led to the basement offices. "You told your sister I was the only one who could use it, and then you have a hissy fit when I come to do that very thing. Vampires! Surely the most unreasonable of all creatures. Whoa! What the—"

Halfway up the stairs from the basement, a long, thin, sticklike object flexed, flopping over into a roll. Behind it a smaller, squat, spiderlike object crawled. A truly monumental scream was building inside me, about to burst out when a horribly dry, crackling noise whispered up the stairwell. I squinted at the brown objects for a second, leaping down the stairs toward them as a misshapen blob thumped its way around the landing.

"What the hell did they do to you!" I yelled, gathering up the (animated) mummy arm and disattached hand before jumping the last few steps over the torso. "Ginger? My God, they tore you apart! Hold on, I'll get you, you don't have to try to move."

I scooped up Ginger's torso, pausing on the way down the second half of the stairs to collect both his legs (which, though separated, were working together to make their way up the stairs) and a second hand. Ginger made happy little noises at being held so close, his dried lips making a horrible sort of puckering shape that I had a nasty suspicion was his version of a kiss.

"Hold tight, I'll get you put back together," I told him as

I pushed open the metal door to the basement offices. "What happened to the other . . . oh, no!"

The scene in the basement hallway was like something out of a deranged mummy movie. A very low-budget deranged mummy movie. I don't know if the bits and pieces that made up the other two mummies had been scattered in the hallway, but each individual piece—an arm here, a pelvis there—was crawling, kerthumping, and rolling with single-minded determination toward the door . . . and my voice.

"Stop!" I yelled, unable to watch as the disembodied pieces moved toward me. A familiar head rolled onto its side, its jaws open wide in a happy little coo of surprise. I set the bits of Ginger down on a table, propping his torso up so he could look around. "None of you move! That's a direct order. Just as soon as I take care of a little business, I'll be back to collect you and put you back together, assuming there's a barrel-sized jug of superglue around here."

Ginger moaned something that sounded like a question.

"Oh, don't worry," I told him, plucking a spasming finger from my sweater and setting it next to his femur. "The vamp who did this to you all is going to pay. Now just stay put and wait here for me."

I started to walk down the hallway toward the room that held Asmodeus's statue, then paused to look back. "You might scoot yourselves over next to the wall, just in case those police come in. I wouldn't want anyone to get stepped on, OK?"

Three warbling eons-old voices keened their assent.

"Right," I said, marching down the hall, Asmodeus's ring heavy on my thumb. "Time to kick some serious tail."

Chapter Twenty-two

Sebastian was waiting for me in front of the door to the conservation room containing the ivory griffin-headed figure that held Asmodeus in bondage.

"I knew you would come. Saer doubted it, but I knew you would have to come. I am pleased. Adrian's death will be that much sweeter, knowing you will witness it."

I smiled at him. "You know what your problem is?"

The gloating light in his eyes faded a little, a faint frown forming as I continued to smile at him. "My problem, Charmer, is about to be destroyed."

"Wrong," I said softly, making a fist with my ring-bedecked thumb on the outside. Before he could blink, I punched him in the jaw with everything I had. Evidently the ring added a little extra oomph, because Sebastian flew backward two feet and slammed into the door to the storeroom, his head connecting soundly with the solid metal door. For a second his eyes stared at me with utter and complete surprise, then they closed as his body slid down the door with a *whump.* "Your problem is that you underestimate just how determined a pissed-off Beloved can be."

I stepped over Sebastian's prone body, pushing open the door. "One down, two to go."

This room was about three times as large as the one in the sub-basement that had held Damian, and filled with tall metal shelving units holding a number of packing cases and archival picture boxes. I knew I had the correct room—I could feel Adrian's presence like a warm, comforting blanket.

An incredibly *angry* warm, comforting blanket.

I don't suppose you'd like to show a morsel of gratitude that I love you so much that I'm willing to die with you rather than spend my life alone?

There was no answer, although waves of frustration rolled over me. For some reason, he had refused to merge his mind with mine, no doubt part of his form of protection. I walked past several of the shelves, coming into a section of the room that had been cleared of everything but a table covered in a black and purple cloth, a big, ugly, beigeish statue, and two men, one of whom resembled a pincushion.

Saer spun around as I cleared the last of the shelves, surprise evident for a moment in his eyes before a nasty smile curled his lips. He made an elaborate bow, one hand holding a wickedly sharp, long sword.

I ignored him to look at Adrian. He was skewered to the wall by a number of different sizes and types of swords, blood flowing freely down his body to pool around his feet. His eyes were the color of a blue-tinged full moon, but I judged that all in all, he wasn't in too much danger. The fact that Saer hadn't pulled the swords out acted as a deterrent to the bleeding, and although I knew the blood loss was going to leave Adrian weakened and ravenous, he didn't seem wounded to the point of death. "Hey, sweet cheeks. How are you doing? I mean, other than having all those swords in you?"

Adrian glared at me. "Why did you ignore my command to stay away?"

I put my hands on my hips. Two could play at righteous indignation. "Well, for one thing, we had a plan, and that plan did not include you running off to be a sacrifice. For another, I'm not the command-obeying sort of girl, not when the love of my life is intent on throwing away everything we have just because he's so noble he couldn't fart without first asking everyone's permission."

His eyes grew round with outrage, his irises darkening. "I am not that noble! If I farted—which I do not, because I do not ingest food—I would do so at will, without consideration of anyone's feelings. You are the one who is noble. You refuse to admit defeat, and continue trying to save me when you know that nothing can be done."

I looked pointedly at the five swords piercing his torso. "And which one of us has all the swords sticking in his body?"

His scowl was a thing of beauty to behold. "Hasi, I insist that you leave this room at once."

"No."

"You will do as I say!"

"Nope. Not this time."

"Nell, I will not explain it to you again! There is nothing you can do. Leave now!"

I leaned forward and, carefully avoiding the swords, kissed the tip of his nose. "Make me."

"What?" I thought his eyes were going to bug out.

"I said make me. You can't, huh? That's why I'm here, snuggypants. I'm going to help you cream Saer, and then we'll take care of that curse that I see peeking through the blood."

"I am so glad to know I have not been forgotten in this charming domestic scene," Saer said, a dry edge to his voice. He stood behind me, his arms crossed over his chest, the sword held in one hand.

"Oh, sorry, forgot about you for a moment. Torture, Saer? Was that really necessary?" I glanced over my shoulder to glare at him.

"Not in the least." His smile grew as he gestured with the sword toward Adrian. "But it was very enjoyable."

Fury rose within me—my own fury, not Adrian's. I spun around to face Saer, furious that he could joke about torturing a brother who had spent his entire life bound to pain and anguish. "You know, I think I've had just about enough of you. Say good night, Saer. It's time for you to get what's coming to you."

"And just who do you believe is going to see to my punishment?" He strolled around me, touching me gently with the tip of his sword. I stood still, twisting the ring on my thumb, wondering if it would protect me if he tried to run me through with the sword. "You? A third-rate Charmer who can't even call a charm without weakening herself to the point of insensibility?"

Adrian growled. I have never heard another human being growl the way he did. It was animalistic, deep and intense, a warning so effective it raised the hairs on the back of my neck. Out of the corner of my eye I could see him bracing himself, his hands fisted, his eyes pale with anger.

"You cannot even draw a ward that will last any amount of time," Saer added with a smug look.

"I may not be any great shakes at warding or charming on my own, but you know what? As long as I've got the ring, I am damn near invincible." Saer, making his circuit around me, touched my neck with his sword. I whirled around, batting it out of the way as I held up my hand to show him what I bore. "You have run out of time, little man. *Vigor hausi!*"

As the words of the draining curse left my lips, I gathered up every ounce of anger, every morsel of fury, every part of my vengeance, and slammed it toward Saer, pulling on Adrian's darkness to give the curse form.

A blinding flash erupted between us as the curse whipped against Saer, knocking the sword from his hand, sending him backward a couple of steps, but before I had a chance to gloat, he leaped forward, backhanding me into the wall six feet behind me.

Wrath like nothing I had ever known filled the room as Adrian roared. I blinked, shaking my head to clear my vision, knowing that something had gone wrong. The curse I'd used was meant to drain Saer of all power. He shouldn't have been able to not only withstand it, let alone have enough strength to knock me across the room.

"So, brother, you are at last driven to action," Saer taunted, snatching up his sword and quickly sliding the tip of the cold metal against my neck. Pain stung my neck as the sharp blade cut into my skin. My vision returned enough to allow me to see Adrian standing beyond him, the swords ripped from his body, a bloody curved Saracen's blade in his hand. "I wondered if even your Beloved would be able to rouse a sense of honor in you. It has been lacking for so long—"

Adrian's blade flashed. Saer's head parted company with his body. The body stood for three seconds, then collapsed onto my legs.

I looked down at the headless ex-vampire, and wondered if now was a good time to scream.

Hasi, my Beloved one, how badly are you injured?

I looked at the face that examined me so anxiously, raising up a shaking hand to touch his blood-soaked shirt. "You cut Saer's head off?"

"Yes. He was going to kill you. Lift your chin and let me look at your wound."

"That's it? You just cut his head off?" I stared at Adrian for a second, then peered down to where Saer's body still lay across my shins. His head had rolled to a corner, coming to rest in the pool of Adrian's spilled blood.

"Yes, that's it. Hasi, if you would just lift your chin, I will be able to see to your injury."

I pulled my gaze back to his dear, adorable face. His eyes were clear blue, concern and love warming them. "That's . . . it? You cut his head off, and wham, bam, no more Saer? No more torment? No more threat of him trying to use Damian? It's over?"

It is over, Nell. You are bleeding. You must allow me to see to you.

His hand was warm, but insistent on my chin. I lifted it to allow him to see the small cut on my neck. He tsked over it, tearing off a bit of his shirt to tie a makeshift bandage around my neck. I waited until he was done before screaming, *"Why the hell didn't you kill him centuries ago?"*

He sat back, frowning that my question had been presented as a bellow. "I had no reason to kill him until he abducted Damian. And once you became involved, the matter was made more complicated. I knew he would use you against me as he had used Damian. Until I knew the two of you were safe, I could not strike him. Sebastian alone had returned—I had to make sure that Saer had not found Damian before I allowed you to enter the museum."

I pushed him back, kicking my legs until they were Saer-free, accepting the hand Adrian offered to get me to my feet. Adrian's explanation made sense, but still . . . "It's over. I can't believe it's over. I walk in here, you're playing Adrian-the-pincushion one minute, and whammo! the next you lop off Saer's head and it's over." I shook my head, reeled to the side, and decided as Adrian grabbed me and pulled me up against his chest that head-shaking was going to be off my list of approved activities for the next few days. "No. It can't be over. It can't end this easily."

Hasi, you seem to have some difficulty accepting the finality of Saer's death. Did you hurt your head when he struck you? Are you feeling sleepy or sick to your stomach? Do you see two of me?

I disengaged myself from him so I could give him a really quality frown. "I am not witless, if that's what you're implying, and don't deny you are, because I can read you like a billboard! I cracked my head on the wall, but other than a bruise, I'm fine. I just can't believe that after all this buildup, it's over with one swoop of a sword. I've seen lots and lots of vampire movies, and none of them ever end this easily. No. Something is wrong. He's going to come back to life or something. Vampires always do. Look at Dracula—he was always reforming himself from scattered dust or a blob of blood or a cursed ring . . ."

I looked down to my hand as I spoke, shrieking when I discovered the ring was gone. "Where is it? Where's my ring? Help me find it!"

Nell, there is no need—

"Eeek!" I screamed, kicking aside Saer's lifeless legs to pluck the three pieces of shattered ring from under him. "It's broken! Oh, God, I broke the ring! Now what are we going to do?"

"We no longer need it, Nell. Saer is dead. Damian is safe. Sebastian is not a threat to us. We do not need the ring."

"Yes, we do," I whispered, looking up from where the shards lay in my hand. Tears formed and swelled over my lashes as I looked at him, looked at his blood-soaked shirt. Saer had carefully picked spots on Adrian's body that would cause maximum agony while guaranteeing that his natural restorative powers would keep him from dying. Already the bleeding had slowed to a sluggish dribble, his body beginning the healing process. I touched the cold wetness of his shirt, my fingertip on the apex of a curved red line. "We need the ring to charm your curse."

He looked at me, his eyes filled with sad acceptance. *I have lived almost five centuries bearing the curse, Hasi. If I must live longer bound to Asmodeus, so be it.*

I slipped into his arms, wrapping him in all the love and light and joy he brought me. Inside him, the darkness was still there. His soul was still missing, but at least I knew I could fill the emptiness. But for how long would that be enough? *If you are still bound to him, will he not continue to make you do things? Bad things? To your own people?*

He didn't answer for the longest time, just held me, our beings merged together so our strength was shared. *Yes, I will still have to answer his call. But he cannot destroy you. He knows that your death will mean my own.*

I'm not worried about him killing me, I answered, nuzzling the sweet spot behind his ear. *I'm worried about what his demands will do to your soul.*

It is almost mine, Hasi. You have reclaimed it for me. It is within my grasp.

"No, it's not," I said, pulling away from him, wiping the tears that wetted my cheeks. "We both know what I'm going to have to do, Adrian. I know you've avoided thinking about it, but there is no other way. We can't have a life together if you are still the Betrayer. I love you, but I will not stand for you spending the rest of our lives causing death and sadness to your own people. I have to do what I meant all along to do with the ring—I have to charm the curse."

"You will not put yourself at risk for me. You were right in that the ring protected you before, Hasi. To try to charm without it—"

"I know what it means," I said, moving around him to face the small ivory statue that sat on the purple and black altar cloth. "But there is no other choice. Either I lift

335

the curse, or . . . well, I'm just not going to think about that."

Adrian grabbed my arm, pulling me back to him, his eyes lightening as his anger seeped out. "And what if you fail? What if you have another stroke, Nell? Am I so horrible that you would rather risk permanent injury or even death to spending your life with me? Am I that much of a monster to you?"

Monster? No, I answered, stroking a lock of hair off his brow. *Look in my heart, my love. Do you see anything there but the most profound feelings of adoration for you? I love you with everything I am, Adrian. But you know as well as I that our life together will be tainted if you are not freed from your bondage. I don't want to do this. I'm frightened of what may happen if I try to charm without the ring protecting me. I don't want to have another stroke.*

Then do not try it, he commanded, holding me so tight I could scarcely breathe. *I cannot tolerate even the thought of you coming to harm on my behalf. We will find a way to avoid Asmodeus. We will seek help from those learned in demon lore. There is no need for you to fear the future.*

I drank in his essence for one last moment before stepping back. "I'm more frightened of what will happen to us if I do not do this. No"—I put my palm on the cold wetness of his shirt, holding him back—"this is my decision. I have to do this. So rather than spending the next half hour arguing with me about it, why don't you just pretend we've already hashed it out and I won?"

He opened his mouth to protest, but instead acknowledged that I was determined to go forward with my plan. Grudgingly he gave me a gift—his support. "We will face this together, Hasi. Always together."

I faced Adrian, his hands on me as we stood before the statue, our hearts as tightly bound as our minds. The statue sat inanimate on the table, but from the corner of my eye I could see snakes of power emanating from it, flickering and twisting as if they were alive.

Ready? I asked Adrian, raising my hand to touch the starting point of the curse bound to his chest.

I love you, Hasi, he answered, his eyes so full of the proof of his declaration that I almost wavered in my determination to end his torment once and for all. Instead I pressed my finger to the beginning of the curse, jerking back as my arm immediately went numb from cold.

"Heed me, Asmodeus, lord of darkness, master of night." The cold crept up my arm to my shoulder, toward my head. A sudden warmth stopped the flow as Adrian's hand on my neck kept the cold from freezing my brain.

My finger swept around the first of six knots that made up the curse, untangling it as I spoke. "By my blood, I turn this hex placed upon the man before you. By my bones, your power does now take flight."

Pain and rage crackled along my skin as I moved through the second knot, my hand shaking so hard with cold and fear that I had a hard time keeping my finger on the curse. "By my heart, I disperse your will through and through."

Light, white-hot and filled with a scream of fury, burst into my head. The horrible sensation I'd felt ten years before gripped me, tearing me apart as the need to stop, to preserve myself, warred with the knowledge that I was the only one who could save Adrian.

You have already saved me, Hasi. You can never fail me, no matter what the outcome. You have given me love where I have known none. Beyond that, all else pales.

Adrian's words, soft and warm, insinuated themselves through the light and pain, lessening both until I could focus my mind again.

My finger traced through the fourth and fifth knots. "Where there was pain, now joy remains. Where there was darkness, light will reign."

With a cry that came close to shattering my eardrums, Asmodeus burst forth from the figure, his body mangled and twisted, a personification of evil so horrible I could not bear to look at him. I tried to turn away, but his eyes fixed on me, and as he raised his hand, my body exploded in sheer, unending agony. I arched against Adrian, his presence in my head drowning out in the light that began tearing my brain apart. My body was numb on the outside, the cold gripping it so I could not move, but on the inside, my soul wept blood as Asmodeus's voice echoed in my head.

You will die before I release my servant to you.

Then I will die, I screamed, fighting to make my arm move, to make my finger trace the pattern of the last knot. It wouldn't move. It was locked, frozen with cold.

Pain caused my legs to buckle, but I did not fall. I was blinded by the pain and light, but I knew it was Adrian who held me up. It was his hand that was the warmth I felt on my frozen arm, his love that bound us together and

338

gave me the strength to fight on when I wanted to surrender to the pain. On the verge of unconsciousness, and sick with the knowledge that with each passing second more of my brain was being destroyed by my act of charming the curse, I moved my finger through the last intricate swirls and twists of the remaining knot. "Battered, beaten, torn, and harmed, by my love, this curse I charm."

Die, then! Asmodeus's vengeance swept over me, ripping me from Adrian's arms, swinging me up in a maelstrom of pain, fury, and eternal anguish. The light in my head grew until it spilled out of me, turning the world into one unending moment of agony. I sank into it sick with the knowledge that I had failed.

I can't move my legs.

Can you not?

I can't move my arms either.

Ah. Why is that, do you suppose?

Hmm. Let me think about it. Maybe the large, sweaty vampire draped over me has something to do with it.

Dark One, Hasi. I am a Dark One, not a vampire. I have explained this to you time and time again, and yet you insist on referring to me in the popular vernacular. Besides, it is honest sweat. You cannot scorn it.

I opened my eyes and smiled at Adrian, pulling my arm up from where it had been pinned when he collapsed on me after making the sweetest love possible. I trailed my fingers over the lovely contours of his bicep before skimming my hand down his side to pinch the very firm flesh of his behind. "Even wet with the honest sweat of a job well done—and it was a job very well done, not that you need me to praise your sexual prowess anymore—I adore you."

"As is right," he said smugly, his head dipping to nip the skin of my shoulder.

"Ow! The dining car is closed! You had three courses already, you can't still be hungry."

He growled into my neck. *I am always hungry for you, Hasi.*

I grinned and trailed my fingers across the back of his neck, one of his particularly ticklish spots. "You just like flaunting that soul around, that's what it is. I have nothing to do with it—you'd probably be just as happy making love to a hole in a tree so long as you could do it with your soul enhancing all the feelings."

"A hole in a tree!" he yelled in mock outrage, flashing his fangs at me. "You forget who you are speaking to! I am powerful! I am feared! I am—"

"—sexy as hell, and you know it."

His lips curled into a self-satisfied smile. "Woman, you will be punished for such abuse!"

He rolled over, pulling me with him as he prepared to render his version of punishment, which always ended up in wild bunny sex.

"Are you done yet? It's been three hours!" Came a peevish voice from the doorway.

I eeked and scooted down Adrian's body until the blankets hid most of me. Adrian glared over my head at the boy standing in the open doorway. "I have told you before—now that Nell is with us, you must knock before entering our bedroom."

I slithered off Adrian, shimmying over to the far side of the bed, reaching out from under the blankets to feel for the bathrobe Allie had lent me. I had been wearing it when Adrian ripped it from my body. Maybe it had slipped under the bed.

"I did knock. You didn't hear me. She was laughing."

"Nell has a name. She is my Beloved. You will treat her with respect, and not refer to her as she."

My hand, scrabbling around under the bed, closed around a dry, round object. I froze.

"You like her better than me!" Damian shouted. "She smells funny! How can you stand to be around her?"

Adrian rolled his eyes and sat up in bed. "We have had this discussion before. You are my son. I love you. I will always love you. But I also love Nell, and if you give her the chance and stop rejecting her advances, she will take you into her heart as well."

"Oh, yeah, like he's going to allow me to do that," I muttered as I pulled the object out from under the bed.

"Are we going to the museum or not?" Damian demanded, ignoring his father's request. "She said we could go. I want to see the mummies."

I stared down at Ginger's head. His jaw cracked open in a grin. I slapped a hand over his mummified lips to stop the coo of pleasure I knew he was about to make.

"*Who* said you could go to the museum?" Adrian asked.

Damian sighed a sigh of such martyrdom that only a ten-year-old could produce it. "Nell."

"Thank you. We'll be out in ten minutes. I suggest you comb your hair and change into clean clothing," Adrian said.

I carefully shoved Ginger's head back under the bed. Adrian's arm snaked around my waist, pulling me back until I rested on his chest. "I am not sad that you returned the mummies to their inanimate state, Hasi, but I must admit that it was more convenient when Damian could look at them without requiring us to escort him to the museum."

"Uh . . ." I said, gnawing on my lip, wondering how I was going to tell him that in the confused two days that followed the charming of his curse—my recovery from going one-on-one with Asmodeus taking most of that time—I might have given him the impression that I had actually performed a curse returning the mummies to their previous state, rather than just thinking about it, which was as far as I'd gone what with the whole joyous reunion with Adrian after finding out I hadn't really died.

Adrian's arms tightened around me. "Do not worry about Damian, Hasi. He will come to love you as much as I do. It will just take time for him to adapt to the change in our circumstances."

I smiled into his chest, kissing a pert little nipple that taunted me. "Yeah? Well, until then, I have four words for you."

His breath sucked in as my teeth grazed the tender morsel of nippleness, his hands sweeping down my back to wrap around my behind. "And those words are?"

"Dark One boarding school."

His laughter filled my heart, filled my soul, filled the night with more happiness than the world could contain.